I0634584

Hollywood Riptide

Hollywood Riptide

Joseph Sciuto

IGUANA

Copyright © 2017 Joseph Sciuto
Published by Iguana Books
720 Bathurst Street, Suite 303
Toronto, Ontario, Canada
M5S 2R4

All rights reserved. No part of this publication may be reproduced, stored in a retrieval system or transmitted, in any form or by any means, electronic, mechanical, recording or otherwise (except brief passages for purposes of review) without the prior permission of the author or a licence from The Canadian Copyright Licensing Agency (Access Copyright). For an Access Copyright licence, visit www.accesscopyright.ca or call toll free to 1-800-893-5777.

ISBN (paperback): 978-1-77180-230-7
ISBN (EPUB): 978-1-77180-232-1
ISBN (Kindle): 978-1-77180-231-4

Publisher: Mary Ann J. Blair
Proofreader: Shelley Egan
Cover image: nopow/iStock
Cover design: Jessica Albert

This is an original print edition of *Hollywood Riptide*.

To my lovely wife, Melissa, and my son, Jake

Prologue

I once asked a close friend of mine what had prompted him to become an atheist. He simply replied, "I once called Heaven and they put me on hold."

Naturally I followed up and asked, "Well, how long did you wait?"

He replied, "A couple of hours. I thought that was sufficient time, considering all I'd sacrificed. I'm not a very patient man."

Of course, that wasn't the only reason why he had become an atheist. He had fought in World War II and seen a couple of very close buddies blown to smithereens by the Nazi war machine. He was severely wounded himself, and while healing had the privilege — or misfortune, depending on how you look at it — to be in the same army hospital with General Patton when he unleashed the infamous tirade against a soldier suffering from combat fatigue.

Since the time I last spoke to my friend, I have been through many of the same things he went through, and like him I also made a call to Heaven and was put on hold. But unlike him, I was patient. I didn't hang up and eventually someone answered.

The voice on Heaven's end was at first mysterious then suddenly soothing, like the voice of my grandmother. That voice gave me the answer to my questions, and unlike my close friend, I never lost faith.

Chapter One

Back in the day, at the border between West Hollywood and Beverly Hills, there stood a restaurant on Santa Monica Boulevard called the Palm. The building was originally a garage that serviced all types of luxury cars. When a couple of severe earthquakes hit Los Angeles and the buildings all around the restaurant crumpled, the Palm reported no damage, unless you count one bottle of ketchup that fell off a shelf.

The Palm restaurant, lacking any better description, was a high-class speakeasy that served the finest steaks and jumbo lobster and the best variety of other dishes in the entire Los Angeles area. Besides the vegetables and produce, which were bought locally, all the other food was shipped in from elsewhere: the lobster from Nova Scotia, the steaks from the Midwest, and the Palm's famous cheesecake from the Bronx.

It was rumored that more movie deals were signed, sealed, and delivered at the Palm than at any of the major movie studios in town. It was the place where starlets went to eat when they weren't in the mood to put on makeup. It was the place where industry moguls brought their girlfriends for lunch and their wives for dinner. It was the place where Mafia hitmen in from New York went to eat after resolving business.

Caricatures of the Palm's regular customers decorated the walls. The first four tables were reserved for the most powerful and most loyal patrons in LA. Richard Zanuck, son of the mogul Darryl Zanuck, always got table number one. Tom Mankiewicz — famous director, screenwriter, and son of the great Joseph Mankiewicz — always got a front four table, as did producer, manager, and native New Yorker Larry Brezner, who discovered and represented such giant talents as

Robin Williams and Billy Crystal. And of course, there was the flamboyant producer Bobby Flynn, who had, in the last few years, won consecutive Best Picture Academy Awards for two gangster movies that were box-office blockbusters. Beautiful young ladies always accompanied Bobby Flynn, and it was rumored that they were rewarded with bit parts in his movies — without auditions — if they simply followed his one golden rule, which was "if you want the part, you simply have to fuck."

The waiters and managers at the restaurant enjoyed a comradeship with the clientele that was unique. It was not unusual for a waiter to know about a big deal in the movie and record industry weeks before it ever hit the trades. Major stars had no problem telling waiters personal secrets that even their managers and agents knew nothing about. It wasn't unusual for regular customers to give waiters bags of cocaine along with cash as tips. Girls performed striptease acts — literally taking it all off — while singing happy birthday to some stoned-out actor, as a couple of tables over, the Archbishop of Los Angeles was eating dinner. It was controlled chaos, but if anything actually did get out of hand, the GM, Gigi Del Monte, would reach for his baseball bat behind the bar. Order and justice would quickly be restored.

The Palm had become so infamous that when the Reagan administration and the IRS decided to declare a war on waiters' tips, they zeroed in on the Palm first. Suddenly, waiters, busboys, and bartenders at the restaurant had to declare 100 percent of all credit card tips and at least 15 percent on all cash receipts. Thankfully, the drug tips were not included.

Chapter Two

At 26, Nicholas Joseph Caggiano was roughly six feet tall with dark, wavy hair and movie-star looks. He never wore sunglasses, nor did he ever sit by the pool or go to the beach on his days off. He seldom wore short pants, and when not at work, he still wore the simple black Converse sneakers that he had been wearing his whole life. This matters only because, although Nick had already been living in Los Angeles for four years, his attire was not much different from that of any of his friends still living in the Bronx, where Nick was from. A crucifix given to him by his mother still hung from a chain around his neck, and unlike all his friends in Los Angeles, he still attended church as often as possible.

Nick had come to Los Angeles with his college friend Anthony. Both had been film and English majors back in New York. Anthony, whose family was close to the owners of the Palm, had gotten into the restaurant first, and then after a few months, he was able to get Nick in as well. Neither had worked as a waiter before, but their New York personalities and accents made the transition easy. The staff and customers immediately liked them both.

The Palm, as Anthony was fond of saying, was the perfect place for them to be at the moment. The money was great, and they had access to the biggest names and connections in Hollywood. The Palm was the perfect place to push the scripts they were writing and to learn about entry-level jobs in the film business. With their education and background, such inside tips would give them an advantage in landing a job that would rocket them to the greatness they had every intention of achieving.

Four years had passed when Anthony finally got the break he was looking for, working as a production assistant on a film produced by Larry Brezner. He would be making one-fifth the money he was making at the Palm, but in a few years, he would earn ten times the income that he made as a waiter. He had given his two weeks' notice and was in exceptionally high spirits.

Nick was happy for him. Anthony had been a good friend and a loyal guardian, but with his departure came the realization that Nick had to do something about his future. Or he would become like half the waiters at the Palm, would-be actors who made the pilgrimage to California to work in the entertainment industry but eventually exchanged that dream for roles as lifetime servers. The money was great and the customers unbelievable, and each day provided new and insane things to talk about. Waiting tables at the Palm was a trap, and Nick did not want to be its next victim.

Shortly after Anthony gave his notice, Nick walked into Saint Joseph's Catholic Church in Westwood and sat down. It was a place he often came to between lunch and dinner shifts at the restaurant, to think and pray. Usually his prayers centered on his mother and father back in the Bronx, but this time he was in a much more reflective mood about his future. Unlike Anthony, who enjoyed and took interest in all aspects of the movie business, Nick focused mainly on writing. That was his first true love, and his most prized possessions were his books. He had come to Hollywood to write scripts about important events taking place in the world, from apartheid in South Africa to the civil wars in Central America, especially in El Salvador. He knew that to write honestly about these places he had to visit them, but in the four years he had been in Los Angeles, the only place he'd visited so far was the Bronx, to visit his parents every three or four months.

After lighting a candle for his sister, Nick left the church and drove to the airport, where he bought a round-trip ticket to El Salvador. He would be leaving in two months and staying for a week. It wasn't much time, but it was a start.

Chapter Three

After work the following night, Nick met up with Anthony, who had managed to get his hands on an expensive new video camera that, so far, only news crews were using. They decided to drive around West Hollywood and videotape some of the landmarks and skimpily dressed girls standing outside the nightclubs on Sunset Boulevard. It was packed, as usual. Large lighted billboards advertising the latest movie releases looked down upon bumper-to-bumper traffic and the unrelenting sound of car horns and loud music. Anthony decided he'd had enough of this insanity. He turned off the boulevard and headed toward Santa Monica Boulevard.

They parked behind a limo in front of the Palm as Nick put a new tape into the video camera. Bobby Flynn and two beautiful blondes walked out of the restaurant and got into the limo. Anthony turned to Nick and said, "Maybe we'll follow this clown for a few minutes."

"He's probably just going home," Nick replied.

"Or not."

The limo drove off, and Nick and Anthony followed it. They turned back onto Sunset Boulevard, away from the traffic and noise, and drove into the rich, residential area of Beverly Hills. Rows of palm trees swayed gently on each side of them. The sidewalks were empty, and a scattering of lampposts and traffic lights illuminated the quiet streets.

They turned right off Sunset and followed the limo straight to Bobby Flynn's residence. The gate to the mansion swung open, and the limo drove through and up to the house.

"Told you he was probably just coming home," Nick said. The gate stayed open.

"The gate's stuck. Why not take a tour?"

"Seriously, and what if we get caught?" Nick asked.

"Paparazzi! We have the camera to prove it."

"It's still trespassing."

"For once, Nick, stop acting like an altar boy."

They got out of the car, carefully avoiding the surveillance cameras, and walked toward the house. A light in a window came on. The curtains were pulled aside, and against the dark background, it was easy to see everything going on inside the bedroom.

Anthony stopped under a tree near the window. He climbed the tree and positioned himself on a large branch that gave him a bird's-eye view into the room. Nick handed him the video camera and climbed up beside him.

Anthony turned the camera on. Bobby Flynn, naked, was lying on the bed. He reached over and grabbed a jewelry box filled with cocaine. He took two large hits and placed the box back down.

"I'd like to get my hands on some of that coke," Anthony whispered.

"No shit! I bet that hasn't been cut twenty thousand times."

The two blonde girls from the limo walked into the room, totally naked.

"Wow! That's what you call heavenly," Anthony said. "I seriously doubt I'd last more than a minute before blowing my load."

The girls both took hits of the coke. One then positioned herself just above Bobby's face, her butt a few inches from his mouth. The other girl positioned herself directly across from her friend, with her butt barely touching Bobby's erect penis. The girls started to kiss and, almost on cue, started to defecate all over the famous producer. Bobby's face was aglow with orgasmic delight as the girls smeared and massaged their poop all over his body. They joyfully played with his poop-lubricated penis as he licked the inside of both their butts.

"This is the most disgusting thing I have ever seen," Anthony said, but he continued taping.

"Amazing what a couple of girls will do for a bit part in a movie."

"Oh please. These two bitches are as sick as he is. For God's sake, most guys don't even want to think about girls passing gas, much less getting shit on. Wow! Just when you thought you've seen everything."

"I'd hold that thought for a moment," Nick said, as two blond, naked men, so good looking they had to be models, walked into the room. The girls moved to the side as the men urinated all over Bobby's poop-smeared body. In turn he licked their penises and swallowed their semen as they ejaculated in his mouth.

Anthony looked at Nick. "You studied Freud. Is there even a name for this type of sick, pathological behavior?"

"Not that I can think of." They climbed down from the tree.

"Can you imagine being the poor maid who has to come in and clean that mess up?" They got back to the car and drove off. "Just think, Nick. Here we were giving this shithead our scripts, hoping he'd buy one, when all we had to do was piss on him."

"I don't think we're his type. He seems to be seriously into blondes."

"You know, you're right. I guess blondes really do have more fun."

Anthony went back to Nick's apartment in West Hollywood, where they talked and drank some beers. Anthony was leaving for Hawaii the next day, to work on Larry Brezner's film. It would be the first time in four years that the friends would go without seeing each other for more than two days.

Anthony handed Nick the tape and said, "If the jackass ever gives you a hard time, throw this in his face. It'll shut him up quick. And whatever you do, don't shake his hand."

They hugged each other as Anthony left the apartment. It would be the last time they would ever see each other. A force much greater than anything they could have imagined would keep them apart. Nick drank another beer as he placed the tape in a carved-out box shaped like a book.

Chapter Four

Nick walked out of the Palm and over to his car, holding his restaurant jacket. It was another busy night, but by pure chance, he had gotten out early. All his tables left quickly, so with no lingering customers, he was allowed to cash out and leave. He drove to his apartment, parked in the garage, and grabbed a spare sweatshirt he kept in the back of the car. He pulled it over his white dress shirt and walked down to Mirabelle's restaurant on Sunset Boulevard. The Strip was hectic, as usual. Tourists gathered outside Tower Records, and customers by the dozen dillydallied in and out of Book Soup. It was the bookstore in which you could find books by every author from the time of the Roman Empire to the present, and it was one of Nick's favorite places in all of Los Angeles.

Nick walked across Mirabelle's small outside patio and glanced at a loud Russian customer laughing uncontrollably at his own joke. His bodyguard stood a few feet away. Mirabelle's was a wonderful little restaurant that served really good food at about a third the price of the Palm's. It was a great alternative to the busy clubs and overpriced restaurants that littered the Strip.

The bar was small, with only six bar stools, but the bartender was a Czechoslovakian beauty in her early forties who was simply amazing. Ava was charming, flirtatious, and a master at her trade. She kissed Nick on the cheek and reached down behind the bar to grab a cold beer and a chilled glass, which she placed in front of him. Nick always insisted on pouring his own beer, and Ava had stopped asking after about a hundred tries. The bar was empty except for a glass of wine in front of a stool a few feet away.

"Slow night?" Nick asked.

"No! We were very busy up until a little while ago. I think that loud, disgusting Russian scared everybody off. I swear I'd like to take a gun and blow his head off — along with the rest of his disgusting countrymen."

"But then they'd put you in jail and I would seriously miss you."

She reached over and touched Nick's cheek. "No darling, they would probably give me a medal."

Nick took a long sip from his glass as he glanced down the hallway that led to the restrooms. A beautiful, mesmerizing blonde woman walked out of the restroom and down the hall, and sat down on the stool with the wine in front of it. Ava noticed Nick's interest and immediately said to the young lady, "Nicole, I would like you to meet my really good friend Nick."

Nicole barely acknowledged the introduction but shook his hand. Nick pointed to her nose, which had a smudge of cocaine under it. She looked at him as though he was crazy and asked, "What is it?"

Nick bent forward and whispered, "You have a blot of coke below your nose."

She laughed as she removed the blot and said, "Thanks." She gave Nick a careful look-over.

"No problem."

"So what are you, a wannabe actor playing the role of a waiter?"

"No. A wannabe writer working as a waiter."

"Really," she said. "Well, if you ask me, you have a better chance of making it as an actor. At least the idiots in this town can recognize a handsome face."

"I have no interest in being an actor. I really do like writing."

"That's great! A word of advice: don't give up your day job, because you are never going to sell anything."

Nick shook his head and took a long sip from his glass. She was the most stunning creature he had ever seen, and at the Palm, Nick had seen more than his share of beautiful women. Actresses, models, starlets, celebrities … They all had perfect hair and makeup, outfits with matching shoes and purses, and manicures with matching lips. And their perfume. The scents were intoxicating. He had been in the ultimate Hollywood social setting for four years but had never before seen a woman like this. She had some makeup on, but not much. Her beauty was authentic, natural, and pure. It took him by surprise, but there was no denying it. She took his breath away.

"So what restaurant do you work at?"

"The Palm on Santa Monica Boulevard."

"The place famous for its jumbo lobster?"

"Yeah, that's the place."

"I'm pretty sure my father eats there," Nicole said.

"What's his name?"

"His name is none of your business." She was abrupt and sounded rude. Nick hardly noticed. He was happy just to be talking to her.

"Have you ever been there?"

"No! I don't go to any place my father might visit. What are you, a guinea?"

"Meaning an Italian?" Nick asked. He looked at her in disbelief.

"What else would it mean?"

"Yeah, I'm Italian."

"Like I said, you're a guinea. I knew a guinea once. She had the most beautiful skin, just like you."

"In your entire life, you've only known one Italian?" Nick was incredulous.

"What can I say? I don't get out much."

"Well, now you know two. Would you like another glass of wine?"

"Sure, if you're buying. But are sure you can afford it on your waiter's salary?"

"I had a good night — a lot of generous tippers."

"Cool! I will say one thing about my father. If you had him as a regular customer, you might be able to retire early. He's nothing like those other Jew boys you probably have to deal with. My daddy is a great tipper."

Ava was giving them both new drinks when Nicole reached into her purse and took out a vial of cocaine. She handed it to Nick. "Go treat yourself," she said.

Nick walked down the hall toward the bathroom as Nicole turned to Ava.

"One good-looking little guinea, isn't he?"

"He's a real sweet kid."

Nicole laughed. "Aren't they all … until they break your heart."

Nick stood before the men's bathroom mirror and took two hits of coke. He made sure he had no lingering dust around his nose and walked back to the bar to find the unsightly Russian trying to pick up Nicole.

"I told you, jackass. I'm with someone," she told him.

"And who is this someone? I don't see him." The Russian's bodyguard looked on.

"He's right here." Nicole pointed to Nick, who took the seat right next to her.

The Russian looked Nick over and laughed. "This? This isn't even a man."

"And how would you know?"

"I could put you up in a mansion where a beautiful creature like you should be living."

"I already live in a mansion. You'll have to do a lot better than that, you jackass."

"Why don't you just leave the lady alone?" Nick said. "Isn't it obvious she's not interested in your type of filth?"

"Filth, is that what you call me? You American piece of shit."

"That's exactly what I called you, you Russian piece of shit."

The Russian laughed. He placed one hand on Nicole's leg and with the other, took a swing at Nick, missing badly. In turn, Nick picked up his beer mug and slammed it against the Russian's head. The handle broke in Nick's hand. The Russian fell helplessly to the floor as his bodyguard, reaching for his gun, lunged at Nick. Nick stepped aside, grabbed the man by the back of his head, and smashed his face straight down onto the bar. Then he flung the senseless guard to the floor alongside his boss. Nick took the gun off the floor and grabbed Nicole's hand, saying, "We need to get the hell out of here."

Nicole tossed a couple of hundred-dollar bills to Ava as she stepped over the obnoxious Russian and kicked him in the groin, saying, "And I told you I was with someone, jackass."

Chapter Five

Nick and Nicole were walking quickly down the street when she screamed, "My God, that was exciting! I swear I had an orgasm. Where to now?"

Nick looked down at his hand, which was bleeding profusely. "I need to go back to my apartment and bandage this up."

"That sounds like a plan. Poor little baby got all cut up protecting me."

Nick reached into his pocket and took out the vial of coke. He tried to hand it back to Nicole.

"No! No! You keep that," she insisted. She opened her purse and showed him about twenty more vials.

"My God, you have enough in there to buy an island!"

"A small one, maybe. Where's the gun? I want to keep it as a memento."

"I think it's better if we dump it," Nick replied. He lifted his sweatshirt up and showed her the gun stuck in his pants.

"You could blow something important off, keeping it there."

"Don't worry. I have the safety on." They turned off Sunset onto Larrabee and walked up the hill to his apartment.

They entered Nick's studio. Nicole did a quick once-over then said sarcastically, "Cozy."

"It's not much … Maybe if I had your father as a regular customer, I'd be able to afford a one-bedroom."

"Maybe. The gun, please."

Nick pulled out the gun, released the clip holding the bullets, and handed it to her.

"A gun with no bullets. What good is that?"

"Good enough to keep as a memento for the time being — at least until you decide to buy some bullets."

"Scared I'm going to shoot my little protector and rob him of the treasure trove in this apartment?"

"No!" Nick walked over to the bathroom. "Scared you might eventually use it on someone who simply looks at you the wrong way — or even worse, on yourself." He was sensing that, despite her staggering beauty, a woman with a sharp tongue like hers most definitely had some baggage. She was not a sweet, docile maiden. This incredible goddess was a tough broad. Nick felt apprehensive and intrigued at the same time.

He opened the faucet over the sink and let the water run over his bloody hand. He picked out the shards of glass stuck in his hand and threw them in a small trash can.

"Wow! That looks like it hurts," Nicole said. She stood a few feet away from him.

"Believe me, it's nothing." He took a bottle of peroxide out of the medicine cabinet and poured it over his hand. He laughed and said, "Now *that* stings."

Nicole offered to help bandage the hand, but Nick insisted on doing it himself.

"You've done this before?" she asked.

"Not in a while."

They stepped out of the bathroom and into the tiny living area.

"No girlfriend?"

"No girlfriend."

"So what, do you just play the field?"

"No, that's not my style."

"What? A bad breakup with the girl of your dreams?"

"No!" Nick walked over to the refrigerator. "Would you like a beer? That's all I have."

"No, I hate beer. Can I use your phone?" She picked up the phone and called Turner's liquor store, putting in an order for ten bottles of Far Niente Chardonnay.

"What's the address?" Nicole asked.

"136 Larrabee, unit 3B. Caggiano."

She repeated the information and hung up the phone. "Should be here in twenty minutes."

"You know, you just ordered ten bottles of a very expensive chardonnay."

"Do you like it?"

"Yeah, it's great."

"That's all that matters." Nicole took a vial out of her purse and took two huge hits. She walked over to Nick and without asking, put two large hits up his nose.

"This stuff is really good."

"I only buy from the best. Some dealers around here cut the shit so many times that it serves more like a laxative than a high."

"Are you saying that all that coke in your purse is for personal use?"

"Of course, it's for personal use. What did you think, I'm selling the shit?" Nicole sat down on the couch. "I swear, what you did back there with those Russian dicks was such a turn-on. I'm actually wet down here." She pointed to her crotch. "You want to feel?"

"Um, no, I believe you."

"So tell me more about yourself, Nick. What part of New York are you from?"

"The Bronx."

"I should've known. That's where all the tough boys come from. Is your family in the Mafia?"

"No! Why would you even ask such a thing?"

"Because you're Italian, and I thought all Italians are in the Mafia. It's nothing to be ashamed of. They do wonderful work."

"They kill people, Nicole."

"So they do what they need to do to survive. I don't have a problem with that."

"What about you? Born and raised here in LA?"

"Yeah, does that surprise you?"

"No. It's just that I haven't met many people your age who were born and raised here."

"I'm twenty-one and almost all the people my age I know were born and raised here. You're just hanging out with the wrong set of assholes."

"That must be it."

Nick sat down in a chair across from the couch. "So do you hang out at Mirabelle's a lot?"

"I don't hang out at any one place very much, but I've known Ava for years, and I try to stop in at least once a week. She's so cool."

"Yeah, she is."

"Are you in love with her?"

"No, but I'm quite certain that many of her regular customers are."

"I'm sure it makes for good tips."

Nick agreed. "It doesn't hurt."

"So tell me, Nicky, do your parents still live back in the Bronx?"

"Yes. In the same house I was born in. They'll never leave that neighborhood. That's where all their friends and family are."

"Why did you leave?"

"I told you, to pursue a career as a writer."

"No, seriously, why did you leave? Didn't get along with Mommy and Daddy?"

"Actually, I love my mother and father more than anything on this earth," Nick replied.

"Then why did you leave?"

"I just told you why. I go back to New York every three months or so to see my parents, and I talk to them all the time on the phone."

"That must cost you quite a bit, especially on a waiter's salary. I'd really like to meet your parents. I don't know many people who are close to their parents like you are. Do you think they'd like me?"

"I barely know you, Nicole, but I don't see why not … as long as you weren't doing blow in front of them."

"Maybe they wouldn't like me because I'm not Italian."

"That doesn't matter to them."

The doorbell rang.

Nick opened the door and let the deliveryman into the apartment. He placed the bottles of wine on Nick's small dining table as Nicole reached into her purse and took out a stack of $100 bills. She paid the man over $400 for the wine and gave him a $100 tip. As he left the apartment, Nicole handed Nick a bottle and said, "Why don't you show me how good you are at your craft?"

Nick took a corkscrew out of the kitchen cabinet and opened the bottle. He poured some wine into a wine glass and handed it to Nicole, who took a sip. "Very nice, Nicky. Good choice."

"You're the one who chose it."

"Oh yeah. Please, get yourself a glass. We have ten bottles to go through."

"I'm fine with the beer."

"No, you're not. So far you're perfect, except for the fact that you drink beer. Surely, you don't want to upset your guest."

Nick grabbed a glass and filled it. "Who am I to say no to such fine wine?" He raised his glass. "To the sweet life."

They clinked their glasses to toast. Nicole asked, "Why 'to the sweet life'?"

"*Far niente* is Italian for 'without a care.' You learn that in waiter school. All part of the craft."

"So you don't speak Italian but your parents do?" Nicole had a serious look on her face.

"No, I really doubt my parents know five words of Italian. I don't even remember my grandparents speaking Italian."

"That's strange. I thought all Italians speak Italian, even the ones born here. You see, you learn something new every day."

"I thought you have a friend who's Italian."

"I did, but that little wop was born back in the old country. I actually think I understood her better when she spoke Italian than when she tried to speak English, and believe me, I don't speak Italian."

"Were the two of you close?" Nick asked.

"Why would you even ask that?" Nicole reached down for the vial of coke and took two enormous hits. She handed Nick the vial, and he took two normal ones then set the vial down.

"Take a few more hits, Nicky."

"No, I'm fine. Thanks." Nick looked suspiciously at Nicole. He couldn't figure this girl out. All sorts of red flags were starting to fly in his mind, but the wine and the coke and her gorgeous face all kept him from paying attention.

"Please do another hit," she said in a sultry voice.

"Okay." He picked the vial back up and took two more hits.

"To answer your question, yes. The two of us were very close until she decided to do something really stupid."

Nick took a long drink from his glass as the coke jolted him into an even higher euphoric state.

"It really does help, doesn't it?" Nicole asked.

"This stuff's amazing. I seriously doubt I have ever had coke that even comes close to this quality."

"It's the best money can buy."

"Should I even ask what really stupid thing your friend did?"

"No, you shouldn't. It would only upset me."

"Well, I wouldn't want to do that."

"No, sweetheart, you really wouldn't."

Nick stood up. "I have to run to the bathroom."

"That's fine. Just don't be too long." Nicole laughed as she picked up her wine and took a long, seductive sip. She watched him walk away.

Nick closed the bathroom door and stood there for a long, hypnotic, blissful moment. Finally, he pulled down his zipper and urinated. He flushed the toilet, washed his hands, and walked out of the bathroom to find Nicole looking through his closet.

"Find anything useful?"

"What's with all these books?" She was looking at his bookshelves, lined with hundreds of titles.

"I like to read."

"Apparently." She looked through his limited wardrobe. "Not much in the way of clothes, and no women's garments. I guess you weren't joking when you said you never get laid."

Nick was quick to answer. "I never said that."

"You insinuated it, and from the look of things, you weren't joking."

"Maybe you should look under the bed while you're at it?"

"I already did. Less under there than under any bed I've seen in my life. Not even a pair of dirty socks."

Nicole closed the closet and motioned for Nick to follow her back to the couch. Nick followed like an obedient child. He had only known Nicole for a few hours, but she already had him under a spell.

"Why don't you open another bottle, Nicky?"

Nick opened another bottle and refilled both their glasses.

"Do you work?" he asked.

"No, why on earth would I want to do that?"

"I don't know. It's the way most people are able to live and survive."

"That's fine for most people, but I have a filthy-rich father. I stay out of his life, and in turn, he provides me with a healthy allowance each month."

"Well, from what I can gather so far, it must be a supremely healthy allowance."

"Fifty thousand a month." She yawned.

"That's probably more than my father has ever made in an entire year. Shit, it's way more than I make at the Palm in a year, and that's one of the best server gigs in town."

"Would you like to exchange fathers?"

"Never!"

"Then don't judge," Nicole snapped. She picked up the vial, took two big hits, and handed it to Nick. "You know, you really are one drop-dead, good-looking little wop. Your parents must be gorgeous."

Nicole said this as Nick took two big hits. "You think your parents will really like me ... half as much as you do?"

"And how do you know I like you?"

"Don't be cute. I'm the girl you've been dreaming about your whole life. I knew it the moment you saw me coming out of the bathroom at Mirabelle's. It was all over your face. Good thing you don't want to be an actor."

Nick looked at her closely, but despite an urge to reach out and touch her, he simply put the vial of coke back down.

"Am I wrong?" she asked.

"No," he replied honestly.

"Good! Now that's out of the way, we can move on to other things."

Nicole took her shoes off and spread out across the couch. "So tell me, did you beat up a lot of guys at home in the Bronx? You seemed pretty sure of yourself back there at Mirabelle's."

"That guy was a creep. He had it coming."

"Yeah, no denying that. And God, did he smell terrible. I bet he's a child molester."

"You think?"

"Oh yeah. A pig like that? Absolutely. Probably grabbed ten-year-old girls off the streets back there in the old country and forced them to have sex with him."

"That's disgusting."

"I know but freaks like that exist in every part of the world. Let's just imagine that you and I got married and had a lovely little girl and it turns out that the freak living next door was molesting her. What would you do?"

"What do you mean what would I do? I would cut the freak's balls off and shove them in his mouth. There's nothing more despicable and cowardly than taking advantage of a child. Why are we even talking about this?"

"Well, we'll never have to worry about it because I don't plan on ever having children. Please tell me you didn't have your heart set on children?"

"Honestly, I've never really thought about it, but I'm pretty sure my parents are fairly set on the idea of grandchildren. You may or may not know how Italians are about children. They're second only to God."

"Well, we'll just have to find a way around that, won't we, sweetheart?"

Suddenly, they were discussing children and she was calling him sweetheart. How did this happen? Nick had always thought he'd ask a girl on a date first, but the wine and coke were making him feel invincible. He decided to roll with it. "How about adoption, or are you dead set against that, too?"

"I see the possibility of a compromise there, as long as they come toilet trained. Would that satisfy your parents?"

"I guess, but we'd have to lie to them and tell them we tried and you just couldn't get pregnant. Would that be okay with you?"

"I guess. I mean, I'd hate to lie to your parents, but if it was the only way to nab their son, I suppose that'd be fine."

"Cool! I hate to lie to them too, especially since they'll probably be saying five thousand prayers a day that we have healthy children. But you can't do what nature won't allow."

"Are they very religious?"

"Have you ever met Italian parents who weren't?" Nick asked this absentmindedly and then corrected himself. "Oh, I forgot. You've only known one Italian. Was she religious?"

"If laughing and being happy are a form of praying, then I guess she was very religious. She wore a chain like you have around your neck."

Nick looked down at the crucifix around his neck and said, "My mother gave this to me."

"And like a good son, you'll wear it until the day you die."

"I'll probably be buried with it."

"Is that your wish?"

"Yes."

"Okay, I'll try to remember that when it's time to bury you."

"That would be nice. Thanks."

Nicole handed Nick the coke and said, "Cheer up, Nick. That won't be for a really long time — unless, of course — you do something really dumb to me."

"Well, you do have the gun," he reminded her.

"But no bullets."

"A mere technicality for someone like you."

"And what's that supposed to mean?"

"Nothing! Just that with your money, you can probably just make a phone call and have bullets delivered."

"Or you can just give me the bullets that came with the gun."

"I don't think so. It's not every day that the girl of my dreams walks into my life. Why complicate the situation with a loaded weapon?"

"Fair enough."

"So the mansion you live in, is it in Beverly Hills?"

"What makes you think I live in a mansion?"

"Because you said so, back in Mirabelle's, to the Russian."

"Yeah, I did. I grew up in a mansion, but I haven't lived there since I turned eighteen. My father still lives there. I imagine it must be lonely for him. But then he does have all those wonderful memories to keep him company. Would you like the address? You could visit him. He's like you. He loves to read."

"I don't think so. At least not until we're married."

"And what makes you think we'll be visiting him once we're married?"

"I don't know. Isn't that kind of customary?"

"Maybe for you Italians but not for me. Sorry, but you won't be inheriting any in-laws when you marry me. Hope that doesn't complicate anything."

"No, but you will be inheriting my parents once we get married. I can guarantee you that."

"I can't wait, Nicky."

"They don't live in a mansion."

"I didn't think so, but maybe we can build them one right there in the Bronx so they won't have to leave any of their friends and family."

"They wouldn't go for that but it's a nice sentiment. Thanks."

"No competition for who has the biggest and most beautiful house in your parents' neighborhood?"

"Not that I ever noticed. That'd be petty, and that's the last thing my parents are."

"Maybe it's just because they've never had the opportunity?"

"No, that's not it at all. My parents simply know what matters in life and what doesn't. Having a big house and the nicest car in the neighborhood is of little importance to them!"

Nicole sipped her wine. "Why are you getting so angry?"

"I'm not getting angry."

"Yes, you are. You're protective of your parents and that's honorable. I imagine that, in your sheltered little universe, that's the way all children should feel about their parents."

"I would hope so, but I know that's not the case. And not for nothing, but I imagine the universe you were raised in was way more sheltered than mine."

"And why is that? Because my daddy is rich and powerful and unlike your father, he was too busy building an empire and cheating on Mommy to have time for his precious little child, never mind protect her?"

Nick picked up the coke and took two big hits as Nicole continued. "Too much for you to handle, Nicky?"

"No, but I'm not going to comment on a man I don't know — never mind your *father*."

"You're so chivalrous — "

"But I will tell you this, Nicole. I would never allow anyone to hurt you, and that's a promise."

"I think you've already proven that tonight, haven't you?"

"No, what I did for you tonight I would have done for any girl being harassed by that asshole, but since I'm getting to know you more, the narrative has changed."

"So now you'd protect me like you would your mother?"

"Well, I would protect you like someone I'm starting to care about." Nick looked at Nicole stretched out comfortably on the couch … so mesmerizing, so alluring, so unattainable, like a Roman goddess.

"What are you thinking about, Nicky?" Nicole reached for the coke again.

"How many boys, throughout your life, have you had knocking on your door? A thousand? Two thousand?

"None that I've ever let in."

"I find that hard to believe."

"And why is that, Nicky?"

"Because no girl as beautiful as you could turn away that many suitors as unacceptable."

"I have high standards, which isn't to say I haven't had my fair share of sex. I'm sorry to inform you that you're not going to be marrying a virgin. I hope that doesn't complicate things?"

"Not one bit."

"As long as I don't tell your parents?"

"Exactly! And it's not like they'd ever bring the subject up."

"I didn't think so."

Time is the one constant in life, yet when one is doing coke, especially really good coke that hasn't been cut a million times, time seems to move at an exceptional speed. Unlike the hallucinogenic drugs of the sixties and seventies, when the experience was purely personal despite the number of people in the room, cocaine is a social drug. As long as there's an audience — whether it's one person or ten — there will be no end to the conversation as long as the coke lasts. Eight hours had already passed since Nick and Nicole entered his apartment. The sun had already made its appearance through one window. Nicole closed the curtains while Nick was in the bathroom.

The edginess and jitters that usually accompany a coke binge were absent — possibly because there was so much that there was no fear of running out or because it was so good the effects were far more authentic. It showed the difference between hardly cut, pure cocaine and what most people would get from the average street dealer.

Nevertheless, Nick realized that if he didn't get some sleep soon, it was going to be a very long night at the Palm. After leaving the bathroom, he opened the top drawer of his desk and took out two Quaaludes.

"I need to get some sleep, otherwise I'm going to be a mess at work." He shook another one into the cap and offered it to her. "Do you want a sleeping pill?"

She put the pill on the coffee table. "Surely, you're joking? There's no way you're going to work tonight. Just call in sick."

"I can't. That wouldn't be right."

"Then I'll call in for you. I can be very persuasive."

"No, I really have to go."

Nicole reached into her purse and asked, "How much would you usually make on a night like tonight — two hundred, three hundred?"

"It has nothing to do with the money, Nicole."

She counted off six $100 bills and threw them on the coffee table in front of Nick. "You're working a private party tonight, and this customer gets what she wants."

"No, but thank you very much. I could never take money from you. I already feel bad about doing so much of your coke and drinking so much of your wine. That's really sweet of you, Nicole. Thanks again, but I have to go to work."

"Are you fucking kidding me?" she asked angrily. "I'm offering you double what you would probably make, not to mention my enchanting company for the rest of the day and night, and all you can say is 'no thanks'? Whatever, Nick. Whatever! At least take a few more hits and have another glass of wine."

Somewhere deep inside, he knew he shouldn't. Red flags were waving, but he wasn't seeing them. He could only see the stunning woman in front of him, the curve of her face and something childish in her eyes. Nick picked up the coke, took a few more hits, and then poured another glass of wine. He also took a Quaalude and said, "Please don't leave when I fall asleep. It would really be nice to wake up and know this hasn't been a dream."

"I'm not going to shatter your dream. You get some rest, and when you wake up, I'll be right here."

Chapter Six

Nick slept for six hours, and when he woke up, Nicole was right there as she had said she would be. She was still astonishingly beautiful. It had not been a dream.

She was still doing coke and drinking wine, and she was watching cartoons on television. Nick's head throbbed, but the sight of this gorgeous creature on his couch lessened the pain a little bit. The only quick cure was a few beers. He sat up on the bed.

Nicole greeted him. "Good afternoon, sleepyhead. Did you dream about me?"

"Like you said last night, I've been dreaming about you my whole life." He gently touched her as he got up.

"And what was that all about?" She continued to look at the cartoons.

"Just had to make sure you were real, that's all." He walked over to the refrigerator and opened it, but to his surprise, there was no beer. "Where did all the beer go?"

"I threw it out, Nicky. Have some red wine. I ordered it a few hours ago. Far Niente … like the chardonnay. Simply delicious."

Nick poured himself a large glass of red wine as Nicole continued. "Have some coke, Nick. It's the best way to get over the hangover. And take this money, please." She pointed to the $600 on the table from last night. "I'd really appreciate it if you'd simply stay here with me tonight instead of going to work. I promise you'll have a much better time. And by the way, I ordered the cartoon channel from your cable provider. Hope that's okay."

"That's great. I love cartoons."

"My God, Nicky, you just keep getting more and more perfect."

Nick sat down on the couch next to her, and she handed him the coke.

"I really shouldn't. I'm going to be a zombie at work."

"Just do it. And please, stop talking about work."

Nick took a few hits, put the coke down, and took a large gulp of wine.

"How do you feel?" he asked her.

"Wonderful. I do have a question, though. Please don't take it the wrong way, but last night I gave you every opportunity in the world to get me into bed, and not a thing out of you. You're not one of those undecideds, are you? Not sure if you like guys or girls?"

"What are you talking about? Do you think I'd be talking about marrying you if I was gay? Or undecided or whatever you call it?"

"In this town, you never know. After all, you do live in West Hollywood, the first recognized gay city in the United States."

"Yeah, but I live above Sunset."

"And what difference does that make? Below Sunset they're 99.9 percent gay, and above Sunset they're 90 percent gay."

"Nicole, I'm not gay! The only reason I didn't make a pass at you is because I didn't want to take advantage of you while you were high."

Nicole looked straight at him. "Are you from another planet?"

"No. I was taught to respect women. That's how I was raised. I'm sorry if I offended you."

"Wow! You're for real." She snorted two large hits of coke.

"I don't understand. Would you rather marry a guy who takes advantage of you or one who respects you and loves you?" As soon as it was out of his mouth … He'd stunned himself. He had only known this woman one night! This wasn't like him at all. Nick was a romantic, he knew that, but he wasn't the type to fall so hard and fast. Was all this marriage talk for real or only a joke? This woman was casting a spell on him. It wasn't only her striking beauty. There was something about her. She was harsh, but she was childlike, too.

"Oh please, don't ask me such a stupid question. Surely, a person who reads as many books as you do would never confuse sex with love. They're two separate things."

"That's true, but it still doesn't give me the right to take advantage of you."

"I was asking for it, jackass. It would've been consensual. And now — my sweet, adorable little wop — you're going to have to wait."

The doorbell rang and Nick looked at Nicole. "Did you put in another order?"

"Yes, from Neiman Marcus. Surely, you didn't want me stinking up the place?"

Nicole opened the door, and the deliveryman walked in carrying two heavy garment bags. Nicole had him place them on the bed.

"Just need your signature, Ms. Weiss." Nicole signed and handed him a $100 tip. He left the apartment as Nicole opened Nick's closet and hung up the garment bags.

"And now, Nicky, you have some female clothing hanging in your closet. So just in case your morals sway while I'm not here, why don't you use them as a reminder that there will be some serious consequences if you decide to cheat on me? And believe me, I will find out, and you and the little bitch will pay dearly."

Nick picked up the coke, took two large hits, and then refilled his glass with more red wine.

"I'm still going to work tonight, Nicole."

She laughed. "I have no doubt, but that's just another issue we're going to have to resolve."

Nick continued to drink and do more coke, but his determination to go to work stayed strong. He took a shower, got dressed, and made sure all his waiter tools were in his restaurant jacket, which was draped over one arm.

Nicole looked up at him as he was about to leave the apartment. "Oh my, don't you look nice? Why don't you put on the jacket so I can see the whole package? I can only imagine how proud your parents would be to see you right now, after spending all that money on your college education."

"That's not funny, Nicole."

"It's not meant to be funny. I'm just stating the facts. Are you okay to drive, sweetheart, or would you like me to call a limo?"

"I'll be fine."

She reached into her purse and threw him a vial of cocaine. "You're going to seriously need that. You can thank me later."

Nick put the coke in a pant pocket and left the apartment just as Nicole picked the $600 off the coffee table and threw it in the direction of the door.

She was right, of course. During his seven-hour shift at the Palm, Nick made more trips to the bathroom than he had made in the previous six months. For once he could say that he was just as high, on the very best coke, as any of the customers. By the time he checked out and walked to his car, the coke was just about gone. For good measure, he snorted what remained and dropped the empty vial into a trash bin.

When Nick opened the door to his apartment, he saw Nicole sitting on the couch watching the cartoon channel, just like before he left. She was still doing coke and drinking wine.

She asked, "And how was your night, darling?"

"Let me tell you, Nicole, I wouldn't have made it without that coke. Thanks." He reached into his pocket and took out all the money he had made. Putting it on the table next to her, he said, "Take it, please."

Nicole laughed as she picked up the money, around $300, and threw it at the door, where the $600 from earlier remained on the floor. "That sorry amount wouldn't cover the down payment for the stuff I gave you."

"Sorry, but that's all I have."

"Did I ask for anything? What I asked for was that you simply stay here with me, but you couldn't put your precious career on hold. That's going to change. Don't you worry about that, sweetheart. Now why don't you go change out of those disgusting clothes?"

Nick looked at her, shook his head in disbelief, and walked toward the bathroom. He took a shower and put on different clothes. When he walked back into the living room, Nicole looked at him and smiled that radiant smile. "Now don't you feel better?" He did.

"Would you like a fresh glass of wine?" he asked.

"Yes, that would really be nice, Nicky."

Nick picked up the wine glass she'd been using since he left for work and placed it in the kitchen sink. He took out two clean wine glasses and opened up a new bottle of the red wine. Typically, he would have let a nice red like this breathe for a bit, but they were both so coked up it wouldn't matter. Their taste buds weren't at 100%. Before pouring, he dropped two powdered Quaaludes into Nicole's glass. He handed it to her and sat down on the couch beside her. She handed him the coke and he took a couple of hits.

"So besides looking at cartoons, snorting coke, and drinking wine, did you do anything interesting while I was gone?"

"I went to the bathroom a few times. Would you like to check my butt to make sure I cleaned it properly?"

"That's disgusting, Nicole."

"Sorry, Nicky. I didn't realize that bodily functions upset you. There was also a time when I was really gassy, but I think I passed it along with the poop."

"Okay, Nicole. I get the picture."

"My God, Nicky, you are so cute. I can't stand it. I have goose bumps all over my arm just sitting next to you. Feel, please?"

She put out her hand and Nick felt the tiny bumps. "Maybe it's because it's a little chilly in here?"

"I don't think so, cutie." She winked at him and touched the tip of his nose. "It's all you, Nicky."

"I doubt that," he muttered. Nicole reached over to pick up the coke but suddenly fell forward. Nick grabbed her to catch her fall. "Are you okay?"

"Wow!" She exclaimed. "I got really light headed there for a moment."

Nick took the coke out of her hand and rested her head back on the couch.

"You son of a bitch, you drugged me."

"Now, Nicole, you know how insane that sounds. You have enough drugs in you to get a small country stoned."

She fell asleep. "Sorry, sweetheart, but you gave me no other choice." He picked her up and placed her on the bed. He pulled the sheets up to her chin and looked at her for a long time. "I only hope that when you wake up and see things more clearly, you'll still love me."

Nick sat back on the couch and picked up the Quaalude from the night before. He took the pill and washed it down with a healthy gulp of wine.

Chapter Seven

The following morning, Nicole — freshly showered and sparkling, wearing a designer white blouse and matching short pants — stood over Nick, who was still asleep on the couch, and poured a glass of cold water over his head. He woke up sputtering. "What the hell, Nicole!?"

"It's not nice to trick a girl like me."

"I'm sorry, but — "

"Stop apologizing, jackass. I know why you did it. Now go clean up and let's go out and get something to eat. I'm starving."

Nick got into the passenger seat of Nicole's Porsche 940. She drove west down Sunset and into Brentwood. She pulled into the parking lot of an upscale restaurant, handed her car keys over to a valet attendant, and winked at another attendant. They walked into the restaurant, which was exceptionally crowded, and over to the hostess stand.

"A reservation?" the hostess asked.

"No."

"There's a forty-five-minute wait," the hostess said without looking up. "Would you like to leave your name?"

"Nicole Weiss."

The hostess looked at Nicole, picked up two menus, and asked, "Would you like to sit inside or outside on the patio, Ms. Weiss?"

"I think outside. I've been sort of cooped out inside for far too long. What do you think, sweetheart?" All the other customers who were waiting for tables looked at her.

Once seated at a table on the patio, Nick said, "Everyone in the restaurant is looking at you, Nicole."

"It's not what you think, sweetheart. It's just that I happen to be the daughter of the man who, with a snap of his fingers, could take away their snug little lives." She took off her sunglasses and looked around the restaurant with a sentimental eye.

"You come here a lot?"

"I used to, a very long time ago. They have excellent food here."

They both ordered iced teas. Nicole had a large bowl of noodles with just butter and absolutely no greens and Nick, a club sandwich.

The check came and Nick was quick to pick it up. He opened his wallet and paid the bill with cash. Then he excused himself and walked to the bathroom, but not before Nicole asked if she could see the picture on his driver's license. He handed her his wallet and walked off.

At the valet stand, Nicole handed her ticket to the attendant she'd winked at earlier. "Do you remember me, Richie?"

"Of course I do, Nicole. It's been a long time. You're as beautiful as your mommy."

"Thank you, Richie." Nicole reached over and kissed him on the cheek. He opened the door to her car, and she handed him a $200 tip as she and Nick got in. "Hopefully, we'll be seeing a lot more of you."

Tears started to flow down her cheeks. She quickly wiped them away and put on her sunglasses. She got back onto Sunset and drove toward the beach.

"Are you an only child, Nicole?"

"Yeah, but don't jump ahead of yourself, tough guy. I'm quite sure I'm nowhere to be found in my father's will. That treasure trove will go to his army buddies and Margaret."

"Who's Margaret?"

"Seriously, Nicky, you want to be a writer in the motion picture industry and you don't know who Margaret is?"

"For God's sake, Nicole, I didn't figure out who your father was until today."

"Well, Margaret has worked with my father forever, and she's probably the only person in this town who's feared more than Daddy."

"Really? And do you hate her, too?"

"No. I love Margaret very much."

"Are you being sarcastic?"

"Not at all. She is perfect and I love her. There was a time when my father refused to have any industry people at the house. No parties, no business, no entertaining. The only people allowed to come were Margaret and her husband, and she always brought me gifts that no else would ever have thought to give me. They were always so perfect … just like her. Thoughtful, on point."

"Your father was in the army?"

"Yeah, fought in some stupid war."

"A stupid war like World War II?"

"Yeah, that stupid war. Apparently, it had a big impact on him, so much so that if one of his army buddies called, he would walk out of a meeting with the president of the United States to take it. I gather, from what my mother told me, that he saw a lot of his army buddies killed and the ones who survived formed a pact that they would always keep in touch."

"That's really something," Nick said.

"Yeah, it is, but it won't seem nearly as nice when they're reading his will and we get nothing, and all his little buddies and Margaret get everything."

"I don't have a problem with that. If it wasn't for men like your father and his buddies, we wouldn't be free today. That alone is worth all the money in the world."

"You know something, Nick, you are a real fucking jackass, just like my father! You know what he believes? He believes that true heroism can only be found on the battlefield."

"That's what a lot of great men have believed. It's what many of our founding fathers believed."

"And this is the type of bullshit you learned in college? If I were your parents, I would definitely ask for a refund."

"I never said that I believed it."

"You don't have to. Just the way you are defending the son of a bitch, I can tell that's exactly what you believe!"

Nicole, exasperated, drove to the end of Sunset and came to a stop at the traffic light to turn onto the Pacific Coast Highway. The highway runs along the Pacific Ocean, up and down the majestic coastline of California.

"Left or right, my courageous little warrior?"

"What are you talking about?"

"You have two choices. One is to go left and to San Diego, and the other is to go right and to Santa Barbara. Or you can just have me decide, and you can continue contemplating whatever warriors like yourself think about."

"Nicole, you need to turn around. I need to be at work in less than two hours."

"Sadly, that is not an option, Nicky."

"Okay. Then just let me out and I'll take a cab from here."

"I don't think so, sweetheart. Not with no money in your wallet and your lone credit card missing."

Nick pulled out his wallet and opened it up to find no money and no credit card.

"And for the record, sweetheart, your driver's license photo doesn't do you any justice."

The traffic light changed and Nicole turned left. "San Diego it is."

"Nicole, I can't just be a no-show for work. Please..." She continued to drive.

"Don't you worry there, sweetheart. I took care of work for you. Talked to some little ditz named Kelsey. Told her I was your neighbor and that I found you in the hallway, vomiting and shitting uncontrollably. Took you to the hospital where they are currently doing tests but strongly suggested that it was food poisoning, which you almost certainly got from some contaminated food you ate at their famous restaurant."

"Seriously?! That is what you told her?"

"Yes, sweetheart, that is exactly what I told the little ditz. Are you banging her?"

"I'm not banging anyone, especially not her."

"Well, whose fault is that, Nicky? You had your chance a few nights ago and decided to go the chivalrous route, unless, of course, you took advantage of me last night when I was passed out."

"Are you crazy?"

"I know, you would never do such a terrible thing. You tucked me in so nicely, and I bet you even gave me a little kiss on the head."

"You know, Nicole, when you get tired of me in a week or so and drop me like a hot potato, none of this is going to seem so funny when I have no job and no way to pay my bills."

"Poor little Nicky. Do you actually think I would do such a thing?"

"Honestly, Nicole, I don't know what to think anymore."

"Of course you don't, Nicky. You're just an adorable little wop from the Bronx, lost in a world you don't understand yet fortunate enough to have met the girl of your dreams, who is madly in love with you. Let me ask you, sweetie, how many times you've been to the beach since moving to lovely Southern California four years ago."

"I don't know, Nicole." Nick was frustrated.

"Oh come on, Nicky. Play along, please. How many times?"

"A few times."

"Like, two or less?"

"Yes. Like two or less," he admitted.

"Simply amazing. Most people who come to Los Angeles can't get enough of the beach, and yet after four years, you've only managed a couple of appearances. Have you ever even worn sunglasses, Nicky?"

"I can't stand anything on my face."

"Of course you can't. But have you ever even tried to wear a pair? A nice pair of sunglasses to go along with your movie-star looks?"

"What's your point, Nicole?"

"My point is that you're a relic, and that's just one of many reasons why I love you."

"Okay, 'a relic.' If you say so. You know, ever since you took control of my life, I do feel more relaxed." Nick looked lovingly at the beautiful young lady beside him.

"Of course you do, sweetie, and it's very big of you to admit it. You need a mommy in your life, and since your mommy is back in the Bronx, I'll try to do the best job possible to be a wise and capable stand-in."

"That's really nice of you, sweetheart. Maybe when we get back home, you can cook dinner for us?"

"If that'll make you happy, of course I will, my little angel. Anything to keep my boy strong and healthy." She reached over and squeezed his cheek. "You're so adorable I can't stand it." She came to a stop at a traffic light, put the car in park, and kissed him passionately as she ripped at his clothes. Nick tried to hold her off but to no avail. The light changed and drivers started beating their horns, which Nicole simply ignored.

A frustrated driver — a big, burly guy in a T-shirt and torn dungarees — knocked violently on the window of Nicole's Porsche, yelling, "Hey bitch, what the fuck is wrong with you?"

Nicole turned and rolled down the window, "What did you say, asshole?"

"What the hell is wrong with you, bitch?" The guy reached down into the car and grabbed Nicole by her arm. With no hesitation, Nick reached down into Nicole's purse and took out the gun from last night at Mirabelle's, putting it up against the disgruntled driver's head.

"Now, is that any way to speak to a lady? First, apologize, and then walk back to your car so we can get this show on the road."

"I'm sorry." The driver stepped slowly away from the car and began walking away.

"Of course you are, fuckhead. Now get out of my sight," Nicole said.

"Drive, Nicole." Nick put the gun back in her purse and looked down at all the vials of cocaine. "You need to turn into the next parking lot and turn around."

"Why?"

"Because if that jackass calls the cops and we get pulled over, we'll have a lot of explaining to do."

Nicole turned into the parking lot of a seafront restaurant and parked in the back.

"I am so turned on, Nicky. I could fuck you right here."

"What's going on with you, Nicole?! Put some ice down your pants before you get us arrested."

"Why? Why, Nicky, must you spoil the moment?" They got out of the car and walked toward the restaurant. She suddenly stopped and pushed Nick onto the hood of her car, then started to pull at his clothes. He got hold of both her arms and wrestled her off.

"Seriously, Nicole, there are people watching!" Nick yelled. She quickly turned away and walked toward the back entrance of the restaurant.

"I need a drink," she yelled back at him. Nick looked at her in disbelief.

Nicole sat at the bar and ordered two frozen margaritas with salt. Nick entered the restaurant and sat on the bar stool next to her.

"Twice, Nick! Twice! You got me all worked up and then came up empty."

"Will you please calm down, Nicole?" Nick pleaded with her as the bartender put down their drinks.

"What's this?" Nick asked as he looked at the margarita.

"This drink is the closest I could get to 'ice down my pants.' Twice!" she said. She put two fingers up to his face and said it again. "Twice!"

Nick sighed deeply and looked around the empty restaurant.

"Don't ignore me, you son of a bitch," Nicole yelled.

Nick whispered into her ear, "I recommend that you get rid of the gun and the coke in your purse if you insist on making a scene."

"Seriously, Nick, what am I supposed to think? Are you some type of closet fag? One moment I'm the girl of your dreams, and the next moment you are pushing me away like I have some dreaded disease. Or is it that you've had so many beautiful women I'm no big deal? I'll tell you what, we can still get married, but we'll need to make some arrangements."

Nick took a sip of his drink and reached over to gently run his hands through her hair. "Are you sure you don't have some Latin blood running through that beautiful body of yours?"

"And what does that have to do with anything?"

"Well, Latinas are known for their passion. Surely, you've heard of love Italian-style. Don Juan…?"

She placed her pearly-white arm next to Nick's dark arm. "Do I look like I have Latin blood in me, Nick?"

"No, you look one hundred percent WASP. But your father is Jewish and Jews are a very migrant people, so maybe somewhere along the line a little Spanish or Italian blood made its way into your lineage? That would be a good question to ask your dad," Nick suggested.

"Are you insane? My father bleeds red, white, and blue. Never once has he brought up his Jewish heritage to me — never once."

"It was just an idea."

"A very stupid idea. The only thing that man has in common with Italians and Spaniards is that he's a pig, like the rest of your kind. Let me ask, Nicky, are your parents the passionate types who cheat on one another?"

"Don't you dare bring my parents into this insane conversation."

"Oh, I almost forgot. Nicky is very protective of Mommy and Daddy. Well, they had to be passionate at least once, otherwise you wouldn't be here. Would you, my sweet little Nicky?" She leaned over and kissed him passionately. "You see, not so bad, is it?"

"Great! Maybe we could practice a little later."

"Do you plan on doing something heroic between now and then?"

"Like what?"

"I don't know. Why don't you surprise me?"

Nick looked past Nicole at two policemen entering the restaurant through the front door. He reached over and kissed her, whispering, "Two cops just walked into the restaurant."

"Great! Just what I need to ruin the evening."

The two cops sat down at a table and looked over the menu as a waitress walked over to greet them.

"Why don't you go to the bathroom, Nicole, while I pay the bill? I'll meet you outside."

"Okay." Nicole slipped Nick some money, got up, and walked to the bathroom. He paid the bill and walked out the back entrance. He waited by the Porsche until she walked out of the restaurant. Then they got into the car and drove away.

"Where to, tough guy?"

"Let's get off this highway. Why not go back to the restaurant we ate at." Nick glanced down and saw the gun and coke still in Nicole's open purse. "Seriously, Nicole, you didn't at least get rid of the gun?"

"And why would I do that, sweetheart? That's a memento from the first night we met. I will forever cherish it." She turned off the highway and drove back onto Sunset. They entered Pacific Palisades, and she pulled suddenly into a parking spot directly in front of a restaurant. "We're far enough off the highway. Besides, I want to be able to smell the ocean air."

"That's fine. How about we leave the gun behind, and about nine vials of the coke?"

"So reckless and yet so cautious." Nicole pinched Nick's cheek. She put the gun and most of the coke under her seat.

They sat at a table on the outdoor patio at the back of the restaurant. She'd insisted that they sit outside despite the chill in the air and the screeching of wandering seagulls. She was so manic and happy Nick was quite certain — despite the fact she hadn't been out of his sight for nearly an hour — that somehow she'd managed to inject a large dose of cocaine up her nose. She ordered two frozen margaritas, slipped the waiter a hundred dollars, and made a toast to the seagulls.

"Beautiful birds, aren't they, Nicky?"

"Lovely."

"Now, be honest. Aren't you happy I called in sick for you?"

Nick looked closely at the dimpled, blue-eyed, blonde-haired beauty. "I could die happy just looking at you, Nicole. Does that answer your question?"

"I'll take that as a yes … and thank you very much, my brave little warrior."

Nick, sensing an opening, thought this might be the ideal moment to tell Nicole about his planned trip to El Salvador. The trip was only a few weeks away, and he couldn't keep it from her much longer. He hadn't expected to meet a woman and suddenly have her in his life full time. And he certainly never expected her to be as possessive and unpredictable as Nicole. She was difficult and frustrating, and she had a gritty edge to her, but there was something about her that went deeper than her surface beauty. She had an innocence about her, and she seemed to cling to Nick like she needed him.

He figured that if he played the entire thing down and actually went so far as to invite her, maybe she wouldn't go insane. Maybe she would react calmly. Never could a man be so wrong.

"Nicole, how would you like to go with me to El Salvador for a week?"

"El Salvador? Is that some sort of resort in Mexico?"

"Not exactly, sweetheart."

"Well, I don't care where it is. If you're going, I'll be going right along with you. Be sure you get reservations at the best hotel, and first-class tickets. I don't fly coach. We can make it a prehoneymoon getaway."

"It's in Central America, Nicole."

"Central America … Where is this place, like in the middle of the country? Like in Kentucky?"

"No, it's a group of countries that connect North America and South America. Guatemala, El Salvador, Nicaragua, Honduras ... "

"And why the hell would you want to go there? Don't a bunch of savages who are constantly fighting live down there?"

"I wouldn't call them savages."

"And why not? From what I understand, they still wipe their asses with their fingers. That's a savage in my book. Forget it, Nick. Neither you nor I will be visiting that god-awful place. Where do you even get these ideas?"

"I have to go. I'm already booked. The arrangements were made months ago."

"You don't have to do anything except love and protect me. The rest of the narrative, I get to write. Are we clear on that?"

"No, Nicole, we're not clear on that. I'm writing a screenplay on the civil war going on in El Salvador, and I need to go there and at least get a feel for what's really going on."

"Did your mother accidently drop you on your head when you were a baby? Is that the reason you come up with these crazy ideas? Is it, Nicky?" Nicole was screaming, bordering on hysteria. Her emotions were more than anger that he would leave her for a week. She seemed desperate to keep him close.

"Don't be foolish, Nicole."

"Don't be foolish, Nicole!" She mimicked him. "Are you kidding me? Only a fool would write a screenplay about a place that no one gives a shit about, much less go visit the shithole to get a feel for the place. You really don't get it, do you, Nick? You stupid little wop, I'd have both your legs broken before I ever let you visit a place like that. So start making other plans unless you want to be walking around on crutches for the next six months. Are we clear?" She got up and kicked Nick really hard in the shins, then walked off, leaving him bent over in pain.

The customers on the patio were all looking at him. A lady sitting at the table next to him leaned over and said, "If I were you, son, I'd listen to her, especially if you want to have a career in this town."

Nick looked up at the lady and didn't say a word. Nicole returned to the table and sat back down.

"So are we clear, Nicky?" Reaching over, he rubbed the cocaine from her nose and placed it in his mouth.

"I think you broke my shin, Nicole."

"Good! That saves me the money of having your legs broken. God! No one can ruin a good time quite like you, Nick. You should put that on your business card, next to 'Loser.' Seriously, you are fucking amazing. Do your parents even know about this?"

"No! Besides you and every customer on this patio, no one knows. Can't we talk about this later?"

"No! I'm going to call your parents right now and tell them. It's about time we were introduced, and what better way to bond than over their idiot son's safety?"

"What am I, some kind of child in your eyes? My parents have already been through enough hardship. You don't know anything about it, or about them. You hardly know anything about me. I don't need this shit. Who do you think you are, trying to take over my life like I can't make decisions of my own? I was doing just fine until you came along. You think because you're rich and gorgeous I'm just going to let you walk all over me? You can go screw yourself, Nicole."

"I'd never mistake you for a child. A child can blame his mistakes and poor judgment on age and innocence, but you, Nicky, you are a college-educated jackass! All grown up, working as a waiter, subservient to every asshole who sits at your assigned table. You call that 'doing fine' before you met me? Four years since moving to LA, still waiting tables, no scripts sold, and barely any beach time. You call that living?"

"Fuck you, Nicole," he said, slowly and deliberately.

Nicole stood up, finished her drink, ordered two more, and once again walked off to the bathroom.

Chapter Eight

Nick sat alone, rubbing his head. Then the lady sitting at the next table leaned over once again and said, "I'd do whatever she says, son, especially if you ever want to have a career in this town."

"What are you, part of a Greek chorus?"

"I was blacklisted because of my beliefs and had to go underground to simply make a living. It's unfair, but that privileged little bitch has the ability to offer you a clear — if troubled — path to your dreams. Not easy, but it's better than living your life in the shadows."

"At least the shadows offer some cover," Nick said sadly.

"But shadows don't pay bills, son. And she's right about one thing, and that's that no one gives a shit." The lady stood up, placed a consoling hand on Nick's shoulder, and turned to leave. "Good luck."

She walked away as Nicole sat back down. "Made a new friend while I was gone?" She ran her hand across her nose.

"You're a mess, Nicole."

"Is that so? Is that what your new friend said about me?"

"She's nothing but a shadow, and as you know, no shadow is ever going to lay a hand on you."

"What the hell does that even mean?" The waiter placed two more drinks down on the table.

"I'm going to El Salvador, Nicole, so why don't you do yourself a favor and simply accept it?"

"You just don't get it, do you? What chance do you think you have of making it in this town without help from me? Zero, that's how much. The only thing you have going for you is your connection to me, so why would you jeopardize your only hope by making me mad? That is simply insane."

"Here's the thing, Nicole. From the moment I saw you, I haven't been able to tear myself away. It has nothing to do with your money, or your powerful Hollywood father, or your threats to hurt me if I go. At first I thought it was because you're so fucking beautiful, and you're right, I did dream of a woman like you my whole life. But now I know that isn't it. Your looks aren't why I love you, or at least not the only reason."

"Oh really? How do you know my ravishing beauty hasn't completely smitten you? You think you're too tough to fall for me?"

"No, that's just it. I have fallen for you. If it were only because of your looks, that wouldn't be enough. It wouldn't be enough for me to stay when you're treating me like shit. I wouldn't tolerate you coming into my life and taking over if I only cared about what you look like. There's something about you, Nicole. You're wild, unpredictable, angry, fierce, and a little scary, I admit it. But there's also an innocence about you, a frightened, panicky, childlike innocence, and I want to protect you. I want to keep you safe from any bad guys, and keep you safe from yourself. I'm in love with you. I love you, but I'm going to El Salvador, and that is final."

"You're really starting to stress me out, Nick. I mean, you're really stressing me out, you son of a bitch." She slapped him across the face, stood up, and walked back to the bathroom once again, to powder her nose.

Nicole sat on the toilet in the bathroom and snorted an entire vial of cocaine. She stood up and looked at herself in the mirror; cocaine dripped from her nose. She licked the residue off with her tongue and spoke to her reflection, "Don't let him do this to you, Nicole! Don't let him!"

Nick looked at Nicole as she sat back down at the table. Pale as a ghost and sweating profusely, she took a sip from her drink. Alarmed, he asked, "Are you okay?"

"I'm wonderful."

Nick picked up a napkin and tried to wipe the perspiration and coke dust from her face, but she slapped his hand away. "Stay away, you pervert!"

Nick backed off as Nicole closed her eyes and tightly pressed her hands together. She took a few deep breaths and said, "My chest is so tight it feels like it's going to explode."

"Take a few more deep breaths. Try to relax."

"It feels like a knife is cutting right through my chest, and you're telling me to relax, you stupid son of a bitch."

Nick took a $100 bill out of Nicole's purse and threw it down on the table. He picked her up like a piece of paper and carried her out of the restaurant. In a heartbeat, he pulled out of the parking lot, driving her car. She sat in the passenger seat with her eyes closed, breathing heavily. Nick turned onto Sunset and sped down the boulevard, turning left on Hilgard and into the emergency room entrance of the UCLA medical center.

Chapter Nine

He got her immediately checked in and walked beside her as they wheeled her into a small room and placed her on a bed.

Dr. Ronald Cotlair looked down at her. "You're a little too young to be suffering from a heart attack."

"Why don't you have them put that on my tombstone, doc?"

The doctor checked her heart and a nurse took her blood pressure.

"A hundred and forty over ninety," the nurse said.

"A little high," the doctor said nonchalantly. "A little stressed, Nicole?"

"Yes, I'm a little stressed, and if I die, I want you to have him arrested for killing me." Nicole pointed to an anxious Nick.

"Why? Did he force the cocaine up your nose?"

"No, but he stressed me out so much that I took more than usual."

"I don't know if that defence will hold up in court." The doctor turned to Nick. "You're not supposed to be in here, young man."

"I'm not going anywhere." Nick stood firm, like a sentinel.

"Apparently not." the doctor said. He looked back down at Nicole and chuckled. "He doesn't seem like such a bad guy. Why would you want to put him in jail for the rest of his life?"

"Because he's an asshole, that's why! He just informed me that he's going to El Salvador so he can get a better feel for how those savages live. Oh, and by the way, he's in love with me. What the fuck?"

"Interesting! I spent a little time down there helping out those poor savages. I wouldn't recommend it as a vacation spot, but—"

"Oh my God! You're a bigger jackass than he is. He's just plain dumb, but you're a doctor. What the hell, doc?"

"Well, thank you so kindly for that wonderful compliment, Nicole. It's not every day I get called a jackass."

"So, am I going to die?"

"I seriously doubt that, not today at least. But I'm going to have this lovely nurse take some of your blood anyway, mainly because I'm interested in seeing the ratio of cocaine to blood in your body. Then I'm going to have them do an EKG, not that I actually think there's anything wrong with your heart, but while you're here we may as well check you out. Who knows, maybe a few of your insurance dollars will get earmarked for those savages."

"That's not funny."

"Oh, sure it is, sweetheart. Now, do this jackass a favor and count to ten." The doctor took a needle from the nurse. "I don't hear you counting, Nicole." He stuck her with the needle and she immediately fell asleep.

The doctor turned to Nick. "A rambunctious little creature, eh?"

"You don't know the half of it, doc. Sorry about the insults."

"No problem! We get about half a dozen cases just like her every week. Students stressing out over tests, overmedicating themselves in order to stay up, and then rushing in here complaining about chest pains."

"Is she going to be okay?"

"She's going to be fine, but I don't need to tell you the dangers of cocaine use. Looking up her nasal passages was like looking up the nasal passages of a severely burned firefighter. She's been using for quite a while, and if you love her nearly as much as she loves you, I recommend you get her some help."

"What makes you think she loves me?"

"Because no one acts and behaves like that while suffering from severe chest pains unless they are full-blown crazy for the person they direct all that energy to. Why don't you go get some rest, son, because your girlfriend is going to be out for a while. I gave her an extra milligram of the tranquilizer I injected into her arm. She needs the rest, and you might want to take some time to figure out how you're going to handle her when she wakes up. I doubt she'll be any less angry."

The doctor left the room as Nick watched Nicole getting hooked up to a heart monitor. She looked so pale and lifeless that it sent an agonizing chill through his body. He decided right then to call her father. He went through Nicole's purse and found her father's home phone number.

Nick called the man known as the most powerful person in Hollywood. Mr. Weiss answered himself and, without hesitation, assured Nick that he would be at the hospital right away.

Nick was sitting beside Nicole's bed holding her hand when Richard Weiss walked into the room. Nick dropped Nicole's hand and looked up at him.

"You can continue holding her hand. I remember when that simple pleasure made me the happiest man in the world." Clearly distraught, Weiss looked down at his daughter. "Who are you, her dealer?"

"Her dealer!? What are you, crazy? Her dealer?! I'd kill the son of a bitch if he were here in front of me."

"Sorry, but the last update I got on my daughter said that she had no friends — only dealers."

"Well then, you might want to hire better investigators."

"So you're her friend, or maybe more than a friend?"

"I care about your daughter very much, Mr. Weiss. I thought some parental intervention and caring might go a long way toward averting another situation like the one we're looking at."

"I guess my daughter hasn't told you much about our relationship?"

"She's told me enough. I don't know why that matters. You don't suddenly become less of a parent when your child hits a certain age."

Weiss walked to the other side of the bed, across from Nick. He gently reached down and ran his hands through his sleeping daughter's hair. He sighed deeply as tears rolled down his cheeks.

"Your daughter has hinted at the fact that you love books. Have you ever read *Dante's Inferno*?"

"The entire trilogy, a number of times."

"Well then, you are aware that the last circle of hell is reserved not only for Lucifer but for all those people who could have made a difference and did nothing."

"Look, I don't know who you are or what you think you know, but it seems you do care about Nicole, or you wouldn't be here. You certainly wouldn't have had the guts to call me if she didn't matter to you, and I appreciate that. Young man, I don't owe you or anyone any explanation, but for the record, I've tried to make a difference in my daughter's life — tried many ways for the longest time — but all she ever does is push me further away."

"From what Nicole has told me, you fought against the Nazi war machine. You survived some of the bloodiest battles in modern history. You were part of the Allied forces that helped liberate Paris. And yet the way I hear you tell it, this lost, bitter young woman, your child, is too much for you to handle? There's nothing you can do because she pushes you away? Forgive me, sir, but that sounds lame coming from a man like you."

"You don't know the whole story, son. What exactly are you asking me to do?"

"Get more involved in your daughter's life. Stop enabling her. She knows how much you love her, and she takes advantage of it. Every time she pushes you away, you need to push forward that much harder."

"And what's your stake in this game?"

"I'm just trying to hold on to a dream, Mr. Weiss. Nicole entered my life like a tidal wave, and I don't want to see her get washed away in a sea of cocaine."

Nick and Richard Weiss conversed for a long time, but it became apparent to Nick that the older man was not at all interested in disclosing any secrets that might help explain his daughter's behavior.

Weiss was impressed with Nick's character. The frustration and anguish on the young man's face every time he looked at Nicole were genuine. He'd been determined, before entering the hospital, that it was time to take extreme measures to ensure his daughter's safety and health, but after talking to Nick, Weiss recognized qualities in him that were similar to two other people who had been close and had a positive influence on Nicole. Those people were both gone now, and it made sense that Nicole had been drawn to this young man. He was willing to give Nick a chance, an opportunity to navigate the mind and heart of his only offspring and — hopefully — set her on the right course once and for all.

Weiss reluctantly left the hospital before Nicole woke up. Nick thought it would be better if Nicole didn't wake to the sight of her father. After nearly eight hours, she finally opened her eyes and looked at Nick. He was still sitting next to her, holding her hand. He looked tired.

Nicole angrily pulled her hand free. "I guess I'm still alive because if I was dead and in Heaven, I seriously doubt they'd allow an asshole like you in."

"Now that's not very nice, Nicole. I've been here the whole time, by your side, praying that you would be okay."

Martha, a middle-aged Hispanic nurse, walked into the room and smiled at Nick. "So you finally took my advice and kissed the sleeping beauty?"

"Oh please." Nicole rolled her eyes. "I can't even get this clown to kiss me when I'm awake."

"Don't listen to her, Martha. She's delusional."

"How do you feel?" Martha asked, as she took Nicole's blood pressure. "Good enough to go home?"

"I guess, but does it have to be with this jerk?"

"Well, that depends. Do you have any other boyfriends as good looking and caring as he is? I could give them a call."

Martha asked Nick to leave the room so she could examine Nicole.

"That young man is madly in love with you. I should think that would make you happy. Don't you love him?"

"Honestly? I'm crazy in love with him." Nicole paused. "I've done nothing but give him a hard time, but he's still here," she said quietly.

Chapter Ten

Nick opened the car door for Nicole as a hospital attendant wheeled her out to the curb. He closed the door, and Nicole slouched down into the passenger seat. As Nick was driving away from the hospital, Nicole said, "Nurse Martha thinks you're the greatest thing since Swiss cheese. If only she knew the truth."

"She's really sweet."

"Delusional, that's what she is. Did anyone ever tell you, Nick, that you drive like an old lady?"

"Yes, Nicole, virtually everyone who's ever driven with me."

"Well, it's good to know that I'm not the only one … So when do you plan on telling me, Nick?"

He didn't answer. He kept his eyes on the road.

Nicole screamed, "Don't you pretend not to hear me, you son of a bitch. When did you plan on telling me that you called my father and had him come to the hospital? Is there anything you won't do to sabotage our future?

"What are you talking about?"

"How friggin' dumb can one human being possibly be? Surely, it had to dawn on you that my father holds the strings to our future and seeing me lying there comatose is not a good omen."

"Ah, so it's about the money. Is that what you're trying to tell me? Well, I don't give a shit about your father's money. I only care about you, and if cutting you off is what it takes to keep you alive, then all the better."

"I could strangle you right now. You ignorant, stupid fool!"

"Shut up, Nicole."

Nick pulled into the garage of his building. They got out of the car and walked to the elevator. She looked in her purse as Nick opened the door to the apartment. He closed the door behind them and locked it.

"Where's all the coke?"

"Flushed down the toilet at the hospital."

"WHAT??! Are you fucking kidding me?! No!" While Nicole emptied her purse on the kitchen counter, Nick opened the bottom drawer of his desk, surreptitiously taking out a pair of handcuffs. He walked up behind Nicole and grabbed her by the wrists, cuffing her from behind.

"What the hell are you doing? You sick bastard!" Nicole screamed as Nick dragged her to the railing separating the living area from the bed. "You're hurting me!"

"Stop pulling at the cuffs and they won't hurt." He tied a rope from behind the handcuffs to the railing.

"You sick bastard. I'm going to kill you!" Nicole screamed over and over again as she struggled with the cuffs.

"You can kill me later, Nicole. In the meantime, for right now, why don't you just shut up?"

"You have no idea who you're dealing with! I swear I'll have your head!"

"I know exactly whom I am dealing with, Nicole — a spoiled, rich brat I've had the misfortune to fall in love with. You see, in my stupid little religion, it's a sin to commit suicide and an even bigger sin to stand around and do nothing while someone you know is trying to commit suicide. I'm already riddled with guilt, Nicole, and I have no intention of standing around and watching you destroy yourself."

"What are you, some kind of religious nut? Is that the reason you run away from me like the plague anytime I hint at getting romantic? Is that it?"

"Shut up, Nicole, and please don't confuse respect with some type of sickness. The moments you've chosen to get romantic were the worst places and times for romance. Just because I won't demean you or myself by giving into your coke-fueled whims, you don't get to accuse me of having some kind of problem. My only problem has been the desire to treat you right. I never thought it would be so fucking difficult to be a fucking gentleman!" Nick took out a padlock from behind his bookcases and placed it over the door lock.

"These cuffs are cutting into my wrists."

"Stop moving around. It's not like you're going to get out of them. They're police cuffs, and not even a seasoned criminal like you is going to pick them."

The phone rang and Nick picked it up. "Hello, Mr. Weiss. Yes, she's right here … handcuffed to a railing and a bit upset."

"Daddy!" Nicole screamed. "He's insane — he's going to kill me!"

"No, Mr. Weiss, she's fine. Of course." Nick carried the phone over to Nicole and put it under her chin.

"Daddy, listen to me. He's insane. You need to get down here before he rapes and tortures me and throws my mutilated body into a dumpster." She looked at Nick and said, "Do you mind? A little privacy, please."

Chapter Eleven

Nick walked toward the bathroom as Nicole continued to talk to her father. "Daddy, please. Don't believe anything he's told you. If you want to see me alive again, you need to get some men down here and knock down this door. No police! The address… " Nicole paused and then yelled out to Nick, "Hey, jackass. What's the address here?"

"It's 136 Larrabee, apartment 3B," he yelled back. Nicole relayed the address to her father. "And Daddy, whatever men you send, make it perfectly clear to them that if they so much as scratch my little Nicky, I will personally kill them. He might be a little crazy, but he's mine. And with a little help, I'm sure he'll be fine." She screamed at Nick again. "Hey, jackass, my father wants to talk to you."

Nick took the phone. "Yes, Mr. Weiss, she's absolutely fine. She's the last person in the world I would ever hurt, and once she calms down, I'll take the cuffs off and she can move around all she wants … No, not a problem. Yes, I'll talk to you soon. Thank you." Nick hung up and looked across at a shocked and appalled Nicole.

"Oh my God. This is one I did not see coming. You're in cahoots with my father?! First you cozy up to the daughter, and now you're best friends with the big man. I totally get it now. You slimy piece of shit."

"Shut up, Nicole, unless you want to stay handcuffed to that railing forever. You have no idea what you're talking about."

Nick reached into the top drawer of his desk and took out a roll of duct tape. He cut off a piece and placed it over Nicole's mouth, which immediately shut her up.

"Finally, some quiet." Nick picked up the telephone and called the Palm. "Hello, Kelsey, I won't be able to come into work tonight. Still suffering from the food poisoning... What do you mean, I should call Gigi later and tell him myself? Listen, you little twat, why don't you just do your job and relay the message to him when he comes in? God almighty." Nick slammed the phone down and angrily punched it off the counter. It flew across the kitchen floor. He looked at Nicole, sitting there taped up, and stunned at his outburst. "You see, I'm starting to sound and behave like you."

As he walked over to pick the phone up, it suddenly rang. "Yes?!" Nick listened as he slid down the back of the counter to the floor, out of Nicole's line of sight.

"No, mom, everything's fine. Just got out of the shower, that's all." Nick listened as his mother talked, then finally replied, "No, Mom, how could I ever forget? Yes, I've been to church and I always light candles." He started to cry, trying to breathe and hold back the sobs. As Nicole listened to the pain in his voice, the stern, angry expression on her face dissolved into a soft, caring one.

"I miss you and Dad so much. Soon, Mom, very soon. I love you and Dad more than anything... Yes, I promise. Love you."

Nick hung up and sat there, crying quietly. Nicole made a sudden move that snapped him out of his sad thoughts and memories. He wiped his eyes, stood up, and looked down at her. He shook his head, unlocked the padlock, and placed it on the counter. "This is too insane. I can't deal with it. Please just promise me you won't start yelling and screaming once I untie you."

Nicole nodded as he looked into her eyes. "I've never meant you any harm. I don't know what you're into or why. I just hope that whoever you find in the future will care about you and love you half as much as I do. You need someone to protect you from yourself. I'm sorry it won't be me."

Nick gently pulled the tape off her mouth and then took the cuffs off her hands. "Hang on a second. Let me get some lotion to put on your wrists."

Nick ran to the bathroom and came back with a bottle. He took Nicole's hands and rubbed the lotion over the spots already starting to bruise on her wrists.

"Is your mom okay?" Nicole asked quietly.

"She's just having a bad day. She'll be fine."

"Do you want to talk about it?"

"I can't right now, but thanks. You can take the lotion with you."

"Are you kicking me out?"

"No, Nicole, not in a million years would I ever kick you out, but I thought by the way you were talking that you didn't want to have anything to do with me."

"That's not true, Nicky," Nicole said, tears in her eyes. She threw her arms tightly around him. "That will never be true. It may not make any sense, and I know I'm far from easy to deal with, but I need you. Please don't ever leave me. I don't want to be without you."

They stayed there for a long time, embraced in each other's arms. Nick felt her warm tears from seeping into his shirt. It seemed she was finally ready to let some of her guard down, and it touched the inner sanctum of his heart.

Chapter Twelve

Nicole sat a few rows back from Nick's gate inside the Pam Am terminal at the Los Angeles International Airport. The arrival of his flight from El Salvador had just been announced, and Nicole's stomach still rumbled like it had been doing for the entire week since Nick left. She had gambled and let him go when he put his foot down about the trip, and for once, it had paid off. Nick was different. He'd kept his word. She had allowed him his Hemingway moment and seriously hoped it would be his last act of reckless stupidity.

Hispanics surrounded Nicole, and she was amazed at how beautiful the little boys and girls were. The teenage girls were quite sexy, even if their outfits were a little over the top and their makeup was applied a little too heavy. She couldn't help thinking that, in a couple of years, all these sexy little girls would be plump like their mothers and grandmothers. Once married, they would undeniably start dropping babies nonstop for the next twenty years. Between that and the burritos and tacos, how could they avoid getting obese? And why did they all seem to smell like burned grease? You would think that, after so many years in this country, they would have discovered soap.

Passengers started to disembark from the plane and were greeted by family and friends. Nicole finally spotted Nick, but she fought off the urge to run to him and hug him. Instead she waited for him to spot her, and as he walked toward her, she finally got up and greeted him with a simple kiss on the cheek. "Not even a real kiss after a whole week, Nicole?"

"I reserve real kisses for people who deserve them..." She looked over her suntanned boyfriend carefully. "You're so dark you could pass for Nat King Cole. What did you do down there, go to the beach?"

"El Salvador is close to the equator so the sun's very hot."

"The sun's very hot here too, Nick, but in all the time you've been living in southern California, you couldn't find a beach until you met me. Now, in one short week, you come back to me looking like some dumb-ass surfer dude searching for the perfect wave."

"I don't know what you're hinting at Nicole, but on my grandmother's grave, I swear I did not go to any beach, or sit by any pool, or think about any girl except you. In the whole time I was gone, I doubt that ten minutes ever went by in which I didn't think about you, and that's the truth."

Nicole looked at him and couldn't help smiling. "Well, I am the best thing that's ever happened to you after all."

They got into Nicole's car, drove out of the parking area across from the terminal, then turned onto Sepulveda Boulevard.

"For the record, I have been an extremely good girl since you left — no coke."

"Really? I'm very proud of you, Nicole."

"And very well you should be ... considering the agitation and anxiety you put me through."

"I'm sorry that you suffered so much, but I'm back now and happy to see you. Thank you for coming to pick me up."

"Whatever!" Nicole pressed down on the gas pedal.

As they neared Nick's apartment, Nicole turned left off Sunset. The car suddenly accelerated as they climbed through the Hollywood Hills.

"Where are you taking us?" he asked. "I just want to go home."

"And who said we aren't going home?"

"Because even I know I don't live up here."

"Wow! Did you actually pick up a sense of direction down there in Central America?"

"You're running on all cylinders tonight, aren't you?"

"I've had a whole week to prepare myself." She slammed on the brakes and came to an abrupt stop next to a guardrail that protects cars from going over the side of the mountain. She inched slowly along the guardrail, which opened on to a large plot of isolated land overlooking the city of Los Angeles. She parked the car in the farthest corner of the plot.

"Nice view, Nicole, but I'd still rather go home."

"Shut up, asshole." She lowered the back of her seat and looked up at Nick. "Are you waiting for an invitation?" She lowered her pants and panties.

"Seriously?" Nick asked.

Nicole reached up and grabbed him by the shirt, pulling him down over her. "Will you please just fuck me?" She impatiently clawed at his pants.

"I thought you were mad."

"Can't I be two things at once, mad and horny as hell?"

"Of course you can!" Nick lowered his pants. "I really did miss you."

"Of course you did." Nicole let out a pleasurable groan.

Less than two minutes later, Nick, embarrassed, fell flat on top of her. "Sorry. At least you know I wasn't with anyone else."

"It's okay, Nicky. I'm pretty sure even Valentino misfired occasionally. I like knowing you were faithful to me while you were gone."

Nick lifted himself up and put his pants back on. He looked down at her, lying naked below the waist and staring up at the ceiling of the car. He couldn't tell what she was thinking, but she was calm and quiet and he didn't want to ruin it. After a minute, she put on her clothes and they drove off.

"Don't be such a grumpy little bear, Nicky. You're still my hero. You're so brave, going down to that third-world country and trying to save one savage at a time. Tell me, do they still wipe their butts with their fingers?"

She reached over and tried to pinch Nick's cheek affectionately, but he put up his hand to thwart her gesture.

Chapter Thirteen

Nicole parked the car directly in front of Nick's building. She opened the door to the apartment, and as they entered, he looked instinctively down at his answering machine.

"No new messages after being away for a week?"

"Oh, you had plenty of messages but I deleted them all, except the ones from your parents. I called them back. Don't worry, everything's okay."

"You talked to my parents?!" Nick asked in disbelief.

"Yes, I spoke to your parents. Don't sound so shocked. They're lovely, and so sweet. I can't wait to meet them."

"Who did you say you were?"

"Your fiancée, who else?"

"You're joking."

"No, I'm not joking. Why would I lie to them?"

"When did we become engaged?"

"Do you seriously need to ask?"

"Yes, Nicole, I seriously need to ask."

"A week ago. When you left me at the airport. You selfish piece of shit! You don't deserve parents like yours. I bet your father never left your mother to take an extended vacation in some third-world country."

"My father isn't a writer."

"And as far as I'm concerned, neither are you. Real writers get paid, but so far, I haven't seen any pay stubs from Simon & Schuster. Or did you just forget to show me?"

Nick walked over to the refrigerator and took out a soda. "Where did you tell my parents I was?"

"On a retreat."

"A retreat? Where, Nicole? Where did I go on this retreat?" Nick yelled.

"To Santa Barbara. A mountainous retreat owned by the Catholic Church. I told them you felt it necessary to cleanse your soul before we got married."

"And they believed you?"

"Of course, they believed me."

"I must admit, Nicole, that is one hell of a lie."

"I felt terrible having to lie to my future in-laws, but what choice did I have? I feel more love for them at this moment than for you, and I haven't even met them yet."

"Regardless, still one hell of a lie."

"Thank you."

"Would you like a soda?"

"You know I don't drink soda or beer, Nick. It makes me feel bloated and gives me terrible gas."

"How could I forget?"

She reached for the remote to the television and turned on the cartoon channel.

"I see your taste in TV hasn't changed. Exactly what ideas go through your mind when you're watching Bugs and Daffy and Porky Pig?"

Nick looked at the TV and the wild shenanigans of Bugs and his friends. "Amazing!" He walked toward the bathroom and a hot shower, shaking his head.

Despite Nicole's bizarre behavior, Nick slept like a baby until the next morning, when the sound on the TV was turned up high and cartoon voices came ringing like an alarm clock through his ears. Nicole was wearing a dress shirt from his closet and panties, lying seductively on the couch and watching Looney Tunes.

"Did you sleep at all last night?" Nick asked.

"Yes, like a kitten."

"What time is it?"

"A little after 8:00 a.m. Time to get up, sleepy boy."

"Do I have to?"

"Yes, Nicky, you have to. We're moving today," she said.

"But I thought you liked it here."

"Yeah, it was great when I was doing three bags of coke a day, but now that I can see clearly, it's lost its appeal. In sober daylight, it's a depressing little dump in the middle of Fagville. I hate it."

"Well, don't hate it too much and don't waste your time searching for a place, because I don't plan on moving anywhere for the time being." Nick turned over in the bed and closed his eyes.

Nicole walked over to the bed and looked down at him. "The movers are going to be here in less than an hour."

"If you can just let me sleep a while longer, we can talk about this later." Nick's jet lag kept his brain in a haze, preventing the news from penetrating his brain while keeping out the outrage, confusion, and anger.

"There's nothing to talk about, lover boy. We're moving to my condo in Studio City. The lease on this dump has officially expired. And by the way, don't expect to ever see your deposit." Nick turned over in the bed and looked directly at her.

"I had to pay that little fag manager — you know, the one with the crush on you — one thousand dollars to agree to get rid of all the garbage in this place."

"What garbage, Nicole?" Nick asked angrily. He sat up.

"Every piece of furniture."

"Seriously? Everything in this place, I bought new!"

"Oh, that doesn't surprise me. New or old, it's ugly. Forgive me for saying it, Nicky, but it all has that college sophomore look to it. For someone who takes pride in all the great literature you read, you'd think that, somewhere along the line, you would've picked up an idea of what real furniture looks like." Nicole had an air of utmost disdain in her voice.

"Where are my books, Nicole?" Nick slowly stood up from the bed. He was mildly stunned and upset up to now; he'd gotten used to her antics. But when he didn't see his books, Nick nearly had smoke coming out of his nose. He was fuming.

"Where are my books, Nicole?" He repeated the question as his voice rose to a feverish pitch.

"In the same place they've always been." Nicole slid open the closet door and revealed boxes filled with books. Each box was labeled with the titles and authors of the books inside. "Don't bother thanking me, asshole. I can't even tell you how long it took me to label each box and keep them all in the same order you had them arranged on those stupid shelves. But because I love you so much and know how much those books mean to you, I did it anyway."

"Where are my work clothes?" He grabbed her tightly by the hand.

"I put them in a box and personally returned them to your former employer."

"What?"

"You heard me. You no longer work there. You quit the Palm, or, to phrase it correctly, I quit for you, because you never would've had the balls to do it yourself."

"That's insane. Number one, you can't quit my job for me. And number two, my boss would never believe a psychopath like you."

"One, I can do anything I want, and two, I can be quite convincing." She broke Nick's hold on her hand with a forceful shove. "And don't you ever call me a psychopath again. This time I'll let it slide because I understand you're a little stunned over the sudden move, but next time there will be consequences you can't begin to imagine."

Nicole stormed into the bathroom and slammed the door. Nick, for a long, uneasy moment, stared vacantly into space. He felt like a fighter surprised by a left hook and sent to the canvas with a follow-through right cross. He regained his composure by entertaining the thought that it was simply an elaborate joke. She was like a little girl, copying the plot from a cartoon. He picked up the phone and called the Palm, then listened as Kelsey, the hostess, recalled the day Nicole had come into the restaurant and quit on his behalf.

"Yes, Nick, about an hour before opening. She walked in, passed the hostess stand, and ignored my warning that we weren't open yet. She walked straight up to Gigi, who was sitting at the bar looking over the reservation book, and dropped a box on the bar. She told him that they were your uniforms and that you quit. Gigi laughed and told her to get lost and take the box with her, or else he was going to call the police. And that's when the insanity started.

"She picked up a bottle and threw it through the mirror above the bar. It made such a loud noise that, at first, I thought she was shooting up the place! When Gigi went to grab her, she kicked him so hard in the genitals that he screamed and fell to the floor. She then very calmly placed a bundle of money on the bar — it turned out to be five thousand dollars — and said, 'That should easily cover the damage.' And that if he ever got the crazy idea to rehire you, the damage she did that day would look like child's play compared to the damage she would eventually bring down on this dump. Then she walked away from Gigi and told me to have a pleasant day. And told me not to forget to smile when guests asked me about the broken mirror.

"She was crazy! Is she your girlfriend?"

"My fiancée," Nick said. He felt numb.

"Wow. Really?! Interesting choice."

"Yeah, tell me about it. Is Gigi in now?"

"Yeah, but I wouldn't bother coming in. Believe me, he does not want to see you. Afterward he went on a rant about how he told you guys never to mingle your personal lives with the job. I'm sorry, Nick, but you're out of here."

Despite Kelsey's warning, Nick grabbed what looked like his car keys and ran out of the apartment. Even though his manager was known to be a venomous lunatic who got immense satisfaction out of seeing other people suffer, Nick somehow believed he could talk Gigi into letting him keep his job. Considering how crazy everything in his life had become, it seemed like a viable possibility.

Nick paced back and forth in the elevator as he rehearsed what he was going to say to his lunatic boss, or ex-boss. The elevator door opened, and he walked toward his reserved parking space, dropping to his knees when he saw that the space was empty. His car was gone. Kneeling on the grease-stained garage floor, he slapped his hands against his head, a slain and defeated figure unceremoniously betrothed to the conqueror.

Nick returned to the apartment and flipped the keys onto the counter. Nicole greeted him with a big smile. "For a moment there, Nicky, I thought you ran away."

Chapter Fourteen

Nicole was dressed in white shorts and a cropped white T-shirt, sitting on the couch, watching cartoons.

"Can I ask you one question?" Nick asked.

"Of course, sweetie. It's not like I'm one of those dictators you rave so passionately against."

"Not in that outfit, you're not. White … an interesting choice."

"You like?"

"What's there not to like, Nicole? By the way, what did you do with my car?"

"I sold it. It was for your own safety, Nicky. I mean, let's face it, you're a terrible driver. But that's not your fault, sweetheart. I've never met a New Yorker worthy of a driver's license, especially not one from the Bronx."

"And how much did you get for it?"

"Seven hundred and fifty dollars."

"Seven hundred and fifty dollars." Nick repeated the number in disbelief. "Just last year, I paid thirty-five hundred for that car."

"And that's what you call throwing good money away, Nicky. Surely, you're aware that 1985 is the worst model year in GM's history?"

"It didn't even have a scratch on it, and I doubt if I put a thousand miles on that car. And seven hundred and fifty dollars was the best you could get?"

"Yes, Nicky. It was the only offer I got."

"No, what you really mean to say is that it was the first and only offer you took on the car. Am I right?" He was seething inside but also exhausted from fighting with her, and she looked so damn hot in that white outfit.

"Yes, Nicky, you're right. I didn't have time to waste showing people that stupid piece of junk. Believe me, seven hundred and fifty is more than that car was worth."

"And where's the money?"

"It's gone. I used it to pay the movers and to buy a few necessities for the condo."

"Is that so? At this moment, Nicole, I have exactly forty-seven dollars to my name. I am a twenty-six-year-old man with forty-seven dollars to his name. You know what? I'm in serious need of a drink." Nick walked over to the refrigerator, opened the door, and found all the wine in the refrigerator gone.

"What happened to all the wine?"

"I threw it out. I knew that you wouldn't be able to handle all this change and that the first thing you'd reach for was some booze to dull the pain. Well, honey bun, I just can't handle you getting drunk at eleven o'clock in the morning. Not after all the stress I've been through this last week."

"And yet, Nicole, you're stoned right now. I can see it in your eyes. You're turning my life upside down and enjoying it. Why are you doing this to me?"

"I smoked half a joint early this morning. I'd hardly call that stoned. And before you mosey along, cowboy, I have a few questions I need you to answer." She poked him in the chest.

"Can't it wait, Nicole? I'd like to shower before the movers get here."

"No, it can't wait," Nicole held up a photo of a pretty blonde in a skimpy outfit. "Do you know this bitch?"

Nick looked at the photo. "Where did you get that picture?"

"It fell out of one of your stupid books while I was packing. Just tell me, who is this bleach-blonde little bimbo?"

"A friend I haven't seen or talked to in a number of years."

"Did you fuck her?"

"What?"

"Don't bother. The 'what' said it all."

"I don't see the point in this argument, Nicole. What went on between her and me took place a number of years ago — way before I met you."

"I'll tell you the point, Nick, because bitches like this never forget the past, and eventually always come back knocking. I just want to be prepared."

She lifted a second picture up to Nick's face, this one of a pretty teenage girl in a Catholic school uniform.

"And this preppy little cheerleader, with the Ali MacGraw haircut. Did you do her too?"

"Give me that picture, Nicole." Nick was angry. His voice had suddenly changed. Nicole hid the picture behind her back.

"A simple yes or no will suffice. Did you fuck her or not?"

"You stupid bitch. That's my little sister. Now give me back that picture before I walk out of here for good."

There was a moment's pause as Nicole digested this information. "Sister? You never told me you had a sister." She looked closely at the picture and quickly realized that Nick was telling the truth.

"She was killed in a freak accident eight years ago, and you know what, Nicole? She was everything you're not. She was decent and kind, she had the manners of a young lady, and she was caring. She put others before herself. She loved to laugh and go to the movies and be around people. She would've done something with her life." Nick grabbed for the picture but Nicole refused to let go.

"Do you have any other siblings I don't know about?"

"No, it was just her and me. Now I'm all they've got."

"My God, Nicky, what a selfish son of a bitch you are. Knowing how despondent your parents must still be over the loss of one of their children, and what do you do? You take a stupid and dangerous trip into the jungle to study a bunch of savages? You could've been killed by one of the spears they throw at each other. How inconsiderate can you be? Imagine the pain your parents would have felt if anything happened to you. I really hope you had a wonderful trip because that was the last one you'll be taking. You jackass."

Nick grabbed at the photo of his sister again but Nicole said, "No! I'll put it in a beautiful frame and put it in your study. This shouldn't be hidden in a book. Here." Nicole handed him the other photo of the bleached blonde. "I'll allow you to keep that just in case you get tired of having sex with me and need to jerk off. On second thought, give that back." She tore it up into a hundred pieces and threw it at Nick. "How stupid am I, actually thinking someone could get tired of having sex with me. Isn't that the most ridiculous thing you ever heard?"

Nick spent the final minutes in his apartment on the bed staring up at the ceiling while Nicole sat on the couch looking at cartoons on TV. Shortly before taking refuge on the bed, Nick had called his parents. He hadn't heard them so excited and happy in many years. Apparently Nicole had won them over in a big way. His mother said that her prayers had been answered and Nicole was God's way of taking care of her son. She said Nicole had sent them some pictures and that she was not only beautiful but she glowed like the Madonna. She talked so respectfully and never used that terrible language that so many girls her age were using these days. Many of the pictures she sent of herself had Nick in them, and she'd written beautiful quotes on the back of each one. His mother was over the moon.

Nick was sure the photos Nicole sent to his parents must have been laced with some type of drug. It would have passed into their bodies through their skin when they touched the pictures. His mother had compared Nicole to the Madonna. Surely, his poor mother was hallucinating.

It wasn't enough that Nicole had discarded all his possessions except for his books and manuscripts. She'd also gotten him released from his job and had sold his car for one-fourth what it was worth.

And now she was after his parents?! The way things stood, she was well on her way to becoming a loving member of the family. Nicole was a cocaine addict and a cartoon addict, and his mother was thrilled they were together. You couldn't make this stuff up.

Nick turned his head and looked at Nicole. She was undeniably stunning. If he were to snap a picture of her at this very minute, he would have to title it *Innocence*. What a joke. Here he was, engaged to this psychopath, and he hadn't even proposed. Psychopath! He didn't know how he could love her, only that he did. He couldn't imagine his life without her and didn't want to go back to the same boring routine day after day. In some ways, he missed the comfort of stability, but Nicole brought an excitement to his life that had been missing. She made each day unpredictable, an adventure.

Nick looked back up at the ceiling. She had totally annihilated him, stripped him down to his bare essence, and robbed him of his own parents. And now she was ready to start building her own version of the perfect man … her own little Frankenstein. Nicole had determination, audacity, and an abundance of confidence on her side, and she possessed a reservoir of energy like those cartoon characters she so loved.

The movers arrived, and Nicole told them what they needed to move. They looked at her, confused. "Is that all?"

"Absolutely!"

The movers looked across at Nick. "Yeah, that's it, guys," he said.

"Gentlemen, if you might like any of this fine furniture for yourselves, please feel free to take." Nicole said. Then she took Nick's hand and led him out of the apartment. "Say good-bye, Nicky. Despite its depressing squalor, this place will always be dear to my heart."

Chapter Fifteen

Nicole put down the top on the Porsche, and they got into the car. Nicole decided to drive over Coldwater Canyon Avenue, a longer but much more scenic and beautiful route to Studio City. At Doheny and Sunset, near the border between West Hollywood and Beverly Hills, she came to a stop at a red light. She playfully grabbed Nick's hand and waved it up and down.

"Say good-bye to West Hollywood, Nicky. To the Rainbow, Gazzarri's, sweet Mirabelle's, the Palm, bookie, bookie soup... "

"Nicole, I don't understand. It's not like you won't be back here sometime in the future."

"And why would I come back here? I'll avoid this place like the plague. I'm not like you. I know when to let go." She put on a pair of expensive sunglasses. Nick stared at her as she started to drive again.

"What are you thinking, Nicky?" She turned onto Coldwater Canyon.

"It never fails to amaze me how beautiful you are."

"Thank you. And for the record, I never get tired of hearing it." She smiled her most dazzling smile. "You know, Nicky, I know a little place off the road a little farther up. We can stop and ... you know, do it."

"When did you become such a fan of having sex outdoors?"

"What do you mean?"

"You know, last night and now today."

"Oh, don't be such a prude, Nicky. I'm just having fun. Now, do you want me to turn off the road and go to that little spot I just told you about?"

He sighed as she blew him a kiss. "Too late now, Nicky. We already passed it."

"Thank God!"

"How dare you! You pass on a chance to have sex with me and you say, 'Thank God'? How insulting is that? You hurt my feelings … but you need to know that I love you more than anything in this world. And I also love your parents. What you have with them, the bond between the three of you — especially after losing your sister — that's the kind of family connection I never had. I see that your love and respect for your parents is so real. I want that too. I love you so much, Nicky."

"Surely, there has to be some relative you love — a kindly grandma, an aunt, an uncle, a cousin?"

"No, I hate them all."

"Not your mom?"

"Especially her, that cowardly bitch."

"Nicole, please, don't talk that way about the dead … especially your mom."

"Why, am I supposed to canonize her now because she's gone? That woman failed her child, her only child, in the worst way possible. She failed to protect the one good thing in her miserable life. I hope she's burning in hell."

"Okay, how about we move on? Who's your favorite cartoon character?"

"Who do you think, Nicky?" She replied as though Nick should know the answer.

"I don't know. That's why I asked."

"Bugs Bunny! Who else could it possibly be? And your favorite?"

"I guess Bugs, too."

"No, Nick! Your favorite can't be Bugs. You're nothing like Bugs."

"Then who?"

"Porky Pig, that's who."

"Okay, that's great. I like Porky."

"You know Bugs is originally from the Bronx and Brooklyn," she said.

"No, I didn't know that."

"You couldn't tell it in his voice?"

"I'll be honest with you. I never really thought about it."

"It figures. Did you go to Brooklyn a lot when you were living in the Bronx?"

"A couple of times, maybe. People from the Bronx don't go to Brooklyn unless they really have to."

"I don't understand. Aren't they right next to each other?"

"Yeah."

"So after all those years living in the Bronx, you only went to Brooklyn a couple of times. And yet you had no problem going off to Central America, thousands of miles away, to live among the savages and drive me insane?"

"But look how much you got done while I was away." Nick grinned at her and she couldn't help smiling back.

Nicole turned onto Ventura Boulevard and drove farther into Studio City, past Jerry's Famous Deli. "Welcome to the Valley, Nicky. I already feel cleaner."

"I thought the air pollution in the Valley is even worse than over the hill."

"So technical, Nicky. Can't you just enjoy something without analyzing it to death? Be honest, four years in Los Angeles and you've never even been to the Valley, have you?"

"I really don't know."

"Of course you don't. After twenty-two years living in the Bronx, you still don't know if you went to Brooklyn," she teased.

"I didn't say that, Nicole. I know I've been to Brooklyn, but only a few times."

"But not enough times to catch the Brooklyn dialect in Bugs's voice?"

"No, not that many times. You're not only beautiful, sweetheart, but so very smart."

"I know. When we go to visit your parents, you can rest assured we'll be taking a trip to Brooklyn. You simply amaze me at times, Nicky. You don't go visit landmarks right next door to where you live, and yet you want to go to all these stupid countries where they don't even speak English. It would do you good to stop reading the *New York Times*."

"I don't see that ever happening, sweetheart."

"Whatever, Nicky. If you want to continue wasting your time reading that left-wing communist newspaper, go right ahead… "

"But don't you want to see a world in which all people enjoy the same freedoms we do?"

"Of course I do, Nicky. As long as it doesn't involve you traveling. The next time you get such a crazy idea, I'll have your legs broken."

"Oh, here we go with the broken legs again."

"I have a lot of money, sweetheart, and can easily outsource my dirty work."

"Now, Nicole! Surely, that's not the girl my parents think is so perfect?"

"Well, it just goes to show you how smart your parents are. They haven't even met me, and they already see all the wonderful qualities I possess. It's sad that the man I'm about to marry is so blind to my many gifts."

"They actually believe you're like the Madonna."

"Madonna!? Why the hell would they think I'm like that talentless little whore?"

"Not the singer, Nicole. You know, Jesus, Mary and Joseph. The Virgin Mary. Madonna."

"Oh, oh … okay. That's so sweet, Nicky. Now that I think of it, I don't think we should have sex again until we're married. Out of respect for your parents. They think I'm the Madonna, for Pete's sake."

"Seriously, Nicole? I know we haven't had a perfect opening to our love life, but what about the other guys you've been with?"

"Oh please, Nick. It's not like I even remember them."

"You can't suddenly become a born-again virgin, Nicole."

"Oh really, Nicky? Wait until later, when your pistol is looking for a home."

"You know, it's not too late for you to become a nun. Just the idea of you in one those old-time habits, with only your beautiful face showing … what a turn-on. Ingrid Bergman aside, you would be the prettiest and sexiest nun ever. And the Catholic Church can always use a gentle, caring, and loving person such as yourself."

"So that's it, huh? It's nuns that really turn you on. I should've known. Twelve years of Catholic school … It was twelve years, wasn't it, Nicky?"

"Yeah — twelve glorious years."

"Twelve years of Catholic school and you turn into a pervert who gets turned on by women dressed in black Victorian costumes."

"Now that's not very nice. What have nuns ever done to you?"

"Nothing, Nick … but now that I know what really turns you on, I'll look for a nun's habit to wear on our honeymoon."

"Promise?"

Nicole turned left on Colfax Ave and then right onto Moorpark. She parked the car in front of her condominium — a sprawling, six-unit complex with a swimming pool and tennis courts. She took off her glasses and looked directly at Nick.

"I have a very serious question to ask you, Nicky. Are you still mad at me?"

"It's all over with, Nicole … all in the past. I can't help whom I love, and I love you more than anything. You can turn my life upside down and inside out, you can try to control every detail of our future, you can even manipulate my parents. I don't care. I just want to be near you and be your guy."

"You didn't answer the question, Nicky. I have no doubt you love me. After all, you'd have to be the biggest fool in the world not to love me. Now back to the question. Are you still mad at me?"

"No, but in all honesty, I was very mad at you before. You literally trashed everything."

"Okay, Nicky, no need to rehash the past. All you need to know is that everything I do is because I believe it is in your best interests. I never had anyone stick up for my best interests. No one fought to make sure I was safe and on the right path. I believe, when you truly love someone, that's the least you can do." Nicole shut the ignition off and got out of the car. Nick lingered for a few seconds, trying to process her latest remark. She only revealed tiny bits of herself at a time.

She grabbed his hand as they walked across the complex. The door to her condo was open as the movers carried in the last few boxes. The movers handed Nicole a receipt, and she tipped them with two $100 bills, $100 each. They graciously thanked her, left the condo, and closed the door behind them.

"So how do you like your new home so far?" she asked excitedly.

"It's beautiful, Nicole. Very white." Nick looked around the gigantic living room with its white carpet, white three-section sofa, and white reclining chairs. Across from the sofa, a sixty-inch TV sat adjacent to an expensive, top-of-the-line sound system. Nicole opened a curtain and revealed a large sliding door that opened out onto a balcony. She opened the glass door and they walked out. The balcony overlooked an Olympic-size swimming pool. The place was beautiful.

A stunning brunette, perfectly tanned and wearing a diamond-laced bikini and black sunglasses, sat by the pool pretending to read a magazine. She looked up from the magazine, smiled faintly in the direction of Nick and Nicole, and looked back down.

"Quite lovely," Nick said, about the property and the pool.

"Do you know how to swim, Nicky?"

"I used to." Nick's eyes slowly moved in the direction of the lovely brunette.

"You either do or you don't, honey. There's no in-between." Nicole screamed, in the direction of the girl, "Hey, sweetheart, nice bikini. Did you pick it up at Kmart?"

The girl, Michelle, shook her head and pretended to read the magazine.

"Hey you, I asked you a question. Don't pretend not to hear me. Surely, your parents raised you better than that."

"What do you want?" Michelle screamed back at her.

"You. What else would I want?"

Nick grabbed her by the hand. "What are you doing, Nicole?"

Michelle got up and walked toward the two of them.

"A little discretion would be nice," Michelle said.

"I don't do discretion, sweetheart. How much for the two of us?" Nicole asked. The girl looked both of them over.

"Two thousand for the whole night," the girl replied. Nicole reached into her pocket and pulled out a stack of hundred-dollar bills.

"What are you doing, Nicole?!" Nick asked.

"Shut up! I'll deal with you later." Nicole counted off $1,000 and handed it to the girl.

"What's this?" Michelle asked.

"That's the easiest money you're ever going to make. The next time you plan on advertising, be sure to do it on the other side of the pool, or else you'll need money to fix your face."

Michelle moved to the other side of the pool. Nicole angrily poked Nick in the chest and slammed the sliding door shut.

"What the hell is wrong with you?" Nick said.

He started to walk away, then turned back as all signs of restraint disappeared. "You're sick, Nicole, a psychopathic, sick bitch. It's no wonder you don't get along with anyone ... not with your father, no one. Why don't you have any friends? Do you have any girlfriends? You have nothing but too much time on your hands and too much of your daddy's money. How dare you presume to know what's best for anyone else. Fuck you." He turned away from her again.

She leaned against the sliding door. The sun was shining brightly into the condo, in contrast to Nick's drab apartment that they'd left behind in West Hollywood. Nicole watched Michelle pack up her belongings and leave the pool area. She knew Nick was leaving for good, or at least planned to, but where would he go with no money? "Where are you going?"

"Go to hell, Nicole. Go to hell." Nick replied as he opened the front door and left the condo and complex.

"And this is my reward ... my reward for all the suffering and pain he put me through. What a fool," she whispered, and then started to laugh. "Like he won't come back for those stupid, fucking books."

She stood by the sliding door for a very long time, brooding over Nick's indiscretions.

Chapter Sixteen

Hours later she sat on the couch, rocking back and forth, looking at cartoons. The idea that Nick had not come back was starting to trouble her. It had been nearly eight hours since that stupid incident. Surely, he was over it by now.

He must have gotten lost. After all, he had lived four years in Los Angeles and couldn't travel a half a block from home without getting lost. He had never been to the Valley before today, and God only knew where he might be. Her first guess was a bar, but he didn't have much money. He was used to leaving big tips, so he'd probably steered away from a saloon. But he had enough money to buy booze at a store, so he was probably laid out on a park bench by now, unconscious and stupid.

Nicole grabbed her car keys, left the condo, and jumped into her car. She traveled slowly around Studio City looking for Nick, stopping at the two parks in the area and searching the benches. She heard church bells in the distance and drove toward the St. Charles Catholic Church on Moorpark and Lankershim. She parked in front of the church in a no-parking zone. She climbed the front steps, opened the door, and walked into the beautiful and spacious church. It was dimly lit and empty except for Nick, who sat toward the back of the church in the middle of a pew. She sighed deeply as she walked toward him. She slid into the pew and lightly touched his shoulder.

"What are you doing here?" He was furious.

"I was worried."

"What you should be worried about, Nicole, is that God doesn't strike you dead right here and now."

"And why would he do that?"

"Because you're evil." His voice rose and echoed back at them.

"Don't say that, Nicky. I'm sorry. I admit I overreacted to you looking at that girl, but it was your fault. All week I was worried sick about you, and then you said those terrible things."

"If you really want to make it up to me, just lend me five hundred dollars so I can buy a plane ticket back to New York. I need to rethink my life."

"No!"

"You can give a hooker a thousand dollars to move to the other side of a pool, and tip movers a hundred dollars each for moving ten boxes, but you can't lend me five hundred dollars, which I will wire back to you when I get to New York?"

"We're engaged, sweetheart. Surely, you didn't forget that already. What would your parents think if you suddenly and unexpectedly show up at their door without me?"

"Please don't use my parents to justify your actions. You're drop-dead gorgeous, Nicole, and rich. You can buy yourself all the friends you need and get yourself a stud to satisfy you in bed. You don't need me."

"Is that what you want for me? Paid friends and hired sex?"

Nick turned away from her and looked at a statue of Saint Joseph. "Of course not," he replied, shaking his head.

"I thought I'm the girl of your dreams, Nicky, or is that no longer the case?"

"Oh please, Nicole ... enough with *The Love Boat* moments. It's so not you."

"Since you left, I've picked up the phone a half dozen times to call my dealer but didn't because I knew how mad you'd be if you found me high on coke. I promise, it won't happen again."

A priest, Father Francis, walked over to them. "Is everything okay, Nick?" the priest asked.

"Yes, Father. This is the little devil I told you about." Nick introduced Nicole.

"She doesn't look like a devil, Nick. She looks much more like a beautiful angel."

"As you know, Father, the devil can come in many shapes and forms."

"Yes, my son, but I'm pretty sure that this young lady is no devil. Forgiveness is a sign of strength, and we both know God makes boys from the Bronx extra strong."

"Yes, he does Father, especially this one," Nicole said.

"God bless, my children." The priest walked away.

"Let's go, Nicole. This time you've been saved by divine intervention. Next time you may not be so lucky." Nick took her gently by the elbow and led her out of the church. They got into Nicole's car and drove off. A few minutes later, Nicole parked in front of her complex, and they got out and walked into the condo together.

"Nicole, is it all right if I lie down on the couch a few minutes?"

"Of course, sweetheart. Why would you even ask such a question?"

"Because my clothes are dirty." He looked at the white sofa again. "Maybe you should get a towel?"

"Don't be silly, Nicky." She gently nudged Nick onto the couch, where he lowered his head and stretched out his tired body.

While he rested, Nicole went to take a hot shower. After a prolonged time in the bathroom, she walked back into the living room, dressed in a white nightgown and sparkling clean. Her hair glistened, and there wasn't a single blemish on her face. She tapped Nick gently on the arm and smiled down at him as he opened his eyes.

"My God, Nicole. You are so unbelievably beautiful."

"And clean."

She pulled a reclining chair next to the sofa and sat down. She rubbed her hands through his hair as he tried to stay awake. "And you smell so nice."

"Thank you, Nicky."

"You know, I had the strangest thought while I was sitting in church earlier. Don't get me wrong. I really do like Porky Pig and Bugs … but my favorite character of all is Charlie Brown."

"That's a wonderful choice. I love Chuck. Like you, he never gives up on people."

Nick fell asleep. Nicole took his hand and held it tightly. "You're definitely like Chuck, with a little bit of Snoopy thrown in."

Nicole fell asleep on the recliner, still holding Nick's hand. She was nearly as exhausted as he was but managed to get up hours before he did. A little thing like exhaustion wasn't going to get in the way of her big, albeit slightly revised, plan. Despite her tendency to fall asleep on the couch watching cartoons, she was delighted to see Nick's face first thing that morning. For once she wasn't disappointed to open her eyes to something other than Bugs Bunny and friends.

Nicole went about her morning as usual, taking another shower. She hadn't missed how Nick looked at her after she came out of the shower last night, steamy clean. She combed and dried her hair in front of the bathroom mirror and, after a close inspection of her face, decided to go without makeup.

Nick finally woke up and, for a long, unfocused moment, thought he was back in the Bronx. The rich, pleasant smell coming from the kitchen was the same aroma he was used to waking up to back in the Bronx, when his mother would surprise him with his favorite of all breakfast meals, French toast. The crazy idea that Nicole had kidnapped his mom and flown her out here was real enough that he jumped off the couch and rushed to the kitchen. Nicole stood over the stove, dipping seasoned bread into a frying pan just like his mother used to.

She greeted him with a big smile. "Good morning, sleepy head."

"Nicole! You're in the kitchen, cooking. Do you feel all right? I didn't realize you knew how to turn on a stove."

"Don't be silly, sweetheart. There are many wonderful things you don't know about me. Your beautiful mommy gave me the recipe. I hope I haven't messed it up too much."

"Well, it smells just like my mother's. I'm sure it's great."

Nicole opened the refrigerator and took out a bottle of fresh-squeezed orange juice. She poured a large glass for Nick, who sat down at the kitchen table in front of the perfect setting she had created for him. She finished cooking the French toast and then placed a large dish in front of him, along with maple syrup. He poured a large amount of syrup on top of the toast as Nicole sat down beside him.

"Aren't you going to eat?" Nick looked at her closely.

"I already ate, hours ago."

"Nicole, there's something different about you. I noticed it last night before passing out but figured it was just my mind playing games with me."

"I have no idea what you're talking about, sweetheart."

"There's a glow about you. I mean, more than usual … plus ten. You're not high on anything, are you?"

"Don't be silly, Nicky. I haven't been high since yesterday morning, and I feel wonderful."

"That's so great, Nicole. I can't begin to tell you how proud I am." Nick tasted the French toast. "My God, this is as good as my mother's."

"You like?" She was clearly pleased that he liked it. "I'm going to try to stay clean and sober, Nick. I promise to do my best. I want this to work for us. I really do love you."

"Nicole, nothing would make me happier. Does this mean you'll be making me French toast again?"

"That and a whole bunch of your favorites. Your mom sent me a list of the recipes for all your favorite dishes."

"You and my mom are really hitting it off." Nick was chewing, happy.

"And why wouldn't we, Nicky?"

"No reason. You know, it's just a little strange since you two have never met."

"We talk a lot. Unlike you, I call them twice a day to check on them."

"Of course you do." Nick finished the last piece of toast, using it to wipe up the maple syrup on his plate. "I think it's great that you're getting along so well with my parents."

Nicole moved his dirty plate to the side and said, "I've had an epiphany."

"An epiphany? Have you been looking through a dictionary between cartoons?"

"I'm converting to Catholicism."

"Now that is funny." He laughed.

"I'm not joking." She let go of Nick's hand.

"But you don't even believe in God. You're a devout atheist. How many times have you told me that?"

"I told you, Nick, I had an epiphany." She was getting angry.

"What does that even mean? Did God come to you, tap you on the shoulder, and tell you that you were a chosen one?"

"Don't you speak to me like that, you dumb-ass. I confided in you about something that's really important to me, and you joke about it? Not very Christian."

"Okay, just hold on a minute. You've bombarded me with so much stuff it's difficult for me to digest, much less unravel the mystery that goes by the name of Nicole."

"You know what your problem is, Nicky? You're a Neanderthal. Anything that even resembles 'change' in your life sends you into a panic. You're like a teenage girl. Now I'm going to talk to the priest we met in church last night."

"Please, sit back down." Nick took her hand and she sat back down. He looked into her eyes. They were clear and sober, but he knew he couldn't be too careful. "Promise me you're not going to lose it when I ask you this question."

"I promise."

"Do you want to convert because you think it would make my parents happy?"

"No, Nick, but you know that's an excellent reason."

"Just for the record, my parents don't care what religion you are. Just as long as you don't tell them you don't believe in God, you're okay."

"But I do believe in God now, Nicky. Seriously and honestly."

"Well, have you thought about simply practicing one of the religions you were born into? The Jewish and Protestant religions are both very beautiful faiths."

"And why would I want to practice either of those? My father is Jewish and I hate him. My mother was Protestant and I hated her. You're Catholic and I'm madly in love with you, and I want to share the same religion that's so important to you."

"Okay, then I'll go with you to visit Father Francis if it's that important to you. If nothing else, it'll make getting married easier."

"And when are we getting married?"

"Well, considering I just found out about us being engaged a few days ago … I guess it's customary to wait six months to a year."

"I don't do customary, Nicky, and I can't wait that long."

"Three months?"

"Fine, if you think you can go three months without sex, that'll be great."

"What do you want to do, Nicole, get married today?"

"Today would be wonderful, but in this stupid state with all the paperwork, we have to wait five days. Don't worry, I have my lawyer working on it, and in five days, we will be a legal union."

"Nicole, you're forgetting one big thing, my parents. They just can't fly out here. My father is on dialysis, and they'd have to make arrangements with a hospital."

"I know, Nicky. And believe me there's no one in the world who wants your parents at the ceremony more than I do, but just think about the stress for a minute."

"It's not so easy, Nicole. My parents haven't been right since my sister died. Every day I feel guilty for leaving them and moving out here. To just tell them over the phone that I got married … That wouldn't be right."

"Sweetheart, just listen to me a minute. I know I'm no substitute for your baby sister, but there's one thing I am sure of and that's that the thing that worries them the most is you being alone out here. They're so overjoyed that I'm in your life. I think that telling them we got married and assuring them that, when we come to New York, we'll have another ceremony and a beautiful reception will be a giant relief for them. And then there will be no more lying about us living together. And whereas I am no substitute for your sister — may she rest in peace — I know that your mother would love to have a girl back in the family, if for no other reason than to be able to share her feelings with another female."

"That's beautiful, Nicole. You're full of pleasant surprises this morning, but if I agree to get married in five days, you have to agree that we can't go on a honeymoon until we first visit my parents."

"A honeymoon? No! No, Nicky! I wasn't planning on a honeymoon. You have a job and you start tomorrow. The job doesn't allow for any days off until you hand me a finished script."

"Okay, that sounds like a plan." Nicole took him by the hand and led him down a long hallway. She stopped at a closed door and told Nick to close his eyes. He refused at first, but with enough teasing and pressure from Nicole, he agreed. She opened the door and led him into a beautiful, picturesque study. He opened his eyes and shook his head in disbelief.

"It's all yours, sweetheart. Now don't you ever say that your fiancée doesn't have exquisite taste in both men and furniture."

"My God, this place is beautiful. I love it."

Mahogany bookshelves reached from the floor to the ceiling, and lined three walls of the room. A large, antique desk — with a framed picture of his baby sister and a picture of his parents — sat between two of the bookcases. Nicole sat on top of the desk and folded her legs, spreading her hands out like a commercial model.

"The dealer told me it belonged to some famous writer. Hunter something. Some real stupid name which I can't believe I forgot."

"Hunter S. Thompson."

"Yes, that's it. You're so smart." Nicole reached down and opened a cabinet with a small, built-in refrigerator.

"Is that where the beer goes?"

"No! Remember our deal. We both remain clean and sober. When you sell your screenplay, then we can celebrate."

Nicole grabbed Nick's hand and turned toward a closet. She slid open the door and revealed a rack lined with Armani suits, shirts, and sportswear.

"If you're going to be successful, Nicky, you need to dress the part." She beamed as he gingerly touched his new clothes.

"I cannot even imagine how much all of this must have cost you." Nick looked around the room again. "I can't imagine any other person in the world, except my parents, doing this for me."

"And don't you forget that," Nicole warned. Then she opened another door to reveal a stunning, royal bathroom. "Take some time to settle in with your new space and things. I'll be out there." She left him alone.

Nick stepped into the shower. He had a crazy idea that cold water might snap him out of this dream he was living, but that didn't work, so he quickly turned the water to a comfortable temperature.

As the hot water washed over him, Nick remembered an old phrase that his aunt used to repeat: "Even a dog knows not to bite the hand that feeds him." The phrase had particular relevance now. Despite all of Nicole's solemn, heartfelt promises of better times, he understood without any doubt that he was the dog and she was the master. At first she allowed him space to roam, then gradually she tightened the collar, and now she appeared to be closing the deal.

It was important to remember that Nicole wasn't just rich, but very rich. Her allowance of $50,000 per month was more than many Americans make in a year. Spending money was no sacrifice for Nicole, especially now that she'd given up drugs — even though Nick knew he couldn't count on her staying clean and sober for long. Sobriety is rarely a journey without bumps in the road.

He grabbed a towel and dried himself off. Laid neatly on the sink were a pair of expensive dungaree shorts, a tennis shirt, white athletic socks, and a new pair of Nike sneakers that probably cost more than his entire wardrobe before meeting Nicole. The clothes fit perfectly, and as bizarre as it all seemed, he couldn't deny the fact that they felt and looked really nice.

Nick stepped out of the bathroom and back into the study. He sat down at the desk — Hunter S. Thompson's desk — swirled the chair around. Once again he was amazed at the authentic decor of the room. The ten boxes of books delivered by the movers sat on the floor across from him, and later that night, he and Nicole agreed that they'd put them onto the bookshelves in the order that made him most happy. The one thing Nicole didn't mess around with was his books and manuscripts. Apparently, they were no challenge to her, so they weren't of any interest to her.

Nicole was proud that she didn't waste her time reading, or watching the news, or caring about history or the environment. She didn't pay any time or attention to any of that stupid nonsense. She despised love poems, and the mere mention of poets such as Byron and Keats made her want to vomit. She had warned Nick many times not to waste his time writing her any sort of love poems. She would simply tear them up and deposit them in the garbage, where they rightly belonged. Words had no meaning to her. She was a girl of action. She had gotten through high school paying other students to do her homework. Male teachers had been pawns to her. Fully developed at a young age, stunning and flirtatious, she'd had no problem blackmailing male teacher after male teacher — secretly taping their after-school conversations, sessions that always ended with a confession of true love for the underage teenager.

Nicole's two favorite movies were *The Godfather* and *The Godfather, Part II*. She strongly related to the character of Michael Corleone, played by Al Pacino. When asked if she liked Mr. Pacino in any other roles, she replied, "Why would I waste my time looking at him in anything else? He is never going to be better than he was playing Michael Corleone." As for going to see a movie in a theater, there was simply no point. Movies were for couples who ran out of things to talk about, lonely losers whose only means of escape was to fantasize about things they were too scared to do in real life. Besides, going to a theater and sitting there with a bunch of smelly perverts was not something that held any appeal for her. There were already far too many perverts she had to deal with in real life. Being surrounded in a closed space by even more miscreants would only increase her chances of committing murder and going to prison.

Nick wasn't even sure if Nicole liked sex. She constantly reminded him that he was inept at lovemaking, but never once did she push him to satisfy her with his hands or mouth or toys that girls used to satisfy themselves. Actually, he wasn't even sure if Nicole was sexually attracted to men. Never once did she mention other guys as being handsome or hot, and she wasn't one to hold back her opinion. For all he knew, she was into other girls.

Nicole was adamant about never getting pregnant. The idea of spending nine months of her life getting fatter and fatter, feeling miserable, bloated and gassy, simply had no appeal whatsoever. She apparently possessed no maternal instinct.

Despite it all — the hard exterior and general lack of compassion for her fellow human beings — she could be hurt. Like the time the lights had gone out at his apartment while she was watching her cartoons, like every time she spoke to her father, and especially at the airport, when he left her to go visit the "savages," as she liked to call them. Her look at the airport was the worst. Nick had come within a split second of turning around, abandoning the savages, and running back to her. If it hadn't been for the heavyset lady behind him accidentally pushing him forward, the trip might have evaporated in the arms of a beautiful, calculating, manipulative damsel.

Nick shook his head, got up from the chair, and walked out of the study into the living room. Nicole sat on the couch, transfixed by the cartoons on the TV. Nick didn't say a word; he didn't want to startle her. He quietly walked into the kitchen, opened the refrigerator, grabbed the fresh-squeezed orange juice, and poured himself a glass. He watched Nicole from a distance. She literally did not move. Her concentration on those cartoons was so intense that it was almost frightening. She could sit mesmerized for hours on end. It was one thing when she had been using, but to be in such a trance while totally sober caused him concern. Nick thought that never in his life had he seen someone so intently and deliberately alienated from the real world.

Nicole snapped out of it as a commercial break interrupted her concentration. She looked across at Nick. "I thought you'd never be ready."

"Sorry, I lost track of time. I couldn't pull myself away from that shower, and the study. The whole suite is simply amazing. Thank you so much."

"Just remember who loves you more than life itself." Nicole picked up her handbag. "Can you think of anything I might need to bring to church?"

"No, what did the priest say?"

"To just bring myself and you. Ready?"

"Yeah. Let's go."

Nick had expected at least a question or two about the Catholic religion from Nicole, but as she drove down Moorpark, she talked instead about how glad she was that Charlie Brown was Nick's favorite cartoon character. She never referred to Chuck as a cartoon character, but as a "character." His resilience was so refreshing. Whereas Nicole hated all sports, especially baseball, she loved that Chuck never gave up, regardless of how many hits or runs he allowed.

Nicole parked the car in the church's parking lot. Nick knocked on the door of the rectory, and Father Francis greeted them and led them into a small office. He sat behind a desk, and Nick and Nicole sat across from him in separate chairs.

"I was very glad to hear from you this morning, Nicole. If you don't mind me asking, are you currently a member of a different religion?"

"Well, Father, I'm sort of a hybrid. My low-life, crap father is Jewish, and my deadbeat, crap mother was Protestant. Thankfully, she killed herself about ten years ago. Now the world is blessed with one less cowardly, despicable excuse for a human being."

"Nicole, please, you're in a church … Watch your mouth and show some respect," Nick pleaded. He knew she was all about pushing people's buttons but couldn't understand why she would do this to the priest, who had been nothing but kind to her.

"Please, Nick! You see, Father, you need to understand that Nick doesn't do change very well. I need to take the initiative on everything, otherwise nothing would get done. My future husband is perfect in every way, except he can't relate to the fact that I hate my father and mother. Nick's parents are unbelievably wonderful, so I'm nearly as excited about becoming a member of his family as I am about marrying him."

"I think it's wonderful that you love Nick's parents, Nicole. That's usually a touchy subject with newlyweds. Hopefully, down the road, you might find it in yourself to forgive and love your own parents."

"That will never happen."

"So let me understand. Your father is Jewish and your mother was Protestant? Did you at any time follow either of those religions?"

"No, Father. In all honesty, until yesterday I didn't even believe in God. I figured that all religions were one big con. But then after that terrible fight with Nicky, I had a revelation … an epiphany. I was driving around aimlessly, looking for him, and then it's like a voice in my head said, 'Go to the church.' And lo and behold, I went and there was my Nicky, sitting right there in the pew. The comfort that I saw in his face — the relief this religion gives him — seemed to pass right into me. I actually felt it, Father! At first I thought it might be some residue cocaine still in my system, but the feeling lasted throughout the night, and this morning I knew that it was God. He entered my body."

"Seriously, Nicole, that's your story?" Nick asked in disbelief.

"Seriously, Nicky," she replied as Father Francis took her hands.

"That is beautiful, child. Very beautiful. I can see the glow in your face. It's as though the Holy Spirit is inside you."

"You see, Father? You see the glow, too?" Nick asked. "I thought I was imagining it. What have you done differently, Nicole? Did you lighten your hair?"

"You heard the Father, Nick. It's the Holy Spirit."

"Oh please, Nicole. You don't even know who or what the Holy Spirit is."

"And neither did Paul, when he was struck down off his horse and visited by the Almighty," Father Francis remarked.

"No disrespect, Father, but equating Nicole with Paul is just not right. She's as likely to go out and preach the word of the Lord as she is likely to become a nun."

"Why so skeptical, son?" Father Francis asked.

"Because I know her, Father." Nick stood up and walked behind Nicole. He gently rubbed his hands into her shoulders. "You see this magnificent creature, Father, this beautiful, glowing little creature? Well, I love this woman more than anything in this world."

"More than your stupid books?" Nicole asked.

"My books can be replaced, but nothing can replace you." Nicole spun around, stood up, and kissed Nick long and passionately, right in front of the priest.

"I might hate poetry, but that's the most beautiful thing anyone has ever said to me. Kiss me."

"Nicole, we're in a church … She's very passionate, Father. If it wasn't for the golden blonde hair, blue eyes, and pearly white skin, one might actually take her for Italian." Nick laughed weakly as he looked Nicole straight in the eyes and said, "Remember why we are here, sweetheart? Your conversion to Catholicism?"

"Yes, of course, Nicky. Sorry, Father, but you know how it is, when you find something so perfect, so unexpectedly, that you just lose control."

"Yes, finding the Lord can be ... exhilarating," Father Francis agreed politely.

"Not the Lord, Father, my Nicky."

"There she goes again, Father. Just joking, right sweetheart?" Nick pleaded with his eyes.

"No, why would I be joking? So Father, what's the fee to join this club?"

"What club?" Father Joseph was bewildered. He tried to filter and decipher Nicole's train of thought.

"You know, how much does it cost to become a Catholic?"

"There's no fee," he replied.

"No fee?! That's ridiculous, Father. These days there's a fee to join everything. It's the American way."

"We're a religion, young lady, not a gymnasium. We follow the word of God and try to carry out his work on earth."

"And doesn't that cost money?"

"Yes, of course it costs money, but thankfully we have parishioners who give generously to the church, and their support helps us care for the poor and homeless."

Nicole stood up and walked over to a number of framed pictures on the wall behind Father Francis. The pictures were of poor, Latino families that the church helped support and feed.

"And are these pictures of people that the church helps?" Nicole asked.

"Yes."

"All Mexicans?"

"Not all. Some are from El Salvador, Guatemala, Haiti... "

"Yes, yes, I know. All the same, they're savages who need saving," Nicole said, as Father Francis looked across at Nick.

"Don't look at me, Father. You're the one in the business of saving souls," Nick said.

"I would not use the term 'savages' though... "

"Of course not, Father. The word implies something without a soul, without any morals, a despicable excuse for a human being like my scumbag father. Yes, even I can tell that these Mexicans in these pictures have souls and are worth saving," Nicole said pensively. She turned around and picked up her handbag. "I want to be one of those parishioners who helps." She took her checkbook out. "So tell me, Father, whom shall I make this check out to?"

"To St. Charles Catholic Church," Father Francis replied.

It did not take long after Nicole made out the check for her to start on the road to being a Catholic. Father Joseph changed garments and quickly baptized Nicole as Nick stood witness. After the baptism, Nicole decided to take a solemn, pensive walk around the church. Nick decided to skip the walk and simply sit in a pew and watch her.

Father Francis sat next to Nick. "Quite an interesting fiancée you have there."

"Yes, Father, you don't know the half of it. She could teach Al Capone a few things."

"And yet you love her unconditionally."

"Yes, Father. She's cast a spell on me that would make the most powerful witch in the world jealous. I'd take a bullet for her, jump in front of a car to save her life. Living without her isn't an option. I spent a week away from her, and all I could think of was getting back to her. I am completely smitten. It's as if she is inside my head. My dreams are all about her ... the ones I can remember."

"If it is any comfort to you, I have no doubt that she feels the same way about you."

"I have little doubt about that, Father. She tortures me, but I know she loves me. It's like she's always testing me to be sure I'll stay no matter what. She shows the worst of herself to make sure I deserve the best of her. Does that make sense, Father? It's like she needs me to constantly prove that what we have is unconditional.

"I don't think anyone really knows what goes on in Nicole's mind. She's quite open about her feelings and emotions in the moment, but if you pry too deeply and she gets uncomfortable, she'll shut you down in a second. Nicole doesn't follow. She leads. But in the midst of her petulant, stubborn, spoiled-brat drama, she'll do something so thoughtful, so caring and sweet, that I fall in love with her all over again. Deep down she knows what matters. She wants to embrace decent values but just hasn't had any role models to emulate."

"The check she made out to the church was for twenty thousand dollars," Father Francis said.

"Don't equate her generosity with any type of sacrifice on her part. She's rich and has no problem using money to get what she wants," Nick informed him.

"A lot of our parishioners are rich, but few have been as generous as your future wife. That twenty thousand dollars will provide shelter and food to countless homeless and poor families in our community for months. We appreciate all donations of any size or amount, but I'd be lying if I said a donation of this size doesn't seriously help."

Nicole stopped her crusade around the church at the fourteenth and final Station of the Cross, a depiction of Christ being placed in a tomb after he died on the cross for the sins of all men. The concept of someone dying for the sins of others was such an alien and incomprehensible notion to Nicole that she almost started to laugh at the very idea. The obvious choice to her would have been to seek revenge.

Father Francis gave Nicole books and pamphlets that he thought would help her understand the Catholic religion better and prepare her for what it means to be Catholic. She pretended to be grateful and was actually quite gracious when the priest offered his guidance to both her and Nick anytime they might feel a need to talk.

As Nicole drove out of the church parking lot, she asked Nick, "So how did I do?"

"You were wonderful, sweetheart."

"Thank you, Nicky. You see the lengths I'll go through to please you? And just think how happy your parents will be when they find out that I'm Catholic, too."

"Not for nothing, sweetheart, but I think you won over my parents way, way before you ever walked into that church."

"You can never be too sure. Your parents raised the perfect man. I don't want them to have any doubt that I'm the perfect mate for you. Please, don't ever say anything bad about me to your parents."

"They wouldn't believe me anyway," Nick said, half joking.

"Please. Nicky, promise," she insisted.

"I promise."

"Thank you. Can I ask you a stupid question?"

"Yes."

"Why is Saint Joseph your favorite saint? I mean, of any saint, why would anyone pick him? Surely, any guy who believed that his girlfriend was miraculously impregnated without having sex must have been higher than a kite. Either that or Mary must have been a serious, serious fox. Or maybe Saint Joe was one of history's first closet fags."

"An angel came down and assured him that Mary was pure." Nick was desperate to explain it to her.

"Like I said, Nick, higher than a kite. I didn't even know they had LSD back then, did you?"

"He wasn't high, Nicole."

"Well then, he was either gay or Mary was the hottest chick ever … and boy, did she exert her influence over him. Wow! Truly insane."

"Religion is all about faith — an extension of belief in what seems impossible, a belief in miracles."

"Seriously, Nick, an educated guy like you believing that a woman can get pregnant without having sex? That's precious. It's one of the reasons why I love you so much. You possess an innocence that's usually reserved for toddlers. If I came to you after months of not having sex and told you I was pregnant, would you believe me if I told it you it was divine intervention and not another guy that got me into trouble?"

"I know you would never cheat on me, so I guess I'd have to accept that it was divine intervention. I love you, and love means trust."

"Wow, Nicky, you are on some roll today. If I didn't know better, I'd you're trying to get me into bed."

"You're the one who was ready to do it in the rectory."

Chapter Seventeen

Nick was happy the conversation about Saint Joseph was over, at least for the moment. It seemed to be heading toward that dark zone where no answer would satisfy Nicole's curiosity unless it was the answer she wanted to hear.

They walked into the condo, and she immediately handed him the books and pamphlets Father Francis had given her. "Nicky, can you do me a favor? Read these books and write a short summary for me."

"Would you like me to read them right now, or can I wait a few minutes?"

"Right now would be great." He knew she was serious, but he couldn't help it.

"Seriously?"

"Seriously! I want to be as informed as possible, just in case I get into a conversation about religion with your parents. I know how important being a Catholic is to them. I don't want to disappoint them."

"Okay, Nicole, whatever you say. I'll go into the study and do your homework."

"Why would you go in there?"

"Because that's where one usually goes to read books. Besides, isn't that the reason you built the study for me? So I could read and write in there?"

"Of course. To read and write things that will help you with your screenplay, not to read my stuff. Sometimes I just don't get you. Wouldn't you rather be in here with me?"

"Of course, I would rather be in here with you, but how do you expect me to read, write your summaries, and keep you company?"

"Don't you occasionally look up when you're reading?"

"Of course."

"And what would you rather look up to, those stupid bookshelves or me?"

"You. How could I ever possibly want to look at anything except you?"

Deep down, Nick never felt totally comfortable having sex with Nicole. Even when it was pure lust, like in the car after she picked him up at the airport, the notion that a harsh critique followed every time didn't help. And it went way beyond that. Nicole never gave freely of herself. Even with her clothes off, she had a shield around her, a protective barrier that made you feel, if you tampered with that shield, you might be in for some serious trouble.

After an unusual romantic encounter — minus the usual critique — they settled on the couch in the living room. Nicole rested her head in Nick's lap and fell asleep while he picked up the books and pamphlets and started to reeducate himself about the wonder and joy of being Catholic. The cartoon channel played on the TV. The sound, after an unusual compromise on Nicole's part, was very low, just loud enough for her to hear.

He couldn't help noticing how soft and level her breathing was, like that of a kitten. Her body was motionless. It was the first time he'd ever seen her like this. Not even in the hospital, when she was under heavy sedation, had her body been totally motionless. And as for her breathing, it was always fluctuating, like that of a hungry tiger. She would become totally transfixed while watching the cartoon channel, yet her body would always seem tense and tight, always on guard against some impending threat.

Nicole slept a very long time, long enough for Nick to finish reading and write short summaries for her to look over. She finally woke up, stretching long and wide as she focused on Nick's face. She asked how long she'd been asleep, and Nick replied by handing her the summaries. She smiled gratefully as she glanced through them, and then put them aside. She sat up and kissed Nick on the mouth. It was a rare peaceful moment between them.

Nick reached down and picked up a box off the study floor, placing it on the desk. He had a precise order in which he placed his books, and to Nicole's credit, she had packed them in the same way he had them arranged in his apartment. The dearest books and authors were always placed on a shelf closest for him to reach, so the first box he opened contained all the books written by the great Joseph Conrad. First was *Heart of Darkness*, followed by *Under Western Eyes, Nostromo, The Secret Agent*, etc. There were so many books by Conrad, not to mention huge volumes of his letters, that when packing it all up, Nicole had started to suspect Nick had a boy crush on this guy … but her suspicions subsided when she saw a picture of Conrad and realized he was dead. Next on the shelf came James Joyce, another hunk of a man who in real life looked like he was dead. The list of strange-looking guys and girls went on until suddenly they came to Hemingway. Nicole could not deny she thought Hemingway was quite attractive and manly, and possessed many of the features of her beautiful Nicky, including the stupidity to go to places where bullets were flying and life was cheap.

The idea that anyone would read even one page of any of those books was incomprehensible to Nicole. What could any of those writers have to say that one didn't learn in real life? And even she knew that there were only so many plots, and she had seen them all unroll watching Mr. Bugs Bunny. But she had come to terms with the idea that Nick's one really bad habit was reading these stupid books and idolizing a bunch of dead people. After all, it was better than having him chase other girls.

Finally, Nick picked up the box that Nicole was anxiously waiting to get into — the box containing that wonderful tape of Bobby Flynn tucked into the hollow interior of a pretend hardcover book. Nicole, totally unbeknownst to Nick, had already viewed the tape a number of times, checking it for authenticity. She had come across this fabulous jewel of filmmaking while packing Nick's books in the old West Hollywood apartment, when he selfishly abandoned her for a week to play the part of Hemingway. It was undeniably the pearl inside the oyster, the diamond inside a mountain of useless paper. She so admired the short and compelling film that she had five extra copies made, hiding them in five different safety deposit boxes in five different banks.

There were many things that Nicole never mentioned about her past. After all, why would she want to spoil the pristine and unsoiled image she had been cultivating? Besides, her history might get back to Nick's parents, and she couldn't have that. Hell, no!

Chapter Eighteen

Among the many things she never told Nick was that Bobby Flynn, famous producer and alleged playboy, was her uncle. Her father and "Uncle Bobby" — as she used to call him — were brothers. Their father, her grandfather, was a wealthy businessman from back east who had made his fortune in the garment business, a business neither of his sons had any interest in. Both brothers were attracted to the bright lights of Hollywood, and they both relocated to lovely Southern California after the war. Nicole's father, to his credit, volunteered for the marines right after Pearl Harbor and went on to fight in some of the bloodiest and most historic battles of the war. Her uncle Bobby, to his credit, feigned an illness and injury and was never drafted.

The young Weiss men decided on their way to California that it would be better if one of them changed their last name. Both were booming with confidence and loaded bank accounts. Once they became "big," they didn't want the issue of nepotism and anti-Semitism to hinder their road to greatness. They flipped a coin, Uncle Bobby lost, and just like that, he went from Robert Weiss to Bobby Flynn. Very few people in the movie business ever knew that they were brothers. They didn't look anything alike.

Uncle Bobby had gone into acting at first. He'd always thought of himself as the next Clark Gable, but after a few bit parts — the most famous playing a bullfighter in the movie adaptation of one of Hemingway's short stories — he decided his talents were best exercised behind the camera. So, like his brother, Bobby became a producer, and the greatness and acclaim they both desired was soon achieved.

Nicole picked up the pretend book and acted surprised at how light it felt. She shook the object, listened as the tape rattled back and forth, and opened the book to reveal it.

"And what do we have here, Nicky?"

"That, Nicole, is the most vile and disgusting thing I have ever seen."

"Now don't you lie to me. Is this one of those tapes that little boys hide from their mother, in which naked boys and girls are doing very nasty things?"

"In all honesty, Nicole, there are naked boys and girls on that tape doing unimaginable things, things that only the most corrupt and twisted minds could ever imagine."

"May I ask how you came to have this tape in your possession?"

Nick, never mentioning a name, told her the story of how he and his friend had clandestinely taped the whole thing. Nicole listened and thought, Maybe there really is a God. How else could one possibly explain all these wonderful things falling so neatly into place? Here she was holding a tape that her fiancé and his friend made, neither of them immoral enough to realize the possibilities — not to mention the financial gain — that this piece of trash represented. Surely, this was living proof that a college education was a total waste. That, or that boys from the Bronx were really stupid.

His friend Anthony had given Nick the tape to do whatever he wanted with because it so grossed him out that he was scared it might affect the way he looked at girls. And there was Nicky, working as a stupid fucking waiter, stashing the tape away in a hollow, carved-out book, waiting to get up the nerve to burn the vile and disgusting evidence of the filthy, deviant behavior of a pillar of the industry. It was totally unbelievable. What world were these two from?

Nicole handed Nick the book with the tape inside. "I can't believe that you would put this vile piece of garbage next to your cherished books. I mean, isn't that like putting poems written by the devil next to the Bible?"

"You know, Nicole, you are one hundred percent right. I'm going to dump this trash right now."

"Do you mind if I keep the book? It would be nice to keep my most cherished mementos stashed away in."

"No, I don't mind. Go right ahead." Nicole took the book and threw the tape into the trash can next to the desk.

The last time Nicole had seen her Uncle Bobby was over twelve years before. The day would forever remain locked in her mind as though it was yesterday. Early that morning, her useless mother tried for hours to burn curls into Nicole's hair with a curling iron. She wanted to show off the only thing she had produced in her life to all of Hollywood's elite. All the big shots were going to be at the bash Uncle Bobby was throwing in honor of his fiftieth birthday. Nicole's mother had gone so far as to order a $1,000 dress from an Italian designer for her little girl. The dress was dark red and quite beautiful, and after the party, Nicole had every intention of soiling the dress in front of her mother.

Nicole's mother, Elaine, had been a teenage beauty queen from Washington State. She aspired to be an actress but, in reality, had no talent. She nevertheless caught the eye of Nicole's father, who it was rumored started banging her shortly after she received her crown at the tender age of seventeen. At the age of twenty, while she was pregnant with Nicole, they secretly married. The lust in their relationship lasted until about two years after Nicole was born, and then Daddy got tired of the aging beauty and started looking for new conquests in the teen magazines. He had an eye for young talent and immediately started banging a number of teen models, a few who went on to be major movie stars.

As far back as Nicole could remember, Daddy and Mommy never really communicated with each other. She spent his money, kept her eyes closed to everything that could negatively affect their marriage, and between bouts of severe depression, occasionally spent time with her sole offspring. Daddy was very content with this marriage. To him it was the perfect relationship. He screwed everything he wanted, and Mommy disappeared further and further into a dark corner ... too fucking stupid to ask for a divorce and too cowardly to even contest her husband's behavior.

Her parents had always kept separate bedrooms, and Nicole remembered barely controlling her desire to kill both of them. She had planned it all out. Her mother was the easy target. After spending the day drinking and downing pills, she would be passed out at night and Nicole could easily walk into her bedroom and stab the cowardly bitch in the heart. Sometimes Nicole would actually daydream about watching the life drain out of Mommy's body. Then she would move on to Daddy. She would curl up close to him in bed — he could never resist the feel of a warm, young body — and she would stab the son of a bitch right in that disgusting thing that grew large and tear a hole right up to his heart. She felt elated every time the plan ran through her mind. They had both failed her miserably. She wanted them to pay.

The ride to Uncle Bobby's party was not unusual, except that Mommy seemed happy. It was apparent that she had already been drinking, and her happy pills had probably just kicked in. She kept smiling as though she was reliving her days as a beauty queen. She was still quite beautiful at twenty-nine but could easily be mistaken for thirty-nine. Her makeup was a ghastly white, and her lipstick was an unearthly dark red that made her look like a clown. Nicole giggled every time her mother turned toward her to warn her not to wander off at the party, to please stay close to her. Daddy seemed preoccupied with last night's conquest.

Mr. Weiss parked the car in front of the valet stand. He handed the valet the keys and a $100 tip. "Please keep the car close, just in case I get lucky and get called away from this shithole." He waited impatiently as his wife looked in the car mirror to apply even more make up to her already overpainted face. "Elaine," he yelled, "for the love of God, can we please get going?" He turned to the valet. "She's playing the lead in the remake of *The Bride of Frankenstein*. She's simply trying to stay in character."

Nicole walked over to her father and the valet. "Do you get to drive all these great cars?"

"Of course he does, sweetheart," Mr. Weiss said. His daughter looked across the makeshift parking lot at all the Porsches, Ferraris, classic Mustangs, and Mercedes.

"Did you ever crash any?" Nicole asked the valet.

"No," the valet said timidly.

"Sweetheart, if he crashed the cars, he wouldn't have a job for very long." Mr. Weiss turned back to the valet and commented, "If you can believe it, that creature inside the car fixing her makeup used to look almost as beautiful as this stunning child. That was in another life."

"I can definitely believe that, sir," the valet said.

"If I could drive all these cars, I would crash them all into each other. That would be so much fun."

"Of course you would, sweetheart. That's what makes you, you."

Elaine finally stepped out of the car.

"At last." Mr. Weiss reached into his pocket and handed the valet another $100 bill. "That's for listening."

The family walked toward the party, which was mostly taking place beside an Olympic-size pool. Elaine stopped for a moment and bent down to look at Nicole.

"How does Mommy look? Does Mommy look beautiful?"

"You look like Bozo the Clown."

"Don't be mean, Nicole. Why must you always be so mean?" Elaine tearfully reached into her purse and pulled out a tissue. She wiped the tears away as Mr. Weiss looked at his daughter.

"Tell your mother how beautiful she looks," he commanded.

"Why?" Nicole remained defiant.

Now her daddy pointed a finger at her and slowly, forcefully demanded, "I said, tell your mother how beautiful she looks."

"No! You tell her. You're the idiot married to her."

Elaine looked at her husband. The pain and humiliation on her face was too much for even him to bear. He took the tissues out of her hand and wiped off a couple of layers of makeup. "You look beautiful, Elaine. Very beautiful."

"Thank you." Elaine suddenly put on a big smile and walked toward the other party guests with her family.

Richard Weiss was immediately greeted by an army of powerful agents, lawyers, celebrities, directors, producers, and politicians. Mr. Weiss was the polar opposite of his brother, whose schizophrenic and hyperkinetic personality made him very difficult to deal with. The Hollywood elite almost unanimously found Richard Weiss gracious, courteous, and easy to deal with. He never made known his disdain for most of the younger generation — suit-and-tie executives, producers and agents — whom he saw as pompous, no-talent assholes riding the coattails of some very talented young writers and directors.

Four years in the military — witnessing death and mayhem firsthand — had left a profound and lasting impact on Richard, even though he had never once discussed his military service with anyone outside of the men he served with. The Vietnam War was a matter of great contention for him. The way Hollywood flip-flopped on the issue was very bothersome to him, and during his tenure as head of a major studio, he never once knowingly green-lighted a film in which the major players were draft dodgers.

He never once partnered with his own brother, a draft dodger during World War II. Bobby always thought it was because Richard feared people getting wind that they were brothers, but that was only part of it. The real reason was because Richard saw Bobby as a cowardly human, gleefully evading his responsibility to his country while benefiting greatly from the sacrifice of millions of other Americans.

It was nearly an hour before Richard was able to settle at a makeshift bar away from the bulk of the guests. By that time, Elaine and Nicole were out of sight.

Elaine, between hits of the cocaine that she carried in her purse —
in a vial with an attached spoon — was comfortably situated at another
makeshift bar, far away from her husband. Her daughter was nowhere
in sight, and Elaine's only thought of the little bitch was a hope that she
wouldn't see her again tonight.

Elaine conversed with the bartender, who kept busy mixing her one
drink after another. She was unusually flirtatious and after a while,
started sharing her cocaine with him. She knew that he found her
attractive. He had told her that she was the most beautiful girl he had
served all day. Elaine had never dared to cheat on her husband before,
but it had been years since she had heard wonderful compliments from
a young man.

Between shifts Elaine and the bartender made their way to a room
inside the mansion that was away from everything. Within minutes he
had his pants down and Elaine's panties flung across the floor. Her legs
held up high, she laid on the bed as the bartender easily slipped his
penis into her wet vagina. She moaned and begged, "Fuck me harder,
fuck me harder," and just as the bartender climaxed inside her, she saw
Nicole, sitting in a chair, watching them intently.

"Oh my God! Oh my God!" Elaine screamed. The bartender started
to apologize for ejaculating too soon. "No, no," Elaine said, pointing to
her ten-year-old daughter sitting in the chair.

"What are you doing here, Nicole?" Elaine asked, as the bartender
quickly put on his pants and ran out the door.

"You told me to stay by you and not wander off," Nicole reminded her.
Elaine grabbed her panties off the floor and clumsily tried to put them on
as sperm dripped down her legs. "Did you pee yourself, Mommy?"

"No, sweetheart. The young man was just helping me with my back.
You know how my back gives out sometimes."

"Is that why you were telling him to 'fuck you harder, fuck you
harder'? He wasn't pushing hard enough?"

"No, sweetheart. I wasn't telling him to fuck me harder. I was telling
him to push harder on the sore spot."

"No, Mommy. You were telling him to fuck you harder. I heard you. I was right here. And how could he push harder on your back when you were lying on your back?"

Elaine finally managed to get her panties back on, which immediately started to show signs of leakage.

"Mommy, are you sure you didn't pee your pants?"

"Yes, sweetheart, I did. I was just too embarrassed to say so."

"And that man, did he pee on you?"

"That man was helping me, Nicole. He was a very nice man."

"Then why did he run away? Was he afraid that Daddy was going to find him helping you?"

Elaine grabbed her purse and Nicole's hand, and they walked into the adjacent bathroom.

"Please, Nicole, help your mommy. I love you so much," Elaine begged. She reached into her purse, turned away from Nicole, and took out the vial of cocaine. She took numerous hits, placed the vial back in her purse, and turned back to Nicole.

"What were you putting up your nose, Mommy?"

"Medicine, sweetheart. It helps me breathe."

Elaine sat on the toilet and tried desperately to get herself together. She picked up a washcloth and had Nicole wet it for her. She ripped off her panties, placed them in her purse, and cleaned off her legs, thighs, and vaginal area.

"Maybe you should start wearing diapers, Mommy."

Elaine looked at her daughter with dilated eyes and her mind racing like a runaway train. *I really hate her sometimes. No one would believe for a minute that I would be capable of such thing. She's evil. That's what she is ... pure evil.* She smiled as she reached out to her child. "Come here, sweetheart. Give your mommy a hug, please." Nicole, like an animal smelling and sensing danger, moved away. "No, not until you put on a diaper."

"That's a very good idea, sweetheart, but can't your mommy get a hug first?"

"No! You're disgusting!"

Elaine suddenly snapped out of her trance and realized she had been entertaining the idea of killing her own child. She shook violently and lowered her hands. "You're so beautiful, Nicole. So beautiful. You know, when I was your age, I was beautiful like you."

"Daddy still thinks you're beautiful. He said so. Remember?"

"Yes, I remember, but he didn't mean it."

"Did that man think you were beautiful?"

"No one thinks I'm beautiful anymore," Elaine said sadly.

Elaine stood up and looked in the mirror. She studied her reflection — a disturbing, unrecognizable snapshot — and saw a crude image of a woman who once wore the innocence and beauty that won her a state-wide teenage beauty pageant. She was a girl who had been recognized by Hollywood — wined, dined, and seduced by one of the most powerful men in all of showbiz. She eventually married that man and gave birth to his only child, and then he discarded her like an expired fashion magazine once the facade was removed and the contents were empty.

Elaine could suddenly taste the cocaine on her tongue, and with that sensation came a whole new high, replacing the jittery, anxious feeling one usually gets after using cocaine for many hours. The image in the mirror suddenly didn't look so bad, and her figure was still as incredible and fantastic as when she was eighteen. Yes, she had stepped out on her husband — and maybe for a few minutes actually felt like a cheap hooker — but her husband had been stepping out on her every other night for the last ten years. Surely, she was entitled to one encounter.

Richard had hinted on numerous occasions that he didn't care if she slept with other guys, as long as she didn't get pregnant and she never brought them home. He would never ask for a divorce and if she ever did, he made it quite clear, she would meet with an untimely and unfortunate demise.

Elaine redid her makeup, applied fresh lipstick, and fixed her hair. Nicole had wandered off while her mother fussed in front of the bathroom mirror, going through a mental and physical transformation. Energized with a new confidence and aided by a few more hits of coke up the nose, plus a large dose on her tongue, Elaine walked out of the bathroom. Unconcerned about her ten-year-old daughter and what she had seen, Elaine went back to the party and took a seat at another bar, away from the handsome bartender who had dropped a load in her in less time than it takes to recite the alphabet. She sipped a glass of white wine, crossed and recrossed her legs, and started to giggle as a warm, light breeze passed under her dress.

Mr. Weiss remained at the same bar where he started, unconcerned about his wife and quite sure that his daughter was getting into some type of trouble. After conversing with his cockeyed brother, the famous Bobby Flynn, he was quite sure that the award-winning box-office champion was the luckiest motherfucker on the planet. Never was he more certain of their decision thirty years ago to keep their relationship a secret. If he didn't know better, he would have thought his brother was suffering from dementia. Bobby made no sense; he was incomprehensible and he smelled like a sewer.

Besides the insufferable time he spent listening to Bobby, there was seldom a moment in which some "dick" didn't stop by and try to push something on him. Richard's usual response was, "Give me a call and hopefully we can set up a meeting." His only respite from the onslaught was a conversation with the bartender about the Los Angeles Dodgers. He was a huge baseball fan, proud of his friendship with the Dodgers manager, Tommy Lasorda.

Nicole, in the meantime, had climbed the stairs to the second floor of the mansion. She had been up here a few times before with Uncle Bobby, who always gave her wonderful gifts and always reminded her to never tell her parents. Because if she did, he would unleash a monster upon her that would not only eat up Mr. Bunny but would chop her into little pieces and cook her for dinner. First she had to pee, badly, which was a good thing because Uncle Bobby loved to watch her go to the bathroom through a hole in the bathroom wall. She put down the toilet seat, lowered her panties, pulled her lovely red dress above her waist and sat down. She urinated for a long time and tried really hard to poop, but nothing would come out. She saw Uncle Bobby's eye against the hole but pretended not to see him. That was part of the game … that and not flushing the toilet after she was finished. She got up from the toilet, rolled up her panties, and straightened out her dress. She washed her hands like a good girl and tried to pass some really loud gas, but even that was a no.

She checked the hallway before leaving the bathroom to make sure no one was walking by, then walked down to the adjacent room, where Uncle Bobby secretly watched her go to the bathroom. He was a little disappointed that all she could do was pee, but he told her he had a new game they could play that would make up for her inability to poop. Nicole was happy to play another game because Uncle Bobby promised her really exciting gifts, and it stopped the monster from getting her and Mr. Bunny. Besides, she had a toy that she wanted to share with him.

Uncle Bobby dropped his pants and introduced her to Little Bobby. She pretended to be in awe, but in reality, she had seen the same version of Little Bobby before. Uncle Bobby liked to change his name and would always ask if she would like to hold his penis, or whatever name he was using during the game to describe his manhood. Nicole, like always, placed her hand on Little Bobby and started rubbing it back and forth. Uncle Bobby groaned as his penis expanded and then he asked if he could see her little Nicole.

At first Nicole did not understand because this was new to the game, but dear old Uncle Bobby explained where Little Nicole was situated and touched the spot in her dress where she was located. "They could become friends, Little Nicole and Little Bobby," Uncle Bobby suggested.

Nicole was excited and said she loved to make new friends, and Uncle Bobby said, "Well, sweetheart, just roll down your panties and pull up your dress like when you go to the bathroom. They can meet and touch each other."

Nicole was intrigued by this prospect but insisted that she wanted to show Uncle Bobby a toy she brought for him, and first he would have to close his eyes. He agreed and closed his eyes. Nicole reached into the pocket her useless mother had sewn into her dress and pulled out a small canister of high-intensity pepper spray she had purchased at school. As Uncle Bobby begged her to get on with it, Nicole sprayed his elongated penis with the spray. At first Bobby felt a warm and pleasant sensation, and then, like a match thrown onto gasoline, he exploded in agony, letting out a scream that could wake the dead. Nicole laughed as Uncle Bobby hobbled around the room with his pants down around his knees.

He screamed, "Get this shit off me, you little bitch!" and fell to the floor as he tripped over his pants.

"No! No, Uncle Bobby, that's not part of the game." Nicole sprayed enough poison into his eyes to blind an eagle. He rolled out the door — with a little help from Nicole — and into the hallway. "Help! Help! She's trying to kill me!" He grabbed onto the banister and lifted himself up, his pants still around his legs. The party guests, the royal elite of the Hollywood establishment, looked up in astonishment.

"Help! Help! I'm blind. I'm blind!" The guests didn't move. Without the help of a script to read from, they were totally paralyzed with indecision. Bobby, in the meantime, helplessly clutched the banister as he hobbled toward the top step, his calls for help unanswered, a pathetic pervert at the peak of his game suddenly exposed by a child. He desperately tried to balance himself on the stairs as Nicole gave him a swift kick in his butt that sent him flying down the stairs like a character in a cartoon.

Bobby landed at the feet of his guests — barely conscious, his eyes bloody, Little Bobby exposed and deflated. He quivered in pain. The guests finally snapped out of their shock and ran toward him. Screams for an ambulance echoed throughout the mansion as Nicole calmly walked down the stairs. As some guests attended to Bobby, the rest looked up at the doll-like little child dressed in red. She pushed her way through the crowd surrounding Uncle Bobby and bent down, then touched Little Bobby. She gently petted the shriveled little guy and said, "Poor Little Bobby. Poor Little Bobby."

In the distance, still seated at the same bar, Richard Weiss saw many guests from outside suddenly rush toward the mansion. He thought at first that maybe they were getting ready to sing "Happy Birthday" to his brother and that as soon as that was done, he could depart from this gaudy shit show. That pleasant thought quickly vanished as the sound of an ambulance and police sirens grew louder, and louder again as they entered the property. Deep down in his gut, he knew that somehow, some way, his lovely daughter was probably involved.

Richard hadn't seen Nicole since they'd arrived, but even at four feet tall, that little beauty stood out in a crowd, especially in that dark red dress. He finished the drink in his hand, asked the bartender for a double Johnny Walker Blue neat, and downed it. He graciously thanked the bartender, left him a $200 tip, then walked slowly but deliberately toward the mansion, no longer simply entertaining the possibility that his daughter was involved but quite certain.

The reality was that Elaine was incapable of keeping an eye on Nicole. As a three-year-old toddler, Nicole had outsmarted her mother. At ten she was a pint-size Einstein compared to Elaine. He should have brought the maid along and glued them together.

The crowd parted as Mr. Weiss entered the mansion, and naturally, there was his lovely daughter, in red, looking down at the supine figure of his brother. He turned to a guest and asked, "Is he dead?"

The guest replied, "I don't think so."

A number of guests tended to Bobby as Nicole looked up at her father and smiled. "We were playing, Daddy, and then Uncle Bobby had an accident. Poor Uncle Bobby."

Mr. Weiss reached down and picked up Nicole. He whispered into her ear, "Be quiet." She refused at first and Richard covered her mouth with his hand, whispering once again. "Be quiet, Nicole, otherwise there will be no cartoons for you. You can tell me everything later, in the car." He swept her away as the paramedics and police rushed toward Bobby.

Richard carried Nicole toward the valet and asked, "Where is your mother?"

"I don't know, Daddy. The last time I saw her she was upstairs asking a nice man to fuck her, to fuck her hard."

"Well, I hope she was having a good time." He placed Nicole in the front seat of their car and put on her seat belt. He drove away as Nicole told him the whole story about her and Uncle Bobby — the games they had played and that tonight had not been the first time. He grimaced throughout but didn't say a word until he parked the car at home. Then he said, "Give me the pepper spray, Nicole."

"No! It's my toy," she insisted, and unfastened her seat belt.

"Okay, have it your way, but when the police come and find that pepper spray, you'll be going to jail for a long time. And Nicole, there are no cartoons in jail."

She frowned, handed over the pepper spray, and said, "But I want it back when the police leave."

"There will be no more talk of pepper spray, Nicole. No more. Do you understand? I can't protect you if you don't listen to what I am telling you. You are in big trouble, young lady, big trouble. Uncle Bobby may have had it coming — in fact, from what you're telling me, he definitely had this coming and worse — but you hurt him badly and there are consequences for your behavior."

"Why? Uncle Bobby wanted to play. He liked our games."

Mr. Weiss gave instructions to Nicole to go up to her room, take a shower, put on her pajamas, and place everything she was wearing into a bag. Nicole obeyed for the first time in years and did everything her father said. Mr. Weiss disposed of the clothes and the pepper spray. He knew that these were only half-measures in an attempt to protect his daughter. There were enough witnesses at the scene who could place Nicole on the second floor with his brother, and there was no way to cover up her involvement. He had already gotten word that his brother would survive, and the extent of the injuries would not hamper a full recovery. His collarbone and one leg were broken from the fall down the stairs. His eyesight would recover fully in a day or so, and his genitals, after a period of intense soreness, would be back in play in less than a week.

Mr. Weiss, as expected, welcomed the police into his house a few hours after he and his daughter departed the party. Like any wise and powerful man, he had a wonderful relationship with the local police department and with all law enforcement agencies throughout the state. He was a large contributor and had spearheaded a drive to get all uniform police officers new bulletproof vests. He was so liked by the LAPD that he was asked to speak at many of their events.

Bobby, on the other hand, was an irritant. The top brass and local politicians made it quite clear to the foot soldiers in the battle against crime that Bobby Flynn — unless he committed the most deranged of crimes — was not to be arrested. Instead of being arrested for drunk driving, possession of drugs, and/or reckless endangerment behind the wheel of a car, he was given police escorts back to his mansion. To the rank-and-file, honest cops trying to do their job, the practice was unholy. But they knew that if they arrested him, within days they would be patrolling the streets of south-central LA, and that was frightening enough for them to break the law and show favoritism.

The two police officers at Mr. Weiss's house made it perfectly clear that they were not there to arrest anyone, only to verify statements given by some guests at the party. Apparently, when Bobby Flynn regained consciousness, he told the police that he was using the toilet when Nicole barged in and started spraying him. She thought it was a game, and he was quite sure that she did not understand how dangerous the spray was. He had no intention to press charges.

Richard, a master at disguising his true feelings, could not hide the burning, livid expression etched on his face. "On the toilet, is that what he said?" The police officers immediately responded by telling Mr. Weiss that if he saw anything else or knew of a different story, they would be pleased to take his statement. The first officer went so far as to say, "This whole episode is quite bizarre, pretty deranged. Yes, this is deranged."

Richard immediately picked up on the officer's willingness to pursue this investigation further and showed his approval with a wink of the eye. In truth, he had been sitting at a makeshift bar talking baseball with the bartender when all this insanity had gone down. He hadn't seen anything, and after finally entering the mansion, his only thought had been to protect his daughter and get her out of there. His daughter had been unresponsive the whole trip home and insisted on going straight to her bedroom and taking a shower.

The officers apologized but insisted that they needed to see Nicole before they would be able to write their report. Mr. Weiss took the officers to her room, knocked on the door, and walked in. "Nicole, these nice police officers would like to talk to you for a few minutes." Nicole was dressed in her pajamas, sitting on her bed and watching cartoons. She was so absorbed in what she was watching that she didn't even show any signs of recognizing the presence of anyone in her room. The police officers tried kindly to elicit responses to their questions, but Nicole only shook her head. The officers looked to Mr. Weiss, and he motioned to them to just leave her alone.

The men left the room. The officers, apparently taken aback by Nicole's stoic and unresponsive demeanor, offered Mr. Weiss the chance to have an LAPD psychiatrist talk to her. Mr. Weiss graciously refused, but made it perfectly clear that his daughter would be seeing a family doctor as soon as the next day.

The officers left, got into their car, and chatted seriously about whether they should recommend that this case be closed or whether further evidence was needed. Mr. Weiss, in the meantime, poured himself a drink and took a slow walk up to Nicole's room. He stood in front of her and blocked her view of the TV.

"Are they going to arrest me?"

"No."

"Are they going to arrest Uncle Bobby for touching me?"

"Is that what you want?"

"Of course, that's what I want. He's disgusting, like you."

"I'm only trying to protect you, Nicole. If they arrest him, it could turn out bad for you, and that I do not want. I'll take care of Uncle Bobby without police involvement."

"Are you going to kill him?"

"I am going to make him pay, dearly. That I promise you."

"All I want from you, Daddy, is for you to kill him. Don't you owe me that much?"

"If I kill him, I'll be going off to jail for the rest of my life. Do you really want that?"

"What I want, Daddy, is to see him dead."

"Nicole, I love you more than anything in this world." And as he said it, Richard knew he meant it.

"Maybe that's the problem, Daddy. You love me too much."

"That's not possible, sweetheart. God would never allow it."

"I don't believe in God, Daddy. Only stupid people believe in God. Very stupid people, like Mommy."

Mr. Weiss looked carefully at his beautiful daughter. The shock value in the things Nicole said or did had long worn off. She was to be taken seriously, and that was the major advantage she had over both her parents.

"Nicole, you cannot speak to anyone about the things that happened today. Do you understand me?"

"Only if you promise to kill him."

"Okay, Nicole. I promise, but not a word to anyone."

Hours later, Richard, unable to sleep, sat in his study drinking an ice-cold beer. He had a refrigerator in a cabinet that was part of the large bookcase next to his desk. Cold beer had been his favorite drink ever since he joined the Marines. The refrigerator was kept at thirty-four degrees. Beer, like water, froze at thirty-two degrees. In public he seldom drank beer because for him, one beer was too much and ten beers not enough. And he didn't want to be running to the bathroom every ten minutes to pee. Three Scotches neat had less fluid in them than one beer and required no bathroom trips.

Richard heard the front door open at exactly 4:00 a.m. He waited a moment as he heard his wife's footsteps coming up the stairs. He called out to her, and she did a double take at the sound of his voice. Elaine was sure he was still asleep, and the thought of encountering him in her present condition was frightening. Her hair, makeup, and clothes were a mess, and there was no quick fix to her appearance. She walked into the study, unsteady and wobbly, and tried to avert his steely gaze.

"Why don't you take a seat, Elaine, before you fall down." She took his advice and managed to drop into a chair across the desk from him. "Take a few more hits, Elaine. I want you half conscious for this conversation."

"But..."

He interrupted her. "I said, take a few more hits."

Elaine pulled out a vial of cocaine and took three hits up each nostril. She absorbed the rush and for a moment, closed her eyes.

"I hope you had a wonderful time today, Elaine. On a day that I told you to watch our child, you decided it was more important to get stoned and fuck the first guy who showed any interest in you."

"That's not true," she replied.

"Don't lie to me, Elaine. You reek of sex — not with one lover, but multiple lovers — but that doesn't interest me. I have given you the green light, my blessing, for the last five years, to fuck whoever you want. I just figured that even a stupid bitch like you would have enough sense not to start having sexual liaisons with different men at a party with so many powerful and important people, especially when your daughter was running around wild. Do you even know what happened today?"

"Yes, I heard."

"And yet it took you twelve hours to get back home after the incident occurred, precious hours you could have spent with your traumatized daughter."

"Seriously, Richard, our daughter hates me. She's evil. Do you understand me? Pure evil."

Richard stood up and walked behind the chair Elaine sat in. He pressed his hands against her head and whispered into her ear, "Don't you ever let me hear you say that again. She's our daughter, Elaine, the by-product of two terrible parents, and because of that, she has to carry around the scars we have inflicted upon her for the rest of her life."

"And what do you expect me to do, Richard?"

"I expect you to be a better mother. I expect you to take an interest in her, to be concerned with her welfare. Dressing her up in thousand-dollar dresses doesn't make up for a lack of hugs, or a lack of emotional bonding."

"Really, Richard, is that your answer to our child's problems? A lack of hugs? I lock my bedroom door at night. You know why? Because I am scared shitless that our child might walk in during the night and stick a knife through my heart. And not to alarm you, but I'd start locking your door, too. Why don't you start with the hugs, and if that works out for you, I'll follow your lead."

"Maybe, Elaine, if you put a stop to all the drugs and booze, you might not be so paranoid?"

"The drugs and booze are what give me the courage to even live in this house with that creature."

"What did I just finish telling you, Elaine?" Richard pressed his hands tighter against her head. "I will not tolerate you talking about our daughter like she is some type of monster. If you keep it up, you'll be the one I put into an asylum."

Richard released his hold on his wife's head and sat back in his chair. He opened another beer and looked closely at Elaine. The thought of how battered and agitated she looked was frightening to him. Her eyes appeared abnormally large, and her skin had the complexion of someone suffering from a severe vitamin deficiency. She reminded Richard of the women he encountered during the war. The image of those women is one that he had tried to erase from his memory, but still, some thirty years later, the reflection of all those ladies was staring back at him in the figure of his wife.

He said, without any hint of malice, "You've gotten so old at such a young age, Elaine, but I can help you. I want to help you."

Richard Weiss was not a religious man. After seeing so many of his buddies killed right before him, some only inches away, it was impossible for him to imagine — much less pray — to a higher being that was so merciless. He was appalled by the inhumanity one person could bestow onto another human being. Yet between the time he had left the service until this very moment, he had become one of the monsters, and it was evident in the face of his wife, the mother of his child. "Yes, Elaine, I want to help. I need to help," he repeated with complete sincerity.

It was the nicest thing her husband had said to her in years, and she believed him. The truth was difficult for Elaine to handle, but this one time she wouldn't balk at his invitation but accept the fact that unless she got help, she'd never have a chance of getting better. Two days later, with her husband at her side, she checked into a rehab center in Malibu, overlooking the beautiful Pacific coastline. She would spend the next three months there, with her husband and daughter visiting on weekends.

Richard had managed to convince his defiant daughter that unless she behaved and started treating her mother with respect, there would be no more cartoons, and his promise to kill Uncle Bobby would also be off the table if she didn't help him support Elaine in her recovery. He promised her that if she behaved, he would arrange a meeting for her with Mr. Bugs Bunny and Mr. Daffy Duck. Needless to say, that was the turning point in the negotiations ... the carrot that snatched the bunny. Nicole could not resist Bugs Bunny, and like any wonderful actress, once the curtain went up, she transformed herself into the ideal child.

Elaine was taken aback with the love and affection her husband and daughter were showing. For the first time in many years, she did not fear Nicole but basked unselfishly in the beauty and perfection that she had produced. It was not long after entering the facility that Elaine's natural beauty started to return. The toxins were removed from her body, she had love and support from her family, and suddenly, she didn't have to search for approval and affection because they were, once again, in the eyes of everyone around her.

Richard and Nicole were also on better terms than he could recall in a long time. His daughter was more forthcoming and warm than he had ever seen her, and although deep down, he still had doubts, it was a welcome surprise to see her smile joyously, not vindictively. They finally seemed to be coming together as a family, as a unit that supports each other rather than separate parts at war with each other.

On the way back from the rehab center, driving along the Pacific Coast Highway, Nicole turned to her father. "Don't you think Mommy looks beautiful?"

"Yes, sweetheart, she looks very beautiful."

"And now that she's beautiful, does this mean you're going to love her again?"

Richard hesitated and looked curiously at Nicole. "I have always loved your mother, Nicole."

"No, you haven't. If you love her, why do you have so many girlfriends?"

Richard was on the verge of denying the whole thing but realized that his daughter knew the truth, and that by lying to her, it might very well shatter the truce that had grown between them. "That's all over with, Nicole. I've done some bad things, and I'm sorry for all the pain I caused … Do you believe me?" He wasn't used to being humble, and his own sincerity surprised him.

"I don't know if I believe you, but I guess it only matters if Mommy does."

"That's not true, Nicole. It matters to me just as much that you believe me."

Nicole looked out her window at the waves shattering against the beach.

"What causes the waves in the water?"

"The wind, sweetheart," her father replied.

"Is that all? It seems like there must be something more."

"Earthquakes under the surface of the water can cause waves, violent and destructive waves."

"Am I the reason Mommy got so sick?"

"No, Nicole! Why would you even think such a thing? I'm the reason your mother got sick. If you blame anyone, blame me."

"I don't think so, Daddy. I've heard Mommy say how evil I am, that the reason she drinks is because she's scared of me."

Richard pulled the car over to the shoulder and stopped. He took Nicole by the hands and looked her straight in the eyes. "Now you listen to me, young lady. Your mother might've said those things, but it was only because she was sick and not herself. She didn't know what she was saying then, but now that she's getting better, you'll never hear such things again. Your mother loves you."

"I don't think so, Daddy."

"You have to think so, Nicole. Please, you have to think so."

"Why? Why is it so important that I believe Mommy loves me?"

"Don't you want your mother to love you?"

"I really don't know, but I do know that I've never loved Mommy. I have often thought about killing her. I dream about killing her and how nice it would feel." Nicole spoke as if she was in a hypnotic trance. "But maybe now, I think I could love Mommy. She seems different. She looks different and smells different. She laughs and smiles, and she doesn't look scared like a frightened mouse. Yes, Daddy, I think I might be able to love this new Mommy, and maybe she could love me."

Richard didn't respond. He could not speak to reply. It was as if his vocal chords had been severed just as he was forced to hear and acknowledge an undeniable truth, something he had heard many times before but didn't want to see or believe. He had long ago accepted that Nicole was different. Even her radiant beauty seemed to be a veneer, a mask designed by a greatest artist to conceal a terrible evil. Richard had come to expect the unexpected. He'd sensed at his brother's party that she was involved in the mayhem even before learning any of the facts.

He knew that the maid and staff at the house were afraid of her. They thought she was an agent of the devil, a demon, and whenever they were close to her, Richard could not help noticing how they clutched their crucifixes, which they all carried on their person.

At times Nicole spoke in a terrifying monotone that reminded him of serial killers portrayed in the movies. Instead of her growing up to be a great doctor — a determined scientist who discovers cures for terrible diseases — at this point, he was just hoping that she wouldn't grow up to be a cold-blooded killer or gun for hire. She spoke of killing people without understanding the consequences of such actions, without the moral barriers that stop sane people from doing such things. She was only ten, yet children younger understood the differences between right and wrong. She been abused and hurt, and there was no immediate cure for that. She had been abandoned by the very people who brought her into this world, but Richard was determined that they would become a close family, a unit in which all parts work together not against each other. Once again he looked closely at her. "Smile for me, Nicole?"

She smiled and suddenly all the evil and wickedness dissipated like a vapor of smoke. Devoid of any malevolence or pretense, she continued to smile, revealing dimples that reflected an inner innocence and purity. "Do you like my smile?" She started to giggle as a seagull landed on the hood of their car and looked curiously at her. "I wonder what he's thinking?"

"I think he's thinking that you're the most beautiful creature he's ever seen," Richard replied.

"Don't be silly, Daddy. I bet he's hoping we'll feed him." The seagull flew away, and Nicole's eyes followed his majestic flight toward the sea. "It must be nice, to be able to fly away like that."

"Where would you fly to?"

"I think I'd fly into a cloud and hide there forever. Do you think anyone would miss me?"

"I would miss you greatly."

"Why?"

"Because I love you so much. Don't you believe me?"

"I guess."

"Would you like to take a walk by the water?"

"Yes, Daddy, that would be great."

He lifted his daughter over the guardrail and onto the sand. He reached for her hand and she grasped it. The simple feel of her hand was unlike anything he had felt in years. At that moment, that place in time, holding Nicole's hand had more importance than any handshake to close a major deal. It was the first time since she was a baby that she had unconditionally accepted his protection and safety.

Nicole took off her sandals as they reached the water's edge and handed them to Richard. She giggled and laughed as the tide rolled up and between her toes. The seagulls shrieked and the one lone cloud that she wanted to hide inside had disappeared, evaporated into the untold mysteries of the universe, as trust between father and daughter was recovered, if only for a moment.

Richard had one small piece of business he needed to take care of before Elaine came home. The revelation that he had turned into everything he despised and that the most important thing in his life was crumpling before him was a painful eye opener. He had woken up on the night of his brother's birthday party to see that he had become the very same oppressive monster he had fought against.

Since that night, Richard had not been in touch with Bobby at all. He nevertheless kept tabs on his brother's recovery and business dealings, and the news was all cheery for the cowardly little pervert. Part two of the gangster saga he produced had recently opened in theaters around the country to rave reviews and record-setting box office performances. The movie was already being mentioned as an Oscar favorite for Best Picture. His recovery was going well, and it was reported that he would soon be back to work in his office. The studio was planning a huge welcome back party, with celebrities from across the country being flown in for the occasion … including the reclusive Robert De Niro.

Bobby Flynn lived for those celebrations, especially when he was the guest of honor. Despite the unfortunate circumstances that put him in the hospital, and eventual house arrest for the last three months, he was still the King of Hollywood and wearing the crown that went along with the title.

As Richard walked into his study and opened the bottom drawer of his desk, he wasn't thinking about any celebrations, only about old-fashioned revenge. He took out his revolver from the war, loaded the chamber, and stuck the gun into a deep pocket of his jacket. The gun had not been fired in a couple of years. He used to take it to the firing range at least once a year to air it out, and afterward he would carefully clean the gun, like a precious jewel. There was never a time that he sat down at his desk and didn't think about the gun. He was always aware of its presence in that drawer next to his leg. It represented both life and death. He had killed a couple of German soldiers in the war with this gun, kids no older than himself, and in turn the weapon had saved his life. In short, he turned out to be a better shot than the Germans he encountered.

Unless one is a sociopath, killing is not easy. To be able to look your intended target in the eyes, simply shoot, and then watch them die is a horrifying experience. Even if the entire thing lasts no more than a few seconds, even if you are totally justified and it is for a much greater good, it is always as though the eyes have the final say, conveying that the curtain has come down for the last time and there are no acts to follow.

Richard had no idea what he was going to do when he got into his car and drove to Bobby's house. Besides the gun, he had a tape recorder hidden in the breast pocket of his shirt. The promise he had made to Nicole to kill Uncle Bobby had nothing to do with this unannounced visit; this was strictly between the brothers. Nicole was the victim, and her father was simply defending her against one of society's miscreants.

He parked his car in front of the house and entered Bobby's gaudy, extravagant habitat without even knocking. He walked into the parlor and watched as his brother did a long line of cocaine. He knocked on a piece of furniture and Bobby turned quickly around, nearly jumping out of his skin when he saw his brother.

"My God, Richard, you nearly scared me to death. No one even told me you were coming, or that you arrived." Bobby pointed to the coke on the table. "Take a hit. It's great shit!"

"You know I don't use that garbage."

"That garbage, as you call it, was the drug of choice for Sigmund Freud. Who am I to argue with such a genius?"

"Even Freud eventually rejected cocaine as a drug with limited positive effects and way too many negative effects."

"Is that so? Well, if he was using this shit he might rethink that theory."

"Take a seat, Bobby. We have much to discuss." Bobby hobbled over to a chair and sat down. "I see you're recovering quite nicely, just in time to bask in the success of another huge hit."

"Lady luck, brother. Lady luck," Bobby said proudly. "I'll tell you what, I'd enjoy it a lot more if it wasn't for that psychotic daughter of yours. I told you to abort that child when she was in her mother's womb. If you had any sense, you'd divorce that wacko wife of yours and give her full custody. I don't care what it costs. In the end, you'll make out like a bandit, because it will be just a matter of time before that psycho Nicole kills off mommy Elaine, and then you'll be free of the two biggest mistakes you ever made. Your wife will be dead and gone, and your daughter will spend the rest of her life in an institution for the dangerously insane. My God, talk about a real-life Rosemary's baby… "

Richard reached into his pocket and took out his gun. He pointed it directly at Bobby and said, "Please, keep on talking. Tell me more about my ten-year-old daughter that you molested."

"Are you crazy, Richard? You're going to take the word of a ten-year-old psychopath who carries around pepper spray over the word of your brother? You can't be serious!"

"I heard that you and Nicole have played many games I wasn't aware of. Why don't you fill me in?"

"Harmless games … hide-and-seek. Nothing like you're suggesting. What type of human being do you take me for?"

"A very sick, twisted human being. Rumor has it that you get off by having young ladies shit and pee on you. That's the type of human being you are."

"All rumors, Richard. Sick, disgusting rumors."

"Really? Back to the party, Bobby." Richard moved the gun closer.

"I have nothing else to say. Read the police report if you don't believe me. Your daughter attacked me while I was taking a shit. That's all there is to it."

"Not good enough, brother." Richard pulled the trigger and put a hole in the wall just behind Bobby's head. "Next time you might not be so lucky."

"Are you insane? Kill me and you'll ruin yourself and everything you've worked so hard for. Is that what you want?"

"What I want is the truth." Richard put the gun to Bobby's temple. "I won't miss from here."

"Okay, okay … but take that gun away."

"From the beginning, Bobby."

"We have this game where she goes to the bathroom and I watch her through a hole in the bathroom wall, and after she's finished, I give her candy and gifts."

"So you watch Nicole go to the bathroom, and that gives you a hard-on. Is that right?"

"Yeah, sort of… "

"Go on."

Bobby began to sweat profusely. "Please, I need another hit," he begged.

"Go ahead, you sick son of a bitch."

Bobby snorted another big line of coke before he continued. "Well, on my birthday she could only pee, and part of the deal we have is that she needs to pee and shit and leave it in the toilet for me to see."

"Of course, what's the thrill without being able to see the whole handiwork? Go on… "

"So to make up for not being able to shit, she agreed to touch and rub my penis."

"The thing she was calling Little Bobby?"

"Yeah, and then she told me to close my eyes because she wanted Little Bobby to meet her Little Nicole, and when I closed my eyes, she pepper-sprayed my dick and eyes. That sick little bitch!"

Richard pulled the trigger a second time and a bullet whizzed close enough to his brother's ear that Bobby felt the air next to his head move.

"Tell me, Bobby, where do you want the bullet? Between your eyes, through your heart, through Little Bobby? It's up to you, brother. Choose wisely, because there are no second chances."

"Please, I'll make a true confession to the police. Anything, just don't kill me. Please don't kill me, Richard."

"How are you going to make it up to Nicole? Tell me that. Ten years from now, when all this comes back and haunts her dreams, what advice will you have for her then? What comforting words or gestures will you provide? What Freudian witticisms will you use to rationalize your savage behavior?"

"I'm sorry. Do you honestly think I want to be like this? Do you think that I want to enjoy, and take pleasure in, what other people find disgusting? I was born like this … What choice do I have?"

"You have the same choice we all have, and that's to resist the temptation and seek help. But like always, you choose the road the devil leads you down — destroying lives and whatever else might get in your way — simply to satisfy your vile desires."

"That's not true!" Sweat poured down Bobby's face. "Look at all the good I've done, all the people I've helped." He pointed his finger around the room at all the plaques from different charitable organizations.

"All symbols of one big lie. That's all it's ever been for you, one big lie. Never an unselfish action, every action calculated with the same underlying, greedy goal of enhancing your own image."

"I can change. I know I have the ability to change." Bobby pleaded with Richard, who stepped closer to him. Bobby, in turn, crouched down into a kneeling position with his hands up before his face. "Please, Richard! For God's sake, I'm your brother!"

"That's been my grave misfortune. The King of Hollywood! Look at you. If only they could see you now … such an unflattering pose for royalty." Richard kicked Bobby in the head, and he fell over like a rag doll.

"If you ever go near my daughter again, I will kill you." Richard shot another bullet into the wall behind Bobby, who was crying, in a fetal position. "If I ever hear of you abusing or touching any child at all, I will kill you. And if I ever hear that you have been talking trash about Elaine, or uttering a single word about my family, I will kill you. Are we perfectly clear?" Richard sent another bullet whizzing past Bobby's hair into the wall, and then bent down next to his brother. "You see, I have plenty of bullets, Bobby, and any one of them can have your name on it. Tread very carefully, brother."

Richard walked out of the mansion, got into his car, and drove off. Back at his own house soon after, he walked into the study and locked the door behind him. He pulled the tape recorder out of his breast pocket and shut it off. He sat down, took the gun out, pulled the last bullet out of the chamber, and started to clean the gun with the precision and patience of a devoted craftsman.

That night Richard sat down at the dinner table with Nicole. Elaine would come home from rehab soon, and their quiet father-daughter time together would end. They ate pizza, Nicole's favorite. She drank a soda and he sipped a simple glass of tap water. He asked her about school, and she responded like a normal ten-year-old. "It was okay." He told her what he expected from her once Elaine got home. She nodded as sauce ran down her chin, and he reached over with a napkin and cleaned it off.

Richard hadn't lived the normal day-to-day life of a husband and father, but it was time. He'd never imagined doing this domestic family thing, but here he was. He actually cared. He didn't want his wife or daughter hurt anymore. Once again he told Nicole in no uncertain terms what he wanted and expected from her when Elaine arrived the next day.

"You seem worried, Daddy. You think I won't behave?"

"No sweetheart, I'm not worried. We have an agreement, and I'm simply confirming that if you don't live up to it, you will be very, very sorry. It's important that you understand, from now on, that there will be consequences for the choices you make. You and your mom both have a lot of healing to do, and I'm going to make sure that neither of you keeps the other from what you need. We're all going to start owning our actions around here, being responsible to ourselves and each other for a change."

"And what about your responsibility to me, Daddy? What if you don't live up to your end of our agreement?"

"I live up to my agreements, Nicole, so don't go worrying your pretty little head about it." He placed his napkin on his plate and listened as Nicole shifted the conversation back to Bugs Bunny.

Later that night, Richard met with the maid and kitchen staff. He apologized for the indignities and insanity they had put up with for years. He handed each of the three of them $10,000 in cash, as a bonus for being so loyal. He explained to them that his lovely daughter would no longer be calling the shots and that he would appreciate an accounting of her behavior on a regular basis. As for the lady of the house, she would no longer be walking around drunk and on drugs, and he would appreciate an accounting of her behavior, too. Rather than hiring spies, he liked to think of it as rallying his household troops to help manage his family. If he was going to do this responsible husband-and-father thing, it wasn't going to happen without help.

Richard informed the staff that he expected to be home every night for dinner unless he had important business and couldn't leave the office. He did not foresee many of those nights. When traveling, from now on, Elaine and Nicole would be accompanying him. After the brief meeting, the staff was given the rest of the night off and Richard walked into his study. He sat down, opened the refrigerator, and took out a cold beer. He enjoyed a number of beers … the last beers he would enjoy in his house for a long time. Understanding Elaine's illness, he had made sure all alcoholic beverages were taken to the basement. The bar in the living room was now stocked with soft drinks and bottled water. When guests came over, they would simply have to accept and respect the new rules. Every temptation, every reason to break with her sobriety, was being removed from the house, including the smell of booze on his own breath.

On the way to his bedroom, Richard stopped at Nicole's door. She sat on her bed, looking intently at cartoons. He entered the room and sat down beside her. "Why aren't you in your pajamas and in bed? We have a big day tomorrow."

"Yes, Daddy, I know, but I have to finish watching this." Nicole spoke in a frightening monotone. He glanced at the TV and the wild, hysterical antics of the cartoon characters. Then he kissed Nicole on the head, said good night, and walked out of the room. Her level of concentration was astonishing. She had seen every one of those cartoons hundreds of times, but it was as though her mind and soul had been removed from her body. The only thing left was this beautiful shell and reflection of a little girl.

The following morning, Richard stopped by Nicole's room to wake her up, but she wasn't there. Her pajamas were flung on her ruffled bed, and the TV was on her favorite channel. Not daring to shut the TV off, he simply left the room and walked downstairs and into the kitchen, where he found Nicole sitting at the table, eating a cold slice of pizza, and drinking a glass of milk.

"Nothing like cold pizza in the morning," he said with a smile.

"Yes, Daddy, it's delicious."

He sat next to her at the table. "You know, when I was your age, my daddy, your granddaddy, used to take us to New York City to visit, and the best part for me was the pizza. New York has the best pizza in the world. Did you know that?"

"No, Daddy, but maybe we should move there."

"Well, in a couple of months, I have to visit New York on business, and both you and Mommy are going to come with me, so we can eat plenty of pizza then. Would you like that?"

"Yes! I would love that."

Richard planned to drive down Sunset through Bel Air, Westwood, Brentwood, and Pacific Palisades to Highway 1 and on to Malibu. It was a Saturday morning and the traffic was light, and the scenery was way more beautiful than taking the freeway. This was always one of his most cherished routes, especially early in the morning. He loved it when the sun was still rising through the trees, and the freshness and cleanliness of a new day beginning were all around … in the smell of the ocean air and the fragrance of freshly cut grass, in the song of seagulls and the aroma wafting from family-owned bakeries nestled into residential neighborhoods.

He had done this drive too many times to count and couldn't believe it had taken him so long to recognize that, of all the beauty filling his senses, none could rival the splendor and untold loveliness of his only child, who sat beside him. Nicole clutched a plastic bag of goodies she had prepared for her new friends, beholden to the sea, unfettered and unchained to the land, and better known to the common man — sailor and fisherman alike — as seagulls.

Richard found a safe place to pull off the highway, and they got out of the car.

A flock of gulls gathered around Nicole as she generously reached into her bag of goodies and fed them. She did not seem to mind the wailing and squawking, and once she finished feeding them, she appeared to take great pleasure in seeing the gulls fly off, wings flapping as they climbed above the ocean to glide peacefully, searching for even more food.

Richard would never mention it to Nicole, but he was no fan of these loud, noisy scavengers. In fact, if it were not for her sudden obsession with these creatures, he never would have allowed her to be around them. The crazy idea that one of these things could lift her up and fly off with her like in Greek mythology was all too real for him every second she just stood there, watching them in awe. In a near panic, Richard finally reached down and picked his daughter up, then carried her back to the car. He placed her in the passenger seat and securely strapped her seat belt.

"What's wrong?" Nicole anxiously asked.

"Nothing, sweetheart. We're just running late and I don't want Mommy to worry."

"But I didn't even have time to say good-bye."

"We can send them a letter explaining the situation. I'm sure they'll understand." Richard drove away.

Elaine waited patiently in her room with her bags packed. She was terrified to go home and had even considered staying an extra month. The love and support her husband and daughter had shown her the last three months was wonderful, but she feared that once she got back home, it would all disappear. The desire for drugs and booze was still there, but she knew it would always be there. If staying sober was her only concern, she had no doubt that she could and would win that battle, but there was so much more.

Richard's and Nicole's personalities were so strong that they could kill the optimism and faith of Mahatma Gandhi, much less a mere mortal like Elaine. Her husband had reassured her countless times that things would be totally different now, that they were going to be a real family — no more girlfriends on the side, no more disappearing acts into the study, no disparaging remarks, no more separate bedrooms. And under no circumstances would Nicole reign supreme anymore.

From now on, their daughter's misdeeds would be met with appropriate consequences. Rules and respect would be clear and enforced. Nicole was only ten. There was still a chance to help her become a young lady instead of a vulgar, selfish monster. She had been terribly neglected and harmed, and that was on them. Richard knew he had to make it better, and he was finally ready to try. Elaine so wanted to believe it all, but one of the disadvantages of being sober was that one was not so easily fooled or distracted from the truth. The lies would be more difficult to mask and broken promises, not so easily justified.

Except for the last couple of years, Elaine was still undeniably beautiful. A few months shy of her thirtieth birthday, she could once again take comfort in the fact that she was stunning, and very desirable. Elaine was the first to admit that she was no genius; she had barely finished high school. If not for Richard's generosity, she might not even have achieved her diploma. Her scholarly acumen hit an all-time low when she could not even help Nicole with her second-grade homework. The fact that she was drunk and stoned probably didn't help, but it certainly enhanced Nicole's confidence that she could easily manipulate, control, and eventually dispose of her mother with a knife to the heart.

After the first few days in rehab, Elaine had learned a valuable lesson — that if she ever intended to succeed as a wife and mother and if she had any plans to be a happy, productive human being, she would not only have to get control over her addiction but also take control of her own life. She could no longer be reactive but had to become proactive. She had to educate herself, not only through books but also through experience. She could no longer live simply in Richard's shadow; she needed a path independent of him. Most of all, she had to erase her fear of Nicole and make it quite clear, in no uncertain terms, that if fear and intimidation were the game Nicole was resorting to, well then, she was in for the battle of her young life.

Once the family of three was comfortably seated in the car, Elaine turned to her daughter in the backseat. "How is school, sweetheart?"

"It sucks," Nicole replied curtly.

"And why is that?"

"Because it simply sucks." She spoke with more than a hint of arrogance.

"Well, Nicole, that is not an answer, and until you have a concrete reason why school sucks, I don't want to hear you say that again. Do you understand?"

"What?!" Nicole tried to stare her mother down, but Elaine determinedly held her gaze.

"You heard exactly what I said, young lady. Your poor grades will no longer be tolerated."

"And are you going to help me improve my grades?"

"If that's what it takes, I'll be happy to help you. That's what mothers do. And if by some chance your grades don't improve, we'll hire a tutor for after school."

"I'll kill you first." Nicole hissed. She was seething. How dare her sick, drunk, stoned mother disappear for three months and suddenly waltz back into her life like she was in control. This was so unfair!

"I wish you hadn't said that, Nicole," Richard said quietly. "That little remark just cost you your TV privileges tonight and for the rest of the weekend. No cartoons."

"DADDY!! Do you hear what this bitch is saying?!" Her father pulled over to the side of the road and parked.

"Did you just hear what you called your mother, Nicole?"

"Yes, I heard what I called her. I called her a bitch, a stupid bitch!"

"You know, if I ever called my mother a bitch, my father would have beaten me senseless."

"I don't care what your father would have done."

"That's too bad, Nicole. Apparently, it didn't take you long to forget everything we discussed over these last few months."

"I haven't forgotten. She's the one who started it." Nicole suddenly realized that both her parents were looking directly at her with irritated and unforgiving expressions.

"So what's the plan, to kill me and dump my body? Now that the two of you are born-again lovebirds, and I'm just a massive inconvenience?" Nicole asked this only half joking, with a sinister smile.

"No!" Elaine protested. "Your father and I are just trying to be the best parents we can. We both really messed up these last few years, and we owe you our best attempt to be full-time, attentive, caring parents now. It can't be too late for us, Nicole. We sincerely want what's best for you. Can't you at least give us a chance?" Elaine kept her voice strong and steady, but she was pleading.

"I guess, but only if you let me watch my cartoons."

Elaine looked at Richard, who nodded his approval.

Nicole felt lucky to have wiggled out of that situation. It was the first time ever that both parents had attacked her at the same time. Usually her father took her side and her mother was so out of it that she didn't even know there was a side to be taken. Now Mommy was awake, was going to help her with her homework. Before Mommy went away, Nicole was pretty sure that she didn't even know what grade her daughter was in. Exactly how long Mommy would remain like this was anybody's guess, but one thing was for sure, that this new and improved, very beautiful Mommy was a challenge Nicole never imagined or expected.

After Richard carried Elaine's luggage up to their bedroom, he stopped for a long moment at the top of the stairs and watched as Elaine happily conversed with the staff. Nicole might have felt lucky to wiggle out of the situation in the car, but her father was simply overjoyed that it had come to a happy ending. At first he was shocked by Elaine's attitude toward their daughter. Nearly two months ago, he'd told his wife that Nicole's report card was a travesty, but that was the last they had talked about it. When Elaine brought up the subject of her daughter's grades in the car, it was nearly as shocking to him as to Nicole, but when she did not back down and calmly added more gasoline to the fire, it nearly made Richard's heart flutter. Usually Nicole would reduce her mother to tears in any argument. But this time, probably the first time ever, Elaine had turned the tables and put Nicole on the defensive, suddenly and unusually unsure of her footing. It helped that Richard had sided with Elaine, but in the end, it was her determination that won the day. After peace had been obtained, Nicole sat quietly in the backseat as her parents conversed happily for the rest of their ride home.

At the dinner table that evening, Elaine carried the conversation without forcing any issues. She asked Richard about work and a couple of new movie projects she had read about in the trades. It was the first time in years that she had asked him about work. After her acting career had failed to take off and she became pregnant with Nicole, she never again broached the subject of his business. At the time, she blamed him for her failure as an actress. After all, he was extremely powerful but never helped her get even a bit part in a movie even though he made major stars out of less talented actresses simply because their asses were shaped a certain way. What Elaine didn't know was that Richard had seen her in a number of screen tests, and she was so bad that he felt the need to protect her from the ridicule and embarrassment that would follow any of her performances, regardless of how small.

Nicole had her face buried in a large bowl of noodles and butter. It was her second favorite dish after pizza. She was happy, for once in her life, that the conversation was not about her. She was still trying to figure out the motives behind this totally transformed woman she called Mommy. Even though she had visited Elaine every weekend at the rehab center with her father, it was never real for her until now that Elaine was home with them. Even her father seemed totally enthralled with her mother, and only glanced at Nicole a few times. Previously he would chat with Nicole during these awkward dinners and totally ignore his wife. Somehow everything was upside down.

Nicole suddenly sensed that her dominance over her father might be slipping and that the promises she had made to him might lead to her ruin. She looked up from her bowl of noodles and smiled meekly at both her parents. "Can I please be excused? My tummy hurts."

"Oh no! Is there anything I can do to make you feel better?"

"No, Mommy." Nicole then unexpectedly hugged her mother, saying, "I love you, Mommy, and I am so happy you're back home."

Elaine hugged Nicole back as the young girl looked across at her daddy with a devil's grin.

Elaine was touched by her daughter's gesture, but not for a moment did she believe that there was a shred of sincerity in Nicole's behavior or words. She might have been a terrible actress, but her daughter could give Bette Davis a run for her money. She never believed, even when high, that hugs were the answer to Nicole's bizarre and disrespectful behavior. Over the past number of years, the only conversations that took place between her and Richard had been about Nicole, and Richard always took the child's side ... regardless of how appalling Nicole's actions were.

Tonight, once Nicole left, Elaine switched the conversation to her plans and future goals. She told Richard that she would like to go to work in the design and wardrobe department at the studio if he could help her get in — not as an employee, but as an intern. And not as Mrs. Elaine Weiss but as Ms. Elaine Hampton, which was her maiden name. Richard joked, asking if she was ashamed of her husband or just in the market for a new spouse.

Elaine laughed and said, "If I was looking for a new husband, I wouldn't be asking to intern in the wardrobe department. Don't think I'd have much luck there."

Richard agreed to get her into the department and thought it was a wonderful idea. Despite the lack of intimacy in their marriage, Elaine had never expressed a desire for independence. Because of the flexible hours as an intern, she still planned on being home for Nicole when she got home from school. After allowing her daughter a few hours to decompress after a long day at school, she would sit down and help with her homework. She hoped and prayed that Nicole would welcome her help and support, but if she didn't, her many privileges would, one by one, be taken away, and Elaine expected her husband to back her up 100 percent. She understood and sympathized with Nicole's troubled, abused past, but that was not going to be an excuse for Nicole's continual failures in school and her disdain for other human beings. If the child's attitude did not change, Elaine was prepared to seek professional help for their daughter.

Unless his wife had suddenly become a wonderful actress, Richard believed everything she said. Gone was the faltering and illogical train of thought that had accompanied their previous conversations. Gone were the timidity and uncertainty, and gone was Nicole's automatic veto power. Elaine was in control of herself and ready to do right by her family. As long as she stayed sober and kept making sense, Richard would have her back.

"What about your brother, Richard. What have you done about him?" Elaine's dark and calculating tone left her husband temporarily speechless. "Do I need to go over there and kill the son of a bitch myself?"

"I took care of him, Elaine. He will no longer be a problem for this family. That much I can guarantee you."

"It's too bad we can't save the rest of humanity from that miserable predator."

"Maybe someday, Elaine. Maybe someday."

On his way to bed, Richard looked in on Nicole, who sat on her bed watching cartoons. He sat beside her and Nicole asked him, "And where are you sleeping tonight?"

"With Mommy, Nicole. Married people sleep in the same bed."

"Since when?"

"Since today, Nicole." He ran his fingers through his daughter's hair. "Why don't you ever smile, sweetheart?"

"Why?"

"Because you make other people happy when you smile."

"Why?"

Richard, frustrated, leaned back and rested his head on her pillow.

"What's wrong?" Nicole asked.

"I have a headache from listening to you ask 'why' over and over again. When you smile, you make me feel happy. Does that count for anything?"

"No! You're disgusting."

"And why is that, Nicole? Why in the world would you say that? Just tell me."

"Because Uncle Bobby told me you were, that's why." Nicole said this with a self-assurance that made Richard sit upright on the bed and take his daughter by her arm.

"And why would you believe that disgusting pig?"

"Because he's your brother and he knows everything about you."

"And what makes you think that he knows everything about me? What has he told you?"

"He has superpowers, Daddy!"

"Like Superman and Spider-Man?" Richard looked at his beautiful daughter and almost reconsidered his decision to let his brother live.

"Yes, like Superman," she said. "The boys at school told me about the pepper spray. It's the only thing that can kill him. If you're really going to kill Uncle Bobby, you need to get a lot of pepper spray and spray it all over his body. That's the only way."

"You don't need to worry about Uncle Bobby anymore. He's dead," Richard told his daughter. It hurt him to lie to her yet again, but the pain and fear she exhibited were so overwhelming and so genuinely expressed that he felt he had to alleviate her suffering by any means available … if only temporarily.

"What?" Her eyes narrowed and she focused intently on her father.

"Uncle Bobby is dead and he will never hurt you again," he assured her.

"But how? How did you kill him? Did you use pepper spray?"

"No angel, a silver bullet to the head." Richard touched his forehead with his finger. "No more Uncle Bobby."

"But how could a simple bullet kill Uncle Bobby? He's a superhero. A bullet can't kill him … only the pepper spray."

"No, sweetheart, not a simple bullet, a *silver* bullet. Silver can kill all kinds of demons and superheroes. A lot of people don't know that because superheroes don't want it to get out that silver can kill them."

"So Uncle Bobby is really dead?"

"Yes, sweetheart. You never have to worry about him again."

"And how about Little Bobby? Is he dead, too?"

"Quite dead, angel. He shriveled up right before my eyes."

"Did you take any pictures, Daddy?"

"No, I had to get out of there as quick as possible, before the police came. You can't tell anybody. You understand, Nicole?"

"Yes, Daddy, I understand."

Richard watched his daughter try to process what she was just told. Her complexion was a ghastly white, and her eyes seemed to pull away from this world into a dark, unimaginable place. Richard was tempted to shake her, but she was rigid and he actually thought he might break her with any sudden movements. He whispered, "Nicole, are you okay?"

"I'm tired, Daddy. I need to go to sleep." She crawled under the covers.

"Don't you want to put on your pajamas, sweetheart?"

"No, Daddy. Not tonight." She closed her eyes and fell asleep almost immediately, under the watchful gaze of her father. Her features relaxed as anxiety left her body and she transformed back into an innocent little girl who, not long ago, was happy feeding seagulls.

Richard walked into his bedroom and unexpectedly found Elaine in the bed. He had totally forgotten that he and his wife had agreed to sleep in the same bed from now on. At first he felt uncomfortable, and then the powerful image of their helpless and damaged daughter overcame him. He sat down beside his wife and told her almost word for word everything that he and Nicole had just discussed. Elaine listened intently as concern for their daughter became a strong cohesive bond between them.

Richard took a long time getting ready for bed, which was highly unusual for him. The military had taught him many things that remained with him for the rest of his life. One of those things was time management, and despite every contrary desire, he never slept more than seven hours a night, never took a shower longer than three minutes, and never spent more than a few minutes shaving or combing his hair.

Even before his recent transformation into a family man, Richard never spent more than two hours a night with any women he slept with. He always made it perfectly clear to them that it was sex, not love, and that perks they received —whether a small part on a sitcom or the lead in a movie — were purely accidental and nothing more. In truth, of course, it was far from accidental that many young ladies he slept with went on to have wonderful careers in the entertainment industry.

But night, time was eternal for Richard Weiss...

The following morning, when he awoke, Elaine was already up and out of the room. He didn't even remember falling asleep, or kissing her, or the wonderful scent of her body. He put on a robe and opened the bedroom door. He could hear voices in Nicole's room as he walked down the hallway. He paused a few feet from the door and listened as daughter and mother conversed about Bugs Bunny. According to Elaine, Mr. Bunny was from New York City. To Nicole, the idea that Bugs had the same birthplace as the best pizza in the world made her very happy. She definitely had to visit.

Nicole sat at the breakfast table and ate her leftover noodles from the night before. She looked at a map of the United States and the circle her mother had drawn around New York City. She explained to her father how important it was that they visit the Big Apple very soon. She picked up her map and placed it between both her parents, asking her father how long before they could travel there. After explaining the distance and the time, they agreed that they would go the following weekend, but only if Nicole behaved at school and did all her homework.

Nicole tried to explain to her parents that she had paid a boy at school to do her homework, so they need not worry about that.

Richard simply shook his head and said, "And how has that been working out? Apparently, the boy hasn't been living up to his side of the bargain. Because if he were, your grades wouldn't be so bad."

Both her parents explained that her little arrangement with the boy would no longer be tolerated. From that day forward, she was to bring all her homework home and her mother would sit down with her each day to help with her assignments. Nicole naturally resisted at first. After all, why should she waste precious time doing her own homework when she could simply pay someone to do it for her? She promised that she would recruit a smarter, more reliable student to do her homework, but this approach did not go over very well, and she agreed to do her own homework and allow her mother to help. It was either that or forfeit the trip to New York, and there was no way she would let that happen.

The following morning, Richard dropped Nicole off at school. During the entire ride, all she could talk about was the impending trip to New York. Before getting out of the car, she unexpectedly reached over and kissed her father on the cheek. It was the first genuine show of affection she had ever shown him. He watched as she left the car and mingled with the other children. The whole scene was like a dream sequence in a movie — one moment so frighteningly real, and the next moment totally surreal. He had never seen Nicole interact with other children. In fact, he had never seen his daughter play with other children at all.

Richard arrived at his office shortly after dropping Nicole at school. The simple kiss on the cheek had ignited a flame in him that was worth all the box-office receipts in the world. He looked at a picture of his wife and daughter on his desk and smiled. Maybe this second chance would repair and win back the most important things in his life. He canceled all his upcoming dinner reservations. There was not an actor, director, producer, or agent in the entire town who he had to personally wine and dine. He was the chairman and a major stockholder of the most powerful studio in town. He was respected and well liked, not simply because of his powerful position and wealth but because he knew how to treat people, rivals and foes alike, with dignity.

He arranged to have the company plane over the weekend and booked a suite at the Plaza Hotel in New York. Despite his veiled threat to cancel the trip if Nicole did not live up to her side of the bargain, he knew deep down that, unless his beautiful daughter did something outrageous, there was no chance that they would skip this family excursion.

After all the arrangements were made for the New York trip, Richard called the wardrobe department and explained that he had a friend, Elaine Hampton, who wanted to intern in their department. He explained carefully that she should receive no special treatment and that in no way was she a threat to anyone's job. He was quite certain no one would recognize her. Over the last five years, Elaine had virtually disappeared from the public eye. She never accompanied her husband to any of the major Hollywood events that he was compelled and expected to attend. Actually, the last time she had been seen among many of Hollywood's elite was at Bobby's birthday party, and between then and now, she looked and behaved like a totally different person.

Elaine arrived early to pick Nicole up from school. It was the first time in over three years that she had picked her up. By three o'clock, when Nicole got out, Elaine had usually been half-stoned out of her mind. Today she parked in front of the school, got out of her car, and waited patiently for the school bell to ring. Limousines and luxury cars of all makes lined up in front of the school. Chauffeurs, beautiful nannies, and a few mothers got out of their cars and, like Elaine, waited for the children to be released. Dressed in a stylish skirt and comfortable shoes, her hair softly caressing her lovely face, Elaine Hampton Weiss stood out like Grace Kelly. The school bell rang and children, accompanied by teachers and safety guards, rushed out of the school. Elaine spotted her daughter and waved. Nicole hesitantly waved back as teachers and children alike seemed to stand still for a split second, looking in the direction of Elaine. A teacher bent down and asked Nicole, "Who is that?"

"That's my mother."

"My God, your mother is beautiful."

"Yes, my mother is very beautiful," Nicole acknowledged, looking proudly at the amazing lady who, a few months ago, had looked like a clown. She hugged her mom and got into the car. Nicole had sensed months ago that her power over her father and the kingdom they called home was slowly slipping with every passing day. What she had not counted on was the empowering intelligence and confidence that came with her mommy going sober and transforming back into the beauty queen she was over a decade ago.

Like a fairy tale, like a dream, a beautiful and loving alliance developed between mother and daughter, and together with Richard, the strength and unity of a real family flourished. Nicole's grades greatly improved, and Elaine thrived as an indispensable member of the studio wardrobe department.

Chapter Nineteen

Nicole handed Nick the last of the books, which he placed on the farthest shelf from his desk. He looked around the study proudly, turned to her, and kissed her on the lips. "Thank you very, very much. It's like a dream come true."

They were married four days later in a simple ceremony at the Little Brown Church on Coldwater Canyon Avenue. There were no witnesses except for the preacher, a photographer, and a lady playing the organ. Less than fifteen minutes after they were pronounced husband and wife, Nicole was making passionate love to her husband. A short time after that, she was on the phone with Nick's parents, telling them the wonderful news. And a short time after that, she was on the phone telling her father, who responded by saying, "I can only hope you married the boy I met at the hospital."

"Yes, Daddy, who else would I have married? He's perfect!"

Nicole suggested to her father that, as a wedding gift, it would be nice of him to buy them a condo in Manhattan, preferably overlooking Central Park. She indicated that it was the least he should do for his only child.

Richard hesitated, saying, "I'll think about it." He then insisted that, before he started giving out any wedding gifts, maybe the three of them should meet and have dinner together.

Chapter Twenty

Nicole agreed to have dinner with Richard. If nothing else, it was another chance to show him her wonderful husband and her rehabilitated, sober self. Richard made the reservation at his favorite restaurant and arrived early. He ordered a whiskey neat as he sat at his favorite table, thinking. He had not seen Nicole since his visit to the UCLA emergency room. He could usually get a face-to-face meeting with the most powerful people in the world — the president, governors, senators — within a few days of a request, but not with Nicole. After tonight he hoped the long breaks in their relationship would change.

Nicole was aware that Nick and her father had been secretly and regularly in touch with one another since they met at the hospital, but she didn't know how short each conversation was, usually less than a minute. Mr. Weiss disclosed very little to Nick about his daughter's past, and Nick kept the details of Nicole's present behavior and health to a minimum.

Nick and Nicole entered the restaurant and walked toward Richard's table. She was stunning; his daughter's beauty never failed to take Richard's breath away. Nicole was ten times as beautiful as her mother, and that was saying something. He got up to greet both of them, kissing Nicole on the cheek and shaking Nick's hand.

They sat down across from him, and Nicole asked, "So how is the world of entertainment these days, Daddy?"

"No complaints, sweetheart. Margaret wanted me to tell both of you congratulations and to tell Nicole that she seriously misses you."

"You should have brought her along. She is the one person, other than Nicky here, who I seriously, sincerely love and respect."

"I will definitively pass that along to her." A waiter poured bottled water into Nick and Nicole's glasses and refilled Richard's glass.

"Sobriety seems to be having a wonderful effect on you, Nicole. You look absolutely radiant."

"Well, thank you, Daddy," Nicole replied graciously.

The waiter took their dinner orders, and Nick excused himself to go to the bathroom, as if on cue. Richard leaned forward and looked directly at Nicole. "So, now that you're married, what are your future plans?"

"I'm going to give Nick some time to finish what he is writing, and after that, probably move to New York for a while. By the way, have you given any thought to my wedding gift idea?"

"You mean the condo overlooking Central Park? No, I haven't given it any thought, because I'd like to spend a lot more quality time with you right here in Los Angeles."

"You've got to be kidding."

"No, sweetheart, I'm not kidding at all."

"Surely, you're aware I can just buy my own condo in New York."

"Of course you can, but that would require savings from the money I send each month, and I'm quite sure you haven't saved a penny. Plus, I don't think any bank is going to give you a loan while you are unable to show any income. And if I get wind that you plan on moving away from Los Angeles, your monthly allowance will not follow you to your new destination. Not a penny of it. So keep that in mind."

"You son of a bitch!"

"And that type of disrespect, Nicole, will have you waiting tables right here in Los Angeles."

"I don't understand. I've been good. No drugs or booze. I'm married to a man that women dream about in fairy tales, and this is my reward?"

"Don't look at this as a punishment, Nicole. It is a simple reprieve. For the time being, stay put. Set aside time in your busy schedule to have dinner with your father once a week and continue to behave, and your allowance and other perks will continue as usual. This is the best I've seen you doing since before your mother passed away. I'm proud of you."

"Fuck that cowardly bitch, and fuck you."

Richard grimaced, deflated but determined. "Don't test my resolve, young lady, because before long, your husband will be begging for that waiter job you got him fired from, and you might very well be working right beside him."

Nick returned from the restroom, and Nicole got up. "Excuse me, gentlemen, but now it's my time to use the restroom. I've suddenly got this terrible urge to vomit."

Once Nicole walked away, Richard had to ask. "So tell me, Nick, which of my beautiful daughter's wonderful qualities do you find most appalling?" He looked straight at Nick, like a prosecutor determined to get the truth.

"What?" Nick replied like a dumbfounded witness stunned by the question.

"No need to act coy with me, son. I am quite aware that my daughter is possessed by more demons than Lucifer has in all of hell."

"We're trying to tackle those one at a time, sir."

"So a slow but steady exorcism is the plan the two of you have come up with? Is that part of her reason for converting to Catholicism?"

"I had nothing to do with her conversion, Mr. Weiss. Actually the whole damn thing is a sham. I've always known that, but Nicole insisted."

"And what Nicole wants, Nicole gets."

"She speaks her mind. There's no denying that."

"And her demons have no effect on you? Nothing she says bothers you?"

"Our conversations are private, Mr. Weiss. I won't break that trust. I'm sorry, but what goes on between Nicole and me is our business. Your daughter is bewitching, and yes, she is troubled, but that is a challenge I've willfully accepted."

"Nicole was sexually abused as a child. Did she tell you that?" Richard revealed this in an uneasy and unsettling tone of voice that ignited a chilling blaze through Nick's body. "You didn't know, did you?"

"No!"

"Repeatedly. It happened repeatedly before we found out and put a stop to it."

"Who? Who did that to her?"

"A relative. Let's just leave it at that."

"And the name of this relative?"

"That doesn't matter, Nick. This all happened years ago. The problem has been taken care of."

"If the problem has been taken care of, then you should have no problem giving me the pervert's name."

"No."

"I don't understand. If Nicole doesn't want me to know, why did you tell me?"

"Because I think you need to know that despite your love for her and her love for you, there's no denying that my beautiful daughter is very troubled, that her behavior is erratic at best, and that the things she says are quite often appalling. There's a lot more at play with Nicole than meets the eye, Nick. By telling you this, hopefully it will give you a better understanding of what you just married. Nicole tells me that you have lovely parents."

"Yes, I've been very blessed. Nicole reached out to them, and now she talks to my mother more than I do."

"You know, there was a span of about four years where we were an actual family. My wife had overcome her addictions to drugs and booze, and for the first time in my life, I put my family before work. It took Nicole a little time to adjust, but once she did, I don't think she was ever happier in her life. We had dinner together every night. We took trips together. Nicole and her mom went from being enemies to best friends, something I never thought I'd see. Suddenly, the two most precious girls in my life were a team, and together they took great joy in vetoing any family decisions I made. I was never happier.

"Elaine had become not only an exemplary mother, but … She took an intern job in the wardrobe department at the studio, and without any help from me, worked her way to the top of the department in just a few years. We planned on having another child, but instead she was diagnosed with pancreatic cancer.

"Nicole was never told about Elaine's illness. My wife had overcome a serious addiction — a sickness fueled by my neglect and numerous affairs — and postrecovery, became what only a few of us ever really accomplish, a great parent. She was a wonderful, creative worker and as courageous as any person I have known since my time in the war.

"One morning after I left for work and Nicole had gone off to school, Elaine walked into my study, sat behind the desk, and swallowed a whole bottle of the pills she was taking for the cancer. It was ruled a suicide but I knew differently. She didn't want to put us through the agony of seeing her waste away. She left a simple note: 'Thank you for caring. Love, Elaine (mother and wife).'

"Nicole was devastated. She refused to listen to the fact that her mother had already been dying from cancer. She simply concentrated on the notion that Elaine had committed suicide and left her. After that, everything really fell apart. I cannot begin to tell you how much it pains me to hear Nicole call her mother a… " Richard paused as Nicole came back from the restroom.

"So, did you two men have a good time talking about me?"

Richard looked at Nicole and back at Nick, then finished his sentence. "I can't begin to tell you how much it pains me to hear my daughter call her mother a 'cowardly bitch.'"

Nicole pretended not to hear her father and simply sat down beside her husband. The rest of the night went along smoothly. Before getting into his car to go home, Richard reached over and kissed Nicole on the cheek. "You are a very lucky and fortunate young lady to have found a man like Nick. I think he'll make a fine husband." He drove away as the valet pulled up with Nicole's car.

Chapter Twenty-One

Nicole and Nick got into the car and drove off. After a few awkward moments, he said, "That didn't go so badly. What do you think?"

"The son of a bitch took the condo in New York off the table, at least for now. Our wedding gift, if we ever want to see it, comes with stipulations. In answer to your question? Yeah, Nicky, it went simply wonderful."

"Sorry, Nicole."

"Sorry doesn't do shit for us. The man gave me an ultimatum, and when my father makes a threat, he's serious. So from now on, when my father calls and asks us to meet for dinner, the only answer is yes … unless we want to see a serious drop in our lifestyle."

"Honestly, I don't think that's such a bad idea. In the long run, it's a good thing that you see your father more often."

"You really are a simpleton, aren't you? In less than five minutes, my father was able to turn you. Remind me next time to wear a diaper, so if I need to pee, I can just do it at the table instead of taking the risk of leaving you alone with him. That man eats children like you in his sleep."

"No one turned me, Nicole." Nick was trying to be patient.

"My God, you are so fucking naive. It would do you a world of good to take your head out of those stupid books you read and observe what goes on in the real world."

"You know what, Nicole, it would do *you* a world of good if you stopped being so paranoid. The world is not conspiring against you."

"You're right. The world is not conspiring against me, but the man who controls our livelihood is doing a wonderful job. How would you like to go back to waiting on tables? Or did my father offer you a job, or money, or a string of high-class hookers to keep him informed of my every move?"

"Your father seriously loves you, Nicole, and the sooner you open your eyes to that, the better off we will all be."

It was easy to judge Nicole's crazy, illogical mind, but now it made sense that she had developed a ruthless shield of armor to protect herself. Nick had always surmised that Nicole's childhood had been one hell of a bumpy road. One didn't turn out like her without going through some horrifying trials — imagined or real — but he had never suspected sexual abuse. The crime of violating a child was such a taboo in the Bronx neighborhood where Nick was raised that a person even suspected or rumored of doing such a thing would eventually meet with a grisly demise, the neighborhood police typically handing out a final and fatal verdict.

Nick looked at her face, the face of an angel, and reached over to gently touch her cheek. "You know what, sweetheart, I know that each day I wake up, I am fortunate just to open my eyes and see you beside me. That's how much I love you, Nicole."

"My God, Nicky, you really are the wonderful writer I imagine you to be."

"It's not a line. I mean it."

"I know you do." Her voice cracked in a rare moment of leaked emotion. "I know you do. Thank you."

Nick looked at her as she tried to hold back unaccustomed tears. After a few awkward moments, she said, "I'm sorry I'm so damaged."

"Not to me. To me you're perfect. Challenging, but oh so perfect."

Nicole regained her composure and had to ask the question that had been bugging her all night. "So what else did you and my father talk about?"

"We talked about your mother."

"Really."

"Yes. And from what your father told me, she was quite a lady."

"I guess he didn't tell you about the early years."

"Yes, he told me about her addictions and problems and how she neglected you when you were young. But overcoming those problems and eventually becoming the person she was before she died makes her even more extraordinary."

"She killed herself. Isn't that a sin in your religion?"

"She had pancreatic cancer. She was already dying."

"So people fight cancer all the time and survive. She chose to be a coward."

"Many doctors consider pancreatic the worst form of cancer. The survivability rate is very, very low. If I was diagnosed with it, I hope I would have the courage to take my life so I wouldn't put you through the unbearable toll that illness takes on an entire family."

"I thought family members are supposed to stay strong and united during good and bad times, in sickness and in health. God forbid your mother was diagnosed with pancreatic cancer. Would you tell her it was all right to kill herself?"

"Of course not, but love can be very selfish. I know that I wouldn't want my mother to stay alive in terrible pain and agony just because I wasn't ready or willing to let her go."

"It's that painful?"

"It's terrible. It would have been awful for her to go through and awful for you to see. I believe she was trying to spare you, Nicole. But it isn't easy losing your mother and best friend, is it?"

"No, Nicky. It's been easier to blame her all these years. I was so angry with her for leaving me, especially after everything I'd been through. Once she finally came back to me, sober and whole, I didn't want to let her go. I felt terribly cheated. It never dawned on me what she must have been going through. I guess I owe her an apology."

They walked into the condo, and Nicole immediately sat down on the couch and turned on the cartoon channel. Nick walked into the study and sat in the chair at his desk. He looked across at the picture of his baby sister that Nicole had put into a beautiful frame. Death was the great equalizer, and Nick was fond of reciting the poet William Butler Yeats's famous line "Whatever is begotten, born, and dies." The only problem was that death did not discriminate, and in the cases of Nicole's mother and his sister, their premature deaths were both sins against nature. No pastor, priest, or rabbi could rationalize those injustices.

Nicole walked into the study. Determined, she asked, "What else did my father tell you?"

Nick got up from the chair and stood next to his wife. "Nothing else, sweetheart. You were only gone a few minutes."

"You're lying. You see, the problem with good people like you is that you are terrible liars. What else did he tell you?"

"I promised him I wouldn't tell you, but I'll make an exception if you promise not to tell him and you answer my questions truthfully."

"Okay. What else did he tell you?"

"He told me you were repeatedly molested as a child ... Now my turn. Who did it?"

"A relative ... a disgusting pig. What else did my father say?"

"He was probing for information about our relationship, but I told him that what goes on between us is personal."

"So you stood up for me," Nicole smiled, proud.

"I would never betray you. What's the name of the relative who hurt you?"

"It doesn't matter. The situation has been handled."

"That's exactly what your father said. If the situation has been handled, then you should have no problem giving me the name."

"That's not going to happen, Nicky. The son of a bitch has already taken enough from me. I don't want him anywhere near you."

"So the bastard isn't dead?"

"No."

"Is he in jail?"

"No."

"Then the situation hasn't been handled, Nicole. What's his name, damn it?!" Nick demanded, raising his voice.

"You know, you're really starting to turn me on."

"What?"

"Don't be coy, Nicky. You know how turned on I get when you're protective of me."

Nicole pushed her hands hard against Nick's chest. "Come on, tough boy. How about a little physical contact with your wife?" She pushed Nick backward toward the bedroom.

"What are you doing?"

"If you can't figure that out, sweetheart, then you're not nearly as intelligent as I thought," she said, as she pushed Nick down onto the bed and crawled on top of him. "You asked for affection, and now I'm properly aroused and ready to deliver." She pulled Nick's pants down. "If you have any complaints, you can file them later with the proper authorities."

Chapter Twenty-Two

Nick slept as Nicole gently placed a blanket over his half-naked body. She went into the bathroom to quietly clean herself up, then put on a robe and walked into the living room. Standing by the window, the curtains pulled open, she looked out at the pool, then picked up the phone and dialed. It rang a number of times and then her father picked up on the other end.

"Hello, Daddy."

"Nicole, why are you calling so late? Is everything okay?"

"Everything is wonderful, Daddy. I just thought you'd like to hear that, after all these years, I have finally decided to forgive Mommy. She really was quite an extraordinary woman."

"Really? I'm happy to hear this, Nicole. And what made you finally come to this decision?"

"Well, as you must have figured out tonight, my husband is not only perfect, he is very smart. Nick made me realize that it was a lot easier to blame her than accept the fact that was directly in front of me. She was quite courageous to kill herself in order to save us from seeing her suffer. It took me a long time to see it this way, but it feels like a tremendous weight has been lifted from me. Now I can finally mourn her correctly and speak about her fairly, with pride."

"I don't think I have ever been more proud of you, sweetheart."

"Thank you, Daddy. Maybe there is still some humanity left in me."

"Maybe enough to forgive your father, too?"

"No, Daddy. You've known all along what that'll take. Deliver on that promise and we can once again be a family."

"I love you, Nicole."

"I know you do, Daddy. Good night."

Nicole hung up the phone and lay down on the couch. Isabelle, the last nanny in a long list of nannies after her mother's death, had been her first true love, the love you never forget. Isabelle had been twenty-one when her father hired her. Her skin was golden, and her face and eyes bright. She was unlike any creature Nicole had encountered. Isabelle was always laughing, and even though her command of the English language was not great, it was like poetry when it came out of her mouth. And when she spoke her native Italian — even though Nicole didn't understand a word — the sounds that came out of Isabelle's mouth were like music.

Early one morning, just after her father left for work, Nicole walked into Isabelle's room as Isabelle was coming out of the shower. A simple towel covered her glistening body, and Nicole looked at her, mesmerized. Isabelle dropped the towel and took the sixteen-year-old Nicole into her naked bosom. They kissed repeatedly as Isabelle led the teenager to her bed. They made scintillating and passionate love, Isabelle touching Nicole in a way the young teenager had never imagined possible. It was the first time since her mother's death that Nicole felt whole, as though the hole in her heart had finally been filled.

For the next year and a half, Nicole and Isabelle shared the same bed, the same pleasures. They made plans for the future. The only thing holding them back was Isabelle's insistence that Nicole finish high school. Richard quickly caught on to the relationship but allowed it to continue. It was the first time in years that Nicole seemed genuinely happy.

Then one very sunny day, Isabelle, laughing and giggling like always, climbed the steps to the diving board in her two-piece bathing suit, with Nicole looking on. As the beautiful Italian girl walked to the edge of the board, she slipped and cracked her head, then fell lifelessly into the pool. The water turned red, and Nicole's rediscovered joy and happiness vanished once again.

Chapter Twenty-Three

Unlike other women, when Nicole looked in the mirror, she didn't have any doubt about her beauty and sensuality. She undeniably looked like her mother, but in all honesty, she was even better looking. Now that she no longer held the burden of hating her deceased mother, she suddenly felt even more liberated. The threats made by her father at dinner didn't seem nearly as dire as she had originally feared. Cutting her off from the endless money train he provided was unrealistic, especially after Daddy so avidly approved of her husband, and after she confessed that she had been wrong about Mommy.

Nicole, for the first time since Elaine's death, could truthfully acknowledge and debate what type of person she might have turned out to be if she hadn't lost her mother so young. She could finally acknowledge and own the lasting influence her mother had on her. Elaine had shown a resilience and strength that was hard to deny. She had been a living example that one could survive the dark and impenetrable place deep inside all of us, where we seek false refuge and inevitably succumb to chemical assistance and delusions disguised as allies, unflinching in their desire to destroy us. Nicole had also escaped that dark and impenetrable place, but unlike her mother, her wounds still remained and the scars occasionally were difficult for her to ignore.

Nicole closed the door to the study and left her darling husband surrounded by those god-awful books and the silence he required to write. The idea that he was taking this long to write a stupid script was seriously getting on Nicole's nerves. She simply couldn't get it through his thick head that nobody in Hollywood reads. The only thing that mattered was the pitch. She purposely had not put a television or record player in the study so that he wouldn't be disturbed or distracted. What she hadn't realized at the time was that those stupid books would be the biggest distraction, but then what was she to do ... burn them? Instead of writing during the time she left him free of her wonderful company, she often peeped in and found him reading one of those books, or even worse, looking sentimentally across at that stupid picture of that little guinea bitch.

What in creation was she thinking when she had that picture of his sister framed? Didn't he realize that looking at her constantly was not going to bring the bitch back? She was dead, gone, like Isabelle and her mother. In fact, every time Nicole looked at that picture she thought of Isabelle, who probably looked very much like Nick's sister at sixteen ... except for the hair.

Isabelle's hair was full and voluptuous and smelled wonderful. Isabelle was perfect. By now they would have been living in Paris and everything she had been planning would be accomplished. It was all wrong. Isabelle had been so full of life. The idea that someone like her could so easily be taken away forever was unimaginable. Even after five years, Nicole still struggled with the harshness of reality and how everything can change in a split second. Even if Nicole wanted to go and visit Isabelle's grave, it was almost impossible. Her body had been shipped back to her tiny village in Italy, where her family lived.

The only things Nick knew about her sexual history were the small tidbits she chose to tell him. He was good about not exploring previous relationships. On the other hand, Nicole never stopped looking into his past. Nick was good looking, and no guy who looked like him and drank so much alcohol remained a virgin for too long past the age of fifteen ... so that was exactly how far Nicole had her sources look back into Nick's past. He'd had a number of sexual partners, but nothing close to the amount that any other guy with his looks and personality would have had by his age. And he'd never had anything close to a committed relationship — no long-term girlfriends. The son of a bitch must have been too busy reading his stupid books, because although she'd had some initial doubts, there was no fucking way he was gay.

Nicole was absolutely determined to never let Nick know about Isabelle. Even her father knew never to broach that subject with Nick if he ever wished to be part of their family. It wasn't so much that Nicole didn't want her husband to know she had been in a long-term lesbian relationship. It was more because Isabelle belonged solely to Nicole, and no one would ever intrude or be privy to that as long as she could help it.

Nicole teased Nick about his sexual shortcomings, but the truth was that whether the sex between her and her husband lasted one minute or one hour, it did not matter. A man could never satisfy Nicole, not even the man she so dearly loved. A man's sex organs were disgusting to her. A penis was the most appalling body part in all species. There were many great qualities about Nick, but the best was that when it came to sex, he never ventured outside the box. There was no oral sex or anal sex, no penis between her breasts. Nicole owned a vibrator but she never used it. She satisfied herself the old-fashioned way, using her fingers and fantasizing about Isabelle.

Nicole pulled open the living room curtains and looked out at the pool area. It was another beautiful day in Los Angeles, and she could feel the sun on her face, warm and comforting and inviting. She opened the sliding door and walked out onto the balcony. At the far end of the pool, she saw Michelle, the little whore she'd paid $1,000 to simply relocate to the other side of the pool. Nicole stared at her glistening, brown skin lathered in suntan lotion, her healthy body lying seductively on a lounge chair. The strange, intoxicating smell of chlorine, Michelle's inviting figure, and the warm feel of the sun touching her face triggered a dangerous desire in Nicole that she had hoped was long conquered and gone. She walked off the balcony and closed the door behind her, then pulled the curtains shut as she looked at the closed door of the study, with her most precious possession safely stored inside.

She walked out of the condo and suddenly found herself pulling up a chair next to Michelle.

"Still too close to your balcony?" Michelle was slightly startled by Nicole's sudden appearance.

"No, bitch, you're fine. How's business?"

"A little slow, but it always manages to pick up," she said with a wink.

"Maybe you should try a different advertising strategy, besides sitting out here by the pool."

"Why? It works quite well. You're here, aren't you?"

"What's that supposed to mean?"

"Oh please, Nicole. That was a wonderful performance you put on for your boyfriend, and I appreciate the money, but you were the interested party, not the boy toy. That whole little drama was for your own entertainment, and you know it."

"He's not my boy toy. He's my husband."

"Like that changes anything."

"You know, for a girl who sucks and fucks anything for a price, you sure are one smart bitch."

"No need to get nasty. I'm on a semivacation. I'd love to spend some quality time with you, no charge, no strings attached. The truth of the matter, Nicole, is that I find you exceptionally attractive despite your god-awful personality." Michelle reached over and touched Nicole's face.

"Do you party?" Nicole asked.

"Occasionally if that's what a client wants, but you're not a client."

"But I want to party. Don't worry. It's on me."

"Great! Why don't we relocate to my place?" Michelle picked up her belongings and they both walked toward her condo.

"After we're all finished, you're not going to get all guilty on me, are you, Nicole?"

"Do I seem like the type who carries guilt around in her handbag? Get serious! Just remember, what my husband doesn't know won't hurt him, but what you know can be quite deadly."

Michelle laughed as she opened the door to her condo. Her place was sparsely but richly decorated, with the latest electronics and artwork.

"Make yourself comfortable, Nicole. I'll be just a minute." Michelle walked toward the bedroom, calling over her shoulder, "Open a bottle of wine. There's a wonderful Caymus Cabernet."

Nicole walked over to the wine rack, which was fully stocked with expensive reds. "Gifts?" she asked, as she took the bottle of Caymus off the rack.

"Each and every one. I like expensive things, but I'm also a practical girl."

Nicole watched Michelle's reflection in the bedroom mirror. She took off her bathing suit and stood naked, looking like a bronze goddess. She put on a short silk robe and tied it loosely around the waist, then walked back into the living room and looked at Nicole.

"What's wrong, Nicole? That bottle of wine isn't going to open itself."

"You have beautiful skin," Nicole said thoughtfully.

"Thank you." Michelle walked over to Nicole and took the bottle of wine out of her hand. "Don't know how to unscrew the cork?"

"Honestly? No!"

Michelle opened the bottle and poured two glasses. "Let me guess. Italian?"

"Michelle Romero, one hundred percent wop."

"It's like you Italians have a monopoly on beautiful skin … This is delicious."

"Happy you like it. Have you been with many girls, Nicole?"

"Only one, but it was for over a year. If she hadn't gone off and died, I'm quite positive we would still be together. Her name was Isabelle. She was Italian like you. Actually, she was literally off the boat, as she used to say. Isabelle was a perfect creature. We were going to live in Paris… "

"I'm sorry."

"Yeah, so am I." Nicole drank the rest of her wine and Michelle refilled her glass.

"Does your husband know?"

"No, but it's not for the reasons you'd think. Nick might be Catholic but he's fairly open minded. He's all for gay rights and all that shit."

"Is it because telling other people about her makes you feel like she's slipping even farther away?"

"That's exactly it. I'm just a selfish bitch, and what went on between Isabelle and me I will never share. Are you Catholic?"

"Yes. I think the vast majority of Italians are."

"I converted to Catholicism before Nick and I got married."

"Was that a condition?"

"Not at all. I just thought it would be a nice thing to do. It's not like I actually believe in any of that nonsense."

"Not to get too personal, but if your most important relationship was with a girl and you're about to step out on your husband with another girl, why did you even bother to marry Nick?"

"I love Nicky more than anything in this world. As men go, he is perfect. Without hesitation, he would step in front of a bullet for me. The night we met, he smashed a beer mug against some jerk's head. The guy was hitting on me, and then the asshole's friend came to help, so Nicky took him by the head and smashed his face directly into the bar. In less than ten seconds, he had knocked both guys out. There was blood everywhere. I was so turned on — literally, no bullshit — I had an orgasm right there."

"Really? Wow. Did you fuck him right after?"

"No! That's where it really got interesting. We were both doing coke that night. We got back to his apartment and continued partying for hours, and the whole time, I was waiting for Nick to make a move on me, expecting him to make a move, giving him every sign in the world that it was okay. I mean, any other guy in the world would have had his dick out, but not my Nicky. What did he do? He took a 'downer' and went to sleep. Left me on the couch partying.

"The next morning when he woke up, I was still there partying away, but I had absolutely no desire to have his dick or any other dick inside me. Thankfully, true to form, Nicky didn't even give a hint that he was interested in fucking me."

"You must have thought he was gay," Michelle said.

"Of course, I thought he was gay. After all, his apartment then was in West Hollywood, fag capital of the world. I mean, my Nicky is just too good looking, and he never mentioned anything like 'Jesus will save us all' … so there was nothing for me to think except that he was gay. Guess why it took him so long to fuck me? Just guess."

"Because you were his dream girl, and he didn't want to soil you before you got married."

"No, but that's a good one."

"There's a lot more to being a hooker than just spreading your legs."

"I bet. It has to be the worst job in the world, spreading your legs for different guys just to put food on the table. I wouldn't last a day before castrating one of those pigs."

"Some guys never even take their dicks out. They just want to talk. Dinner at the Palm and talk the night away. Believe it or not, most of the time I'd rather just fuck and get it over with."

"Why not just spike their drinks?"

"Return business keeps me afloat and allows me to drink expensive wine. Can't get much return business if they don't remember anything."

"I guess not. Don't you prefer women clients?"

"Oh no. The few women clients I have are older, married, have lived their lives in the closet… Before they're ready to take that plunge, it usually takes two bottles of wine and five hours of therapy."

"Wow. That sucks!"

"And not half as generous with the gifts as the guys."

"Off the clock, who do you prefer?"

"An empty bed and a good book. I haven't had a real relationship since high school. Honestly I never really gave much thought about sleeping with girls until I moved out here and got into the business. For God's sake, I come from Staten Island. My father is a cop and my mother's a nurse. Now my two brothers are ready to become cops.

They're Catholic and Italian, with old-fashioned ideas. My father belongs to the Knights of Columbus."

"What's that?"

"A Catholic organization that raises money for the Vatican and Catholic charities. He's been a member so long, I think they made him a Grand Knight."

"Get out, really? You mean, he can order hits?"

"What?" Michelle asked in disbelief. "My father would never kill anyone."

"Of course he wouldn't, but he has men who would?"

"No, Nicole, they're not the Mafia. The Knights of Columbus do good work. They help people. They don't murder people."

"Sorry! It's just when I hear Italian and Catholic, I figure they're in the Mafia, especially if they're from New York. My two favorite movies of all time are *The Godfather* and *The Godfather, Part II*. I don't get turned on by many men, but Michael Corleone I would fuck in a heartbeat."

"Really?!" Michelle refilled both their glasses with wine.

"So what would your parents do if they found out you sleep with girls?" Nicole asked.

"They'd disown me. And if they found out I was working as a hooker, they'd send my brothers out here to kidnap me and throw me in a monastery."

"That's insane."

"No, that'd be normal for any of the families I grew up around, whether they were Italian, Irish, German, Spanish, or Jewish. The people in my neighborhood don't understand, and they certainly don't approve of girls having sex with other girls, or guys having sex with each other."

"Well, not getting that guy-on-guy shit I totally understand. That's truly disgusting. I would outlaw that if I could. I can't even imagine being in the same bed with two guys trying to fuck me. Why the hell are you even working as a whore, Michelle? You're beautiful. Surely, all it would take is placing yourself in the right location at the right time to snap up one of those Jew moguls and be set for life. And even better, you'd be dictating his life."

"You make that sound easier than it is."

"No! I know from firsthand experience how easy it is. My father is Richard Weiss."

"Your father is the president of Burbank Studios?"

"My father owns Burbank Studios, and his empire keeps growing."

"Wow! I can't even imagine what life must've been like growing up around all those famous people." Michelle was in awe.

"My father did a really good job of shielding my mother and I from all those assholes. I don't remember one party at the house where celebrities were invited. Once a year, on Memorial Day, he would throw one big party for all his army buddies. He'd fly them in from all over the world and put them up at the Beverly Hills Hotel for as long as they wanted to stay. I still remember, before the party began, they'd read out loud a list of their friends who'd been killed during the war. Those were the only times I ever saw my father pray."

"Does he still throw the party each year?"

"I guess. I haven't lived at home for a number of years. It's not like he'd send me an invitation."

"And why is that? Surely, he'd want to show his beautiful daughter off to the men who mean so much to him."

"Because I don't give a shit about the war they fought, or the fools who were stupid enough to get themselves killed, or his buddies who survived. More than half of them are disabled. I just don't give a shit."

"How can you say that? They're the reason we're here today. You can't dismiss the sacrifices they all made."

"Now you sound like my Nicky. You can see him turn red in the face when I say things like that."

"You know, even I am starting to get angry over the things you're saying. I lost relatives during that war you don't give a shit about. My father still suffers terribly from being shot in the legs numerous times."

"I'm sorry, Michelle, but would you rather me not be honest?"

"Have you even read about World War II, or seen any movies about the war?"

"No, and why would I? My father had firsthand experience and never talked about the war with me."

"Did you ever think it was because he was simply trying to protect you from the worst kind of horrors many human beings ever had to endure?"

"Maybe. You know, Michelle, it's too bad my daddy isn't available. He's still mourning the death of my mother nearly ten years ago, but you'd make a great second wife. You're just his type — young, beautiful, and understanding. Maybe if he decides to get back in the game, I can at least get him as a client for you. He's very generous."

"That's disgusting."

"Oh please, don't go soft on me. I'm so ready to be a naughty girl." Nicole reached over and kissed Michelle on the lips.

"You never did tell me why it took your husband so long to fuck you."

"Because he didn't want to take advantage of such a young and vulnerable druggie like me. Can you believe that? Me, vulnerable? I'm probably the most dangerous thing he'll ever encounter in his life."

Nicole tried to kiss Michelle again, but she backed off and walked toward the stereo.

"What's wrong?" Nicole asked.

"Now I need to get back in the mood."

"Seriously, Michelle. You're a hooker. I thought you were required to always be in the mood."

"Did I ask you for money?" Michelle angrily looked through her selection of albums.

"I'm sorry."

"I bet that's something you don't say very often."

"No, I don't. But I'm truly sorry if I offended you," Nicole said.

"What type of music would you like to hear?"

"Anything but the Beatles."

"Wow! That's usually the first choice among my clients under forty."

"I'm not a client, or did you already forget? I love their music, but it's Nick's — and was my mom's — favorite band. You can understand, right?"

"Of course. How about some Gresham?"

"Who's that?"

"Someone I'm pretty sure you have no emotional attachment to." Michelle placed the album on the turntable. The music started and she walked over to the wine rack. "Ready for another bottle?"

"Sure. Do you mind if I have a package delivered here?"

"Just don't make it a habit."

"They're very cool." Nicole picked up the phone and placed her order with her drug supplier. "In forty-five minutes," she said, as she took eighteen $100 bills from her pocket.

"My God, how much did you order?"

"Enough so it won't become a habit. Three hundred is a tip."

"Wow! Maybe I could give up my night job and just be your personal delivery person."

"Back in the day, that would've been wonderful. I haven't used in over five months."

"I don't need any coke to get turned on by you, despite your rude personality and insane, uncaring opinions. You're just way too yummy looking to resist."

"That's sweet. Thought for a moment you were becoming a little too sensitive." Michelle refilled Nicole's glass with Chianti.

"Delicious," Nicole said, as she tasted the new wine.

"Italian." Michelle slipped behind Nicole and started to nibble at her neck. "Thought since you were in the mood for Italian, we might as well go all the way."

"So very thoughtful of you." Nicole turned around and kissed Michelle softly on the lips. Michelle opened her silk robe and let it fall to the floor. They started to kiss passionately as Michelle pulled down Nicole's shorts. They touched each other's bodies, and Michelle took Nicole by the hand, leading her into the bedroom.

Chapter Twenty-Four

Nicole slid her tongue down Michelle's body like a wine connoisseur enjoying every last drop of a celebrated vintage. She stopped at Michelle's vagina and fondled it like a precious jewel. She softly licked her clitoris and Michelle let out whimpers of pleasure. The doorbell rang and Nicole lifted her head, looked at Michelle and said, "Talk about poor timing."

"It's not like you're not coming back," Michelle replied. Nicole got up off the bed and walked to the front door. "Don't forget to put some clothes on," Michelle reminded her.

"Jose is such a flaming fag you could put a cigarette next to him and it'll light itself." Nicole picked up the $1,800 and opened the door. She gave the money to Jose and he gave her a large bag of cocaine.

"Gracias, Miss Nicole."

"Gracias, Jose." She shut the door and sampled the cocaine. She walked to the bedroom and looked across at Michelle, who was playing with her clitoris. "Seriously, you couldn't wait a minute?"

"Sorry, sweetheart, but it takes me time to get heated up these days. I couldn't risk that moment slipping away."

"Want a hit? It's real good."

"Just get your lovely ass back into this bed." Nicole licked a large hit of cocaine off her hand, and once again licked Michelle's vagina while her hands played with her clitoris. Michelle's body stiffened as she started to have an orgasm.

Nicole, in turn, stuck her finger in the bag of cocaine and then put her finger in Michelle's mouth. They kissed passionately as Michelle rearranged Nicole's body so their legs intertwined and their vaginas connected. Like a pair of scissors, they slammed at each other's vaginas like a heterosexual couple copulating.

"You like taking charge, don't you, Michelle?"

"I usually don't have a choice," she replied. They moaned and groaned, unsupervised and uninhibited, joyfully fulfilling each other's desires.

Nicole could tell that it was getting late. It was nearly dark outside, and she had to make a decision. If she went back to her place, Nick would immediately know that she had been out partying, but he almost definitely would not suspect her of cheating. She turned to Michelle, who lay naked beside her on the bed, and spread two large lines of cocaine across her flat, bronze stomach. Then she took a straw and sniffed both lines up her nose. She threw her head back as the rush of the cocaine immediately hit her.

"I need your opinion," Nicole said.

"Really? You listen to other people's opinions?"

"Not usually, but what do you think I should do? Go home and deal with Nick, or just call him and tell him I'm at a friend's home and sleeping over?"

Michelle laughed as she turned Nicole over and placed two lines of cocaine on the sides of her ass. She took the straw and sniffed both lines, then waited as Nicole turned over and got on top of her.

"First, I'll tell you what I wish you'd do. Call your husband, tell him the truth about your sexual preference, and tell him it's been great, but you cannot continue to live a lie. Then book us two tickets to Italy, and let's leave this all behind and live happily ever after."

"You speak Italian?"

"Some ... enough to get us by," Michelle replied as she sucked at Nicole's breasts. Nicole ran her fingers through Michelle's dark, luminous hair.

"And how about your family?"

"Oh, that's easy. I simply moved to Italy with my girlfriend, to try a hand at Italian cinema."

"And what else would you tell them about me?"

"That you're a blonde-haired goddess and the two of us fuck like crazy." They both started laughing.

"Life should be so easy."

"Oh, it could be — for me at least. If I truly thought you loved me like you loved Isabelle, I think I could sacrifice it all, the family recriminations and everything else. But *I* am not married."

"I really do love Nicky," Nicole confessed.

"I know you do ... and if he's as understanding as you say, maybe you should tell him the truth, that occasionally you need to step out on him and help yourself to a little pussy." They laughed again.

"Call your husband, Nicole. Tell him you're spending the night with a friend."

Nicole reached into the bag of coke and with a tiny cocaine spoon, took a hit up each nostril. "Now I'm ready," she said as she picked up the phone.

Nick knew from the moment Nicole started to speak that she was high. He didn't accuse her of anything, because that would only make it worse. He knew that if you threatened Nicole, she'd immediately become defensive, a danger to herself and others. He told her to keep in touch, that he loved her and couldn't wait for her to get back home.

Nicole told Nick that she was visiting a sick friend in Arrowhead, about a ninety-minute drive from where they lived, and she didn't want to leave the poor creature until she was sure she was okay. Nick knew she wasn't in Arrowhead because her car was parked outside their place, and he knew for sure she wasn't visiting a sick friend because she had no friends. He figured she was somewhere in the area, possibly at a bar, but he decided not to go look for her because, even if he found her, she wouldn't come.

Nicole wasn't like any of his friends who used coke because, unlike his friends, Nicole's resources were extensive. Money would never be an issue. She could buy coke from now to the end of time and still have money. At the moment, he needed to exhibit patience and hope and pray that the worst didn't happen. The idea that she was cheating on him never even dawned on him. Nicole was as asexual as any creature he'd ever known. Although he occasionally suspected that she might like girls, he never gave it any serious consideration. She looked at girls as indifferently as she looked at guys.

After hanging up the phone, Nicole took another two hits from the coke spoon.

Michelle asked, "How did it go?"

"He knows. He's been here way too often not to know, but I'd bet my life he has no idea about you. I'll be staying the night if you don't mind, and possibly by tomorrow, we'll be on our way to Italy."

Michelle sat down beside Nicole and said, "Honestly, I don't want you to ruin your marriage over me."

"I won't. Now, where were we?"

Chapter Twenty-Five

The night continued, and after using virtually every part of their bodies as launching pads for snorting coke, they went for a more traditional launching pad, the black album cover. The cocaine was exceptionally good quality, and even after hours of partying, the girls were still getting that really good feeling. They had already finished off six bottles of wine, but it had little effect. That was the beauty of coke. You could drink your ass off and never really feel the effect of the booze.

Nicole had convinced Michelle to turn the music off and put the cartoon channel on. At first Michelle thought the whole thing was a joke, but after seeing how engrossed Nicole was in the cartoons, she thought differently.

"You really have a thing for Bugs Bunny, don't you?"

"He's an absolute genius. Did you know he's from New York? You both come from the same hometown, Michelle. That's an honor."

"I didn't know that." Michelle took an extra-long hit of cocaine. "I think I'm going for a swim."

"Naked, I hope."

"Someone might complain."

"Seriously? The only person who would complain is a flaming fag like Jose. Oh, by the way, I put in another order. Should be here shortly."

"Really? We're going to be up for days."

"And the problem with that is?"

"Nothing, except you have a husband to answer to, and second, I'll eventually need to go to work."

"First of all, my little sweetheart, I don't answer to anyone — not my father and certainly not Nicky. Secondly, as long as you are with me you'll never again work as a whore, a hooker, or whatever you want to call your profession."

"That's the drugs talking, Nicole."

"You can think that, but my little Nicky can attest to how easy it is for me to change another person's chosen profession. Maybe after this little fling is over, my darling husband and I will have you over for dinner and he can tell you the whole story."

"See you in a few," Michelle told Nicole as she walked out of the bedroom.

"Don't drown," Nicole warned her.

"I'll try not to." Michelle put on her silk robe and walked out to the pool. She anxiously looked around and then, feeling quite certain she was alone, took off her robe and dove naked into the pool. The water was cold, and her body momentarily stiffened as though hit by a bolt of lightning. She rose to the surface, shook her body, and swam to the other side of the pool. She rested against the edge of the pool as she looked up at the sky. This was not the way she'd pictured her day and night unfolding when she originally lay out by the pool this morning. The visit from Nicole had been unexpected. Her body had been violated so many times that she had serious doubts about whether she could honestly feel emotional and physical excitement for another person again.

The idea that Nicole could reawaken that girlish dream — of running away with the one you loved and living happily ever —was totally amazing, but like Nicole, Michelle had no friends. She had paid customers who, at any time, could exchange her for a younger and more exotic model. She had reluctantly continued going to acting classes, which she had found to be a waste of time, instilling a false hope that never amounted to anything in the real world. Her agent was useless, and almost every audition she went on was through a connection she'd made, nothing at all to do with her agent. The truth was, she simply needed to get a new and powerful agent at one of the major talent agencies like CAA or William Morris.

Michelle swam back and forth a number of times, then reached over the edge and pulled an inflated raft into the pool. After a number of failed attempts, she finally managed to get settled. She lay comfortably across the raft, closed her eyes, and floated across the water. The raft hit against the side of the pool, and Michelle opened her eyes and looked directly up at Nick. She had fallen off the raft and desperately tried to hide her naked body behind the rubber boat.

"Where the hell did you come from?" Michelle asked in a panic.

"I live right there," Nick replied, as he pointed to his condo.

"Oh yeah. I didn't recognize you for a moment. I'm so embarrassed."

"Don't be. You haven't seen my wife by any chance, walking around here like a lost, coked-out zombie?"

"Your who?"

"My wife. The crazy blonde who threatened to kill you a few months back and then gave you a thousand dollars to relocate to the other side of the pool."

"No! Why would I see her?" Michelle's breathing got noticeably heavier.

"Are you okay?"

"Yeah, why would you even ask that? I'm fine."

"I don't know. It's just been a long day." Nick turned away from the pool and walked toward the condo.

"If I see her, I'll tell her you're looking for her."

"Thanks. Sorry for the interruption. Have a good night."

Nick walked back to his condo as Michelle got out of the pool, put on her robe, and walked quickly back to her place.

Nicole was sitting on the bed watching cartoons when a nervous Michelle walked in from her swim.

"My God, you'll never guess who I was just talking to."

"My Nicky."

"Yeah! He shocked the hell out of me. I was floating in the pool and he just appeared."

"Were you naked?"

"Yes, I was naked. Don't you remember? It was your wonderful idea!"

"What did he say?"

"He asked me if I would like to fuck, and I said sure, but at the moment, I'm a little busy fucking your wife."

"You didn't!"

Michelle stepped in front of the TV and shut it off.

"Why did you shut that off?!" Nicole asked.

"Because that duck and rabbit are starting to play with your head."

"Do you think Nick knows?"

"No! My God, Nicole, I feel dirty."

"That's funny, coming from a former hooker."

"Remind me again why I find you so attractive?"

"Because I'm beautiful and I get fantastic coke."

Michelle shook her head. "I need to take a shower."

"Why? I was looking forward to licking you dry like a little kitty cat."

"I don't think so. Besides, the chlorine from the pool will give you diarrhea."

"Don't want that," Nicole replied. She got up and grabbed Michelle by the arms, throwing her down on the bed. "What's wrong, and please don't tell me it's because you ran into my husband."

"It's nothing. Just need a few more hits."

Nicole reached over and grabbed a whole new bag of cocaine. "I see Jose made it over," Michelle said.

"Oh yeah. That little fag made himself another three hundred." Nicole dipped the coke spoon into the bag and gave Michelle a number of hits.

"Feeling better?"

"Oh yeah."

"Don't want my beautiful Michelle walking around unhappy."

"Nicole, do you think you could ever love me?"

"Yes, but it's complicated."

"How complicated can it be? Couldn't you just pay off your husband and tell him the truth?"

"You don't pay off my Nicky. He can't be bought. Believe it or not, if I told him the truth, he'd probably understand. All he's ever really wanted from me is honesty. I'm not kidding — he's a perfect human being. His only crime is that he was stupid enough to fall in love with a selfish, destructive, dishonest bitch like me. I'd feel really guilty if I left him, but it's even more complicated than that."

"Your father?"

"Oh, he looms large, but not for the reason you think. Before meeting Nick, Daddy thought Isabelle was the best thing that ever happened to me since my mom died."

"He knew about you and Isabelle?"

"He knew everything."

"Wow!"

"My father has been around this town a long time. He doesn't give a shit about gay rights or who's sleeping with whom. As long as it doesn't interfere with the production of one of his movies, he has very little interest in the personal lives of celebrities and hired hands."

"Then what is it?"

"It's not for me to tell, my beautiful Michelle." Nicole ran her hands through Michelle's hair. "It's not for me to tell."

"What kind of answer is that?"

"It's the only one I have. What did you and Nicky talk about?"

"About my breast size. Duh. About you. He wanted to know if I'd seen you."

"Was he worried?"

"Honestly, I don't know. I was so embarrassed, I could barely look at him. Does he usually stroll around the complex at three in the morning?"

"No!"

"Well then, I guess he's really worried!" Michelle screamed at Nicole as she started to walk out of the room. "I'm going to take a shower."

"Why are you being such a bitch?" Nicole yelled at her, and Michelle turned back around.

"I work as a professional prostitute, Nicole. I'm used to hearing clients express guilt all the time, But you, you are really amazing. Every time you bring up your husband and how fucking perfect he is, do you have any idea how that makes me feel? It makes me feel like the lowest piece of filth in the world."

"I don't know why."

"Because you made this encounter between us personal, and I was dumb enough to fall for it. I should have insisted that it just be sex ... a mutual physical attraction between a spoiled rich girl and an off-the-clock call girl."

"I don't know what you want, Michelle. What is it that you expect from me?"

"I guess the same thing your husband wants from you ... a little bit of honesty."

"Is that so? Listen to me, you little bitch. I told you I was insanely attracted to you. When you asked if I could fall in love with you, I answered honestly and said 'yes.' I'll gladly go to Italy with you, but in the end, I'll always come back to my husband. I'm going to give you something much more important than a stupid relationship. I am going to give you a real chance at a movie career with no strings attached, except that from now on, you'll never work as a hooker except on the big screen. Are we clear on that, pretty woman?"

"Do I have a choice?"

"Not if you want a chance at a career that'll make your family proud, and hopefully very rich."

"Why is it so important to you that I never work as a prostitute?"

"Because it's sickening to me for you to be subjected to the filthy desires and whims of a bunch of pigs. They're disgusting and unprincipled creatures."

"Wow. That's pretty heavy, Nicole."

"Yeah, I guess it is. It must be time for another hit."

"Well, I'm going to go take that shower. Want to join me?" Michelle asked. Nicole took a number of large hits of coke.

"In a few minutes. I'll meet you in there." Nicole waited for Michelle to leave the room and picked up the phone to call Nick. She knew it was too late in the game to pretend or try to fool him. She simply told him she'd had a relapse and that he shouldn't worry. She made him promise not to call her father, and hopefully, she would be home in the near future. He pledged his undying love for her and she did the same, and meant it. She hung up the phone, took a few more hits of coke, and walked into the bathroom, where she opened the shower door and joined Michelle.

Chapter Twenty-Six

Two days later, Nicole was still not home, but fortunately for Nick, he recognized Jose from West Hollywood and saw him making a delivery to Michelle's place. After Nick approached and threatened to disembowel him, Jose gave up Nicole's location and the name of her lover.

Nick knocked on Michelle's door. The unsuspecting girl, thinking it was Jose coming back, opened it, totally naked. She nearly dropped when she saw Nick.

"Guess there isn't a place in this world where you don't go around naked?"

Michelle simply stood there, speechless.

"You tell my wife that if she doesn't get her ass back home in fifteen minutes, the consequences for both of you will be dire." Nick walked away.

Michelle closed the door and turned to see Nicole stepping out of the bedroom.

"Guess the party's over," Nicole said. She opened the door to her condo and looked across at Nick, who stood by the window.

"Congratulations, Sherlock, it took you only three days to crack the case."

Nick looked at her with disgust. "You uncaring little slut."

"Wow! That's a new one — an 'uncaring little slut.' I guess I've moved down a few pegs in the moral stratosphere known as 'Nick's world.' I'm crushed."

"You really don't care about anyone or anything, do you? You don't care about anything except yourself, Nicole."

"Oh please, Nick. What are you more pissed off at, the fact that I relapsed or the fact that I've been fucking the girl you noticed three days ago?"

"Addicts like you have relapses, Nicole. I fully expected that, but I really didn't expect you to have a fling after less than two months of marriage."

"It didn't mean anything, Nick. It was purely physical, and now it's over. I mean, girls in Los Angeles have affairs with other girls all the time. It's part of the culture."

"Do you have any idea how naive that sounds?"

"What, would you have preferred some guy sticking his dick in me the last three days? Would that have been better?"

"You really don't get it, do you? In the time we've known each other, I don't think we've had sex eight times. Do you have any idea how unusual that is? Most married couples have sex eight or more times in just the first two days of their honeymoon."

"You're a gentleman. I've always said that. You're nothing like all those other pigs. That's why I married you."

"No, it's not about me being such a gentleman. I simply respected your desires. Just being near you was plenty for me. I never want you to do anything you don't want to do, and whenever we did make love, it was that much more special. But now that's all gone."

"I don't understand. Why is that all gone? We'll get past this and everything will be fine."

"For God's sake, Nicole, if you like girls, why in creation did you marry me?! Why would you marry any guy, for that matter? You were right. There's nothing wrong with two girls being in love. It's perfectly okay with me, but for us, it means the end of our marriage. Can't you see that?"

"See what? Just tell me what the hell do you mean? I will never, ever divorce you. Do you understand? Never!"

"Nicole, how can we ever make love again without me thinking that you're simply providing me with a service? I can get the same type of service from any prostitute. It's apparent to me that, despite what you say, male organs disgust you. I disgust you."

"No! No, that's not true. If it's sex you want, we can have more."

"Oh my God, I'm giving you a way out that's going to cost you nothing. Can't you see that? Are you just high and not thinking straight?"

"No! It's not because I'm high. I love you more than anything in this world. Can't you see that?" Nicole screamed at him.

"Once again, do you have any idea how insane that sounds? You just spent three days with someone else. It can't be that you want me around so I can impregnate you. You've already told me countless times that you never want children. So why in the world do you want to spend the rest of your life living a lie, unsatisfied, when you can literally have anything you want? Go run off with the girl. What's her name?"

"Michelle."

"Go run off with Michelle. She's your type, even I know that."

"It was just physical. It was a mini-binge. It's over! She's my friend, that's all. There's nothing about you that disgusts me. I am so sorry, Nick, that I hurt you. Please don't do this."

"It isn't possible to be sorry when you deliberately do things that you know will hurt me. You're not sorry, Nicole. You do exactly what you want to do without caring at all how it might affect others. Is there even a shred of sincerity in you? In due time, Nicole, you will thank me. You really are damaged. I thought I could love you enough to make everything okay, but I'm not equipped for this. You need help."

"I thought that's what a husband is supposed to do, help his wife."

"The help you need is so far above my abilities … I'd only be hurting you more." Nick took her by the hand and sat her down on the couch. "If you really want to do me a favor, please get some sleep. Please."

Nick walked out of the condo as Nicole stared up at the ceiling. She reached into her pocket and took out a bag of cocaine. She took two long hits, picked up the phone, and called her father.

"Daddy, I've really messed up. I need your help."

"Tell me everything."

"Please Daddy, I need Nick. Just get him back for me. Please."

Chapter Twenty-Seven

The taste of ice-cold beer is truly one of the great and refreshing pleasures in the world. That's what Nick was thinking as he ordered another from the barmaid, Cindy. He sat on a stool at the end of the bar, occasionally reaching into a bowl of peanuts. The nuts were salty, and they complemented the beer like a fine red wine complements a prime NY steak.

The Starlite bar was somewhat of a landmark in Los Angeles. It had been around a long time, and in some early TV shows like *Dragnet* and *Perry Mason*, its neon sign and exterior made some of the location shots. It was dark, and except for a door in the back where deliveries arrived, sunlight never touched the place. It had a pool table, a jukebox, a TV, and a long, unpolished bar. During the day, it was strictly an old man's bar, the type of bar on every other street corner in the part of the Bronx where Nick was raised. At night the place was filled with young people, and it was almost impossible to get a seat. Thankfully for Nick, it was daytime, and even though he stood out like a blooming red rose on a cold winter day, no one seemed to notice or care.

It was not until Richard Weiss, his father-in-law, sat down beside him and asked, "Are the beers really cold?" that Nick snapped out of his self-induced trance.

"They're nice and frosty," he said.

"Is this your regular hangout?"

"Nah. First time I've ever been in here. I have a wife who can drive a man to drink."

"Strange, I have a daughter just like that."

"Yeah, I think I've seen her. The most beautiful girl I've ever laid my eyes on."

"I'm a little partial, but I have to agree. She's the prettiest girl in the world."

"Heard it could be deadly if one's foolish enough to fall in love with her."

"Yes, I've heard that too, but beauty like that usually comes at a price."

Richard ordered a beer and took a long, refreshing drink. "You were right, ice cold. I had my doctor make a house call and give your lovely wife a sedative that quickly knocked her out. He said she's resting comfortably and her vital signs are stable."

"Thanks, that's the best news I've heard in three days."

"She told me everything, Nick. At least, her version of everything."

"She has an arsenal like no other person I know. Just when I thought she'd shown me all her worst secrets, she threw me a curve ball that would have fooled Ty Cobb."

"She's quite versatile," Richard said with a sigh.

"Did you know about the girls?"

"Yes, but I also knew she had some relations with guys, and in this town, gender and sexual reality are quite different from a regular person's perceptions. When Nicole first told me about you in such glowing terms, in terms I never heard her speak before, I just figured she'd settled on guys, on you. I wish I knew more about the thought processes of my daughter, but I fear if Sigmund Freud ever had Nicole as a patient, he might never have given up using cocaine."

"Have you ever thought about cutting her allowance? Her access to so much money might be part of the problem. I mean, her monthly allowance is probably more than my father makes in a year."

"I don't give her any money."

"Seriously? I guess that fifty-thousand-dollar check that shows up in her bank account each month appears there magically?" Nick sat in disbelief.

"Her grandfather, whom I doubt she even remembers, left his only grandchild — your wife — twenty-five million dollars. It's in a trust that she was totally entitled to at the age of eighteen. Back in the days of my father, I guess eighteen-year-olds were thought of as more responsible. It took a league of lawyers and a very understanding judge to limit the amount she could receive to fifty thousand per month until she turned thirty, at which time she could take all that was left in a lump sum. She knows nothing about the trust, and I'd greatly appreciate it if she never finds out. If you think the amount she receives now is a major problem, just imagine twenty-five million being dumped in her lap."

"The entire world would be in danger." Nick laughed as he ordered two more beers.

"Speaking as one human being to another, if I was in your situation, I would run as quickly as humanly possibly away from Nicole. She's treacherous, dangerous, and very unstable. I'll compensate you very generously for the insanity my daughter has put you through, and I'll help you establish yourself in the industry."

Nick took a long drink from his bottle of beer. "That's very generous, sir — "

"Just let me finish, son. As a father, I am begging you not to leave my daughter. Until she met you, for years I've had the same recurring nightmare. In the dream, I'm back in the army, in a fierce battle with the Germans. All around me, my friends are getting slaughtered. When the battle subsides, the few of us remaining have the gruesome chore of retrieving our dead comrades ... in a heartbeat, their lives snuffed out by a vicious enemy the world will hopefully never have to encounter again.

"Once all the bodies are retrieved and tagged, I notice a body bag without a tag. I zip open the bag and there, inside, is my daughter, and it's then that I always wake up. After surviving the war, I never thought

I could see anything worse than so many of my friends killed and others, severely wounded and crippled for life. But the sight of my little girl in that bag is the most terrifying image I've ever seen. Knowing that I'm to blame for the way she turned out makes me no different than the enemy responsible for killing so many of my friends. I stopped having that nightmare when my daughter married you, and now I'm imploring you not to leave her. I'll pay you whatever amount of money you want … enough so that your family back in the Bronx will never have to worry about money for the rest of their lives."

Nick finished his beer and looked directly at Richard. "Despite what I told Nicole back at the condo, I have no intention of leaving her. When we got married, she officially became my problem and responsibility. She's no longer your problem, and I promise you that I'll do everything in my power to keep Nicole safe. I have dealt with her intimacy problems for the last six months. I doubt we've made love more than five or six times, and I can deal with that. Beyond all reason, I'm madly in love with your daughter. My faith and my conscience would be forever crippled and compromised if I didn't give it my all and save her. I appreciate the generous offer, but it would be against everything I believe in to take a penny. I don't deserve — and will never take any money — for doing something that's my responsibility and something I freely and knowingly accepted."

"How can I ever thank you?"

"There's no reason to thank me, Mr. Weiss. You know, my father carries this strange guilt around with him. He feels like he should have provided better for his family, as though his undying love and devotion weren't enough. He thinks he should have somehow made more money, so we as a family could have had more luxuries … like a color TV and a bigger house. Occasionally when I saw him slip into one of his moods, I reminded him how lucky I felt to have a wonderful dad, a decorated soldier for my father … like you, Mr. Weiss, who sacrificed and helped preserve a way of life far too many Americans take for granted."

"And what was his response?"

"He would always say the same thing, that it was his 'responsibility and duty' to serve his country and that he was one of the lucky ones who made it back in one piece. A sadness would momentarily come over him, and then I would usually detect a smile of appreciation that I recognized his service and the service of so many others who weren't fortunate enough to come back alive."

Richard ordered two more beers and tapped Nick's bottle. "To your father."

They had quite a few more beers, and after the situation with Nicole had been temporarily resolved, they talked baseball and books.

If the conversation with Nick had gone as he expected and the young man had taken money to cut ties with his daughter … Richard had already started working on a second option. He was not going to give up on Nicole. He was determined not to let that recurring, surreal nightmare become a cloud over him. He honestly felt, deep down, that inside Nicole's troubled mind, there still existed that little girl, happily feeding seagulls and watching in wonder as they flew over the ocean.

Richard was not a religious man; he never pretended to be. He respected his colleagues' religious views but never expressed his own views — in public or to his friends — on the subject of a deity or any higher power. Unlike other studio heads, he never reached out to the powerful Catholic Church in Los Angeles or the influential Jewish community. He never once green-lighted screenplays or books that dealt primarily with religion. His support for Israel and its right to exist was mainly a reaction to his war experiences. He never took Nicole's conversion to Catholicism seriously. His only real thought on the subject was to hope they could work a miracle with her. Yet after he had finished talking to his stoned-out daughter, Richard remembered a monastery for nuns on a hilltop in France that he had helped liberate during the war. Many of the nuns, especially the younger ones, had been raped by Nazi occupiers, yet they continued to worship and defy the evil conquerors in a way that was both heroic and inspiring.

They were a very ascetic convent of Catholic nuns. They lived on food they had farmed themselves. They had no electricity, and the plumbing was primitive at best. They made and bottled jams that they sold to local merchants. The little money they made went to the poor in surrounding villages. Occasionally they sheltered Jews in hidden tunnels beneath the monastery.

Before leaving to track down his son-in-law, Richard had asked Margaret to gather updated information on the monastery. As he was leaving, she handed him the limited information she was able to find. True to their calling, that religious order of nuns still occupied the monastery on the hilltop. Apparently, little had changed since the war. They still lived with no electricity, farmed for their own food, and marketed their jams, but now they didn't shelter and hide the persecuted. They openly accepted and comforted the tormented souls that arrived at their door. This was quickly growing in appeal as option number two if Nick responded as Richard expected and left his tormented wife.

Nicole was still passed out from sedatives. Richard was going to have her chartered off to France before she regained consciousness. She would arrive in France and occupy a room in the monastery no bigger than a closet, with no cartoons to watch, no drugs, no money to bribe and pay off the staff. Her screams would go unheard, but on a positive note, she would be surrounded by women, strong and independent women, not just the type she could seduce. Nicole would serve a term no shorter than a month, and if she didn't satisfy her father's demands, that sentence could be stretched out longer. It had been a long time since his daughter had suffered consequences for her actions.

Standing beside his limousine outside the bar, Richard told Nick about the monastery and what his plans were for Nicole if he was left with no alternative. He hoped that Nick would relate this story to his lovely wife. Nicole pretended not to fear her daddy, but in a world filled with demons and dragons, she knew that he was the one person who could slay her if he ever decided to.

Nick declined the offer of a drive back to the condo. He shook Richard's hand and walked off, not quite sure what to make of the monastery option. Then he suddenly turned back around and ran toward the limo just as it was taking off.

Richard rolled down the window. "What is it, son?"

"You need to promise me that you'll never do such a thing to your daughter," Nick pleaded.

"And why is that? I thought if anyone would understand my thinking, it would be you. Surely, Nicole needs a heavy dose of reality."

"Reality yes, but a convent? Absolutely no. With all due respect, sir, that would kill her."

"Well then, son, the impossible job and challenge you've so courageously accepted just got ten times harder."

"But I promised you I'll never leave her."

"Yes, and I believe you, but the beautiful creature you love is a very resourceful little demon, and I doubt you've seen half of what she has in her repertoire. I'll speak to you soon, Nick. Thank you," Richard rolled up the window and watched as Nick walked away.

Peter, the limo driver, asked, "I guess we won't be stopping to pick up that other passenger?"

"Correct! My little bundle of joy has thankfully escaped the cruel dose of reality she so richly deserves."

Richard opened the mini-refrigerator and took out a cold beer. He opened it and took a long drink as he looked out the window at Nick, walking back to the condo.

"Do you believe in God, Peter?" Richard asked.

"I guess so, sir. I really don't give it much thought."

"And your parents, were they not religious?"

"Honestly, sir, I think the only thing they worshipped was the spirits you get out of a bottle."

"I see."

"And the airport, sir, is that no longer on the itinerary?"

"No longer, Peter, unless you want a fully paid vacation to the French countryside."

"No, thank you, sir, but it does sound wonderful. Do you go there often … to the film festivals and stuff?"

"Haven't been back there in over forty years, and hopefully — God willing — will never have to go back again."

"Are they as rude as everyone says?"

"No, the French people are most gracious. It was the Germans who were rude."

"I see, sir."

"Tonight, Peter, we're going to take a ride down to Malibu, but instead of taking the highway, how about we cross over to Sunset and take that straight down?"

"Yes, sir."

Richard took another cold beer out of the refrigerator. Even though it was quite dark outside, he could easily visualize the entire trip down Sunset. He loved this ride when it was early morning and the sun was just making its appearance. At the intersection of Sunset and the Pacific Coast Highway, Richard had Peter drive about a half mile down, and pull over to the shoulder. It was just about at this spot over ten years before that he had watched his ten-year-old daughter happily feed a flock of seagulls.

Richard got out of the limo, climbed the guardrail, and walked down toward the water. He gazed out at the mighty Pacific as he reflected on Nicole's personality, her domineering traits — power, control, and revenge. Finally, he had an answer to the conundrum. It would take a little patience and self-control on his part, but that was a small price to pay to ensure his daughter's safety and well-being and — in the end — assure himself that she would be the rightful heir to the empire he built.

Nick stopped at a convenience store and picked up a twelve-pack of beer. Since the wife was passed out, he figured he might as well indulge himself. Except for the collar, his lovely wife had essentially reduced him to the celibate life of a priest. After all, how could he ever make love to her again when he was quite certain that his male anatomy was appalling to her? Any semblance of enjoying sex with him had been one big lie, and she had just spent the last three days making love to someone else. Maybe Nicole was right after all; he simply did not understand Los Angeles. At the restaurant, he was virtually surrounded by New Yorkers. The waitstaff, managers, and most customers were all from New York. In a bizarre way, it was like he was transported from New York and thrown into a culture that, in every way, was similar to New York except that it was located across the country.

Nick opened the door to the condo and walked into the dimly lit living room. There on the couch was Nicole, comfortably asleep. If not for the breathing, one could easily mistake her for a mannequin. For some reason, Nick had expected something more than the normalcy of walking into a home and seeing his wife asleep. The last few hours had been incredibly filled with drama ... all set in motion by the sleeping beauty on the couch. Nothing in Nick's life had resembled anything close to reality since he'd met Nicole.

Nick opened a beer and sat on a chair in the dining room, right in view of the couch and his sleeping wife. Richard was an extraordinary man, but his last tale about the monastery was a direct threat, a warning that if he couldn't get Nicole under control, her father would take her and put her in a place as remote and foreign to her as humanly possible. Surely, he knew that such a drastic reaction was insane, and dangerous.

Nick was drunk. Before meeting Nicole, he'd often enjoyed just sitting in his apartment in West Hollywood alone, drinking beer. He did not need an audience. At times it was the solitude, the alone time, that allowed him to concentrate on the things that really mattered in his life. He was able to relax and get a measure of control over his thoughts, especially after an exceptionally busy and noisy night at the restaurant, where at times there seemed to be no degree of control or order, only supervised chaos.

Now the chaos was sleeping on the sofa. Richard was CEO and chairman of the largest, most successful studio in all of Hollywood, but he was unable to control his twenty-two-year-old daughter. Nick felt like a bit player in a movie directed by Nicole and financed by Richard, but unlike other movies, this story had no hero, no champion. Only a fool — a regular guy reduced to a tragic fool. As if that wasn't enough, the cast included his mother and father and deceased sister ... resurrected not as her once beautiful and happy self but as a disembodied corpse. They were all innocent casualties of a machine, a beast programmed and fed by an endless money supply without conscience or morals.

Nick fell asleep with his head resting on the dining room table. When he woke up, it was early morning, and he could see through the living room curtains that it was just getting light outside. Nicole was still asleep on the couch. It was as though she never moved during the entire night. She was in the same position, yet breathing normally, and her complexion was nearly back to its natural color. At that moment, she looked six or seven years old — pure and innocent like he remembered his sister — untouched by the demons of adolescence and the winter storms that rattle our existence until the Grim Reaper gathers our remains and turns out the lights.

Nick walked into his study and looked down at the shattered picture frame and the picture of his sister torn into a thousand pieces. He closed his eyes and shook his head as he clenched his fists. He meticulously picked up the pieces of the frame and deposited them in the trash. He had many pictures of his sister and, more importantly, the memories of her could never be erased, so he trashed the ripped-up photo as well.

It was nearly noon when Nicole woke up. Nick had already gone to the store for more beer. After rubbing her eyes, she looked across at Nick, who sat in the same chair at the dining room table.

"Hi, Nicky," she said meekly.

"Hello, Nicole." Nick had very little emotion.

"How long have I been asleep?"

"Nearly an entire day." Nick got up and walked over to the fridge for a large bottle of water and another beer. He handed Nicole the bottle, and she grasped it with both hands. "Drink the whole thing. I imagine you're severely dehydrated."

She drank the water as Nick opened the beer. She asked, "So how long have you been back?"

"A long time. Had a wonderful conversation with your father, but then I'm sure you know that."

"Are you back for real?"

"Yes, Nicole, I'm your husband, and unlike you, I actually take our marriage vows seriously."

"How much did Daddy give you to come back?"

"I didn't take any money."

"Seriously?"

"Seriously. Would you have preferred it if I took his money?"

"It would have been the wise thing to do."

"Are you kidding me? Do you have absolutely no morals? Surely, you understand that what you did was wrong, because you were scared enough to call Daddy to your rescue."

"Okay, Nick, I admit it. I was scared, what I did was wrong, and in a strange twist of fate, I gave you the opportunity to secure your parents' financial future and help us buy the condo in New York. But true to form, you said no. Let me ask you, do you plan on living off my dime for the rest of our lives?"

"You miserable bitch. It always comes back to the money with you people. I had a job making decent money, a job I liked where they liked me. It may not have been a giant income by your standards, but it took care of me just fine until you came along. In fact, everything was just fine until you came along. Now everything is upside down and inside out and I don't know who I am anymore, only that I don't want to be without you."

Nick sat down. He was drunk and tired. Nicole looked directly at him. "I'm sorry about your sister's picture. I was really mad when you left. I'm deranged at times and crazy and irresponsible, but I'm not going to sit here and beg you to forgive me."

"Stop with the insanity plea. You're not coming away from this unscathed. This little fling, as you called it, has seriously compromised our marriage. The drugs, the picture … I can get past those, but sleeping and having sex repeatedly with another girl. That literally puts a cloud over our marriage, and that will take a long time to repair.

"I don't ever want to hear you berating your father and telling the world how much you despise your parents. That's simply not right, especially after everything I've learned about them."

"I've made peace with Mommy, and thanks to you, Nicky, I am getting along better with Daddy."

"That man loves you more than anything in this world."

"I know."

"And yet how many times have I heard you say that you hate him? Every time you get into trouble, he's the first person you call."

"He made me a promise many years ago and still hasn't fulfilled it. When he finally comes through, I'll love him as much as you love your daddy."

"What kind of promise? What did he promise, to introduce you to Bugs?"

"That's not funny, and for the record, yes, he did promise me that."

"And how did that go?"

"Not as well as it should have, but that's not the promise I'm talking about."

"I want to know, Nicole. What was the promise?"

"That's strictly between my father and me. None of your business. Drop it, Nick. I promise I won't speak badly about my parents. Okay?"

Nicole went to the bathroom and spent an extraordinary amount of time in there. She came out combing her hair and looked at her husband. "Sorry it took me so long, but I really needed to shower. Do you want to kiss me, Nicky? I'm all clean."

"No, I don't want to kiss you. My breath smells of beer."

"You're so considerate. It's those small things that make you special." Nicole wrapped her arms around her husband and hugged him tightly.

Nick fell asleep on the couch. The clean, fresh scent of Nicole's hair after a shower had an intoxicating effect on him. He found himself most vulnerable to her charms when she came out with a fresh, glowing, new-car smell and shine. Although she was certain Nick was back to stay, she knew that, once she came out of the shower combing her hair, any lingering doubts Nick might still have would be gone.

She would let him feel like he had the rule of the household for a little while, but that would not last long. Their survivability depended much more on her wits than on Nick's goodness. Already Nick's sense of honor probably cost them an easy million dollars. Her father must have been laughing all the way home after his little chat with his son-in-law, but she would try to salvage at least some of that loss.

The important thing was that Nick was back, and despite her father's stake in all this, she owed her daddy a big thank-you. After pouring out the remaining six beers from the refrigerator, she walked into the bedroom and picked up the phone. The conversation started off pleasant enough. Nicole apologized for her behavior and thanked her father for helping bring Nick back to her safely. But it didn't go so well from there. Richard laughed at her when she suggested that, even though Nick refused to take any money, she felt she should get at least half of the million. After all, she was Nick's wife and entitled to half of all that he had or — in this case — half of what he had been stupid enough to refuse.

Richard told his daughter in no uncertain terms that any other wife would be overjoyed with a husband who returned willingly and freely, without accepting any payoff, simply because he was madly in love with her — especially after her inexcusable behavior. The condo in New York was not even on the table anymore. The idea that she thought he would give her a wedding gift of such magnitude after her infidelity, after only two months, was almost as insane as her asking for half the money he'd offered her husband to go back to her. Besides, there were too many issues to work out right at home. A condo in New York was not the solution.

When Richard told her that Nick had suggested that part of her problem might be access to so much money and a major cut in her monthly allowance might greatly help the situation, Nicole had to gasp for air. She couldn't even respond or entertain the thought. She would deal with Nick later.

It took great courage on her part to bring up Michelle and how she had promised the girl help with her movie career. After a half hour of pleading and Richard repeatedly saying, "No way," Nicole used the two weapons she hoped he would fall for. First was that Michelle's father, like him, had fought in that big war and was wounded a number of times. And second, that if he gave Michelle a role in that Al Pacino movie about him being a writer with all the kids in New York, Michelle would be forced to relocate. Poor Nicole would not be tempted anymore by her astonishing beauty.

Richard finally relented and told Nicole to have Michelle send her resume with head shots to his office ... but no guarantees. Nicole did not push her luck any further because unlike Nick, her Daddy was not in a forgiving mood. She did remember to tell him that she loved him, although that might have been the hardest three words she ever said, especially after the moral lashing he'd just given her.

Nicole was furious with both her father and her husband. The way her father spoke of her husband, you would have thought *he* was in love with Nick. Since when had her father suddenly transformed into some type of moral authority? What a fucking joke. The man had literally taken cheating on his wife to a new level. Of all people to betray her, her own husband. Where the hell did that son of a bitch come off telling her father that a cut in her allowance would be a solution to her problems? *What the fuck?!* The last time she'd checked, she was the one paying all the bills and Nick was the one living off of her. The nerve of some people!

Nicole sensed that her father was plotting against her. He wasn't just angry about her most recent misadventure. She noticed a change in his attitude at dinner with Nick a few nights back. The threats came one after another. She had mentioned it to Nick on the way home, but naturally, her husband wasn't concerned about her apprehensions. Five minutes! Five friggin' minutes was all it took for her father to turn his son-in-law. The boy was clueless. It was no wonder his poor mother and father always sounded so concerned about him. Thank God he had her to look after him. Thank God.

So her daddy had plans for her. That's what he kept saying during their conversation. Plans?! One could only imagine what those plans might be. *Plans. Hmm.*

Nicole finally settled down. She knew that one more mistake in Richard's eyes would be costly. He had been waiting forever to hear her say the words "I love you," but he barely acknowledged it when she finally said them. Until she figured out what his big, mysterious plans were, she had to be the perfect little wife and daughter, because now Daddy had a direct line of communication with an uncensored reporter on her every move.

She sat at the edge of the bed and turned on the cartoon channel, but suddenly, the idea of going into the living room and shaking her husband silly was overwhelming her every thought. He had forgiven her, but in a sick and distorted way, he still got his sweet revenge. She spent three wonderful days snorting coke, drinking wine, and fucking Michelle. Her husband spent only two hours fucking her over, but that two hours would impact her for far longer. Nick had exchanged nasty ideas and stories about her with her father. Now those two were best friends, and she was left with only memories of Michelle … a prisoner in her own condo with a bag of cocaine only a few feet away. The temptation was great, but the punishment would be devastating.

As luck would have it, Nick stepped into the bedroom. "Did you talk to your father?"

She looked up at him and smiled. The desire to tear out his tongue was so strong she could barely control herself.

"Yes, sweetheart. I told him I loved him, twice. Aren't you proud of me?"

"Yes, very proud. I know the history between you has been rough, but I seriously think it's in both your interests to make peace."

"You and Daddy talked about an awful lot. How many beers did you drink together?"

"Quite a few, I have to admit. Your father lived an exceptional life, even before he ever came out here. What an amazing and heroic man."

"Did you tell him about your little trip a few months back?"

"Seriously, do you honestly think I'd bring up such a stupid, unadventurous trip like that to your father? Compared to what your father went through, my little trip was like a vacation to Disneyland."

"Not to me. I spent the entire time you were away worrying about you. Maybe if my daddy had a loving wife like me at the time, he never would have put himself in those situations."

"I don't think that would have made a difference. They were fighting for the survival of our country and our way of life. I don't think any woman would have prevented him from going to fight."

"If you say so. After all, you're the brains in the family."

"Really. Since when?"

"Always. I'm really so fortunate to have two such intelligent and strong men in my life as you and my daddy."

"Are you high?"

"Not since yesterday, sweetheart. You know, my father isn't an easy man to impress, but let me tell you, he just can't stop praising his son-in-law. It wouldn't surprise me one bit if he made you vice president of his company. That's how highly he speaks of you." Nicole momentarily turned her attention to the cartoons, and then nonchalantly said, "Oh. My father kept telling me throughout our conversation that he has plans for me. You wouldn't happen to know what those plans are, would you?"

"Plans? What are you talking about?"

"Plans, Nicky … like how he, my all-powerful father, is going to decide and dictate my future. I just thought that, since the two of you are asshole buddies now, maybe he might have mentioned something to you while you were enjoying quite a few beers together last night."

"As if you'd allow anyone to decide your future? Come on. Who are you kidding?"

"Whatever my father's intentions are, I'm quite sure he means well. I guess my question to you is, if it came down to it, who would you side with — your well-intentioned father-in-law or your wife?"

"I turned down your father's money. I forgave you when any other guy would've taken your father's money and skipped town. I have never betrayed any of the secrets that have passed between us as a couple — not to your father or anyone else. I swore I would always protect and love you, yet you're so paranoid that you actually believe I'd take anyone's side against you."

Nick angrily walked over to Nicole, grabbed her by the arms, and stood her up. "Listen to me once and for all, my little wife. You can put that sick mind of yours to rest, at least when it comes to me. I will never — I repeat, never — let anyone, including your all-powerful father, interfere in our marriage without our mutual consent. Even if your father suggests something to me, I would never decide anything for you without asking you first. Not only do I respect you, but I don't want to deal with the crazy bullshit that is your temper. Haven't we had enough drama, Nicole? Are you ever going to be ready to trust me?"

"I do trust you, Nick."

"Oh please, don't play coy with me. I might not be brightest bulb in the chandelier, but I still can decipher a blatant lie from the truth." Nick let go of her arms and she sat back down on the edge of the bed. "Go back to your cartoons, Nicole. I need to take a shower."

Nick walked out of the bedroom and Nicole smiled faintly. She had to be in control of their relationship. She was the one writing the script and directing the movie of their life, but occasionally, for a few moments, the protective walls surrounding her would collapse and a sense of guilt and shame would trickle into her consciousness. Nick had just lost patience with her again, and she briefly felt a pang of guilt. It didn't last long, but she realized it was wrong to accuse him of siding against her when he had proven his loyalty time and again, tenfold.

That night Nick and Nicole lay beside each other in bed. Nicole wasn't in the mood to have sex, but considering what she had put Nick through, she would have gone along if he gave even the slightest hint that he was interested. But he didn't. They both fell asleep holding each other's hands, and somehow that small gesture of intimacy and familiarity got the healing process under way.

Nicole had been expecting a phone call from her father for nearly a week. Richard wasn't one to delay unless that was part of his big plan. He had sounded quite determined when they last spoke, and that usually meant swift, decisive action. When the phone finally rang that morning in Nick's study, she picked it up with every intention of carrying on the conversation right in front of Nick.

To her surprise, the voice on the other end was an excited and rather loud Michelle, telling her that she got the part in the Pacino movie and wanted to thank her. Nicole casually walked out of the study and into the bedroom, then listened as Michelle thanked her over and over again, asking her repeatedly if there was anything she could do to show her gratitude. Nicole told her that all she had to do was remain her friend and keep the promise to never go back to her former profession. When Nicole finally hung up the phone, she walked back into the study, exhausted, and simply told Nick she was going to the bathroom.

Nicole closed the bathroom door, sat down on the toilet, and started to weep. Michelle had ignited memories and passions in her that refused to die. That beautiful Italian goddess, Isabelle, simply refused to stay buried. Even after all these years, Nicole could still smell Isabelle, feel her touch, and hear that beautiful, melodic laugh. It wasn't fair. Wasn't it about time that Nicole felt free to move on with her own life? Isabelle had to remove herself from Nicole's restless dreams and fade away like people did in the movies. Nicole was so caught up in her own grief that, when the phone rang again, she simply let Nick pick it up. It never occurred to her that, as she wept for her dead lover, her future was being planned and arranged by the two men in her life who had both promised to love and protect her.

Chapter Twenty-Eight

After talking to Mr. Weiss for ten minutes, Nick knocked on the bathroom door and snapped Nicole out of her trance.

"Your father would like to talk to you," Nick said through the door.

"One moment." She looked in the mirror, wiped the tears away, took a deep breath, and opened the door. She looked at Nick and immediately assured him, "Don't worry, I'm fine." She took the phone from him and put on a happy voice. "Hi, Daddy."

"How are you, sweetheart?"

"Great! How are you?"

"I'm good, very good, and in a few minutes, hopefully, I'll be wonderful."

"That sounds scary. Finally figured out a plan to get rid of me without being charged with a crime?"

"No, sweetheart, just the opposite. I want you to come and work with me."

"What? Is this some sort of joke? You want me, the daughter who is your greatest embarrassment, your biggest source of stress, the quintessential, eternal thorn in your side, to come work for you? Doing what? Working in the mail room, sorting mail?"

"Nicole, if I ever made you feel like you were an embarrassment, I am truly sorry. It was never my intention, and that couldn't be further from the truth. I want you to come work directly with Margaret and me. As we speak, I'm setting up your office directly next to mine with adjacent doors."

"What, is this your way of keeping an eye on me? Because if that's what this is about, you're a little too late. I already have a live-in prison guard keeping an eye on me 24-7. I don't even have yard privileges."

"Listen to me, angel, I'm offering you a chance to come to work with me and learn the business."

"How much will I get paid?"

"Nothing! You will have your own office, but your status will be that of an intern. That's just the way it is."

"But I'm your daughter!"

"Yes, and your mother was my wife, and when she came to work here, she didn't get paid a dime for nearly a year."

"That's different, Daddy. Mommy was married to you, and she was already entitled to half of everything you had."

"You're my only child, and you are the sole heir to everything I have."

"Right, Daddy, like I'm even in your will!" She gave a cold laugh.

"You have top billing in my will, young lady, and I'm giving you a chance to solidify that position and carry on and lead our company when I'm gone."

"Wow! Never in my life would I have imagined that you would want me to be part of your company, much less help you run it. Where is this coming from?" Nicole's mind was spinning fast. Rather than being just the daughter of the man with all the power, she could one day be the woman with all the power herself. This was intriguing. "But I don't know anything about the movie business. For God's sake, I barely finished high school, Daddy. What can I possibly do at the studio?"

"You don't see me waving any college degrees around, do you? I learned the business by working my way up from the bottom, and now I'm going to have the honor of teaching you everything I know. You have an active and energized intelligence, Nicole, and together we're going to channel that energy into building an even bigger and better company that you'll run when you are ready."

"How does Margaret feel about this?"

"She's as excited as I am, maybe even more. She's finally going to have another girl in the office, someone to confide in and commiserate with after all these years of putting up with me."

"Are you sure, Daddy? The last time I was in your office, she had to restrain me from doing any more damage than I'd already done. I doubt she's forgotten that."

"That was years ago, and you were under a lot of stress. Margaret isn't the type who would hold that against someone, certainly not you. She loves you, Nicole. You know that."

"I know. She's sort of like Nick. They see the world through rose-colored glasses."

"I don't know about that. I think they see the world just like we do. They just approach it differently."

"Maybe … I swear, Daddy, I think my husband is a communist."

"What? Why on earth would you say that?"

"His lack of interest in money is frightening."

"Would you rather have him interested in your money?? Hasn't he proven himself to you enough times by now? Why do you still doubt him and find fault?"

"Yes, you're right. My Nicky is perfect. I just wish he'd acknowledge that having money is very important. The things that come out of his mouth at times simply drive me crazy. You know, it's better I never went to college. I'm sure that's where he picked up a lot of his insane ideas."

"Don't worry about it, sweetheart. I'm quite sure he'll grow out of it."

"I sure hope so. By the way, Daddy, do I get my own secretary?"

"No. I don't even have a secretary."

"Do I at least get an expense account?"

"No, but nice try."

"What, am I supposed to pay with my own money when I take clients out?"

"When you start taking clients out, that's when you'll get your own expense account, but that's not going to be for a while. Have a little patience. You'll get there quick enough."

"I guess a clothing allowance is out of the question. You do know I'm going to have to buy a whole new wardrobe. I wouldn't want to embarrass you or the company."

"That's very thoughtful of you, but I'm pretty sure your current monthly allowance can easily handle a wardrobe change."

"You know, Daddy, it's not so easy getting things out of you anymore. Still no wedding gift, no paycheck, no expense account… "

"I feel for you, angel, but you'd think that being the only heir to the biggest movie studio in the world would be enough motivation to jump-start your engine. In time it'll all come together for you, and for Nick. I promise."

"Speaking of my communist husband, you do know that my roaming rights have been revoked? He won't let me out of his sight. I gather from your tone that you've resolved this with him directly, and approve."

"Here's the good news. Your sweetie will be working for us also, and accompanying his beautiful wife to and from work every day."

"Seriously, what are you going to have him do? Read books that we might want to convert into movies?"

"Close enough — reading scripts that we might consider buying and making into movies. He'll be working one building over, in the development department."

"Are there girls working over there?"

"Of course, there are women working there, Nicole. What type of question is that?"

"Well then, find my husband another job where there are no women. If you think I'm going to be sitting still while some desperate little bitches are hitting on my Nicky, you've got another think coming."

"Nicole, your husband has proven his loyalty and devotion to you far beyond any sense or reason. I don't think he's stuck it out with you this far only to pick up some other girl."

"Oh please, Daddy, as long as he has one of those functioning things hanging between his legs, I can never fully trust him. He can be my secretary. That would be the perfect job for him. That way I can keep an eye on him, and he can keep an eye on his precious little wife."

"I expect your full attention when you come to work here, not one eye trained on your husband. I'll find him a small office downstairs, away from everyone, where he can read scripts and still have plenty of time to work on his own writing."

"And how much are you going to pay him?"

"Five hundred dollars a week, just like every other reader who starts here."

"Seriously Daddy, only five hundred dollars a week for your son-in-law? How will he ever afford taking me out to dinner?"

"Well, I suggest not spending so much money on your new wardrobe."

"Very funny. Please get that office set up for him right away. If he can't be with me, he loves solitude. It gives him time to concentrate on his writing and reading, and besides, the last thing we want is any of our workers slacking — especially not one married to the boss's daughter."

Chapter Twenty-Nine

Nicole sat down on the bed with her legs tucked under her for a good fifteen minutes. This was a lot to digest. When something seemed too good to be true, it usually was. She was already the recipient of one miracle, Nicky. Her father had never even once mentioned the possibility of her coming to work for him and now, suddenly, after she'd behaved once again like a wretched little child, he was building her an office and inviting her into the highly centralized power structure of the company.

Richard was a very affable boss. He made it his business to know all the employees at the studio — from the grips to the lighting crews to the sound engineers, secretaries, and parking attendants. He visited every department on the lot at least once a month. Great work was always recognized and rewarded.

Richard was liked and admired by virtually everyone in the business, including his most callous rivals and competitors. He listened to his employees, made notes, and encouraged creative, out-of-the-box, forward thinking — but in the end, all major decisions were made by him and his trusted partner of nearly thirty years, Margaret. He and Margaret occupied the entire fifth floor of the executive building. Nicole had known Margaret ever since she could remember. Even after her father's transformation from rogue husband to family man, Margaret and her husband were still regular dinner guests at the house, when all other employees and business associates were kept at a distance.

Margaret was glamorous and undeniably beautiful. She possessed a classiness and elegance that made her unquestionably appealing, and yet she was also down to earth and approachable. Even the irascible Nicole found her impossible to dislike. Margaret could pass for English royalty even though she was born and raised in Lexington, Kentucky, and still possessed her southern accent. Richard adored her and was often quoted as saying that, without Margaret, his company would be "nowhere." Her salary was never disclosed, but it was frequently said that if you wanted final approval for a project, first you had to get it approved by Mr. Weiss and then finalized by Margaret. Very little at the studio happened without their consent and guidance. Nicole knew that the offer Richard made to her must have been approved and finalized by Margaret.

Margaret and her husband had one son, Henry, named after the famous Kentucky politician Henry Clay. He was killed during the Vietnam War, and Richard kept a framed picture of the boy, in full military uniform, on his desk in the study at the house. Nicole used to ask her father about the boy in the picture, but Richard's reply was always the same, "He was a hero who died for his country." Nicole never believed him because to her, Henry didn't look like any hero with super powers. He looked just like a regular boy.

Margaret had reached out to Nicole many times after her mother's death, but it was futile. Nicole always believed that her father had asked Margaret to stop trying, especially after Isabelle entered the picture. Shortly after Isabelle's death and Nicole's destruction of her father's office, Margaret's husband of twenty-six years suddenly died of a heart attack. Nicole did not go to the funeral or the burial, despite her father's pleading for Margaret's sake. Deeply distraught over Isabelle's death, she didn't give a damn about anyone else's grief. It had been a long time since she had seen or spoken to Margaret, but she was sure her father kept his partner abreast of everything that was going on with his daughter, including her marriage to Nick and subsequent fling with Michelle.

Even though Richard had assured her that Margaret was happy she would be joining the two of them in the executive suite — where visitors were welcomed but never invited to stay — Nicole had a hard time believing it. This was the place where even her mother had never been invited, and surely, if anyone in their family deserved to be welcomed, it was Elaine, not the spoiled, unworthy daughter.

Nicole pondered the changes this would bring as Richard knocked on the door to Margaret's office, entered, and sat in a chair across from her desk.

"So did everything go well?" Margaret asked.

"Yes, very well. Nicole will be joining us." Richard sighed.

"Then why the unhappy face?"

"She's a complicated creature, Margaret. I thank God she didn't grow up in Nazi Germany because I imagine her rise would have been quick, and she would've become one of Hitler's most cherished operators."

"For God's sake, Richard, that might be the most awful thing I have ever heard you say. How can you possibly say something so terrible about your own child?"

"It's not easy, Margaret, believe me, but the manipulation never stops. No matter what I do, it's never enough. She's never content. I made her an offer of a lifetime, and she came back with a list of demands!"

"She's a woman, Richard. That's what we do. Surely, you know that by now?"

"A clothing allowance, an expense account, her own secretary?"

"And you said no to *all* of it?"

"Of course I said no, but rest assured, she didn't decline the offer. She's far from stupid."

Margaret looked down at her calendar and, with her pen, crossed out the rest of the day. She looked up at Richard and said, "I'm taking the rest of the day off. I desperately need to go shopping for some new clothes. You don't mind if I ask Nicole to come along?"

"You know, all you're doing is spoiling her even more."

"That's your opinion, Richard. The way I see it, she's our biggest asset and, hopefully, the future face of this company. Who better to spoil?"

"Well, you better get permission from her husband first. Since her last misadventure, she's not allowed out of the house without him."

"That's fine. I've been dying to meet this young man, and besides, you men make such wonderful baggage handlers. I plan on buying a lot."

Richard laughed. "Good luck."

"Would you like to join us for dinner afterward?"

"I'd love to. After all, you are my two favorite girls in the whole world, but I think it would be better if you spend the entire day with her without any interruptions from me. I don't want her to get suspicious and think I'm trying to control her. Believe me, Margaret, since we hung up, I'm quite sure she's been rattling her wonderful mind with the idea that this whole thing is some type of trap or trick."

Richard knew his daughter quite well. He knew if he gave her some space, she'd come around. She was too smart to pass this up.

Chapter Thirty

After driving herself crazy trying to figure out what was really behind this wonderful job offer, Nicole relented and went back into the study. She sat down on her husband's lap.

"Wow! I had a dream like this once, but I never expected it to come true," Nick said.

"Don't be silly. I've sat on your lap many times." She ran her fingers through Nick's hair.

"So did you say yes to the job?"

"Of course I said yes, Nicky. How could I refuse? That's the key to our future."

"I'm proud of you. You're going to make a great executive."

"Thank you. Why do you think it took him so long to ask me to join the company?"

"Long? You're only twenty-two years old. Most kids are barely out of college at twenty-two, never mind working beside the most powerful man in Hollywood."

"I know that, but never once did Daddy tell me he'd like for me to come work with him someday. Never once … and now suddenly out of the blue? This is some turnaround."

"Why can't you — just for once — take a great opportunity and accept it for what it is?"

"Because I'm not like you, Nicky. I didn't grow up in a family where love was unconditional. After my mother turned it around and my father realized how great she was, it was my behavior that was constantly judged. I swear, to this very day, I'm convinced that if my father could've sacrificed me to keep my mother alive, he would've gladly made the exchange. They could've had more children and raised them correctly. I would have been just a bad memory."

"I'm sorry, but I don't believe that. After my sister was killed, I was convinced that my parents would have been happier if I'd died instead. But that isn't a choice they had, and it isn't a choice your father had. Grieving is difficult. Don't fool yourself into believing that your father doesn't cherish you."

"I know he loves me, but it doesn't stop me from having my suspicions."

"You're his only heir."

"That's what he said, but don't fool yourself into believing that my father is leaving his fortune to me. Blood might run thick in your family, but to my daddy, it doesn't mean shit. Despite what he says, I'm quite sure his army buddies — not to mention Margaret — will seriously cash in when he dies. He respects them. He only tolerates me."

"Do you want to know what I really think?"

"Of course I do. Why do you think I'm sitting here on your lap?"

"Forgive me, but I thought it might actually be a sign of genuine affection."

Nicole pretended to be hurt. "I'll let that slide, but only because I've been a bad girl. Now tell me, what do you really think?"

"I think that your father finally stopped looking at your strongest traits as a negative and started to see them as a positive."

"Keep going… "

"Well, you're as strong willed as any human being I know. You're stubborn and persistent, and God help anyone who tries to pull a fast one on you. You're street smart, skeptical, untrusting. You actually would've made a great lieutenant in Al Capone's organization. You could flirt your way out of any situation. Grace Kelly would be jealous of you, not only of your beauty but your ability to twist men around your little fingers like pretzels."

"Wow! You have me figured out. I'm impressed."

"Well, no one has the ability to totally figure you out, which is just one more advantage that will make you a great executive."

"Looking at it like that it makes a lot of sense." Nicole cheerfully ran her hands through Nick's hair. "You're so smart, my darling."

"Each time I look in your eyes, it's like turning another page in a great novel."

Nicole tilted her head and kissed Nick passionately. The phone rang and she reached over to pick it up. "Hello?"

"Hello, Nicole, this is Margaret."

Nicole quickly pulled her lips away from Nick. "Oh. Hi, Margaret, how are you?"

"Is this a good time?"

"Yes, of course. I'm just sitting on my husband's lap."

"So then this is *not* a good time?"

"No! No! I always sit on his lap."

"Really? You must have the happiest husband in town."

"I'd like to think so." Nicole was unusually anxious.

"I'm calling because I just got this wonderful urge to go shopping and spend a whole bunch of money, and as luck would have it, a certain gentleman whom I will not mention informed me that he denied a request for a clothing allowance from a newly hired, very important employee. Can you imagine? How rude! That man doesn't understand women. So can you be free in about an hour and a half?"

"Yes, but you don't have to do that, Margaret."

"Oh yes, I do. I hate shopping alone, and I love shopping for other people."

"Can I bring my husband?"

"Of course. I can't wait to meet this young man. Your father speaks so highly of him."

Nicole hung up the phone and looked directly at Nick.

"That was Margaret!"

"I gathered. She sounds kind."

"She is, in every sense of the word. You have to promise me that you won't fall in love with her." Nicole was completely serious.

"The woman is your father's age, isn't she?"

"A little younger, I think."

"Which makes her around my mother's age. Why would you think I could possibly fall in love with her?"

"Because everybody does, Nick. Margaret has closed deals for my father simply by sitting in the room with her legs crossed. Her flirtatious smile can accomplish more than my father ever has with his wit and supposed genius."

"I'm already impressed. I'll look forward to meeting her."

"Just remember, Nicky, what's mine remains mine. Don't forget a few very important tips. Never — and I mean *never* — speak badly about Margaret to anyone, especially my father, unless you want to see the full weight of my father's power come down and crush you like a cockroach. Not even the bravest journalists in this town who dared to write the worst things about my father have ever so much as mentioned or even *suggested* anything bad about Margaret. My father has her on a pedestal even higher than the one your lovely parents have me on."

"Really? My parents have you on a pedestal? I did not know this."

"That's because you don't listen. They are always comparing me to that virgin lady, who I know is very, very important in your religion."

"Boy, do you have them fooled. Wow."

Nicole punched him in the arm. "That's not funny. They see me for what I truly am ... a miracle from God put on this earth to love their son."

"Okay, if you say so."

"Also, don't bring up Margaret's son. He was killed in one of those stupid wars that you and my father get all excited over. Henry was her only child."

"What war? Vietnam?"

"Yeah, that one."

"How awful. That sucks."

"Yeah, it sucks. He was just a boy, and knowing his parents, he probably would've grown up to be a perfect gentleman, like you. Also, Margaret's husband died about five years ago. They had been married forever and then one day, out of the blue, he had a heart attack and died. Maybe she's been praying to the wrong god, and that's why so much misery has beset such a nice lady."

"What religion is she?"

"How am I supposed to know, Nick? It's not like I ask people about their faith."

Nicole opened Nick's closet door. All the expensive new clothes she had gotten for him hung neatly.

"Wear something real nice, Nicky. It's about time I get to view my exquisite taste on the person I bought these for."

"I think I might need a little help, Nicole. If you don't mind?"

"Seriously, you can't put together a sports coat, shirt, pants, and shoes? My God, your mother is so right. I really am a miracle."

Margaret was nothing like Nick expected. The woman could pass for Ingrid Bergman in *Casablanca*. She looked more like one of the movie starlets he had grown up watching on TV than all the movie stars and actresses he had met and seen working at the Palm. Margaret was elegantly but simply dressed, and she looked better in a pair of high heels than any twenty-year-old. She spoke with a charming southern accent and loved to talk, but never once did she not give her full attention to anyone else who might be speaking. She was the type of woman you would be shocked to hear curse, and she was a woman who got what she wanted without making you feel like you were paying a price or being used.

She greeted Nicole with a bear hug and countless kisses. It was the first time Nick honestly saw that Nicole was not the prettiest creature in his universe. Margaret drove, and Nicole sat in the passenger seat beside her. Nick sat in the back seat behind Nicole, and it was obvious to Nick that Margaret seriously cared about Nicole in a way that only a mother could care and love a child, despite the many years they had not been in touch with each other.

The first stop was Neiman Marcus, and then Saks. Nicole's wardrobe increased at an astonishing rate as Margaret insisted on buying her anything that she even took a slight interest in wearing. The time Nicole spent in the dressing room allowed Nick and Margaret time to get acquainted. She, like Nicole's father, was amazingly knowledgeable, but it was Nick's knowledge of Kentucky history and the great politician Henry Clay that sealed the connection between them. Surprisingly, Nicole showed no signs of jealousy … even though Nick's attention was clearly focused on Margaret. Then again, Nicole knew Margaret was untouchable.

Margaret insisted on taking them to dinner after she had spent a small fortune on Nicole, and it was at dinner that Nick saw a different side of his wife. It was like the veil of darkness that was the hallmark of Nicole's character had been lifted. Gone were the sarcasm, the nasty, demeaning remarks, and the dire forecasts about humanity. The child buried deep inside her seemed to emerge. She laughed uncontrollably and talked excitedly about the future.

Her behavior since reuniting with Margaret and learning of her father's plan to work together proved a theory Nick had secretly believed but never mentioned. The innocence of childhood had never fully developed for Nicole. She had been given every material thing she ever wanted — and yet she had tortured and tormented the house staff and unmercifully insulted her emotionally battered mother. Nicole had never fully enjoyed the most precious of all childhood gifts, the gift of innocence, where make-believe is real and dreams are but a click of the heels away.

Nick politely excused himself from the table, kissed Nicole on her head, and walked off to the bathroom. Margaret reached over and took Nicole by both her hands.

"Your husband is truly wonderful, Nicole. I thought your father was exaggerating about him, but now I clearly see he wasn't."

"Yes, I've seriously struck gold with my Nicky. He's perfect for me."

"Well, not for nothing, but I think he's also struck gold with you. You're as perfect a young lady as I have ever seen."

"Thank you, Margaret. I just have to remember not to self-destruct. I'm sure my father has told you about my latest misadventures. For a moment, I thought I was doomed."

"Listen, honey, at your age we all make mistakes, and besides, forgiveness is essential to any strong marriage. We all have our faults."

"Not you, Margaret."

"Yes, me, sweetheart. My dear husband had to forgive me so many times I lost count."

"Forgive you for what? Being perfect?"

"For being far from perfect, that's what. Just ask your father how perfect I am … you'll see."

"My father!? He'd throw me to the dogs if it was between saving you or me."

"Don't be foolish," Margaret remarked harshly. "Your father loves you more than anything on this planet, and don't you forget that, young lady."

"Okay, but if I was giving a choice between saving you or my father, I would throw him to the dogs."

"What did I just tell you?"

"I know. I just had to say it," Nicole quickly said. "What religion are you, Margaret?"

"Protestant."

"Like my mommy."

"Yes, like your mommy. Why do you ask?"

"Because I just converted to Catholicism, and besides, I've never heard you talk about religion."

"I imagine you must feel very strongly about the Catholic religion to go so far as to convert?" Margaret asked.

"No, not at all."

"But isn't it a long and difficult process to convert to Catholicism?"

"No. I just gave them twenty thousand dollars, had them pour some water over my head, and I was in."

"But why would you even want to convert if you don't care about the religion?"

"I just thought it would be a nice thing to do, since Nicky and his parents are Catholic. He tried to dissuade me and told me his parents didn't care, but you know how Italians are. Six days a week, they're out there murdering each other, but come Sunday, they're all off to church. Do you pray to your god often, Margaret?"

"Yes, and I like to believe that He hears and helps me during difficult times. My religion is a great comfort to me."

"Wow. It must be really nice to have such a cool god."

"Catholics and Protestants pray to the same god, Nicole."

"Oh yeah, I think I could hang with the hippie with the long hair and beard. Jesus seems like he'd be cool." Nicole's eyes wandered to the bar, where Nick sat talking to the bartender.

"Is everything okay?" Margaret asked. Nicole's attention was totally focused on her husband.

"I just don't understand why Nicky is being so rude. It isn't like him."

"I don't think he's being rude, sweetheart. I think he's being a gentleman and giving us two ladies a little extra time to talk among ourselves. He knows we haven't caught up in a long time… "

Nicole's possessive staring and consuming focus on Nick was putting her into a trance. Margaret could see it happening right in front of her and didn't want to lose the rest of this visit to one of Nicole's tantrums, or worse. She had to break the girl's concentration somehow.

"Would you like to change seats so you can have a better view?"

Nicole turned back to look at Margaret. She had actually taken the offer to change seats seriously. "No, that would be too obvious, but thank you. I guess you can say I'm a jealous wife," Nicole admitted.

Nick rejoined them at the table. Nicole remained quiet. Margaret asked for the check.

Margaret drove them back to their car at the studio and reiterated how excited she was that, in a couple of days, they would all be working together. Nicole hugged her for a long time as Nick waited patiently. Then Margaret drove off as Nick and Nicole got into their car.

"So how long did it take you to fall in love with her?" Nicole asked immediately.

"I didn't fall in love with her, Nicole. The only girl I love is you. She's exactly as you described. Lovely, charming, smart, and extremely nice, but she's not you."

"You're such a terrible liar, Nicky. And why such a long time in the bathroom? Did the food not agree with you?"

"I was sitting at the bar talking to the bartender, an old friend."

"And what did the two of you talk about?"

"We actually talked about you. He wanted to know how I got so lucky and landed a goddess.

"And what did you tell him?"

"That all it took was the simple act of selling my soul."

"Oh, that's sweet. You always say the nicest things. Margaret was very impressed with you, Nicky. I must admit though, you have more useless information stored in that brain of yours than any human I've ever known."

Nick squeezed her butt really hard, and she screamed and punched him in the arm.

"What the hell was that?!"

"That was for the rude remark, and secondly, I just felt the overwhelming desire to touch the ass of a goddess."

"Well, you just better watch yourself, young man."

"Let's take a ride to that spot we stopped at when you picked me up from the airport. Do you remember the place?"

"Yes, I remember the spot. How could I forget? Ten seconds of pure bliss."

"Don't be nasty. I was just back from a week in the jungle. Had been thinking of you the whole time I was away. And then you pulled off the road so we could have sex in your car. Do you have any idea how hot that was? Do you have any idea how every teenage boy has that fantasy, or something very close to it? You're so damn beautiful and I couldn't help myself. I still can't help myself now. That may not have been my longest or best performance, but I remember that encounter all the time."

"Do you have any idea where that place is? It's across town, about an hour away."

"Really?"

"Yes, really! For God's sake, Nicky, how in the world did you ever get around LA before you met me?"

"I'm not sure, but I was lucky enough to find you."

"You bet your ass you were. That was the luckiest day of your life."

"You know, Nicole, I bet you'd look superhot in one of those chauffeur outfits with the black cap and white shirt … middle button unfastened … black jacket and tie… "

"Is that another fantasy of yours, Nicky? You know how I love to play games."

"Just seeing you every day is like a fantasy come true. Every time I look at you, knowing that you're my wife, it turns me on all over again." Nick gently touched her hair.

"Wow! You're on a real roll today. I do know a few places near here that are similar to the place by the airport. We can go powwow at one of those spots if you like."

"It's not what you think. There's no emergency here. I want you just as much at home in bed or anywhere as in your car on the side of the road. We don't need to recreate that fantasy if it isn't convenient today. It's just that we're used to being together with free time every day, and that's going to change. Once we start working, we won't be seeing each other as much anymore, so I think we should try to make the next few days extra special. And no, Nicole, that doesn't mean having sex outdoors. Unless, of course, you insist. Just holding you in my arms under the stars is more than I could ever hope for."

Chapter Thirty-One

Nick and Nicole decided against any outdoor adventure that night. Instead, they planned a mini-vacation to Santa Barbara starting the next morning. Before arriving at home, Nick made Nicole stop off at an old bookstore between Lankershim and West Magnolia Boulevard. He insisted that she buy a new biography on Henry Clay for Margaret. Nicole thought the gesture was stupid. After all, the woman just spent $15,000 on her new wardrobe, and here she was sending her a $20 book? It was embarrassing! But the real insanity didn't start until Nick picked out a first edition, first printing of James Joyce's *Portrait of an Artist as a Young Man* for Nicole to send to her father. At first Nicole thought the stupid little book cost maybe $5 — which was about all she wanted to spend on her father — but when she went to pay for the books and the cashier informed her that Joyce's book was $850, Nicole thought he must be joking, and she turned to Nick. "For a minute there, I thought he said $850 for this stupid book." She picked up the book and nonchalantly flipped through the pages as though she was looking at a magazine. "Can you imagine that?"

"That's how much it is, Nicole."

"Yeah, right!"

"Yes, Miss, that is how much the book is … $850," the store owner confirmed.

Nicole once again picked up the book and waved it in front of Nick's face. "What is this piece of shit made of, gold?"

"It's considered by many to be the greatest novel of the twentieth century. For a first edition, first printing and in really good shape? That's a bargain price. Think of it as the Mona Lisa of literature."

"The Mona what?"

Nick said, "Okay, the first pressing of the Beatles' *Sgt. Pepper's Lonely Hearts Club Band*. Surely, you can relate to that?"

"Believe me, miss, this book will be worth three times more in ten years. The person who is getting this book is one lucky individual," the store owner remarked.

"The person who is getting this book has more money than God," Nicole angrily replied.

"She'll take both books," Nick said, and Nicole reluctantly paid the store owner.

Nicole slammed the bag with both books inside onto Nick's lap as they got back in their car.

"Any other great ideas, sweetheart?" Nicole asked as she started the car.

"Yeah, when we get home, you're going to write two thank-you cards to go with the books. One to Margaret, and the other to your father."

"And what am I supposed to say? 'Thank you, Margaret, for spending fifteen thousand dollars on me. Here's a useless twenty-dollar book to show my appreciation. And for you, Daddy, here's a nine-hundred-dollar book to show my appreciation for fucking up my life, you philandering pig! Thanks for destroying my mother and neglecting your only child. It's been a real fucking charm.' Is that what you want me to write, Nicky?" Nicole angrily drove back to the condo.

Nick sat Nicole down at his desk and put two thank-you cards in front of her.

"Write!" he said. She picked up the pen, and he recited, "Dear Margaret, thank you for the wonderful day, and all the beautiful gifts. Love you, Nicole."

Nicole revised his dictation and added, "Love you so, so much, Nicole." She placed the card in Margaret's book and picked up the other card.

Nick recited again. "Dear Daddy, thank you for giving me a chance. I greatly appreciate the opportunity. Love, Nicole."

Nicole shoved the card into her father's book and pushed it aside. She got up and looked at Nick. "Satisfied, dear?"

"Yes. Yes, I am."

The following morning, Nick had both books delivered to the recipients. He then went off for a morning jog as Nicole started to get ready for their trip to beautiful Santa Barbara.

Richard got into work especially early that morning but was not surprised to find Margaret already there, busy at work. Even after thirty years, the sight of his lovely partner put a smile on his face. He knocked gently on the open door to her office before walking in and sitting in a chair across from her. She took off her reading glasses and placed her hands under her chin. "I was expecting a call from you last night, Richard."

"I wasn't sure if I should call. I knew it might have been wonderful, or it could have been absolutely terrible. Once I decided to ring you, I realized it was very late, and I didn't want to wake you. So how did it go?"

"It went wonderfully, Richard. Really, we had a lovely day. She is so smart, doesn't miss a beat. And beautiful as ever. I think she might be even more beautiful than Elaine was at that age, and Nicole seems truly excited to start working with us."

"No hiccups?"

"Not a one." Margaret smiled.

Richard wanted to believe this was a new beginning for all of them, but he couldn't help the doubts that always crept in where Nicole was concerned. He couldn't risk her having another relapse into drugs and God only knew what else. He had to keep her safe.

"You'll protect her at any cost, won't you, Margaret?"

"Why would you even ask that question? Listen to me. That child will only see the inside of a monastery over my dead body. Do you understand? So why don't you just cross that option off?"

"If you say so."

"I should have taken a much more active role in her life after Elaine died."

"You tried. She pushed you away, like she pushes everybody away."

"She was thirteen, Richard. She had been abused. She hardly knew you except that you were a liar and a cheater, and her mother and best friend was gone. That poor girl was lost and lonely and scared. She needed a woman close to her who would listen, who wouldn't give up on her. I should have pushed harder."

"Stop it, Margaret! I am not going to sit here and listen to you take the blame for the way Nicole turned out."

"Well, we've been given a second chance, and this time we're going to do right by her," Margaret insisted.

Nick, sweaty after a long run, opened the front door of the condo and heard the radio blasting in the bedroom. He walked into the bedroom and watched as Nicole lip-synched to Billy Squier's "In the Dark," which played on the radio. She stood in front of the bathroom mirror, unaware of Nick, and pretended to play electric guitar as her hair flew wildly around. The song and Nicole's performance ended, and Nick clapped his hands. "Wow! I didn't know that I was married to Joan Jett!"

She spun around and looked at him, surprised and embarrassed. "Billy Squier, genius. Not Joan Jett."

"I know. I saw him in Central Park before I moved out here."

"Really? That's cool. Now I'm impressed. I thought the only musicians you know sing, 'Love Me Do.'"

"Why so happy, Nicole? Find yourself an extra million dollars under your pillow?"

"Very funny. Margaret called while you were gone. She was so touched by the book and the note that she started to cry. And then, of course, my father called, and he was also touched. And then it occurred to me that the son of a bitch still hasn't given us any gift for getting married! What the hell? So I reminded him of that significant oversight. And as a consolation, until he buys us our condo in

Manhattan, our trip to Santa Barbara this weekend is on him. I have to pick up his credit card at the studio."

"So our little honeymoon is on your father?" Nick asked, feeling bitter.

"Yes, sweetheart. Someone has to pay for it, and it isn't like you can afford to. Go take a shower, Nicky. We need to get out of here and on the road. I already packed your stuff, and by the way, there will be no books allowed on this trip. Your focus is to be totally on me."

"Well, that isn't asking much." Nick walked off to take a shower.

"You bet it's not asking much," Nicole yelled after him. "You seriously don't have a clue how lucky you are."

Nicole's mood improved even more after she picked up her father's credit card and placed it inside her purse. She decided to take the scenic route up to Santa Barbara, which wouldn't be so unusual except for the fact that Nicole had never expressed any interest in or love for nature. She sang along with the radio as she drove the breathtaking Pacific Coast Highway straight into the lovely town of Santa Barbara. If Nick didn't know better, he would have sworn that his lovely wife was high.

After checking in at the hotel, directly across from the beach, they took a walk along the pier and then went to eat at the famous Harbor Restaurant. Sitting at a window table overlooking the water, Nicole decided that she would celebrate the occasion by ordering a bottle of Louis Roederer Cristal champagne, the most expensive bottle on their wine list. Nick hesitated at first, but Nicole was quick to remind him that it was their unofficial honeymoon and it was all on Daddy.

Nicole ordered her favorite dish, pasta with butter, and for Nick she ordered lobster, crab, and steak. When they finished their first bottle of champagne, Nicole immediately ordered another. The waiter saw that Nicole and Nick were both in their twenties and reminded her how expensive the champagne was. He didn't want to be rude but didn't want to get stuck paying for it if he served a bottle to a customer who couldn't afford the bill. Nicole simply shrugged off the waiter's comment and ordered him to get the champagne and not bother her with such minor issues as cost. Nick told Nicole that the waiter was simply doing his job, and Nicole replied, "Of course he was, sweetheart. If it was you doing the ordering, he wouldn't have said a word."

After their third bottle of champagne, Nick was quite sure that Nicole had more on her mind than honeymoon bliss, but when she took out a notepad and pen from her purse, it all became surreal.

"So honey, tell me something that only you and my daddy, and perhaps Margaret, would know?"

"Like what?"

"Like the president of the United States."

Nick paused and wisely refused the instinct to ridicule his wife.

"Ronald Reagan."

"Oh yeah, the actor." Nicole wrote the answer down. "And the vice president?"

"George Bush."

"Oh, that shouldn't be too hard to remember. Bush like the bush between my legs." Again Nicole wrote down the answer. "What else?" Nick downed his glass of champagne and poured some more.

"Something that your daddy, Margaret, and I would know? Like the three branches of government?"

"Okay, what are they?" Nicole was getting impatient.

"The executive branch, which is the president. The judicial is the Supreme Court, and the legislative branch is Congress."

"Seriously, Nicky, do you think anybody really cares about that nonsense? Tell me relevant things, like the manager of that baseball team who my father loves."

"Tommy Lasorda, of the Dodgers."

"Yeah, that jackass. That shouldn't be too hard to remember. Lasorda the jackass! It has a ring to it."

The questions continued and the champagne kept on coming. Nicole's mood grew more and more petulant with each sip of the bubbly. Finally, Nick asked for the check, and Nicole handed over her father's credit card to Nick, strangely enough, without a complaint. He paid the $4,000 bill and left a $1,500 tip. The waiter, uncertain about the huge gratuity, asked Nick if the tip was the right amount. Nick assured him that the tip was correct and then, under his breath, remarked, "Her father is loaded."

It was still relatively early when they got back to their hotel room. Nick, drunk and exhausted, fell facedown onto the bed. Nicole sat beside him and turned on the cartoon channel. Nick reached over and gently touched her. "I had a really nice time tonight, Nicole."

"Me too, Nicky. You're the best thing that has ever happen to me."

Nick ran his hand down her back and decided to simply leave it at that. The notion that this night would end intimately had long passed, back in the restaurant when questions started pouring out of her mouth. Any lingering hope was most certainly extinguished once she turned on the cartoon channel. She would rather have sex with that rabbit than her husband, but that was fine. It was part of the unwritten contract between them, and Nick was okay with it.

He fell asleep quite fast but was awakened by the sound of Nicole talking on the phone. He pretended to be asleep as she took money out of her purse and very quietly walked toward the door. She opened the door just as Nick sat up in bed. "You walk out that door, Nicole, and you will see a side of me that you have never seen before."

"I'm only going for a walk by the beach," she replied with a laugh. "I can't sleep."

"Don't do it, Nicole," he warned her again. He got out of the bed and walked toward her.

"Screw you!" Nicole screamed at him.

He took her by her hand, slammed the door shut, and shoved her up against the wall. He pulled open her hand, took out the large sum of money she was holding, and put it up to her face. "Do you usually need this much cash to take a walk on the beach at four in the morning?"

"What are you going to do?" Nicole anxiously asked, as Nick sat her down on the bed.

"Just sit here, Nicole, and watch your cartoons. Don't get any cute ideas. I'll be back shortly."

Nick walked out of the room with the money in his hand. Two minutes later, Nick reappeared and walked over to his wife, who sat silently on the bed. He pulled a large bag of cocaine out of his pocket. "What, you have connections up and down the coast?"

Nicole sighed deeply as she watched Nick walk into the bathroom and flush the entire bag of cocaine down the toilet. She started to cry. Her hands started to shake. She was furious. He couldn't do this to her! Since when did this asshole think he had control? She was the one who made the decisions, not him — not any man. How dare he flush her coke away?

But deep down inside, Nicole knew that, every time she did coke, she got into trouble. She also knew that if she got into trouble again, even one more time, her father would take away all the good things he was doing for them. And last but not least, she knew if she did drugs again, that Margaret would be awfully disappointed in her, and Nicole didn't want to disappoint Margaret. She was the only woman Nicole had ever truly loved except for her mother and Isabelle.

Nicole made up her mind in that moment that she wanted to try and do the right thing. For once in her sorry life, she would try to be honest and good.

Nick sat down beside her on the bed, and after a few awkward moments, she said, "You married a junkie, Nicky. What else can I say?"

Chapter Thirty-Two

The next morning, with the sun shining brightly and the sound and smell of the ocean in the air, Nick and Nicole sat down at a table at an outside café. She put on a pair of sunglasses as he read the menu. Then he put aside the menu and took out a large sum of money, which Nicole looked at curiously.

"Where did you get all the money?"

"Out of your purse, along with all your credit cards and bank cards."

"Give it back," she demanded.

"Not a chance."

"So you've graduated from a waiter to a thief? That's a giant leap upwards."

"It's really a shame when I have to resort to this petty behavior in the hope of keeping my wife alive. You'll get your money and cards back, but not until we get home."

Nick ordered pancakes, and a bowl of noodles with butter for Nicole.

"I'm not hungry," she protested, and grabbed the waiter's hand. "What I really want is a Bloody Mary."

The waiter looked at Nick, as if to confirm that it was all right to bring her the drink. Nicole saw this and said to the waiter, "Don't look at him. Just bring me what I ask for."

"You can bring her the drink and the noodles, please," Nick assured the waiter. "Thank you."

The waiter brought Nicole her Bloody Mary and Nick, a glass of water. She downed the drink and ordered another.

Nick looked defiantly across at his wife. "You can drink all you want, sweetheart, but you're not getting your money or your credit cards back, and especially not your father's card. Oh, and by the way, I took the liberty of taking these out of your purse, too."

He took her car keys out his pocket and playfully twirled them around in his hand.

"Wow!" she said. "You've covered all the bases. Do you actually plan on driving us home? Because if that's the case, I better call my father and tell him not to expect us at work on Monday. If we leave on Sunday as planned, I expect, on Monday morning, we should be somewhere just south of Canada."

"That's funny, Nicole. Maybe you should put together a show and try your luck at comedy. You're a natural."

"You know, Nicky, the company around here is getting mighty tiresome." Nicole stood up and looked down at him. "You know the beauty about being me is that I can get just about anything I want, even without money." She kicked Nick really hard in the leg and walked off.

Nick grimaced as he pulled out a $100 bill and left it on the table. He followed Nicole at a distance, just far enough that she was aware of his presence. She walked into an open-air bar across from the beach and sat on a stool next to a middle-aged, out-of-shape customer named Benny. Benny wore a tank top, ruffled shorts, and sandals. They were the only two customers in the bar, along with a young, muscular bartender named Lance.

Nicole asked Benny, "Would you be so nice as to buy me a drink? I seem to have lost all my money, and I'm in terrible need of a drink to calm me down."

Benny eagerly agreed and called Lance over. She ordered a Bloody Mary as Benny yelled out to Lance, "Top shelf for this lovely creature in distress."

"Of course," Lance said, as he reached slowly for the top-shelf vodka and started to make the drink. A moment later, he placed the drink in front of Nicole as she told the attentive Benny a sob story about how she lost all her money and credit cards. Benny pretended to care as he eyed Nicole like a prime cut of beef.

"And to make things worse," Nicole continued, "I think I'm being followed by that freak across the way." She pointed to Nick, who sat on a bench about a half block away, looking directly at his wife.

Benny squinted as he looked across at Nick. "Really?"

"Yes. Would you be so kind as to tell him to go away? I'd do it myself, but I'm afraid he might hurt me."

"No! No! A girl like you can't be careful enough. I'll be glad to do it." Benny walked toward Nick.

"Hey, you," Benny yelled at Nick, "Get your ass the hell out of here before I call the cops. What type of freak are you, stalking that young lady up there?"

"That young lady up there is my sister," Nick said.

"No way. The two of you don't look anything alike."

"Same father, different mothers. I'm sorry, half sister. She was just released from Bellevue Psychiatric Hospital in New York. She cut off her fiancé's dick with a butcher knife."

"No fucking way. What do I look like, some kind of jerk?"

"No. I know it's hard to believe, but it's true. I was the jerk for agreeing to take custody of that sick bitch, but she begged and begged and begged until finally I couldn't take it anymore. I tell you what, you go back up there and tell her you took care of the situation. Then innocently run your hand along her leg, and see how she responds. Also, you might want to tell the bartender that she's underage. I'd hate to see the place shut down because of her. In the meantime, I'll take a walk on the beach. Good luck."

Nick stood up and walked away as Benny made his way back to the bar. He leaned against the bar and proudly said to Nicole, "He's gone. Problem solved."

"Oh goody. You're my hero."

"No big deal. Just doing the right thing. Can't stand freaks like that."

Benny ordered a couple more drinks. "Maybe in a few minutes we can leave this dive and go get a bite to eat. What do you say?" he asked.

"Maybe," Nicole replied, as Benny fell for the bait and ran his hand gently along her leg. In a blink of an eye, Nicole grabbed the bartender's slicing knife from behind the bar and put it up against his throat. "I recommend you remove your hand before I cut your balls off. You disgusting pig."

"Of course. I'm sorry!" Benny moved down the bar and away from her. He whispered to Lance, who walked over to Nicole. He picked the knife up off the bar and asked Nicole for proof of age. She reached into her purse and suddenly remembered that Nick had also taken her driver's license. She laughed. "That son of a bitch." She got up off the stool and looked across at Benny. "Thanks for the drinks, pig."

She walked down to the beach toward Nick. "Touché, Nicky. Touché, my love."

"Seriously, Nicole, sending that clown down here to intimidate me. What were you thinking?"

"I could have sent the bartender, but I didn't want to take any chance that you might get hurt."

Nick took her by the hand. They walked for a bit and then sat down on a bench farther down the beach. Nicole laid her head in Nick's lap. "Do you forgive me, Nicky, for being such a bad girl?"

"What choice do I have? It's not like I'm divorcing you, and for some inexplicable reason, I still love you."

"I'm madly in love with you." She looked up at Nick with her big blue eyes.

"My God, you have some strange ways of showing it." Nick suddenly grabbed Nicole's hand, which was halfway into his pant pocket.

"Wow, Nicky! You're the first guy who has ever removed my hand from down his pants."

"Yeah, that's because I'm the only guy who has ever had your money and credit cards in his pants."

"That's rude. I could've had other plans."

"Like what? Cutting it off?"

"The thought has occasionally passed through my mind."

"Of that, I have no doubt."

"Mean, mean Nicky. And on our honeymoon, too."

Nick ran his hand through her hair, twisting and turning, playfully and wistfully twirling, her soft curls around his fingers.

"Nicky, why don't we just pack up and move to Paris?"

"I've never even heard you talk about Paris, and now, suddenly, you want to move there?"

"I've always wanted to live in Paris. I've seen hundreds of pictures and it looks so beautiful, especially in the springtime. Do you speak French?"

"Nope."

"That's okay. You can learn and then teach me. It'll be fun."

"Sweetheart, we can't just pack up and move to Paris. Your father has just set you up with a lovely new office, and it would break Margaret's heart if you don't go work with them."

"They'll get over it."

"Of course they'll get over it, Nicole, but that's not the point. It wouldn't be right."

"You're right, Nicky, like always." Nicole grudgingly conceded the point. "I'm so tired. Can you carry me to the hotel?"

"Nicole, the hotel is four blocks away."

"I'm very light."

"I know you're very light, but four blocks is a long way."

"I thought you were supposed to carry the bride over the threshold on the honeymoon?"

"Yeah, but the threshold is usually two feet, not four blocks, for God's sake."

"Aren't I worth it?

"Of course you're worth it, but… "

Nick didn't finish his thought. He looked down at Nicole, and she was fast asleep in his lap.

His beautiful wife was the most damaged individual he had ever come across, and yet when Nicole's defenses were down, all that obnoxious bravado disappeared. Sometimes when she slept, like now, she seemed downright innocent and fragile. He knew better but also knew that there was still a ten-year-old girl deep down inside who had never been free. It was as though she was begging for help, whispering through an unfiltered curtain of steel.

Nick finally gave in and carried Nicole to their hotel room, where he laid his sleeping wife down on the bed. A few minutes later, he joined her and fell asleep quickly.

Chapter Thirty-Three

A few hours later, Nicole jolted Nick awake. "You need to do me a favor and call my father. Tell him there's no way you can come to work for him unless you work beside me. That you won't even allow me out of the house unless you're by my side the whole time."

"Seriously, *that* is what you want me to tell your father? He's going to think I'm the biggest loser in the world."

"Don't worry about that, Nicky. He already thinks that."

"Oh, stop it. Did he really say that?"

"Not really, but I know how the man thinks. When you turned down all that money and still came running back to me, how could he think anything else? You see, Nicky, unlike you my daddy lives in the real world, where money solves virtually any problem. He would have given you enough money so that your lovely parents would never have to worry about money again — not to mention you and me, at least for a while. Personally I'm still mad at you for that stupid and inconsiderate move, but with a little more time, I'll try to get over it."

"What's wrong with you people?"

"Nothing. Hopefully, one day, reality will set in for you, too. But in the meantime, can you please make that call? You don't want to disappoint your lovely wife on our honeymoon, do you?"

"I'm not making that call, Nicole, at least not now. Give it one day. That's all I ask … one day. If you can't handle it after one day, I'll make the call. I think that's a pretty fair compromise."

"I guess."

"What could go wrong? Margaret adores you, and your father will do anything to keep you safe."

The final two days of their unofficial honeymoon were spent by Nicole asking over and over again, "And what else do you think I should know that my daddy, Margaret, and you know?" By the time they arrived back in Los Angeles, Nicole had filled three notepads with information ranging from Einstein's theory of relativity to the last ten films to win the Oscar for Best Picture. Nick was mentally exhausted. Nicole's irrational obsession with facts and knowledge had literally beaten him into the ground. The fact that he and his lovely wife had not even once come close to having sex was of no consequence.

The following morning, Nicole spent an inordinate amount of time getting dressed, discarding one $1,000 outfit after another onto the bed. Finally, she decided on a black-and-red outfit, matching earrings, and a gold necklace that her mother had given her. She pinned her hair up and turned to Nick for an opinion.

"You're breathtaking."

"That's not the response I was looking for, but thank you anyway, Nicky. Do I look professional?"

"Yes, breathtakingly professional." Nicole closely inspected Nick's own choice of clothes. He was dressed in Armani, a sport coat, shirt, and trousers. He looked like a movie star.

"Surely, Nicky, you don't expect me to let you go off to work looking like that?"

"What? It doesn't match?"

"It matches perfectly, sweetheart, if you're going out shopping for another wife, or a little side action."

"Seriously, Nicole, these are the clothes you bought me. I'd think that you'd want me to look my best on my first day of work."

"Is that what you think, Nicky? That I want you to look your best on your first day? Well, sweetheart, you thought wrong. I want you to look your best when you go out with me, when I'm the only thing attached to your arm. It'll be a cold day in hell before I let you go out looking that good into an environment filled with a bunch of treasure-hunting bitches searching for a clueless and adorable husband just like you."

"You know what, Nicole? Why don't you just pick out my clothes? I don't have the stamina for this right now. I give up."

"Stop with the attitude. Just be happy you have a loving wife who doesn't want you looking too good for other women. I'm only here to help."

Nicole naturally picked out the least flattering ensemble she could put together. The drive to the studio was filled with more questions about everything and everyone that her father or Margaret might be interested in. Three days of drilling on their honeymoon hadn't been enough. She had to cover every base.

At the studio, Nicole insisted on escorting her husband to his office. Everything was to Nicole's liking until they got to Nick's office, which was a hole-in-the-wall decorated with a beautiful young lady from the development department named Maria. Nicole sighed heavily as she looked down at Maria. "And who the hell are you?"

Maria stood up and put out her hand. Nicole ignored the gesture. "I'm Maria from the development department. I was told to come over here and help train a new employee, Nicholas Caggiano?"

"Is that some type of joke, sweetheart? *You* training anyone?"

"Nicole, stop it! Hi, Maria. I'm Nick Caggiano." He shook Maria's hand for a split second before Nicole broke up the handshake.

"Very cute." Nicole looked angrily at Nick and then turned her attention back to Maria. "Look, Maria from the development department, I'm sure you're just doing your job, but your assistance is no longer needed here. Why don't you get your cute little ass back to the development department while you've still got a job?"

"I don't understand. I'm just following instructions."

"Listen, bitch, didn't you hear me? Do you know who I am? Get your ass the hell out of here and don't ever come back," Nicole screamed, as Arthur, the chief security officer, came between the two ladies.

"What seems to be the problem, ladies?" Arthur asked.

Maria spoke first. "Well, this half-breed misanthrope came charging in here, insulting and threatening me for absolutely no reason."

"What the hell did you call me?" Nicole screamed.

"She called you a misanthrope, honey," Nick explained. "It means a 'malcontent.' Great word. I guess we didn't go over that one." He sat in a chair behind the only desk in the room, atop which was a pile of unread screenplays.

"Shut up, you asshole!" Nicole then turned to Arthur. "Can you please call Margaret — "

"Attagirl. Get the boss immediately involved in your delusional, paranoid world," Nick said.

"I said, Shut up, you dick, before I ship you back to the Bronx."

"First class, I hope?"

"Cargo, and on ice, you ungrateful bastard."

"Wow! That's not very nice, not after everything we've been through."

Nicole picked up screenplay after screenplay and angrily threw them at her husband.

"I'm out of here," Maria said, as she picked up her belongings and quickly departed. Arthur finally got Nicole under control by reassuring her that Maria was gone. He called up Margaret, explained the bizarre situation, and was told to escort the blonde lady upstairs.

"What about this jackass?" Nicole pointed to Nick.

"Miss Margaret didn't say, so I guess he stays," Arthur replied, as he closed the door to Nick's makeshift office.

"Do you have a key?" Nicole asked.

"No. Until now this was always a storage room, where people came to get supplies."

Nicole reopened the door and said, "Keep your ass planted in that seat until I come back."

"And where exactly do you think I'd go … back to the Bronx? Where's my first-class ticket, dear?"

Nicole slammed the door shut and turned to Arthur. "If you were married to me, would you bother looking at other girls?"

Arthur pondered the question for a moment, and then sidestepped the answer with a question of his own. "Was *that* what this was over? Your husband was looking at that other girl?"

"No! Why would you even say that? He knows that if I ever caught him cheating on me, I'd kill the bitch and castrate his sorry ass. So tell me, does my hair look all right?"

"Yeah. You have a few loose strands, but otherwise it looks real nice."

"Can you do me a favor and put the loose strands back in place?"

Arthur looked at her nervously. "I'm not any good at that. You can ask my wife."

"What's wrong with you? I don't bite." Nicole looked into the mirror beside the elevator and fixed her own hair. "I'm in a shitload of trouble, aren't I?"

"Don't worry, Miss Nicole. Miss Margaret never gets mad. She sounded as pleasant and calm as ever when I just spoke to her."

"What is it with this 'Miss Margaret' stuff anyway?"

"Respect," Arthur said proudly. "She doesn't like me calling her that, but I can't help it."

"Well, if I don't get fired, you can just call me Nicole. No 'miss' or 'madam' or any of that nonsense. Just Nicole."

They got into the elevator and got off again at the very next floor. Margaret greeted them and immediately hugged Nicole tightly. Margaret whispered into her ear. "First day jitters?"

"I guess. Am I fired?" Nicole asked.

"No, sweetheart, you're not fired. I've waited way too long to reconnect with you. There's no way you're getting away from me that easily." Margaret pointed to a tray of donuts. "Arthur, please help yourself to some donuts. They're simply wonderful. And if you don't mind, can you please hang around a little while? I'm going to need you to escort Nicole around the lot."

"Of course, Miss Margaret."

Margaret took Nicole by the hand, opened the door to Nicole's new office, and watched the delight on the young lady's face as her eyes scanned the exquisitely decorated room. She sat Nicole down at the desk and pulled up a chair next to her. She opened a drawer and took out a piece of stationery with Nicole's name at the top. She handed Nicole a pen and said, "Your first piece of official business is to write an apology to the girl you accosted downstairs. Her name is Maria."

"I really messed up. Not even here an hour yet. I'm so sorry, Margaret."

"Really messing up would have been killing or severely hurting someone. Thankfully, your actions are easily remedied. It's very important, Nicole, that you understand that everyone in this company is important to us and will be treated respectfully. Now start writing, and be sincere." Margaret got up and walked out of Nicole's office.

Nicole wrote an apology to Maria and handed it to Margaret, who had walked back in. Margaret read the short note and remarked, "Very nice." She handed the letter and a $1,000 Neiman Marcus gift certificate made out to Maria back to Nicole.

"I'll give you the money," Nicole promised.

"Don't be foolish. Arthur will show you to Maria's office. I expect you to apologize in person before handing her the note and gift certificate."

"Okay," Nicole said meekly. She walked to the door and suddenly stopped. "At times, it seems like I've lost so much, Margaret — first my mother, and then Isabelle. I can't bear the idea of losing Nicky, too."

Nicole started to cry as Margaret took her into her arms. "I know, princess. I know and we are going to make sure that never happens," Margaret said, as she wiped the tears away from Nicole's face.

Arthur turned to Nicole as they got into the elevator. "You really are Richard's daughter, aren't you? I thought I recognized you, but in the picture on your father's desk, you have your hair done differently. I never asked who the girl in the picture was. I just figured it was some beautiful movie star."

"My father has a picture of me on his desk?"

"Of course he does. Why wouldn't he? If I had a daughter as beautiful as you, I'd have your picture plastered all over the place."

"I figured the less my father is reminded of me, the better he'd feel."

"That's insane. Your father and Miss Margaret are the two most wonderful people I've ever known."

"You know them quite well, don't you?"

"Yes, they're like family to me. I was in the same platoon as Miss Margaret's son. Henry died in my arms in the jungles of Vietnam. He was such a brave young man and really special, like his mom. I took a bracelet off his body, given to him by his mom, with the names of all the horses that had won the Kentucky Derby. I promised him that if I got out of there alive, I'd deliver it to her, and when I was finally discharged, I looked her up. I had no idea who she was, and when I realized how important a person she was, I never expected her to return my call. Well, less than an hour after I made that call, she called me back, and before I knew it, she had me flown first-class from South Carolina to Los Angeles.

That call changed my life, but until this day, I wish I never had to make that choice. She was just like her son had described her, surreal, like an angel from Heaven. When I handed her the bracelet, she fell to the floor and started crying uncontrollably for at least an hour. Never in my life have I ever felt so sorry for a person. It's then that I met your father. He came rushing out of his office and before even looking down at Miss Margaret, he saluted me. I still had on my uniform, and it was the first acknowledgement by another person that someone respected and honored my service."

"That is amazing." Nicole was genuine.

"If I'm certain of anything, it's that only God could create such a perfect person as Miss Margaret. She is not only the most beautiful person on the outside, but inside, where it really counts, she is the most pure and compassionate individual. By the time you clock out tonight, it will all be forgotten."

Chapter Thirty-Four

While Nicole was delivering her apology to Maria, Richard knocked on Margaret's door and walked into her office.

"So did the princess forget to show up for her first day of work?"

"That's not funny, Richard. She is currently running an errand with Arthur for me."

"Okay, there's something a little amiss about that, but for the moment, I'll buy it."

Margaret got up from behind her desk and approached Richard with a contemplative expression. "I think we're going to need to make a few minor adjustments to your plan. I grossly underestimated how anchored Nicole is, both emotionally and intellectually, to her husband."

"Seriously, Margaret, she cheated on her poor husband a couple of months after they married."

"Yes, Richard, I'm aware of that. She needs discipline, not punishment. We missed the boat on her childhood, but she's still a very young adult. If we keep an eye on her and teach by example, she may have a fighting chance. I'm having her husband transferred up here, immediately."

"Millions of married couples work different jobs, many not even in the same town, and yet my privileged daughter can't bear to be away from her husband, who'd be working directly below her?"

"Is there some part of your plan, Richard, that you didn't tell me about?"

"Of course not."

"Then we're still on the same page. The main reason to have her working with us is to secure her safety and happiness, right? Well, if that means having her husband by her side, I don't think we need to discuss this matter any further."

"You know, Margaret, Nicole is quite adept at hurting people. She isn't your responsibility, but if you insist and it turns out that she hurts you in any way, my daughter's happiness will be seriously compromised."

"Richard, your concern for me is touching as always, but we've been given a second opportunity to right a few wrongs, and the possibility that I might get hurt is of little consequence to me. Why don't you go into your office, relax, and read the box score from last night's game?"

"I was at the game," Richard informed her.

"Really, and no invite?"

"If I remember correctly, the last thing you told me on Friday was that you were going to be very busy all weekend preparing lessons for the child."

"I was, but I finished early. You could have called after all. It's not like you haven't done it a million times before."

"Seriously, Margaret?"

"Seriously, Richard."

"Well, it's not like you missed anything. Scioscia struck out with the tying men on base to end the game."

"Maybe they could use me as a pinch hitter," Margaret said

"At least you could draw a walk."

"I think I could do a little better than just draw a walk."

"I'm sure you could, but any pitcher with 20/20 vision would be so bedazzled by your beauty that they wouldn't come close to the strike zone. Sorry, a walk is the best you could ever do, which is a lot better than Piazza is doing."

"That's very sweet, Richard," Margaret said. They both looked toward the lobby and the elevator, which suddenly opened. As Nicole and Arthur walked out, Nicole suddenly hugged him, tightly and affectionately.

"Seems like Arthur has made a big impression on my daughter."

"Of course, Arthur has made a big impression!" Margaret said. "He's wonderful with everybody. Stay here a minute, Richard." She walked out of the office and toward Nicole and Arthur. Richard leaned against her desk and shook his head, thinking, I can only imagine what that errand involved.

Margaret greeted Nicole and Arthur. "Did everything go well?"

"Everything went great, Miss Margaret."

Margaret winked at him. "Thank you very much, Arthur."

Arthur got back into the elevator, and Margaret took Nicole gently by the shoulders. "Your hair is so beautiful, sweetheart, why hide it by putting it up?"

"I thought it would look more professional."

"Nonsense! When I look at you, I want to get the full picture." And then, in a lower voice, she said, "Listen, kiddo, I didn't mention anything to your father about the earlier misunderstanding … so why don't we keep it between us girls and Arthur?"

"Thank you."

The elevator door opened again and Nick stepped out. Nicole looked at him awkwardly, and then turned and looked suspiciously at Margaret, who said, "Go ahead, you can kiss him. You're married now. Besides, from now on, he'll be working side by side with you in your office."

"And my father?"

"He's okay with it. Smile and be happy, child. You're going to be working beside the most handsome young man in the building."

"Oh, thank you so much!" Nicole hugged Margaret tight, then turned and jumped into Nick's waiting arms.

"I love you more than anything in this world, Nicole," he said with a flood of emotion, and she started to kiss him passionately.

Margaret walked back into her office and saw a confused Richard. "What the hell are they doing?" he asked.

Margaret looked back at Nick and Nicole. "I think they call it kissing, Richard."

"Here at work?"

"My God, Richard! When did you get so old?"

"I don't know, Yogi. Why don't you tell me?"

"Yogi! What's with that?"

"Well, now that you're going to be moonlighting as a pinch hitter for the Dodgers, you're going to need a nickname. And what better nickname than Yogi, after the great Yankee catcher Yogi Berra? The most famous bad-ball hitter in all of baseball. Preferred to swing rather than simply accept a walk."

"Very funny, Richard. It's good to see you haven't lost your sense of humor."

Margaret sat at her desk and handed Richard a piece of paper. "The weekend box office."

"Did we make money?" Richard asked, without looking down at the paper.

"Yes, I'd say we did quite well."

"Good!"

"Speaking of which, Richard, you have a meeting with our favorite French distributor, Monsieur Bernard, in exactly one hour."

"Seriously, Margaret?"

"Seriously. I don't need to remind you how greatly the foreign market has increased our overall earnings."

"No, Margaret, you don't need to remind me. But thanks anyway."

Richard walked out of Margaret's office as Nicole, holding Nick's hand, walked toward her new office.

"Nicole, can I speak with you for a moment?" Richard asked.

"In a little while, Daddy. I want to show Nicky around first." Nicole and Nick entered their office and closed the door behind them. Richard shook his head in disbelief.

Chapter Thirty-Five

Monsieur Bernard was a somewhat frequent visitor to Margaret and Richard's offices. The history between the two men went way back. Monsieur Bernard had been part of the French resistance that, along with Richard's division, helped liberate Paris. It wasn't until years later, at a film exhibition in Cannes, that they finally realized they had met during that wondrous liberation. Their friendship grew after that, and the business dealings between the men proved unusually profitable for both parties. The French people loved American films, and Richard got great pleasure introducing great French filmmakers, like Georges Méliès and François Truffaut, to the American public.

Just as Monsieur Bernard was getting up to leave and visit Margaret, Nicole busted in, unannounced. Embarrassed, she tried to leave, but her father called her back and said to Monsieur Bernard, "I would like you to meet my daughter, Nicole."

Monsieur Bernard bowed respectfully, kissed Nicole's hand, and said, "Vous êtes plus belle que tous les anges au paradis." He turned to Richard, warmly embraced him, and quickly walked over to Margaret's office.

"What did he say?" Nicole asked.

"He said 'You are more beautiful than all the angels in Heaven,' and I second that."

"You know, Daddy, you don't have to introduce everyone to me as your daughter."

"Yes, I do. You are my proudest and most precious creation. Besides, if I didn't introduce you to Monsieur Bernard as my daughter, he might have started flirting with you, and after he left the building, your office would be filled with flowers and an invitation to visit his château in France. I don't think Nick would be too happy with that."

"That's disgusting. That man is older than you! What a pig!"

"He's French, sweetheart. It's in their blood. He's been madly in love with Margaret since the moment he met her years ago."

"Like the rest of mankind. She's amazing."

"So what is it that you want?"

"You said you wanted to speak to me."

"That was hours ago, sweetheart. I forgot what I wanted to tell you."

"Well, it doesn't matter. I have a few things I need to discuss with you, if you have the time."

"Of course I have time."

"Now that Nick's going to be working with me, is he still going to get paid?"

"Of course, five hundred dollars a week."

"Personally, I think he deserves a raise. His work with me is much more important than what he originally signed up for."

"No! In less than half a day, your husband went from working in a makeshift room without a window to the executive suites. He's going to be sharing a gorgeous office with the most beautiful girl on the planet. I think that's a pretty big raise in such a short time. And I also think this is coming from you, and not from Nick."

"You know, Daddy, you are one hundred percent right. I should get the raise."

"You're not even getting paid. Besides, you are the only intern in the company with her own office and her own assistant."

"But I'm your daughter."

"Yes, I'm quite aware of that. Eventually, when Margaret and I agree that you've satisfied all the requirements as an intern, you'll start getting a salary."

"And when will that be?"

"That's up to you, angel."

"Okay, but you're going to be shocked at how well I do."

"No, I won't be shocked. I know you're going to do great, but more importantly, I want you to take your time and not feel pressured. I'm sure Margaret has plenty of shopping sprees already planned, and you know how freely she spends."

"Yes, I do. The woman is absolutely perfect. You know, Daddy, I don't want you to worry about Nick. I've already warned him that in our family, we do not tolerate communists. His dislike of money is frightening. It's the only imperfection he has. I can't even tell his parents about it, because it would break their heart."

"But sweetheart, I don't think Nick's a communist. I believe he simply loves you for who you are."

"Of course he loves me for who I am. Why wouldn't he? But that still doesn't explain his crazy notions about money. Remember the 1950s, Daddy, and all the communists running around this town? I bet you didn't have many of them ever admit to being communists."

"No, you're right. They didn't."

"If Nicky wants to move to Russia and practice the teaching of those two idiots Marx and Lenin, let him. But you mark my word, he wouldn't last a day in that terrible country before running back to me."

"I really don't think you need to worry about that, sweetheart. That boy is madly in love with you. If he were planning to go anywhere, he would've gone by now."

"I know. It's so great, Daddy. I can't believe his parents let him out of their sight, much less let him move out here. He's so smart, and yet he can't put on his own clothes without my help. And his sense of direction is so bad that I've forbidden him from driving. He couldn't get from here to Beverly Hills without getting lost twenty times."

"Well, in his defence, New Yorkers aren't known for their driving ability."

"No, they're not, and he's living proof of that. So tell me, Daddy, what do you think about 'Star Wars'?"

"A wonderful movie, sweetheart. It would have been great if Mr. Lucas would've come to us first."

"I'm not talking about the movie, Daddy."

"What are we talking about?"

"About President Reagan's missile defence initiative."

"Oh! Well, I think it has a long way to go before being operational, but I like the idea, and in twenty or thirty years, I think it could work and be a very effective deterrent."

"I agree it's a wonderful idea. We have far too many nuclear weapons aimed at us to just sit around and do nothing. We need a shield. The sooner, the better." Nicole looked at the copy of *Portrait of an Artist as a Young Man* sitting on the shelf behind her father's desk. "So did you read that book I sent you?"

"Yes, sweetheart. It's the best gift I've ever received."

"Well, I don't know about that, but thank you. Do you think I should read it?"

"Yes, I think everyone should read it. Would you like to borrow it?"

"No, Daddy, that's your gift. Besides, I'm sure Nicky probably has five copies at home."

"Margaret is going to be training you and Nick. Is that okay?"

"Of course it's okay. You don't have the patience that Margaret possesses. I feel so bad that I shut her out of my life for so long."

"Well, now both of you have a chance to reconnect."

"Yes, we do. I guess I better get back to Nicky."

She got up from her chair and started to walk toward the door when Richard jumped up from behind his desk. "I remember what I wanted to tell you."

Nicole turned around as Richard walked up to her and said, "I wanted to tell you how proud I am that you've decided to come to work with Margaret and me. Seeing your lovely face each day is a tremendous joy to me. I love you so much, Nicole."

Nicole stood before her father, uncharacteristically speechless, and finally managed to blurt out a simple "Thank you."

"Hey, how about a hug? You seem to be giving them out kind of freely today."

"Of course," Nicole said, and hugged her father.

Richard held her tightly, then leaned down and kissed her head. "I will never forgive myself for not being there when you needed me the most."

Nicole remained silent as she kept her head tucked against her father's chest. Richard continued, "Hey, how about one more thing?"

Nicole broke loose and suddenly said, "Yes, I love you, Daddy." She kissed him on the cheek and then quickly turned around and walked out of the office. Richard remained motionless as the weight of paternal failure and guilt was momentarily lifted from his consciousness. A smile crossed his face as Margaret entered the office.

"Wow! Was that a hug I just witnessed between you and your lovely daughter?"

"You know, Yogi, it must be great to always be right."

"I wouldn't know. I'm not always right."

"I can't think of a time when you weren't."

"That's because, like Nicole's husband, you choose to overlook my mistakes and concentrate on the more important and positive aspects of our relationship."

"Is that it?"

"Of course that's it, Richard. And by the way, I looked up Yogi Berra's stats."

"Of course you did."

"Three MVPs and ten World Series rings. Quite impressive!"

"Not nearly as impressive as you, Margaret."

Nicole took a few minutes in the ladies' bathroom to get her composure back after her encounter with her father. Usually she would dismiss her father's comments as simple lies, but this time, they rang true with such a heartfelt sincerity that she genuinely believed what he said.

She walked back into her office and looked at Nick, reading a huge book on the company's history. "Wow! Don't you look like a big shot behind that desk? What are you reading?" she asked as she sat in a chair next to Nick.

"A book on the history of the company. Listen to this for a minute. 'Interviewer: So tell me, Mr. Weiss, what do you attribute your enormous success in the film and entertainment industry to?

'Mr. Weiss: I was lucky enough to hire the most beautiful southern belle in all the United States, who just happens to have the brains of Einstein, the creativity of da Vinci, and the patience, caring, and nobility of a monk. I made her a full partner many years ago, and since then we have been more successful than I could have ever imagined. That's the secret of my success.

'Interviewer: Of course, we are talking about your partner, Margaret...

'Mr. Weiss: Yes, that is exactly who we are talking about.

'Interviewer: It has been rumored around town that it is all right to criticize you, your movies, or even your friends, but if someone so much as breathes a negative word about Margaret, you will make sure that person never works in this town again.

'Mr. Weiss: First, no one in this town wields that type of power and no one should ever be allowed to. Secondly, after working nearly twenty years with Margaret, I have never seen an occasion in which criticism of her was warranted. The woman is perfect. If a deity does exist, I am quite sure he had a major hand in creating her.

'Interviewer: The two of you have suffered some major losses in your personal lives. How has that affected the two of you working together?

'Mr. Weiss: I lost my wife, Elaine, after thirteen years of marriage. For the first ten years of our marriage, I was a nonexistent, insensitive, and uncaring husband. That is a nightmare and a crime I have to deal with every day. There is no reason to mistreat anyone. The final three years of our life together were wonderful. I can honestly say that my wife, my beautiful daughter, and I were a family, at least for a spell.

'Interviewer: Do you believe that your wife forgave you before she died?

'Mr. Weiss: She was a truly remarkable and talented woman, and also very forgiving. The problem was that I could never forgive myself. For the first ten years of my marriage, I was no different than the monsters I had fought against during the war … and there is no excuse for that.

'Interviewer: Your wartime experiences and commendations for bravery are quite impressive.

'Mr. Weiss: You can stop right there. Half a million Americans sacrificed their lives for what far too many Americans take for granted these days. Millions of young men were severely wounded and their lives severely compromised. I came home alive and in one piece. I didn't do anything different or greater than all those other men and women who served.

'Interviewer: Margaret has also lost her spouse, and her only child, a son, was killed during the Vietnam War.

'Mr. Weiss: Her husband was a wonderful man with a big heart. They were, in my opinion, the perfect couple. He died suddenly and unexpectedly, which made it even more difficult to deal with. Her son, Henry, was a real war hero. He put aside a promising career in the industry, joined the army, and made the ultimate sacrifice, saving a number of his fellow soldiers by using his body as a shield against the approaching enemy. There is nothing worse in this world than a parent losing a child. The very idea, for me, is a nightmare.

'Interviewer: You have one child, a daughter, Nicole. We do not hear or know much about her. What can you tell us about this mysterious young lady?

'Mr. Weiss: In a sense, she is all I have left. She's beautiful, like her mother was. She has tremendous promise, and I am quite certain that she can do anything she puts her mind to.'"

"When did he give that interview?" Nicole asked.

"Three years ago." Nick turned to Nicole. "You are so much more than just a beautiful face. That's what I know, your dad knows, and Margaret knows."

Chapter Thirty-Six

The rest of the day went very smoothly for Nick and Nicole. Margaret ordered pizza for lunch, knowing that it was Nicole's other favorite dish besides buttered noodles. Nicole invited Arthur for lunch, and the conversation was dominated by talk of how poorly the Dodgers were playing. Nicole had no interest in baseball but pretended she did and even made a few comments, directed at her father, about what the Dodgers might do to improve.

Nick was an excellent teacher. He and her father had so many things in common that it was fairly easy for her to fake her interest and knowledge in sports, politics, books, and movies. All she had to do was keep her wonderful husband from rambling on about all this nonsense and simply stick to the facts.

The idea of going to work each day and having to see her father would previously have sent chills down her spine, but Margaret was the cure for all that. Margaret was the virtual blanket that kept Nicole warm and comfortable. She was like a narcotic. How Richard had been able to keep his hands off of Margaret all these years was probably his greatest achievement. If you saw her only once in your life and lived another hundred years, you would never forget her.

Margaret's perfection was undeniable, but inside that beautiful head was still a grieving mother. Only Richard knew about this pain. After her husband's death, Richard had become the only individual Margaret confided in. The woman who could appease the suffering and pain of a dying person by simply touching their hand could not allay the pain and torture she carried inside her over the death of her only son.

Margaret, from the start, had no other intention but to love, comfort, and protect Nicole. If Nicole decided she liked the movie business, that would be a bonus. Margaret would teach her everything she knew at whatever pace Nicole was comfortable with. If Richard felt like he was getting a second chance to be a real father to Nicole, Margaret felt like she was getting a second chance at the best job she had ever had, being a mother. Her son had been taken from her far too soon, and Margaret was determined that Nicole would be around long after she and Richard were gone.

Nick and Nicole went right home after work, and she wasted no time getting out of her work clothes and into the bed. She clutched at the blankets as Nick walked past her, reading the book about the company.

"Nick, please put down that stupid book and come hold me."

He looked at her in amazement. "Did you just say 'Come hold me'?"

"Don't act so surprised, you jackass. Just get over here."

Nick cuddled up next to his wife. "Holy shit, you're naked."

"Keep it up, jackass, and this just might be the last time you ever see this body again."

Nick held her tightly. "What's wrong, sweetheart?"

"Just thinking about things, that's all."

"You feel like sharing?"

"Would you love me more if I was like Margaret?"

Nick turned her toward him and looked her straight in the face. "Listen to me. I know you think you railroaded me into this marriage using a few unconventional tricks — including my unsuspecting parents — but let me assure you, I've been a willing participant on every leg of this journey. I can't get you out of my mind anytime I'm away from you. Your beauty speaks for itself, but it's all the other things that set you aside from any other girl. I find you infuriating but irresistible. Your combatant nature, your fierce jealousy, your quick temper … that all makes you Nicole. Margaret is very pretty and really great, but I'd never exchange any part of you for her."

Nicole affectionately touched Nick's face. "Those girls in the Bronx must be some kind of stupid to have let you get away, but their loss is my gain, and they'll never get a second chance. You know Nicky, after my flare-up with the lovely Maria, I was tempted to run away, get in touch with my dealer, and buy as much cocaine as I could get my hands on. The idea of having to deal with my father was just too much."

"What stopped you?"

"Arthur's reassuring voice, and when I got off the elevator, Margaret was right there to greet me. It didn't hurt that Daddy hadn't shown up for work yet, so Margaret being Margaret, she kept it between us girls and didn't tell him."

"And for the rest of the day, you were the most charming creature on the planet."

"Yes, I was. Thanks, Nicky. I guess with Margaret residing on the same planet, and now in the office across the hall … Each day with her will help me try to be my very best self. That woman is in a class all her own. The idea of even remotely hurting her is enough to keep me on the straight and narrow."

Nicole casually reached down Nick's pants as they were talking. "Little Nicky seems to be growing at an alarming rate. I think you should take off your pants and give him a little air to breathe."

"Are you sure?"

"I wouldn't be lying here naked if I didn't think I was up for the challenge."

Chapter Thirty-Seven

Nick and Nicole exceeded all expectations at work. Once the idea took firm hold in Nicole's mind that they were the likely heirs to her father's and Margaret's empire, the nightmare of going to work each day quickly changed to excitement, anticipation, creative energy, and hunger for success. Her father was true to his word and remained a silent observer as Margaret taught the young couple the day-to-day operations of the company. Nick, like always, did all the reading and neatly and concisely summarized everything for Nicole, who read and reread each summary like she had never done before.

The unforeseen problem for Nicole was the constant reminder of her uncle Bobby, who was a constant topic of conversation in all the trade magazines. She had managed, ever so faintly, to repress her memories of the man. She had lived off the Hollywood radar as much as possible, but now being in the business meant keeping up with everything happening in Hollywood circles, along with the realization that her father was never going to fulfill his promise to kill the son of a bitch.

The picture of the man in the trades and Nick's summarized recaps of all the articles had reignited the flame, the unbridled hatred, and Nicole's burning desire for revenge. She could never tell Nick because, unlike her father, he would kill the bastard. And in the end, she would — once again — become the victim when they sent his ass off to prison. All the money in the world would not be able to keep him out of jail without spilling all the family secrets. Already she could not imagine spending a day without him, much less months or years. She had to be very careful.

Slowly, she would plan her own revenge. She had all the dirt she needed, provided unknowingly by Nick and his friend.

Nicole was giving the proposed budget for the next movie the company was planning on doing. The movie was big, originally a best-selling novel about a major bank heist in New York City. The caper goes unsolved for years until one of the major players is booked on possession and distribution of cocaine, and faces twenty-five to life in jail. Scared for his life and family, he makes a deal with the FBI and snitches on all the other perpetrators in exchange for entry into the witness protection program. The director was the best in the business, hailed by critics and audiences alike as the greatest of his generation. The cinematographer, cameraman, editor, writer — and all the actors — attached to the project were considered the very best, and all worked on previous projects with the same famous director.

The last remaining unfilled piece of the project was a small but pivotal role that could easily reignite a stumbling career or be the launching pad for a new and upcoming actor. The director wanted an Irish-born actor named Colin Becket, age thirty-one, whose early career in Hollywood took off with a number of well-received performances but whose later roles and movies were critical and box-office disasters. Becket had a reputation as an actor who was hard to work with and was rumored to have a major substance-abuse problem. Margaret and Richard were willing to take the chance on Becket, especially since the director had a reputation for getting along wonderfully with all his actors despite their temperaments. The unknown in the whole equation was that where Becket was the director's first choice, he was by no means his only choice. The director had already presented to Margaret and Richard a number of other candidates he would also be happy working with and who, like Mr. Becket, had also auditioned for the part.

Michael Nichen, Becket's agent, was scheduled to meet with Richard early that morning. The two men had a long and successful relationship, and even though Nichen's client was asking for an exorbitant amount — $1.5 million for a one-week shoot — both men knew that this role could relaunch Becket's foundering career. Richard was willing to offer no more than $500,000 and was expecting the negotiations to go smoothly. He also believed this to be a perfect opportunity for Nicole and Nick to sit in on a negotiation and observe the process, something they hadn't done yet. Nicole had done her homework on Mr. Becket and was quite aware of his reputation.

Richard, Nick, and Nicole gathered in Richard's office. Nicole came prepared with notes, the proposed budget, and a sense of professionalism that was truly astonishing to her father. It was as if she had been transformed into another being. He couldn't help thinking that Margaret was truly a miracle worker. He encouraged both Nick and Nicole to participate and to ask as many relevant questions during the negotiations as they felt comfortable with.

Nicole responded by saying, "Don't worry, Daddy. I am fully prepared."

Richard felt a pang of anxiety at Nicole's unwavering response, and as he saw Nichen and Becket walk toward his office from the elevator, his sense of anxiety rose even higher. Becket was not supposed to be present; it went against the protocol Richard had established with Nichen and all other talent agents. Richard greeted both men coldly and responded to Nichen's regretful whisper with an abrupt "That's not good enough." After quickly regaining his sense of composure, Richard introduced his daughter and son-in-law to both men, and they all sat down at his desk.

Becket, after barely acknowledging Nick and Nicole, remarked, "I wasn't expecting an audience."

"And I wasn't expecting you," Richard replied.

"Well, I don't know why not. Surely, I have a right to participate in my own future and livelihood."

"That was a discussion you and your agent should have had before you rudely invited yourself to a meeting you weren't invited to."

"Pardon me, Mr. Weiss, if I choose to take a more active role in my career."

"The way I see it," Nicole interjected, "your agent has been doing a wonderful job of keeping you employed and highly overpaid. Your last three movies combined haven't grossed the one-point-five million you're asking for a one-week shoot with one of the greatest directors of our time."

"Well, well, the beauty queen speaks." Becket looked disparagingly at Nicole, adding, "And she's much more than just a pretty face. She's an accountant to boot."

"Hey jackass, it's one thing to walk in here uninvited, but to walk into my father's office drunk and stoned on coke is highly insulting."

"So sorry, sweetheart. I didn't mean to insult anyone's sensibilities or codes of conduct."

Michael Nichen grabbed Becket's hand and said, "Colin, please."

Richard leaned forward in his chair and placed both his hands under his chin. He said to Michael, "Apparently, your client isn't very well informed. Although he is the director's first choice, he is in no way his only choice. Another belittling word out of his mouth and the only acting jobs your client will ever get again will be at the community theaters back in Dublin."

Richard handed Michael a piece of paper. "That figure is nonnegotiable, unless, of course, your client would like to do the honorable thing and take what he's really worth, which is significantly less."

Michael showed Colin the figure and gestured for him to accept the offer.

"Seriously, Michael, that's one-third what I usually make!"

"It's the role of a lifetime, working with the greatest director on the planet and a cast that's to die for."

Colin looked pensively at Nicole, who said, "In case you didn't hear my father, he said it's nonnegotiable. A simple yes or no will suffice."

"Is it really just that easy, sweetie?"

Nicole grimaced. "Look at it this way. It may be less than you usually make, but it's certainly enough to keep you significantly high and wasted for the next six months."

Colin laughed and replied, "This bitch is a real piece of work. I'd love to see what's hanging between your legs."

Nick suddenly broke his silence and grabbed Colin by the throat, pushing him back in his chair. He kept his hand around Colin's throat as the actor literally gasped for air. "Now is that any way for a gentleman to talk to a lady? I think an apology is in order, don't you?"

Colin tried to speak but was stifled as Nick's grip around his throat tightened. Richard, alarmed, got up and literally tackled his son-in-law to the floor. Colin ran out of the office toward the elevator as Richard got up off the floor, picked up the paper with the salary written on it, tore it to shreds, and threw the pieces at Michael, who he ordered out of his office. He stood pensively by the door and then quickly turned and looked at Nicole, who was busy sexually molesting her husband on the couch, literally tearing off both of their clothes while kissing him passionately.

"Nicole! What the hell are you doing?!"

She suddenly stopped and looked uneasily at her father. "I'm just kissing my husband, Daddy. You saw the way he protected me. For God's sake, if anyone should understand that, I would think it would be you."

"It's one thing to be kissing your husband. It's a whole other thing to be ripping off your clothes."

"Sorry! I got carried away. I'm a little emotional."

"Okay, Nicole, that's fine. Please, just put your clothes back on and try to control yourself."

They put their clothes back on as Nicole said to Nick, "Don't worry, sweetheart. When we go back home I'll show you the time of your life."

"Nicole, I'm standing right here. I don't need to hear this!" Richard was angry.

"Wow. What a party pooper! I actually thought you would be proud of the way I handled myself during that negotiation."

"I am proud of you, Nicole, very proud, but that still doesn't give you the right to have sex in my office!" Richard looked directly at a dumbfounded Nick. "Don't you have any control over your wife?"

"No, none at all! Do you?"

"Oh my God! Oh my God! Talking back to Daddy. I love this newfound aggressiveness in my Nicky. Unless their name is Margaret or Nicole, I don't think anybody in their right mind has the balls to talk back to my Daddy — at least not in this town."

"I didn't mean anything by it. Sorry if it came out wrong, sir." Nick had great respect for Richard. He didn't want to damage or jeopardize the decent relationship he thought they had started.

"Shut up, Nick. Why must you ruin every special moment with some sort of apology? I thought boys from the Bronx were tough, the type to stand rock solid behind whatever they say. Never once have I heard Bugs apologize."

Nick and Richard both rolled their eyes at Nicole's last remark.

"Your husband, just a few moments ago, nearly choked that asshole to death for insulting you. Give him a break."

"You totally miss the point, Daddy. Never once have I said that my husband wasn't the bravest, most courageous, sexiest man on the planet. He's all that a million times over, but he has this terrible habit of apologizing, even when he's right. I'm surprised he didn't run after that little leprechaun and apologize for beating the shit out of him."

"That will never happen," Nick said.

"I hope not." Nicole softly touched Nick's face and then suddenly jumped on top of him and started once again to kiss him passionately.

Richard quickly separated them and spoke angrily to his daughter. "We are not shooting a porno movie here, Nicole. I swear, you keep it up and I'll put you over my lap and whip your ass."

"As if my husband would allow such a thing," she snapped back.

"I'll have Arthur and his crew escort Nick out of the building. Believe me, they are more than up to that job."

Nicole sighed as her father looked at her, irritated. At just about the same time, Margaret entered the lobby of the building and was immediately met by an imploring Michael Nichen. He begged her to intervene and get him back upstairs to talk to Mr. Weiss. Margaret called Richard, who agreed to see the agent as long as his client was no longer with him. Margaret and Nichen got into the elevator as, upstairs, Richard ordered his daughter to sit in his chair behind the desk.

"It's time to close the deal, sweetheart."

Nichen and Margaret walked into Richard's office. Nichen apologized profusely and asked Richard, "Is there still a deal to be made?"

"I don't know. Why don't you ask my daughter?"

Nichen looked suspiciously at Nicole, behind the desk.

"Ms. Weiss, is there any chance these negotiations might still be open?"

"Absolutely not, Mr. Nichen! There will be no further negotiating, but that doesn't mean a deal can't be struck. You've known my father for a long time, and before today, I imagine your relationship has been both courteous and mutually beneficial. In this company, we don't just throw people and clients to the curb, especially after many years of cooperation."

"That is very true, Ms. Weiss. Your father and Margaret run the finest and — undeniably — the most-respected movie studio in the world."

"Despite the fact that your client, Mr. Becket, is a piece of shit in desperate need of rehab, I'm going to make you a nonnegotiable offer of fifty thousand dollars. And the only reason I'm offering that much is simply because I don't need the headache of having to deal with the Screen Actors Guild. The role will resuscitate his quickly dying career, an opportunity he doesn't deserve. You have one hour, Mr. Nichen, and believe me, that's all you have. If you care at all about his career, I wouldn't waste this opportunity. My guess is that your client is at the Smoke House Restaurant across from the studio, downing shots of Irish whiskey and making frequent trips to the restroom. Good luck."

Chapter Thirty-Eight

It took Michael Nichen less than twenty minutes to get back to Nicole and agree to the offer. Like Nicole said, he found Colin Becket at the restaurant, walking out of the bathroom and wiping his nose. After another shot of Irish whiskey, he agreed to the offer and remarked, "Fifty thousand for a week's work. Not bad. It was worth the try."

Nicole sat triumphantly on the couch in her office and watched as Nick finished the last remaining paperwork on the Becket deal.

"You know, Nicky, I saved the company $450,000 today. Do you think I should ask my father for some type of bonus, or at least some cut of the money I saved him? I mean, that's a lot of money, even for a company as large as this one."

"Honestly, sweetheart, I wouldn't rock the boat. You were nothing short of sensational in there today, but your daddy wasn't at all happy with your celebratory advances toward me."

"The gall of that man. For the first ten years of his marriage to my mother, the man literally couldn't keep his pants on, he was so busy screwing every dimwit in this town. Now he has the balls to reprimand me for kissing my husband? He is a real born-again hypocrite."

"Be that as it may, I still wouldn't rock the boat."

"Well, maybe not me, but I want you to go in there and demand a raise. Five hundred dollars a week for all that you do is just downright insulting."

Nick looked up from his paperwork and said, "I don't want a raise, Nicole. I'm happy with what I'm making and all that I'm learning."

"Well, I'm not. How do you plan on supporting a family on five hundred dollars a week?"

"It's only you and me."

"Well, it won't be that way in about seven and a half months. You may not have much lasting power, but you had no problem hitting the bull's-eye. Your swimmers are so good that I have two critters growing inside me."

"Are you serious, Nicole? You're pregnant with twins?"

"My God, Nick, you're so much more than just a pretty face. Yes, twins. I've already told your parents."

"You told my parents before telling me?"

"Yes. I figured that was the only way to protect myself from my desire to have an abortion."

Nick sat down beside her on the couch and said, "I'm really proud of you."

"For what? Being stupid enough to get banged up or for being dumb enough not to have an abortion?"

"For being courageous enough to go through with the pregnancy."

"What is it with you Italians and having babies? From the moment we got married, never once did I talk to your mother when she didn't mention grandchildren and how great it would be to have the little rascals running around the house."

"Your father might not have mentioned it, but I bet he'll be just as happy as my parents with this news. You might not have to ask for a bonus. I imagine he and Margaret will be showering you with anything you want."

"I didn't give much thought to that. Wow! His jaw is going to drop when I tell him. In my little tummy, I hold the future of this giant company."

"I thought you were the future?"

"Yes, that's what they keep telling me, but with my track record, you can't seriously believe it?"

"I do believe it. You were amazing today, a natural. You should've seen Margaret's face when you were talking to Mr. Nichen. She was as proud as any mother could be."

Nicole looked thoughtfully at Nick for a long time and then reached over to take his hand. "Yes, she is divine." She placed his hand over her belly. "I can feel a little bump."

"Oh, they're in there, and this was no divine intervention. They're our little creations."

Richard and Margaret were shocked and beyond joyful when Nicole and Nick told them the news. Suddenly, the stench of Colin Becket was totally washed away. Richard was so overcome with joy that he went instinctively over to the wet bar in his office and pulled out a bottle of Cristal champagne. Margaret quickly stopped him from opening the bottle with a glance that simply meant "no way."

"It's okay, Margaret. It really doesn't bother me," Nicole said.

"That's sweet of you, Nicole, but the sheer joy you've just brought into all our lives with this wonderful news is enough to have us all walking on a cloud. No amount of alcohol is going to make it any better than it is right now," Margaret assured her. "Besides, we have a lot of shopping and planning to do, and there's no better time than right now to start."

Margaret took Nicole by her hand and led her into her office. Richard looked at Nick and asked, "This is for real, isn't it?"

"Oh yeah, if you have any doubts, just ask to feel her belly."

"And you are the father?"

"If it was anyone else asking that question I'd feel insulted, but yes, I'm definitively the daddy. Your beautiful daughter has literally been chained to me for many months."

"Never did I think my daughter would allow herself to get pregnant, and if she did, I thought she'd most certainly have an abortion."

"That option is off the table. If all goes well, you'll be a granddaddy in a little more than seven months. If you don't mind, sir, I need to go finish up some paperwork."

Nick started to walk out of Richard's office but was suddenly stopped. Richard placed a reassuring hand on his shoulder, saying, "I thought you might like to know that I've been having fewer nightmares. Thank you."

They warmly shook hands.

Nicole decided that she would continue working until it simply became too uncomfortable, and when that happened, it would be time for Nick to stop working and take care of her. After work, Nicole got into the habit of going home, getting into bed, and looking at the cartoon channel until she fell asleep. Her stomach was getting bigger quickly, and the opportunity for revenge was shrinking just as fast. It was time, once and for all, to put Uncle Bobby behind her, and the only way to do that was to exact a measure of punishment on the pervert that would hurt but not land her in jail.

Chapter Thirty-Nine

In the morning, as Nick and Nicole got ready for work, she placed the Uncle Bobby tape in her purse.

Nicole had told her father and Margaret the day before that she would be leaving early to go see her gynecologist. It was a regular checkup and she had even convinced Nick to stay at work. She wasn't one of those crazy expecting mothers who insisted on having their husbands along every step of this agonizing process. Richard had offered to have a limo take her, but she said she would rather drive herself. It was nearly four months into Nicole's pregnancy, and unless she was with Margaret, she was literally glued to Nick. Richard hoped that she was simply going to the gynecologist, but instinct told him something else was up. Nicole got into her car and drove out of the parking lot as Arthur, unbeknownst to Nicole, trailed behind in his own car.

Nicole had a friend at one of the talent agencies call up Uncle Bobby's home and inform the staff that they were having a very important script delivered to him by a young female intern at the agency. Uncle Bobby, still in his pajamas, thought nothing of it when his staff notified him of the impending delivery. After all, scripts and documents were sent to his home all the time. Nicole talked her way past the guards and staff at Uncle Bobby's home, insisting that she needed his signature and needed to witness the signing. She was shown into the study, took a seat, replaced the script in the manila envelope with a copy of the infamous tape, and waited for Uncle Bobby to come down. The place was just as she remembered it, tasteless and gaudy.

Uncle Bobby entered the room, mumbling, "Okay, what is it that's so important it needs my signature?"

"Don't be so rude, Uncle Bobby. At least show your niece the courtesy of a little conversation. It has been such a long time."

Uncle Bobby, horrified and frightened, looked at her and had to ask, "How the hell did you get in here?"

"Quite easily. I can be very persuasive, you know."

Uncle Bobby picked up the phone and started dialing.

Nicole said, "I wouldn't do that. It'll only make things worse."

He put down the phone. "What is it that you want, you sick bitch?"

"Now, now. Don't you at least have some candy to offer me?"

"You know, if your father knew you were here right now it would get very ugly."

"For you, maybe, but not for me. Go ahead, give him a call. He hasn't heard from you in ages."

"Enough with the nonsense, Nicole. What do you want?"

"You know, Uncle Bobby, you haven't aged well. My father looks at least fifteen years younger than you. I guess the clean life and having Margaret around all the time can surely slow the aging process. Maybe you should give it a try. Either way, you still look great on film, and for our purposes, that's all that really matters."

"Is there really a script in that envelope?"

"No, Uncle Bobby! It's a gift of a different sort," Nicole replied as she handed the envelope to him. He opened it up and pulled out the tape.

"What is this?"

"On that tape is the performance of a lifetime, the type of performance that could have this town abuzz for years to come."

"What is this, some sort of audition tape?"

"No, you silly man. It's a performance you gave a year or so ago. You might not remember, because I'm quite sure this is just one of many great performances over the years. But luckily, we got this one on tape. Let me refresh your memory. Two beautiful, naked blondes enter your bedroom, where you lie naked on your bed. They turn their luscious asses to you and literally take a dump, at the exact same time, right on top of you, spreading and massaging their feces across every inch of your weasel-like body. Then two handsome model types enter the bedroom, also naked, and proceed to pee all over you as you reach out and grab their penises to direct the flow. When they're done, you service both men and like a true sport, swallow every drop of their sperm."

Nicole paused for a moment and then continued, "Just a minor observation ... I thought it would have been awfully nice if you'd serviced the girls, too. But then who am I to criticize the technique of a master. And in the background... "

"What is it that you want?"

"I want revenge, you decrepit piece of shit, but I will take one million dollars transferred — no later than tomorrow — into my bank account."

"I don't have that kind of money. I've dumped all my money into the movie I'm currently shooting in New York."

"Well then, maybe you should ask your Joker friend for a loan. Surely, that pig owes you."

"It's not that easy."

"Oh, sure it is, Uncle Bobby. You're a mover and a shaker ... a conniver, a liar, a pedophile, and a human toilet bowl. Surely, you have enough shit on people that you could probably raise five times that much in half the time. I recommend that you look at that little gift I just gave you. If nothing else, it will motivate you in ways you never imagined."

"You are one sick little bitch. You should have been aborted from your mother's womb."

"Now, now. Talk like that is going to take my very generous offer off the table, and then your career will really go down the toilet. I'm quite sure that your friend Don Ponte at the *Star* will pay at least three million up front for this epic documentary."

"You wouldn't dare!"

"Oh yes, I sure would."

"That would potentially expose all the family secrets."

"Like I care."

Uncle Bobby opened a drawer in his desk and took out a bag of cocaine. He took four large hits and put the coke back in the drawer.

"Thinking a little clearer now? Or is that just a little pregame boost before you go back into the pigpen?"

"What other options are you offering?"

"I'm not here to negotiate, Uncle Bobby. In case you haven't figured it out yet, I hold all the cards. This time all the monsters are on my side, and sadly, Little Bobby has been slayed."

"How about I give the money to you in installments? A hundred thousand a month?"

"How about you take a few more hits of coke? Apparently, you still aren't thinking straight. Unless, of course, you do the noble thing and call a press conference and admit to the world that the 'Golden Boy of Hollywood' is a sexual pervert, deviant, and pedophile. Then I'll destroy all copies of the tape and you won't to have to come up with any money."

"I might as well just dig my own grave."

"Oh, come on. Hollywood can be quite forgiving! By this time next year, you'll have another blockbuster out and this will blow over like a passing storm. Nothing better than box-office receipts to erase sour memories, right? The same jackasses who will vehemently condemn your sick behavior today will be the kiss-asses praising your genius a year from now. In fact, they'll have their children visit on weekends and suggest sleepovers."

"You got that right, except for the fact that I don't expect another blockbuster anytime soon."

"Well, that's just too bad, Uncle Bobby. A seasoned veteran like you should've known better than to open the bank vault for that egotistical wop who's directing your film."

"He's a genius."

"He sure is, but right now he's probably eating at Sparks Steak House with crew and family, drinking expensive guinea wine while you sit here in this decaying mansion, eating shit and drinking vintage urine."

"Unforeseen problems and delays have plagued this project since the very beginning. Since when do hurricanes hit New York? I ask you, since when?"

"Exactly how much is each day over schedule costing you? About half a million?"

"Something like that." He took a couple of more hits of coke.

"Well, it's been real, Uncle Bobby, but it's time for me to go. Don't forget to watch the tape. Seriously, your performance is a real gem. You shouldn't have given up so easily on your acting career back when you still resembled a human being. My bank account number and all the instructions are included in the envelope. Once the money is in my account, all the other copies of the tape will be delivered to you immediately."

"And how can I be sure of that?"

"I guess you're just going to have to believe me. You destroyed my life and it's been long enough. Now it's time to finally put you in the rearview mirror and never look back, you sick, depraved piece of shit."

"One last question. Where did you get this tape?"

"You wouldn't believe me if I told you. How does the old saying go? 'God works in mysterious ways'? Well, it doesn't get any stranger than the story behind that tape."

Nicole walked out of the mansion, got into her car, and drove back to work. Arthur waited the entire time Nicole was inside the mansion and then followed her back to the studio. He went up to Mr. Weiss's office after everyone had left, including Margaret. Before reporting on Nicole's little trip, he and Mr. Weiss shared a few beers. Arthur sensed that what he had to tell him was not going to make him very happy. He recounted all the details right down to the envelope Nicole was carrying when she entered Uncle Bobby's mansion and the fact that she conspicuously left without it.

Richard looked pensively at Arthur for a long time before saying, "It's an ignorant man who thinks that the crimes of the past can simply be washed away with the passage of time."

Chapter Forty

Richard and Arthur shared a few more beers before Arthur left and went home. It was not until a few more days went by that Richard got the full story from an informant he had placed inside his brother's home years ago. The lowdown on the contents of the tape and the million dollars that was transferred into Nicole's account were further proof that his daughter, despite all outward appearances, was still the vengeful creature that his paternal neglect had spawned into existence.

Richard and Margaret discussed the possible ramifications of Nicole's actions and in the end, decided to act solely on the belief that Nicole had seriously jeopardized her own safety. Bobby Flynn was a paranoid, psychotic drug addict who would forever see Nicole as a risk to his fame and fortune, and no amount of payoff money or the so-called destruction of all those tapes was going to appease his fear.

Nicole and Nick walked into the studio lobby and before she knew it, Arthur swept Nick away, asking if he could spare a few minutes to help him move something. Nicole didn't think anything of the request. After all, Arthur was her friend. If Nick was going to spend any time away from her, it was best he spend it with Arthur.

Nicole took the elevator up to the executive suites, and as she stepped out onto the floor, things felt unusually strange. Maybe it was because Nick was not with her. Margaret was in her office, but there was no sign of her father. The display of donuts, cookies, and coffee that Margaret set up every morning had not been touched. Nicole knocked on Margaret's door, entered the office, and took a seat at the desk across from her.

"Awfully quiet up here today," Nicole said.

"Yes, it is." Margaret looked carefully at her. "How do you feel, Nicole?"

"Heavy!"

"You are carrying a big bundle." Margaret came out from behind her desk. She lovingly caressed Nicole's face. "Every time I look at you, it's like looking back in time at your beautiful mother, but between us girls, I think you're even more beautiful, and I'm quite certain your mother would happily agree."

"I'm in trouble, aren't I?"

"No, sweetheart, you're not in trouble. Your method was not one I would have used, but your intentions were justified. Since the time your father and I found out about your Uncle Bobby's sexual abuse, we have systematically, yet secretly, dismantled his empire. It's no coincidence that he hasn't had a hit in years, and the movie he's now shooting in New York will just about bury him. Sadly, your method of blackmail and extortion gives him a villain to fixate on, and even though we seriously doubt he'll try anything, we're not willing to take that chance. We gave him back the million dollars you took from him, but we didn't touch your bank account. That million dollars is for the superb work you and Nick have done for us, and since we never got around to getting you a wedding gift, I just finished the final paperwork on a large condominium, in both your name and Nick's, overlooking Central Park. You'll be moving in there later today, and you don't have a choice in the matter. Arthur has driven your husband back home, where he's currently packing."

"Does Nick know about Uncle Bobby, that it was him who hurt me?"

"No, and I don't need to tell you it's much better that way. That boy loves you so much that if he ever found out about Uncle Bobby, he'd kill the pervert, and then your children will be without a father."

"What am I supposed to tell him?"

"Just what we told him. That you'll soon be entering the final months of your pregnancy, and we felt it was time you both stopped working and start this new chapter in your life in your new home.

You'll be close to his parents, who will be overjoyed to share one of the happiest times of your lives."

"So wait … We're out of the business?"

"Absolutely not! No way. You are the only heir your father and I have, and even in this short time since you've been here, you've been nothing short of amazing. You're a natural to run this empire someday, Nicole. Whenever you're ready and willing, we expect you to come back and work for us. Besides, we have offices in New York, too."

"I'm sure Nick will insist on working there also. You know how he feels about getting things for nothing. Even with all we have, my Nicky is a proud man. He'll demand to play a key role in supporting our family. He hates handouts."

"Your husband is a wonderful writer, Nicole, and both your father and I have read his script. We've agreed that he is more a novelist than a screenwriter. We gave him a $250,000 advance on the book he's now writing, which we expect to be a number one bestseller and, eventually, a major blockbuster for our company."

"And he took the money?"

"He had no choice. He now has a wife and family to support. And this was fair money, not a gift. It's an advance on a book we have very high hopes for."

"And Daddy, how mad is he?"

"Your father is mad only at himself, Nicole. Despite the fallout from this Uncle Bobby debacle, your father is so proud of the way you've matured and put your life back together. It wasn't very long ago that we were worried sick about you."

"I know." Nicole had tears flowing down her cheeks. "I've been really happy here, I have to say, for the first time since I can remember, since before mom died — especially getting to work with you every day. I love you so much, Margaret."

Nicole hugged Margaret tightly as Margaret reached over and took a tissue from her desk. She wiped the tears away from Nicole's face. "There's no reason to cry. I'll never be out of your life, Nicole, never again … But I do have one burning question, sweetheart. How on earth did you get your hands on that filthy, disgusting tape?"

"I simply opened one of Nick's books and there it was. I guess there's some real truth to what they say, that you never know what you might find between the pages of a book unless you open it."

Nicole told the whole story behind the tape to Margaret, who said, "Wow! Sort of a biblical Lucifer … slayed by the Archangel Michael."

"My Nicky is Michael, right?"

"Yes, my beautiful child. Your Nicky is Michael."

Chapter Forty-One

Nicole was not really surprised that her daddy and Margaret found out so easily about the tape and blackmail. The real surprise was in their response, and the showering of gifts upon her and Nick ... followed by the totally unexpected news that Margaret was going to New York with them for an undetermined amount of time to help set up the condo and prepare for the birth of the twins. The idea that Margaret would be living with them was beyond Nicole's wildest dreams. The only motherly figure she had known since Elaine died would be no farther than a shout away — for a time. It helped to ease a lot of her fears about the babies' arrival.

Richard was not informed about Margaret's impending departure until he arrived at the office. Nicole's bliss had suddenly become his despair. When he arranged for Nicole to come to work with them, he knew that Margaret would be a wonderful influence on his troubled daughter. He didn't think that Margaret would literally take on the responsibility of being a mother and rekindle her own joy of motherhood that was lost when Henry was killed.

Richard listened in silence as Margaret told him of her plans. She had already arranged for a couple of assistants to come up and help with the workload, and she was only a phone or Skype call away if he needed her. After she finished talking and he regained his inner composure, he insisted that they take the corporate jet to New York. And over furious objection, he also insisted on providing twenty-four-hour security for her and the kids for as long as they were in New York. Margaret and Nicole would not be able to leave the condo without bodyguards trailing them, nor would they be able to open the front door and allow visitors in without the bodyguards doing full searches.

The conversation continued, with Margaret saying, "Well, I can't wait for you to come visit so the bodyguards can do a full search of *you*. That should be quite funny."

"I have nothing to hide, so why would I care?" Richard said.

"And I have nothing to fear, so I don't understand why I need bodyguards."

"Because you're just that important to me, Margaret. Do you understand?"

Margaret placed her hands down on Richard's desk and came within a few inches of his face. "For all of your bravado, courageous behavior, and chivalry, you still can't get up enough nerve to say, 'I love you, Margaret.'"

"I thought that was a given." Richard's voice had a rare, meek tone. Margaret laughed.

"It's only a given, Richard, once you say it to me."

"I love you, Margaret. I guess I always have."

"Now that wasn't so hard, was it? Just think of all the extra fun we could have had over the last few years if you'd only said those magic words." Margaret coquettishly kissed him on the lips.

"Would you like to get married?"

"Well, of course I would love to get married, Richard, you fool, but as you know, I'm a southern girl. It's going to take a little more than just a 'Would you like to get married?' for a proper proposal. Why don't you think about that while I'm flying to New York? And by the way, I love you too — a whole lot, in fact."

They kissed again and then Margaret started to walk away. Just as she reached the door to leave his office, Richard asked, "Does this mean we're at least engaged?"

She turned to smile at him, radiant, dazzling. "I'll give you that much, but we have a few more steps to take before we reach the altar. I'll call you as soon as we hit New York."

Richard watched as she walked to the elevator. He had survived some ugly chapters over the years — the fog of war during his youth, the marital indiscretions, the verbal and emotional abuse he put his wife through, and the everlasting guilt he felt for his failure to protect Nicole against his own twisted brother. Through it all, Margaret had been there each morning — gorgeous, smart, ready to take on whatever the day might bring. She was always able to bring him back from any dark place he had been visiting. Never in his life had he known a person he could so easily talk to without fear of repercussions. She was his rock and his best friend.

Until now Richard had been unable to tell Margaret he was crazy in love with her because, after all, everyone was in love with her, and deep down, he never felt that he deserved her. But life is short, and after Margaret helped so much with getting Nicole back on track again, he loved her more than ever. He wanted to tell her. He wanted to tell everyone. It was time. He was finally ready.

Nick rested his head against the back of his seat as Richard's private jet took off from Burbank airport. It was barely a year since he'd been saving money to fly coach back to New York to visit his parents. How quickly things had changed.

He'd hardly had enough time to kiss Nicole when she got back to their condo before they were ushered off to the airport in a company limo. Almost as though it had been planned, Nicole got a call on the car phone that kept her distracted throughout the entire ride. Before the plane took off, she rested her head on Margaret's lap and fell asleep. Nick didn't have the energy to engage Margaret, who at that moment seemed quite content to run her fingers through his wife's hair.

Nicole had been glued to Nick's side for over six months. The pregnancy had made her even more paranoid and clingy. He had to stop jogging because she'd convinced herself that only a guy on the prowl for other women would waste his time running around the neighborhood. The only times they were actually apart were when

"Princess Nicole" went to the doctor, and not even she could get into much trouble during those visits — certainly not the type of trouble that would suddenly launch a cross-country relocation under the guidance of "Queen Margaret."

Nicole seemed calm and content with everything that was unfolding, so for the moment, Nick was okay with it too. But he had the distinct sense that he wasn't being told the whole truth and didn't like red flags popping up. His only concern was Nicole's health and safety — especially now, with their twins in her belly — but he didn't like feeling lied to or manipulated, and that was always possible with this crowd.

The amount of money thrown at them, not including the cost of their Manhattan condo overlooking Central Park, was literally too much for Nick to fathom. The wealth of his wife's family was already a lot to process, and that it was also becoming his wealth was beyond his comprehension. He wasn't even given a choice about taking the advance money for a book he hadn't yet started. Richard had stated, quite bluntly, "You have my daughter and two grandchildren to take care of, and I expect them to be properly looked after and happy all the time. So get over whatever allergy you have to money and enter the real world."

It was the first time his father-in-law had shown him absolutely no respect and literally demanded something from Nick without so much as a please or thank-you. Even though what he was demanding was for Nick to accept incredible generosity in gifts and luxury, it was still an expectation for a grown man to take on a whole new lifestyle. Nick was speechless, and as he was packing, he realized that it was not only Nicole who owned him, but now her father and Margaret and the whole empire of power and greed they represented and controlled. The birth of their twins only gave them more power, and any subsequent children would further tighten their control. He would never truly be the man of his own family.

Nicole had finally gotten back the mother she so desperately yearned for in Margaret. The negativity she had exhibited toward her parents when Nick first met her was almost completely absent from current conversations. The beautiful blonde girl he had daydreamed about while sitting on park benches back in the Bronx was now sitting directly across from him, carrying his children.

The cloud of darkness that Nick felt surrounding and choking him had been put in place simply to protect him. Richard adored the young man, and Margaret quietly thanked God for bringing him into Nicole's life. Their goal was not to make him feel manipulated or controlled but to make him feel welcome, appreciated, and like he belonged. Certain secrets are meant never to be told, and no one knew that better than Nicole. As much as she wished she could tell Nick the whole truth about Uncle Bobby, she knew that would only put him at risk — and ultimately ruin the family they were building together.

The following morning, a messenger from Tiffany's department store delivered a small package to Margaret, with a note. Nicole looked across at Margaret as she read the short note from Richard. "To my Yogi, will you please give me the honor of marrying you?"

Chapter Forty-Two

If one is going to outsource a job like a hit, it is essential to be absolutely certain that the dirty work will be carried out by professionals. Back in the 1980s, the real professionals resided in New York and Chicago. You paid handsomely for their craftsmanship, but you never came away disappointed. Los Angeles, at the time, had plenty of its own hit men, but like everybody else in that town, their real desire was to be in the entertainment business, in the spotlight. They carried out their business like they were auditioning for an acting job, and there always managed to be a leak ... even if the police never caught on.

Uncle Bobby — delirious and suffering from a variety of sexually transmitted diseases, including hepatitis C — was convinced that Nicole had to be silenced. She was a dangerous, nefarious little girl who was constantly plotting against him. So Uncle Bobby hired locally, transported them to New York, and told them in no uncertain terms that Nicole, Nick, and their twins were to be taken out all at once. So on a beautiful spring morning in Manhattan, two LA hit men, dressed handsomely in expensive suits and wearing expensive jewelry, stood guard in their car across from Nick and Nicole's condo. It was Nicole's routine to go for a walk every morning at seven o'clock with her husband and the babies.

The LA hit men arrived early, chatted casually about the movie they saw last night, and drank coffee. A young and very attractive lady, dressed like a professional Wall Street insider and carrying an expensive briefcase, smiled at the men as she walked past their car. They smiled back, slightly stunned by her sleek and confident NY look. Not for a moment did they notice the homeless bum walking toward the car from the back. In less than ten seconds, the bum reached into his baggy, dirty jacket, pulled out an automatic handgun with a silencer at the tip, and shot them numerous times through the open windows of the car. The shooter dropped his gun and walked away just as the sleek professional lady pulled another handgun out of her case, leaned into the car, and emptied the chamber into the bodies of both men at close range, leaving no doubt that their souls were on their way to meet their maker. The lady, like the bum, dropped her weapon and simply walked away.

A few hours later, back in Los Angeles, Richard paid his bill at Nate 'n Al's and left his waitress, Kate, a $100 tip. On the way out, he stopped at the pay phone by the entrance to the restaurant and dialed his brother's number. Bobby, still in bed with two naked blondes from the night before, picked up the phone.

"So you tried to have my daughter and her family killed? Our father would be so proud." Richard accused him with seething hatred in his barely controlled voice.

"Don't be so dramatic, brother. You won as usual. The bitch still walks the planet."

"You really are one sick and deranged creature. Good night, brother." Richard hung up the phone.

A few seconds later, two masked gunmen smashed open the door to Bobby Flynn's bedroom, pushed the girls aside, and unloaded their guns into the decrepit body of the infamous movie producer. They pulled off his pajama bottoms and, with one quick slash, cut off the penis and testicles of the deceased and placed them in his mouth. Then they dropped the guns and the knife and walked away.

Hours later, Richard sat pensively at his desk and looked at a picture of his daughter, grandchildren, Margaret, and Nick. Margaret walked into his office and asked softly, "Is everything okay?"

"Yes. Everything is wonderful."

Margaret left his office as Richard picked up the phone and called his daughter. Nicole sat on the couch in the living room of her New

York condo, watching the news about poor Uncle Bobby. She shut off the television as she picked up the phone, listened for a moment and said, "I love you so, so much, Daddy. Thank you."

She hung up the phone as Nick and their children walked into the living room. The sound of a television from the children's bedroom was still playing.

"Please do me a favor, Nicky, and shut off the television in their room. I never want them exposed to such filth."

Nick and the children walked back into the bedroom as Nicole got up from the couch and walked over to the living-room window. She pushed aside the curtains and looked down at the throngs of Manhattanites coming and going. The shrieks of seagulls were abuzz in her ears as they spread their wings wide and lifted her high into the sky.

Acknowledgments

I would like to thank Tom Mankiewicz and Hal Goodman, who entertained me with fabulous stories about the world of entertainment, sports, and life and whose impact on me has been remarkable.

To Rob Brody, whose conversation and analysis of great literary books and persons were always refreshing and inspiring, especially during the late hours of the night sitting at Dan Tana's Bar.

To Rod Lynch, whose generosity, caring, lively spirit, and amazing friendship is a constant reminder of how truly wonderful human beings can be and the amazing heights they can achieve.

To the West Hollywood Palm Restaurant, whose amazing crew and remarkable customers have left an indelible mark on me.

A very special thank you to my editor and friend, Beth Kallman Werner, and to the wonderful crew at Iguana Books.

www.ingramcontent.com/pod-product-compliance
Lightning Source LLC
Chambersburg PA
CBHW020434030726
47495CB00006B/1802